MEMORY'S DOOR

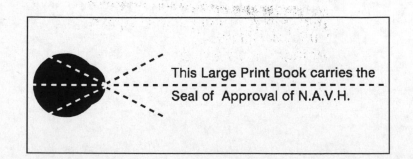

This Large Print Book carries the
Seal of Approval of N.A.V.H.

A WELL SPRING NOVEL

MEMORY'S DOOR

JAMES L. RUBART

THORNDIKE PRESS
A part of Gale, Cengage Learning

GALE
CENGAGE Learning·

Detroit • New York • San Francisco • New Haven, Conn • Waterville, Maine • London

GALE
CENGAGE Learning·

Thorndike Press, a part of Gale, Cengage Learning.

Thorndike Press® Large Print Christian Mystery.
The text of this Large Print edition is unabridged.
Other aspects of the book may vary from the original edition.
Set in 16 pt. Plantin.

LIBRARY OF CONGRESS CATALOGING-IN-PUBLICATION DATA

Rubart, James L.
 Memory's door / by James L. Rubart. — Large print edition.
   pages ; cm. — (Thorndike press large print christian mystery) (A Well Spring novel ; bk. 2)
 ISBN-13: 978-1-4104-6072-1 (hardcover)
 ISBN-10: 1-4104-6072-X (hardcover)
 1. Large type books. I. Title.
PS3618.U2326M46 2013b
813'.6—dc23   2013033738

Published in 2013 by arrangement with Thomas Nelson, Inc.

Printed in Mexico
1 2 3 4 5 6 7 17 16 15 14 13

FOR WILMA,
BECAUSE I KNOW YOU SEE IT;
SOMETHING NEW HAS HAPPENED

"We cannot live our lives constantly looking back, listening back, lest we be turned
to pillars of longing and regret."

FREDERICK BUECHNER,
THE SACRED JOURNEY

ONE

The moment had come to act. There was little doubt and the target was clear. They had to expose the lies being fostered on the world of believers and shout the truth till it reverberated off the highest mountains. He felt it. The others had to sense it as well. The resistance would be significant, but they were ready. All four of them. They fought well together; each complemented the gifting of the others. Three men. One woman. Each fulfilling their roles with precision and strength. And God was on their side. Who could stand against them?

"It is time." He raised his head and drew in the spring air, tinged with smoke from the fire the four of them encircled.

"Have you prayed about this?" The woman turned to her left as she raised her hands to let the flames warm them.

"I've prayed extensively, as I hope all of you have done." The man gazed at each of

9

the others. "The growth can't be ignored any longer. The influence, the appeal . . . it spreads like a virus far beyond themselves, and the time has come to crush it. With God's help we will."

The man to his left adjusted his glasses, bent forward, and stirred the fire with a long piece of kindling. "How long do you antici-pate this operation will take?"

"This is the first Sunday of May. I believe before we reach the first Sunday of July we will have won a great campaign."

"Rock and roll." The third man grinned and rubbed his knees. "I think we'll take 'em down even faster than that."

"Let's pray you're right," the woman said, then stood and brushed off her light blue jeans. "I have to go. Traffic gets worse by the day. But before we break, what's the first step? Tell the millions all about their little band and what they're up to?"

"No, we're going to do something even better." The man rose to join the others and gave a grim smile as he stared into the blood-red coals, then turned to the woman. "I believe in you. That you can make the impossible happen. I believe somehow, some way, you're going to figure out how to get the world-famous Brandon Scott to come on my program and talk about his music and singing career.

"I'll talk to him about those things for a few minutes — get him feeling comfortable — then I'll shift the subject to him and his new friends. I'll hit Brandon with a few questions that will slice and dice him so severely he'll feel like he fell into a shredder. And 14.8 million of my most favorite listeners will hear every word. The truth will come out and the stream of people going through their training will turn into a desert. By the time the show is over, God will have dealt the so-called Warriors Riding a blow they'll never recover from."

TWO

Warm sunlight on his forehead woke Reece on Friday morning and he involuntarily tried to open his eyes. Impossible. They were gone, destroyed during the battle inside his soul ten months ago. The despair once again hit him like a wave but he pushed it aside and sat up, dropped his legs over the side of his bed, and rested his feet on the cool hardwood floor he could now only see in his mind.

God was in this. He had to be. Right? Reece's mind tried to sling the thought into his heart but it ricocheted off. He reached for the watch Doug had bought him, flipped open the hinged covering, and touched the face. Six . . . fifteen. Too early — it was always too early these days — but he wouldn't be able to get back to sleep.

Reece dressed, then shuffled into his hallway past the room his silver-haired mentor had moved into. Part of him longed for

Doug to stay forever and another part wished he would leave this morning. Reece had lived alone ever since Olivia and Willow had died — murdered twenty-five years ago by the demon they knew as Zennon. To have someone, even Doug, take care of him was a bit nauseating.

Reece leaned his ear against his friend's door. A faint clicking sound interspersed with a long, low snore told him Doug was still sleeping. Reece shuffled down the stairs, his hand gripped hard on the railing, his foot reaching out into the emptiness in front of him, not completely sure whether his foot would contact the stair below or never touch anything. An illogical thought. He could picture the stairs in his mind — exactly what his sight counselor had told him to do. But it didn't quench the tingling fear that one day he'd step down and find only empty air.

The thought was ludicrous. A man who had traveled deep into others' souls, as well as into spiritual realms only he and Doug knew about, scared of falling down the stairs? But Reece was. Life was not without irony.

And now the Spirit was telling him to take the other Warriors into those deeper spiritual realms in preparation to soon lead them against the Wolf. How could he do that without his eyesight? Yes, he'd jumped off cliffs and built wings on the way down all his life. But never without the ability to see. Lack of sight changed the game. He needed his part of the prophecy to be fulfilled now and have his eyes restored.

Reece breathed deep, finished his descent, and made his way into the kitchen. When he reached the coffeemaker, he fumbled for the button, flicked it on, and sat at his kitchen table waiting for it to brew. After pouring a cup, he lifted his camera off the kitchen counter and slung it around his neck. Crazy to bring it with him. But it was habit to take it with him during mornings at the fire pit. Even after these many months. Because this might be the morning healing would come and he would once again see the leaves on his towering maple trees lit up with morning sun. This might be the day he watched the fire spit out red sparks and grow dark red embers in its heart. And in that instant he would capture the memory of his vision returning and have it forever.

Reece crept over the grass in his backyard out to the fire pit a hundred yards away. When he reached it, he set his camera on the bench surrounding the fire pit and knelt on the stones in front of it. He fumbled for the kindling Doug had cut and laid in the pine box that now sat next to one of the benches. If Doug ever did leave, how would Reece make the kindling without cutting off a finger or two? But the question was irrelevant. It wouldn't be much longer. He could feel it.

He crumpled up three sheets of old newspaper, put the kindling on top, then laid logs on top of the kindling. Reece lit the paper and sat back, waiting for the kindling to catch, folded his arms, and prayed for his eyes. Five minutes, ten, half an hour, but he sensed nothing, felt nothing from the Spirit.

His counselor said he'd start to feel the size of a room even without his sight. That his hearing and sense of touch would heighten when he stood close to a wall or when people were near. It wasn't happening. Reece had fumbled and cracked his head on his doorway just last night. Not hard enough to truly hurt, but enough to refuel his desire for the healing to come now.

He raised his sightless eyes to the sky. "How long will you tarry, Lord?"

The sound of the wind rustling the trees surrounded him, taunted him, and seemed to whisper, *It's over, Reece. What good are you to the Warriors now? What good are you to anyone?*

"No! I make no agreement with that." He lowered his head, stooped, fumbled for one of the kindling pieces at his feet, and put a stranglehold on the ax till his fingers ached. But didn't loosen his grip. "Heal me!"

Reece imagined a flicker of light and let the stick of wood tumble to the ground. Could the moment be now? He reached for his eyes even though it was foolishness. He laid the tips of his fingers on the scar tissue, then let his hands fall like stones. The voice in the wind was right. He was finished and his belief was burning up and turning into ashes like the wood in front of him.

He groped for his camera next to him on the bench, snatched it up, and flung it out over the yard. It landed with a dull thud mixed with the sound of metal and plastic crunching. He didn't care. Seconds later the silence was filled with the sound of footsteps padding up to him on the grass. Doug.

"Good morning, Reece." The sound of a chair creaking across the pit told him Doug had sat. "This is a May morning with grand finery surrounding it, wouldn't you agree?"

Reece didn't answer.

"Perhaps you're not in the mood to chat,

but regardless it seems there is a grave need for conversation."

THREE

"You need to be fully engaged in the game, friend." Doug's voice had an edge to it.

"I am in the game."

"Really? Is that why you 'dropped' your camera? Was that a result of being in the game?"

They sat without speaking and Reece took a sip of his now-cold coffee.

"You can go back to Colorado anytime you like, Doug. I only asked you to be here long enough to get me back on my feet again."

"I'll go when the Spirit says to. One of the advantages of being retired and a widower is the ability to stay in one place as long as necessary."

"I can take care of myself now. The calendar might say I've had sixty-two birthdays, but this body isn't any older than thirty-three. And I've figured out how to navigate without sight."

The silence returned.

"Is the Spirit in this quest we're both a part of or not, Reece?"

A clichéd question that didn't deserve an answer. If what he believed was true, then of course God was in it. If he wasn't, then his entire life had been a lie. His emotions raged against the small voice of truth buried in the center of his heart.

The sound of paper being unfolded filled Reece's ears. "What's that?"

"I believe if I offered you one guess, your speculation would prove correct."

"The prophecy."

"Of course."

"And you've brought it out for what purpose?"

"Let me read it to you."

Reece fell back and blew out a quick breath. "I know what it says."

"In your head, yes. But you need to hear it again with your heart." Doug's voice started as a whisper but grew as he voiced the words Reece first heard his friend prophesy over him on the shores of Lake Chelan over three decades back.

There will come a day when you will train them — they will be four. The Song, the Teacher, the Leader, the Temple. Keep your eyes open to see, your ears open to listen, your heart open to feel, and your mind open to discern.

When the time comes, the Spirit will reveal each of them to you. You will teach them the wonders of my power they can't yet imagine. And instruct these warriors how to go far inside the soul and marrow.

They will rise up and fight for the hearts of others. They will demolish strongholds in the heavens and grind their enemies to dust. Their victories will spread across the nations. You will pour out your life for them and lead them to freedom, and they will turn and bring healing to the broken and set the hearts of others free.

And when the Wolf rises, the four must war against him and bring about his destruction.

Only they have hope of victory.

And for one, their vision will grow clear,

And for one, the darkness of choice will rain on them,

And for one, the other world will become more real than this one,

And for one, death will come before the appointed time.

Doug didn't get his wish because the words seemed hollow and fluttered to the damp grass before getting anywhere near Reece's heart. He sat in silence, the darkness seeming to draw out the time longer than it probably was.

"Is Brandon still the Song, Reece?"

"Yes."

"And Dana remains the Leader, Marcus the Teacher?"

"Yes." Reece spoke the words to the ground.

"And are you still the Temple?"

Reece rubbed his eye sockets till the stars came. But it wasn't seeing. Only chemical reactions from his fingers stimulating neurons that fired a message to his brain that there were lights in front of him. "What do you want me to say?"

"Whatever you want to."

What could Reece tell his friend that he hadn't already said fifty times? That he wouldn't feel like the Temple again without his sight and waiting for the prophecy to come true was wearing him thin as tissue paper? That at night he dreamed of being on the Skykomish River at dawn, or in the mountains, or at the ocean taking shots no one else would capture in quite the same way?

It wasn't only the death of being able to take photos. An image of his walls of books slipped across his mind. No more grabbing his worn copy of *Pensées* or his heavily highlighted hardback first edition of *Mere Christianity*. No more sitting in the light of his reading lamp studying philosophy or theology till the grandfather clock in his hallway struck one in the morning. And no more leafing through the worn-out Bible he'd lived with for more than forty years.

The healing had to come quickly.

"And for one, their vision will grow clear . . ."

Reece had said it with such confidence the day he came home from the hospital and Dana, Marcus, Brandon, and Doug had stood against Zennon and defeated the demon. But that confidence had been shrinking every day and the fire was close to going out.

"No, I don't want to talk about it. We've talked about it enough. There's nothing more to say."

Doug didn't respond and Reece pictured his friend with a sympathetic smile. But it would soon be followed up with a penetrating question.

Doug's chair creaked as if announcing his inquiry. "When?"

"When what?" Reece grabbed a piece of wood, pictured the fire pit in his mind, and tossed it where the pit should be.

"Nice toss. Right in the center."

"I can't lead them like this."

"Which is the same thing you said to me nearly a year ago. So I'll repeat what I said then. You must. There is no other choice. It is time to tell the four about the Wolf, determine exactly what humans the Wolf will use against us, and strategize our plans of engagement."

Reece shoved his sunglasses higher on his nose. "Not like this. Not until the healing comes. The classes and training we've been doing at Well Spring over the past ten months have been potent. The number of our allies has grown, and those allies are taking the message back to their communities all over the country. There have been significant breakthroughs. Think of the letters and e-mails we get, Doug. It's happening. We'll keep doing that until —"

"You've pushed it off as long as possible. The Wolf grows more powerful daily."

"The Wolf has been growing more powerful daily for ages. We can wait. Give it a little more time, six weeks, a month at least. The Spirit will come through for me and I'll be healed."

"That may be, but we cannot wait. The time to act is now. What has the Spirit told you? I believe Jesus is on his white horse

23

with fire in his eyes, a sword in his hand, his cloak dipped in blood, and he is telling us to ride."

Reece shifted in his chair. "How does the fire look?"

"The fire is fine." Doug sighed. "Reece, we need to —"

"Are we still planning on putting them through the test? To prepare them for the Wolf?"

"Yes."

"Without warning them about what they'll face."

"Yes."

"I don't know if they're ready for that."

"I don't know either. That's the point of them going through it." Doug rested his hand on Reece's arm. "Fret not for the other Warriors. Before the test I believe we should take them into the Wall of Colors. That will give them strength. And I want you to come with me."

"I won't go there without being able to see. It would be worse than not going at all."

"All right, friend. The choice is yours." Doug's chair squeaked and his voice came from above Reece. "Your time is coming. I don't know how it will play out, but have faith, Reece. He will never forsake you."

Reece waited till the sound of Doug's footsteps had long faded before rising from the bench and making his way back to his home. *Come on.* His friend was right. He needed to snap out of it — *had* to snap out of it. Marcus, Brandon, Dana, Doug, and he would gather two days from now, and Reece needed to be strong for them and for himself. This was exactly the web the enemy would want him to become ensnared in. Pity. Self-focus. Only worried about when his sight would be restored. His mind knew the truth of it, but his feelings didn't agree.

Reece breathed deep and sank inside himself. "Lord, speak. Please."

You must ride. This is not about you.

The Spirit's voice was as clear as he'd ever heard it.

"When will I be healed, Lord?"

This journey is not about you, and yours is not to know the future. Yours is to trust.

He took in another deep breath and held it as the truth reached his heart. *I surrender, Lord.*

Peace washed over him and he let the breath whoosh into the cool morning air. Doug was right. They needed to move forward and as impossible as it seemed, Reece would lead the charge.

As he stepped onto his back deck, his cell

phone just inside his house spit out "Break On Through (To the Other Side)" by the Doors.

He flicked open his watch and rubbed the face. Seven thirty-nine. Who was calling him this early? The song stopped as he opened the screen door. Doug must have picked up his cell.

"Hello?" The sound of Doug's footsteps came toward him. "No, this is his friend Doug. Who is calling please?" The footsteps stopped a few feet in front of Reece.

"Please wait and I'll see if he's available." Reece pictured Doug covering up the mouthpiece of his cell phone. "It's Tamera. Do you want to take it?"

Reece held out his hand and a moment later felt his cell phone settle into his palm. "Hello, Tamera."

"I need to come see you." Her voice was clipped and too loud.

"What would we talk about?"

"What happened to me at Well Spring during my training with the other new students."

"And what was that?" Reece eased through the back door and sat at his kitchen table. He didn't need this. She'd been pinging him every few weeks since she ran into Marcus last summer at the Space Needle

26

about getting deeper in with the ministry.

The first time they'd talked Reece suggested the best way to go deeper was to attend one of their training sessions in Colorado at Well Spring Ranch. She'd refused. He said the same thing the second time she called. The third time she said she'd go and she had. He hadn't been there, but Brandon, Marcus, and Dana said things went well.

"I'll explain when we meet. I just want to ask you a few questions."

Reece rubbed his forehead. "Can you ask them now?"

"In person would be better."

"This is a busy time for me, Tamera."

"It's been a busy time for you for the past six months. I went through the training as you suggested. You implied we could get together after I did."

"I did not."

"I think you did."

Reece sighed. "All right, how does Sunday at three o'clock sound?"

"Fine, where would you like to meet?"

"Can you come to my home?"

"Of course."

Reece hung up and squeezed his cell phone.

"What did she want?" Doug's voice came

from his left.

"To make life more difficult."

"The enemy is not going to rest just because you are."

"I'm not resting."

"You're waiting. Holding back. You can't — we can't — afford for you to do so." Doug squeezed Reece's shoulder. "When the Warriors gather here on Sunday night, you need to be ready."

"I came to that same conclusion at the fire pit." Reece raised his face in the direction of Doug's voice. "I'll be ready for Sunday night."

"Really?"

"I'm done with the self-pity."

"Excellent."

Reece heard the smile in Doug's voice, but his tone grew somber a moment later.

"There is little doubt in my spirit that the enemy is going to step up his attack. If he knows we're soon to go after the Wolf and his associates, he'll be coming for all of us in greater measure."

"I agree. I've felt it. With more subtlety this time." The demon Zennon they'd faced ten months back wasn't overt, but he wasn't subtle either. He wouldn't make the same mistake again. And neither would the Wolf.

Reece pulled his beat-up Stetson down on

his forehead. "Have you sensed the attack will be focused on any of us in particular?"

"The one who comes to mind with the greatest frequency is the professor."

FOUR

"Do other realities or universes truly exist?"

A roar of delight broke out on Friday mid-morning in Professor Marcus Amber's class in the physics and astronomy building on the University of Washington campus. He grinned as he stood at the podium in front of forty or so students who whooped and applauded at the question like they were rabid Brandon Scott fans.

That was the question Marcus's class had been waiting to hear. It was the main reason his Physics 401 class was always full, with at least another twenty-three students on the waiting list. It surprised him every quarter that there were people as drawn to the idea of alternate realities as he was. And this quarter it wasn't theory. Not that he truly believed alternate realities existed. Yes, he'd written a book on it — quantum mechanics supported the idea — but he didn't believe there were other universes where you could meet altered versions of yourself or your friends and family.

But he certainly now believed there were spiritual dimensions beyond what most Christians dreamed of, and that at least some of the most seemingly outlandish, mind-bending stories in the Bible were true. He was living them. And in a certain sense, they qualified as alternate realities.

Marcus held up his hand to quiet his students. "I'm going to ask you to boldly go where many classes have gone before. It's your turn to follow in the footsteps of twenty-one classes before you. It has now fallen among you to prove or disprove the existence of other realities and universes."

A shout came from a student in the back of the room. "Do you believe in them, Professor?"

Marcus chuckled. "I take it you haven't read my book."

The young man stood. "No, I have read your book and you don't ever give a definitive answer."

Marcus jabbed his pen in the direction of the student. "I see we have a sharp one among us this quarter. 'Tis true. I do not divulge my personal position on the subject within the covers of my book."

"So are you going to tell us?"

"I understand a number of you already know where I stand with regard to my beliefs in the alternate realities, even though I have sworn all my previous students to secrecy. But even if you do know and they have explained to you why I believe what I believe, I will presume they didn't explain to you the same way I would and with the complete explanation I can. So hopefully you will be enlightened even if you do already know."

"In other words, you're not going to tell us now."

"Yes." Marcus slipped off his glasses and set them on the podium. "I believe in dimensions other than the one in which we typically reside."

The majority of the class cheered, but the student at the back wasn't finished. "And that we can get to them."

"Other dimensions, yes. Alternate realities, no."

"What do you mean by that?"

"There is a high probability that by the end of the quarter you'll find out."

Marcus slid his glasses back on, pulled up a slide on his computer, and pointed to the white screen on the back wall of the classroom. "In case you haven't already heard, here's how the class will work. Half of you will argue for the existence of alternate realities, the other half against. It doesn't matter to me if you believe what you're arguing or not. In fact, I suggest you choose to play for the side whose argument to which you don't subscribe. To convince others of your way of thinking, you must understand completely what they believe, why they believe what they do, and be able to state it with clarity."

Marcus shut his laptop and put it in his satchel. "The rest of the class today will be spent dividing into teams. My capable TA will handle the details. I'll see you on Monday."

As Marcus stood on a street corner just west of campus waiting for the light to change, a man a foot to his right shuffled closer. He didn't stop till his left shoulder was within two inches of Marcus's. A space invader. Great. Marcus wished he could zap the guy into oblivion just like he used to do with that ancient video game he played when he was a kid.

On an airplane? Yes, being jammed within centimeters of strangers was unavoidable due to the airline's penchant for making a profit. But on the corner of the Ave and 45th, it wasn't necessary for this man to snuggle up to him like Marcus and Kat did in front of their big screen on cold January nights.

Marcus grimaced and took a step to the left. So did the man. Marcus glanced to his left. The woman next to him stared at the proximity of his shoulder, then scowled at him. He sighed and willed the light to change.

The man to his right scooted another quarter inch closer, then crept forward till the middle of his shoes were on the edge of the curb. He balanced there, his feet rocking back and forth as if to keep his balance, the edge of his dark red shirt brushing Marcus's as he swayed.

Marcus studied the man's face. A thick black goatee splattered with gray took some of the attention away from his slightly oversized ears. His full head of hair was the same color as his goatee. His eyes were slate gray and the kind that always seemed to be laughing at some inside joke. Fifty? Fifty-five? Somewhere in that age range.

Marcus was about to step backward to get some breathing room when the man cocked his head, looked up, and spoke.

"Finally." He winked.

His gaze roamed Marcus's face as if he knew something secret and was proud of the fact.

Marcus frowned. "Excuse me?"

"We finally get to meet. You and me." He laced and unlaced his fingers three times and stared at them like they might fly away. "I've been waiting, and I'm not always the most patient person in this reality or any other. Especially this one. Because this is the real one. I think. Almost positively sure."

This reality? Oh boy. Either an ex-student or someone who had read his book and had come to believe crossing over into other realities was more than theory.

"I see."

"No, you don't, oh no, you don't. But you will." He smacked his lips and tapped his nose four times. "You will, Professor. I can spot 'em. People like you and me, you know? You've got it on you. He's coming after you. Because you're the key, you see."

"How do you know I'm a professor?"

The man poked his head with his thumb. "Lots of brain cells working overtime."

"And your name?" Marcus didn't offer his hand.

"That will be revealed in due time, *mon frère.*"

"I wouldn't say we're friends."

"We will be." The man rubbed his hands together. "I'm almost positive of that. We

35

could call it a fact. Upon which we should act."

A second later the light changed and Marcus pushed off into the street. Dr. Strange remained on the corner, still rocking on the edge of the curb.

"I'll see you again soon," he murmured as Marcus strode away.

"Is that so?" Marcus called over his shoulder.

"Yes. Absolutely. You need me, you do, you do. I promise it's true."

"Wonderful." Marcus marched forward and waved his hand but didn't turn. "I'm not sure I'll survive the anticipation of seeing you again."

"Nor I," the man called, "so I must be spry, because your choice could pass by in the blink of an eye."

Wow. The man had good hearing. When Marcus reached the other side of the street, he turned to see if the man still stood on the corner but he was gone. A moment later light flashed against the window of the Gingko Tea store and into Marcus's eyes. He squeezed them shut, all sound vanished, and his legs went to jelly. He expected to faint but his strength returned a second later and he opened his eyes.

He almost wished he hadn't. The street,

the buildings, the cars, and everyone around
him had all vanished.

FIVE

Marcus found himself standing on the edge of a soccer field full of young girls, the air filled with shouts from the sparse crowd on either side. What was this? Where was this? He spun in a slow circle. He was in a park surrounded by northwest trees, and the place felt vaguely familiar but he didn't recognize it. Was this a vision from the Spirit? Maybe. If so, it felt so much more real than last time. Could he be in someone's soul? No, he knew that feeling well and this didn't feel anything like that. Plus he'd never gone in involuntarily. And never alone. *Where am I?*

He turned back and studied the girls on the field. Should he know one of them? None of them looked . . . Wait! At the far end of the field it was Abbie, wasn't it? If this was real maybe he'd been teleported here. But why? As he stared at Abbie his stomach churned. Something was off. She looked younger than she should. At least two years. Maybe more.

One of her teammates passed Abbie the soccer ball. She moved to her left, faked to her right, and skittered around a defender. A second later she launched the ball toward the other team's goal. The ball glanced off the goalie's outstretched fingertips and ricocheted into the net.

The crowd cheered and Abbie's teammates hugged her as they bounced up and down on their toes. She turned and scanned the sidelines until she spotted Marcus. Abbie sprinted to him and when she got there threw her arms around his stomach. "My first goal! And you were here!" She gave him another squeeze. "I love you, Dad!" She turned and loped back onto the field.

Marcus stared at her as he staggered toward the middle of the sideline, his mind trying to grasp the scenario. He glanced at the coach's clipboard and the sun flashed off of it, and he shut his eyes. When he opened them he stood staring across the street he'd just crossed.

His new friend was still there, in the center of Marcus's vision just over the top of the cars passing back and forth in front of him. The man leaned against the Compton Building, his arms folded, a big all-knowing grin laminated on his face. Something in his eyes said he knew exactly what had just happened.

As soon as his gaze met Marcus's, the man pushed himself off the wall and strode in the direction of the campus.

"Hey!" Marcus shouted at the man as he popped the crossing button like he was playing a video game, but to no avail. If the light took as long as last time, the guy would be to University Village before Marcus could cross. "Wait!"

The man waved over his shoulder and kept going. Marcus rubbed his thinning brown hair. Over the past year he'd gotten almost used to strange things happening, but this one was new. It didn't feel evil, it didn't feel good, but it certainly didn't feel normal.

A flashback? Doubtful. Even if it was, a flashback to what? He hadn't gone to any games when Abbie was that young. Was it the enemy trying to stir up the old regrets? About what a lousy father he'd — *No. Take the thought captive.* He'd put up a Dead End sign on the road of regrets and he wasn't going down that street ever again.

Marcus pushed the lingering emotions aside and glanced at his watch. He'd have to hurry if he wanted to drop in on Kat at the bakery and still make it to lunch with Tim Schwarzburg on time. He glanced at the street once more but the light still hadn't changed. The glint off an old steel car bumper flashed into his eyes and Marcus half expected to be back at the soccer field but nothing changed this time. He wiped the perspiration from his forehead and marched north up the street.

The bells on the bakery shop where Kat worked jangled as Marcus pushed the door open and the smell of recently baked scones filled his nose. How she stayed so trim was a certifiable mystery of the universe. If Marcus worked in her shop he'd look like the Michelin Man, but the rubber around his middle undoubtedly wouldn't be quite so firm.

"Hey, you made it." Kat appeared through the door leading from the kitchen to the display cases and clipped around a case filled with chocolate éclairs, apple strudels, and oversized maple bars. Her auburn hair was down, which meant she'd finished baking and decorating for the day.

"Did you have any doubts pertaining to my arrival?"

"Not at all." Her brown eyes flashed at

him. "I just know how the first day of a new quarter usually goes, so I didn't know if you'd be able to stop by."

"I was, as you have now most assuredly witnessed." Marcus glanced around the shop. "I wouldn't miss your anniversary."

She frowned.

He opened his arms. "This is your six-month anniversary of joining the work force again."

"Nice of you to remember the date since I didn't." She smiled.

"Still pleased you made the choice to work here?"

"I love it. Lets me indulge my love of baking and get paid for it at the same time." Kat gave a mock curtsy. "And your visit today, oh spouse of mine, is well chosen, for I, your wife of many years, have created a new pastry sensation I'd like you to try."

"Is that so?" Marcus smiled. "By all means, make me the tasting subject of yonder new concoction, fair lady."

She scuttled up to him and poked a round, donut hole-like something into his mouth. "You'll love this." She licked her fingers and stepped back and watched Marcus chew.

It tasted like a glazed donut but had a tinge of orange to it. Not too much, not too little. He swallowed the last of it and stood on his toes to look over the counter.

Kat smiled. "Ah, the gaze that says you'd like another."

"What do you call those?"

"OBs." She traipsed back around the counter.

"Out of Bounds? For the golfing crowd?"

"Orange Balls."

Marcus laughed. "I'd stick with OBs."

"You don't like Orange Balls?"

"Some people might . . . I'm simply suggesting . . . Actually I don't want to suggest anything. I'll simply say in certain circles it would be a conversation starter."

"And in others it'd be an ender." She laughed.

"Precisely."

"Then I shall stick with calling them OBs."

Kat picked up another OB and tossed it in the air toward him. Marcus threw back his head, stutter-stepped to the left, and the Orange Ball plopped into his mouth. "Nuffin' bud ned!"

"Nothing but net?"

Marcus nodded as he chewed on the little puff of paradise. "Remember when we used to do that with olives at your sister's Thanksgiving dinners?"

"It was always the highlight of the day for me."

"Not for her."

"Remember how she scolded us every single time?" Marcus laughed and pretended he held a sign. "And the signs! Do you remember them?"

"The 'Are You My Mother' signs? The ones we brought out when my sister started in on us the next year for the entire gathering to see? The signs that made her barely speak to me for a year?" Kat glared at him. "Those I will never forget."

"Hey, you made them."

"Who gave me the suggestion?"

"I can't remember."

Kat held up an OB and studied it as if it were a diamond and she was looking for flaws. "You really like them?"

To prove his palate had been conquered, he reached over the counter, held his palm up, and wiggled his fingers. Kat placed the OB in his hand and folded her arms, and for an instant the look he'd come to dread appeared on her face. It was only there for a nanosecond, but it was there. The look that said another kind of anniversary was approaching that would rip her heart out once again. And his more than she knew. More than she would ever know because he could never tell her the truth.

Marcus spoke in a whisper. "Do you want to talk about it?"

"About what?"

"You know." Marcus swallowed. "Layne."

She shook her head. "I just want to get through this week."

Relief and disgust flooded Marcus. Relief that he had asked the question like a dutiful husband should and disgust that he lacked the strength to tell her all the details of what had happened that day.

Every year on the anniversary of their son's death he asked Kat if she wanted to talk about it, and every year she said no. In the first months after the accident they talked about it incessantly. Late into every night. Began again early every morning. But as the serrated sting of losing their son turned into numbness and Kat's and his tears came less often, Kat's need or desire to talk about it faded as well. So often the death of a child ripped the parents apart. It hadn't happened to them. But it would if she knew what he'd done.

He buried the thought as he'd become so skilled at doing over the years. The regret so deep that no matter how far down the other Warriors or anyone else went into his soul, it would never be uncovered.

"Do you?" Kat sighed. "Want to talk about it?"

Marcus shook his head and stood in the sweltering silence not knowing what to say, not trusting himself to speak even if he did know what words to offer.

"I'll be okay." She brushed her hands on her tan slacks as if to flick the raw emotions they both carried onto the hard floor. "So will you. We'll get through it like we do every year."

Marcus stared at her slacks.

"Why are you staring at my pants?"

"Are you behind on the laundry? Or did you run out of clothes?"

"Why do you say that?"

"You're wearing the same shirt and pants as yesterday. In all our years together, I've never known you to wear the same outfit two days in a row."

She cocked her head and gave him a quizzical look. "I didn't wear this yesterday. I stepped out of my norm and wore a dress." Kat stepped closer to Marcus and tapped him on the head. "All the neurons firing in order today? You even predicted my tips would be bigger, which turned out to be true."

"That was two days ago." He popped the last piece of the OB into his mouth and

46

savored its sugary coating.

"No, it was yesterday."

"Two days ago."

Kat narrowed her eyes. "Marcus, we had a long talk about choice, that our ability to choose was what separates us from the animals and how we alter our reality in every moment with every choice we make. Remember? You turned choosing a dress over pants into a quantum mechanics lesson."

"No, I didn't."

"Yes. You did." Kat gave him her dead-serious look.

His body felt like it went from 98.6 degrees to 104 instantly. She wasn't kidding. And he had no recollection of the conversation.

"No I didn't." His conviction crumbled and he didn't know what else to say.

"I'm not making this up, Marcus."

"I don't think you are, but we didn't talk about it."

"We did."

He glanced at his watch. "I have to go. I have a lunch with Tim Schwarzburg." Marcus turned to the door.

"Stop." Kat spun him around, her hands on his arms. "Look at me. Are you okay?"

"I'm fine."

"What's going on?"

"Nothing. I honestly don't remember the conversation. I'm probably processing an abundance of stress due to the start of the new quarter." He kissed her on her forehead and then on her lips. "Or possibly I fell asleep while we were conversing. Or maybe you dreamed of the conversation."

"No, I didn't —"

"Then maybe I did. I have to go." He pulled open the door and pretended the jangle of the bells kept him from hearing Kat call his name.

The heat that had started while in the shop grew into an all-out blaze inside Marcus's body. Even though he knew he wouldn't see the man, he still strode back to the corner of the Ave and 45th and stared at the spot where the man had stood. Whatever was going on had something to do with the flashes of light that had come off the window and the car bumper. So what? He couldn't make another flash of light happen because he wanted it to. As he stared across the street, a man to his right jostled him.

"Sorry, man. My fault." An Asian man raised his hands in apology and light flashed off his watch. There was no feeling of vertigo, no feeling anything had changed.

But what if it had?

On impulse he pulled out his cell phone and called Tim. "I'm going to be late for lunch. Sorry."

Marcus slid his cell phone back into the front pocket of his jeans and half walked, half jogged back to Kat's shop. He didn't know how he'd react if he saw what he expected. But he had to check. The bell jingled just as before when he pushed the door open, but that didn't stop his body from going numb because nothing else was the same.

"Hey, I didn't think you were going to stop by. I thought you had a lunch."

"I do. I . . ."

Marcus wiped the sweat from his fore-head. Kat wore a pair of black jeans and a white blouse. No tan slacks, no red shirt, and her hair was pulled back.

"What's going on with you?"

"I'm fine."

"And I'm Tinker Bell. What's wrong, Professor?"

"I don't know. My stomach seized up just now." He bent over. He didn't think she'd buy it, but if she didn't, she kept it to herself.

"Are you going to be okay?"

"Yeah, it's feeling better already. It's likely

nothing more than my breakfast having a spirited debate within my intestines."

"Sorry."

"And it's certainly not enough to keep me from missing out on your new creation, so I'm hoping you're willing to give me a sample."

"What new creation?"

"The one you wanted to try on me today."

"Nice mind reading, bucko. How did you know I've been trying to find something new to make?"

"You haven't made it yet?" The heat returned.

"No. Why, you have an idea?"

Where had he been ten minutes ago? Not here, based on Kat's words and dress. But he *had* been here, there was no doubt in his mind. He needed time to analyze this. Ask the Spirit. Figure out what was going on.

"I said, you have an idea?"

Marcus blinked and frowned at her. "Yes. A glazed donut hole with a splash of orange mixed in. Call them OBs. They'll taste sensational. Trust me." Marcus turned and staggered out of the bakery. For the second time that day Kat called after him and for the second time he ignored her.

He pulled his cell phone out of his pocket and texted Tim, canceling lunch, then dialed Brandon.

"Hey, brain boy, what's up?" Brandon almost shouted over the sound of music in the background. "Sorry about the noise, we're right in the middle of a sound check for tonight's concert."

"No problem."

"You all right?"

"Something . . . two incidents . . . just oc-curred that I can't even start to explain." Marcus trudged down the sidewalk, weav-ing in between other pedestrians, trying to breathe steady.

"You? Not able to explain something? It's a miracle. Did you call to celebrate?"

"This is serious."

"Talk to me."

Marcus explained about the strange man on the corner and what had happened with the soccer game and being in two different versions of the bakery where Kat worked.

"Were they visions?"

"I don't know. It didn't feel like that." He stood staring at the same corner where it had all started half an hour ago. Nothing looked unusual, but now everything seemed odd. The smells, the sounds of the street, the breeze in the air.

"Maybe it was teleportation. The Spirit took you there."

51

"That might explain my visit to the soccer game, but it doesn't elucidate why I was in two different editions of the bakery."

"Elucidate?"

"Clarify, expound, explicate . . ."

"You should have stopped at *expound.*"

"Brandon! I need assistance here."

"Sorry." The music grew softer. The musician must be finding a place of solitude. "I have to go back to it being a vision then."

"As I said, it didn't feel at all like it did during my vision at Well Spring. This was concrete. I know I was there physically both times." The light changed and Marcus crossed the street and strode back toward campus.

"Doesn't mean it wasn't one just because you felt it wasn't. Remember Paul going into the third heaven? He didn't know if it was in his body or in his spirit."

"I know this was in my body, but still you raise a valid point."

"Not a vision, not teleportation, how 'bout a demonic implant was shot into your brain and altered your reality?"

"I'm not exactly in the joking mood. This was strange."

"But we've been in the business of strange for the past year. Think of some of the things that have happened at Well Spring over the past six or seven months. This kind of stuff shouldn't surprise us. We should be more surprised when it isn't happening. I'd shake it off. Let it go."

"Good, good. That's why I needed to chat. To gain a modicum of perspective." The red hickory trees on the edge of campus loomed in front of him. Somehow it seemed getting underneath them would provide a sense of protection and comfort.

"Glad to assist."

Marcus slowed his pace as he stepped into the intermittent shadows of the trees. "And you? Anything unusual?"

The music grew louder again. "I need to get back to the sound check."

"I have a feeling there are abnormalities you've experienced lately as well."

Brandon paused. "It's true. I've got my own version of *Strange Tales* going on these days."

"Would you care to enlighten me?"

"Yeah, soon, but I think I'm going to wait till we all get to hang on Sunday night. I have a feeling by that time I'll be able to tell not only the beginning and middle of this story but the end as well."

Six

Carson Tanner sat in his broadcast studio early on Friday afternoon cradling a scalding cup of black coffee and pulled up the web page for Warriors Riding training at Well Spring Ranch. There was nothing to it. Just a splash page with a picture of a large cabin and white-chalk mountains behind it that shot into a deep blue sky. The only other thing on the page was a contact e-mail.

If Reece and his pals were trying to grow their ministry, this site couldn't be very inspiring to potential trainees to think about signing up. But that was the problem. From what Carson had been able to research after hearing about the ministry from one of his watchdogs, even with almost nonexistent promotion the ministry was growing exponentially. The only time the general public could catch wind of it was at Brandon Scott's concerts. The musician asked people if they wanted to go deeper — told the audience a little about the training — and invited anyone interested to go to the site and e-mail for more information.

That was it and yet little Warriors Riding weekends had popped up all over the country like dandelions gone viral. Men and women who had gone through the training were doing their own retreats from San Diego to New York to Chicago to right here in his hometown of LA — spreading the heresy like rabbits in heat. In *ten* months!

He'd learned about what the Warriors Riding taught from tracking down a few of their more enthusiastic trainees, and it scared Carson. Made him angry. Reece and his pals were a serious threat to Christianity that had to be stopped. And now, they had a target on their backs. He would find a way to get it lined up in his sights.

Carson grimaced and checked Internet stats for himself and his show. Another 2,300 Facebook likes since yesterday. Excellent. Next he checked his blog subscribers, then the number of new fans who had signed up to receive his e-mail newsletter. Just over five hundred during the past three days. Outstanding. The Warriors Riding might be racing to the forefront of Christian culture like an Olympic sprinter going for gold, but the influence of what Carson and his team were doing to bring truth to God's people continued to grow faster than bamboo. The Lord was moving and he would keep following as hard and fast as he could.

He sipped his coffee, letting the blistering liquid burn his lips. Just like God was using Carson's ministry to burn away the heretical elements of Christendom. A rap on the door frame of the studio startled him.

"Hey, a minute and a half till you go on." Sooz Latora, his executive producer, stood in the doorway, her brown hair pulled back hard from her sharp-angled face.

"This show would crash without you." Sooz smiled.

"What about me?" Carson's IT guy poked his head through the door and pushed up his glasses.

"Absolutely." Carson pointed at the two of them. "Have either of you or Grey found anything yet on these so-called Warriors we can use? Or found any of their trainees who didn't have a fun camping experience at the retreat?"

"Not yet, but it's only been four days. Why don't you just go on air and talk about it? Tell people what they're doing. Or try to get this Reece Roth on the show."

"I don't think we're being led to just talk about it. I want to expose it. And having Reece on the show wouldn't do us much good. No one knows him. There wouldn't be any ripple effect. But if we can take Brandon Scott down, word of mouth about the Warriors Riding will spread like wildfire. Any update on reaching him?"

"I've tried his manager, Kevin Kaison, multiple times already. E-mail and voice mail but no response yet."

"Keep trying. And go after Brandon directly. E-mail him. Call him. And dig harder for people who have gone through this warriors training. Find them. Interview them. Draw them out. There have to be some who didn't get sucked into their lies. It can't be that hard. Find ones who are ticked off, ones we can —"

"I know how to do my job, Carson." She frowned playfully at him.

"You're right." He held his hands up. "My apologies. There is no one better at this. You're phenomenal. But I know God is saying move fast on this one." He slid his headphones over his thick blond hair and scooted over to the microphone. "Forgive?"

She smiled, winked, and pointed at the on-air sign above his head. "You're on in thirty seconds."

Carson winked back, then turned to his mic. Sooz was an exceptional producer and exceptional woman. Kind. Smart. Spiritually attuned. A blessing to have her.

A few seconds later his show's pulsing musical intro blasted through his headphones, followed by the recorded voice-over that always pumped him full of adrenaline.

"You want the truth? Can you handle the truth? You can? Then you're in the right spot and you won't want to move a millimeter for the next three hours. Welcome to *The Carson Tanner Show,* where we expose the lies trying to seep into your brain from every direction. We'll inspire, educate, and make sure the truth will propagate! We might even make you mad. But we promise we'll never bore you, 'cause the excitement meter is always pegging on eleven. Now here's your host, best-selling author, internationally known speaker, and voice to almost fifteen million daily listeners — Carson Tanner!"

He waited for the music to fade, then clicked on his mic.

"Without you, my dear listeners, I'd be nothing. Without God I'd be nothing. Without his grace and mercy I'd be tossed in oil and boiled up like a French fry. But with his power we're moving mountains. We're demolishing lies like they're sand castles on the beach. And we are the tide. Relentless and strong. Because of him. Only because of him."

Carson glanced through the glass in front of him and winked again at Sooz. She smiled back and flashed a thumbs-up. It would be a good show. Just like every day.

"Today we're talking United States insanity, folks. Yep, the states are falling like dominoes, my beloved ladies and gentlemen. And that's not a good thing. I'm talking about reefer, Mary Jane, pot, weed, the Jolly Green . . . and the dominoes are the states that are legalizing this drug. Are you kidding me? Will we soon be able to walk into the grocery store and grab a little ganja along with our milk and eggs? What is this country coming to?

"Am I wrong? Talk to me. The lines are open. I don't want to hear from people who agree. I want to talk to those who think I need to open my brain wider. C'mon, tell me where I'm all soaking wet. We're going to a quick commercial break that gives you time to be quick with your fingers. Back in sixty."

By the time the break was over the phone lines were lit up like the running lights on an airstrip.

Carson glanced at his computer screen,

59

then flipped his finger toward Sooz. "We're talking with Kelsey in Virginia. Kelsey, you're on."

"I think every state should legalize it. Why not? It's not even as bad as alcohol and some studies show it's better. Plus, where does it say in the Bible it's wrong? I understand where it's wrong if the government we're under says it's wrong, but now that it's legal, at least in some states, is it still wrong?"

"So you're thinking in the states where it's now legal we ought to do a little prayer, a little study of the Word, and a little lighting up together?"

The caller laughed. "No, I'm not saying I think Christians should necessarily be smoking dope —"

"Hang on, Kelsey. 'Necessarily'? So you think it's okay?"

"If it becomes legal, isn't it their choice?"

"Have you ever tried dope, Kelsey?"

"Personally, no. But I don't see what the big deal is if other people want to — even other Christians. How is it any worse than having a glass or two of wine? I'm simply saying people are going to do it regardless, so why not get some tax money that can offset some of our country's massive debt?"

Carson tapped his fingers on the arms of

his chair. "Here's the problem: When you're drinking alcohol, it's not breaking federal law. Right now, if you smoke pot you're breaking federal law. I don't care what the states say. And there's a difference between someone hooked on alcohol and someone hooked on pot or cocaine or meth. The latter group is breaking the law, the former is not." Carson leaned in closer to his mic. "In other words, the fact it's lawbreaking to do drugs prevents some people from taking that step. We make smoking pot legal, it gives an excuse for a certain segment of our population to step over the line who never would have done so before. And like you just said, Kelsey, that includes Christians.

"There are some Christians who drink. They have a glass of wine and feel a little warm and a little buzzed. Today isn't a day to debate whether that's right or wrong. But I think we can all agree that sometimes, some Christians who drink, drink too much. Right?" Carson adjusted his headphones. "And if pot is legal, then you're going to have Christians taking a little hit of pot to feel a little buzz and get a little relaxed. And then they do a little too much weed. And then they get addicted. And that's a major problem. I'd tell you where that path could lead, but you already know, don't you? Hell.

Thanks for the call, Kelsey."

Carson scrolled down his computer screen and looked at the names of the callers on hold. Sooz always typed in quick notes next to their names. Where they were from, age range, and what they wanted to talk about. There. This guy would lob him a serve he could return to all his listeners at a hundred miles per hour.

"Allen, you're on *The Carson Tanner Show.*"

"I don't think it's the pot smoking or drinking you're really worried about."

"Really. Why do you say that? Talk to me, Allen."

"I think you're worried about Christians always pushing the edge of what's permissible rather than pushing the edge of what's holy. They're getting as close as possible to the edge of the cliff rather than sticking to the middle of the road."

"Bingo." Carson raised his hand and snapped his fingers. "Sooz, do you mind getting Allen's address and sending him a free copy of my latest book?"

Carson jabbed his fingers toward the ceiling like they were guns. "You've nailed it, Allen. He's right, folks. He's sooooo right." Carson closed his eyes, took in a sharp breath, and let it out slowly. "We're to be lights, people! Different. We're to stand apart. Stand out based on the way we behave. Not push the boundaries of sin. The choices we make to stay unstained from the world will infect the world for righteousness! If, if, *if* we choose right. We need to live redemptive lives."

Carson picked up a laminated sheet of paper and wiggled it. "If you don't have our Redemptive Reminders list, what are you waiting for? It'll set you free. You don't know about the list? My bad if you don't. I'll tell you how to get it in a minute.

"It's real simple, folks. You want to be holy? You want to shine? Then think of the movies you're going to. Really? You'd be proud to take Jesus to those movies? Some of the books you're reading? Really? You'd read those out loud with Jesus sitting next to you?"

Carson's head bobbed back and forth as a surge of adrenaline kicked in. This was truth. This was what they needed to hear. "These so-called Christian men who get out on the golf course and stick a big skunk-smelling cigar in their mouths? Hello? That's Jesus? Show me the scripture to back that one up. Ya see, following Jesus isn't just about the warm and fuzzies. It's about taking a stand on behaviors and attitudes. My actions. Your actions. My choices. Your choices.

"You're not in church every Sunday, and I mean *every* Sunday? Why not? They don't have churches where you went on vacation? You need to have your backside inside those four walls every week. When the Word says don't forsake the assembly of the brothers, it means don't forsake it. Not some of the time. All of the time. Don't sit on the beach on Sunday. Get to church. It's the thing you should be looking forward to most on vacation. A chance to fellowship with new brothers and sisters. The chance to hear a different pastor. Hot or cold, not lukewarm. It's time to get serious, folks.

"You're cussin' from time to time — I know some of you are — and you're calling yourself a Christian? Explain that one to me. How can scum-infested water and clear water flow from the same fountain? It can't."

Carson raised his fists toward the ceiling and pumped his arms. "I'm not trying to make you feel guilty. I'm trying to get you to repent. I want to get you through the narrow gate without scraping the skin off your shoulders as you go through.

"Jesus is coming back for what? A blemished bride? No, my faithful, he's returning for an *un*blemished bride. Unblemished!"

Carson slumped back in his chair and went silent for ten seconds. Dead air. Radio 101 said never let there be dead air. But it was right. Let the message sink in. Let God's truth seep deep into their minds.

"Do you smoke an occasional cigarette? Some of you are shocked I'd even pose the question. Good for you. But I'm telling you, there are folks listening right now who just felt the conviction of the Holy Spirit because they're in the habit of lighting up, and I'm talking on a regular basis. Do you really want to be tarnishing the temple like that? Really? You don't, I know you don't. But you need help. You need a little motivation. That's where we come in.

"You don't drive a car without guidelines. There are rules of the road to follow. And the spiritual road we're driving down has more enticing-looking off-ramps than you can count. Off-ramps with lights that look like they're from heaven. But they're not. Get it together, folks. Get on the straight and narrow. Be worthy of your calling. Starting when?" Carson lifted his arms wide. "There is no tomorrow. There is only this moment. So start now. Are you with me? Are you?

"Maybe this is the first time you've listened to my show. Maybe you haven't heard of the Redemptive Reminders. It's nothing fancy. No bells and whistles, just seven simple reminders of what a child of God looks like. But I promise you, they'll change your life. Let me read 'em to you now. Open your mind and hear what the Holy Ghost is saying.

"No cursing. Ever. Let no unwholesome word proceed out of your mouth. Ephesians 4:29.

"No crude jokes. Ever. Same verse.

"No smoking. Ever, in any form. Cigars, pipes, cigarettes. Nothing. The body is the temple of the Holy Spirit. 1 Corinthians 6:19.

"Sin will grow at R-rated shows. Keep yourself unstained by the world. James 1:27.

"A sip at most *might* be fine, but any more is too much wine. Proverbs 20:1.

"No slander, no gossip about anyone. Ever. Proverbs 16:28.

"And the final Redemptive Reminder, no missing church. Ever. Be there every week or you'll grow weak. Hebrews 10:25.

"You can download this list from our website. It will cost you nothing but a click of your mouse. More than five million of you have downloaded it. But that means ten million of you haven't. Print out multiple copies. Put it on your refrigerator. Stick it to

66

your bathroom mirror. Put it on your kids' mirrors. Put a copy in your car, at work. Rise up, friends, and have done with lesser things!

"Time for a break, folks, but one more thought. I'm not saying these things to make you feel bad. It's because I care for you. God has put his love for you in me, and so with his love I love you. But sometimes love is tough. Sometimes love calls you to repentance. Stay strong, folks. And stay there. We're coming right back with more talk, more callers, more truth. This! is *The Carson Tanner Show*!"

SEVEN

Brandon finished the second-to-last song of his first set on Friday evening and scanned the back of the arena looking for the stalker. If the man had come again and kept his pattern the same, he'd stand and walk out within a few seconds. He'd done it every time for the past five concerts when the band finished "Running Free."

No one but Kevin and Brandon's bass player, Anthony, knew about the guy — Brandon hadn't even hinted about it to any of the Warriors except to Marcus earlier in the day. For one thing, he'd been on the road for three weeks and wanted to talk to all of them about it at the same time, and in person. For another, he wanted to figure out if it was just your friendly neighborhood wacko or something darker, like Zennon.

They'd seen little of the demon during the past ten months. Yes, there had been minor skirmishes, but most of their days had been filled with going deeper into the Spirit and helping set others free. But now? Maybe this was part of Zennon's resurgence. Maybe the stalker was Zennon. Brandon had asked the Spirit repeatedly about the tall, well-built man who stuck to the shadows of the halls they'd played in over the past two weeks, but he'd gotten no answer, not even a deeper insight into what action to take.

Brandon pushed back his longish, dirty-blond hair and squinted against the glare of the spotlights bathing his band and him in dark reds and blues. Where was the guy? Was it over? Maybe he'd stopped coming. Brandon scoffed. Yeah, right.

"Wake up, Song Boy. One more tune." His bass player bumped his shoulder into Brandon's. "You with us?"

"In a second." Brandon scanned back over the crowd. Each time the guy sat on the left side of whatever hall Brandon was playing, two-thirds of the way back.

"Are you looking for the guy again?"

"Lucky guess."

Anthony thumped out a bass line, probably to keep the crowd from wondering why the concert had screeched to a halt. "If he was stalking you, he'd have approached you by now, sent a note, sent flowers, done something. Let it go. Maybe he's just a megafan."

"Yeah, a megafan who just happens to have an ax in the trunk of his car."

"Men don't stalk men."

"They don't?"

"Well." His bass player grinned. "Not typically."

"I'll be sure to mention that to the guy when he shows up knocking on my bedroom door at two in the morning with an Uzi in his pocket. I'll call you, hand the guy my cell, and you can tell him he shouldn't be there."

Brandon made another scan of the room. Nothing. Wait. There. Sitting five or six rows back from the spot he usually sat in. Was the guy blond? Wearing a T-shirt? Hard to tell with the lights in Brandon's eyes and the audience buried in shadows. Two concerts back Brandon asked security to talk to the guy, find out who he was, but they hadn't been able to corner the man. Which didn't make sense. He would be hard to miss. The guy had to be almost as tall as Reece.

If he was a stalker, why didn't he ever try to get to Brandon? And why spend the money to see the same concert over and over again? Tickets to his shows these days

70

weren't cheap. Between plane fare and buying a ticket for each show and food while traveling, the guy had to be dropping upward of five hundred dollars per city.

He'd had strange fans before. Those wanting him to sign non-PG areas of their bodies, those whom God supposedly told they were to become a member of his band; there were even a few who thought they were told to come to his house, set up tents, and pray for him every morning at five thirty because "Jesus rose early to pray, so we're following the path he has showed us." But something about this guy was different. He wasn't your ordinary whack job. Which meant the enemy was most likely involved.

Anthony bumped his shoulder again. "Did you see him?"

"Yeah."

"That's cool. Can we start playing again?"

"Sure." Brandon blew out a quick breath and called out the next song to the beat of his foot thumping on the stage. "One, two, three, go!"

An hour later the concert was over and Brandon stood in front of the stage praying with people, hearing their stories, signing autographs, and scanning the back of the room. There was no use — the stalker had never shown up after a show — but he couldn't help himself.

As the last concertgoer turned and waved one more time at Brandon, Kevin clicked up to him on his right. "Done?"

Brandon glanced at the crew milling around the stage, breaking down their gear. "The stalker was here again."

"Yeah, Anthony told me." Kevin nodded. "And we were ready. The guys watched hard."

"And?"

Kevin stepped closer and lowered his voice. "They saw him tonight."

"What?"

"Apparently he left from a door fifty feet from where two of them stood. They went after the guy."

"Talk to me." His heart pounding, Brandon stared at Kevin. "Who is he? What does he want? What'd the guy have to say?"

"They didn't get to talk to him."

"Hold it. They see the guy leave the concert, they're only fifty feet away, and they couldn't find him?"

Kevin shook his head. "I don't know what happened. They say they ran after him. Turned the same corner the guy did three seconds earlier, but when they got there the hall was empty. There were only two doors and both were locked."

Heat washed over Brandon. Zennon. Had to be. Or someone who had learned Reece's teleportation trick. The former was more likely. Fine. Zennon wanted to stalk him? Brandon would hunt the demon in return.

"Next concert I want security racked and stacked every ten yards. We're going to corner this guy and find out who he is. And if he's not human, I know who and what he is, so we'll get ready for that possibility as well."

"Something right here" — Kevin pointed to his stomach — "tells me there won't need to be a next time."

EIGHT

Brandon stared at Kevin and gave a slow nod. As he'd told Marcus that afternoon, his gut was saying the same thing.

Twenty minutes later Brandon hefted his Nike bag onto his shoulder and strode for the back door of the arena. Just before he got there, two of his bodyguards fell into step with him, their black steel-toed boots clicking on the concrete floor of the hallway.

"Thanks, guys."

"No problem, Mr. Scott."

"You keep calling me Mr. Scott, either of you, and I'm going to lay you both out with one punch."

The second bodyguard cleared his throat. "I have grave doubts you'd be able to accomplish that, Mr. Scott. I don't believe you could do it with ten punches."

The first bodyguard gave a mock cough. "Maybe twenty."

Brandon put his hand against the back

door and grinned. "That's why I love being around you two. Let's go."

Brandon saw the man's moving silhouette the instant he stepped through the backstage door leading to the roped-off parking lot. The streetlight above and behind the man cast a long shadow of him that ended at the bottom of the steps in front of Brandon and his bodyguards. If the man saw them, he didn't acknowledge it and continued to saunter across the huge parking lot with his head down.

"Hey!" Brandon called.

The man stopped but didn't turn to face them until five seconds had passed. When he did, he lifted his head and gave a single nod.

Brandon glanced at his bodyguards. "That the guy from earlier tonight?"

"Without a doubt," the one on his right said.

"Ready to find out who he is?"

Brandon didn't wait for an answer and marched down the steps, guards at his sides, toward the man who stood staring at him, legs shoulder-length apart, hands behind his back, blond hair thick and cut short.

From the stage the man had looked close to Reece's height. Up close it was obvious the man was at least a few inches taller. At least six six.

Brandon stopped ten yards from the man. "Can I help you?"

"You're the one who called to me. So perhaps I'm the one who can assist you." The man folded his hands in front of him.

"You've been showing up at my concerts."

"Really?" The man tilted his head and gave an astonished smile. "I'm surprised you've spotted me. I tried to be more discreet than that."

"Is there something you want from me?"

The tall man studied each of them for at least ten seconds before responding. "No. Not yet." He turned to go.

"Who are you?"

"Someone who would rather talk to you another time."

"You've been coming to every one of my shows for two weeks now."

The man turned back around. "As I said before, I didn't realize you saw me. I've always left before your concert was over. I wouldn't want you to think you had a stalker, nothing as unsettling as that."

A hint of laughter in the man's eyes seemed to say this statement wasn't quite true.

"I think you did want me to spot you." Brandon glanced at his bodyguards who both looked ready to jump the guy. Good.

"This is true." The man clapped his hands together three times, softly enough that there was no sound. "Well done, Brandon Scott."

"Well done that I've seen you?"

"Yes. But to repeat myself, this is not the time to talk. But when it is time I wanted us to have met so you'd be more open to further conversation. I mean you no harm."

"If we had a conversation, what would it be about?"

The man stared at the sky as if waiting for instructions. "That would take more than a few moments to explain, and I'm sure you are exhausted."

"The only thing on my schedule tonight is going back to the hotel, and my energy level is peaking at the moment." He motioned to the bodyguards on his right and left. "My friends and I have plenty of time to hear why you've been tracking me. So start talking."

The man took a stride forward and glanced at Brandon's bodyguards. "Can we do so alone?"

"Not thinking that's going to happen."

The man pursed his lips. "It would be better if we spoke alone."

"Do you want me to repeat what I just

said, or would you like to play it over in your head by yourself?"

"I understand." The man looked up to his left as if studying the bright quarter moon that cast a dim light on the parking lot. He glanced at Brandon's bodyguards, frowned, then turned back to Brandon but remained silent.

Brandon pulled his bag from his shoulder and reached into it. "Listen, how 'bout I give you a few signed CDs and a couple of signed photos and you stop following me around on tour."

"If that were possible, I would do it."

"Who are you?"

"One who would help you."

"Sure. Got it. You're going to help me."

"Yes. I would like to."

"Great. Then it's settled. Stop coming to my concerts. Thanks. That will help a lot." Brandon glanced at his guards. "Time to go."

"As you wish." The blond man put his hands behind his back again and stared at Brandon with eyes that seemed to cut holes in his head.

"Wait."

"Yes?"

"Are you Zennon?"

The man frowned and his eyes grew dark.

"My name is Tristan, and I look forward to meeting with you again soon, as well as with the rest of your band."

"My band?"

"The Warriors Riding."

"How do you know about them?"

"In time I'll explain that to you."

Brandon slung his bag back on his shoulder and glared at the man. "Just Tristan? No last name?"

"Barrow. Tristan Barrow."

"And if I don't want to see you again?"

Tristan pointed to the sky. "That's not my choice, and not yours." He smiled. "Don't worry, I'm on your side."

Doug's e-mail yesterday with Sunday night's agenda had hinted that an increased attack from the enemy was coming. Maybe Reece's mentor was right: Brandon had Tristan the stalker, Marcus was seeing visions that seemed to be more than visions, and Reece was struggling with the loss of his eyes.

Dana flashed into his mind but that didn't mean the Spirit was giving Brandon a specific warning about her. She filled his thoughts unbidden on a daily basis. An hourly basis. And he didn't want her to leave his brain but he should. She'd made that abundantly clear after the fourth time he'd asked her to have coffee — just the two of them — and she'd made him promise to stop asking. There was no hope for them. Why couldn't he get that through his head?

Regardless, whatever kind of assault was coming against Reece, Marcus, and him would include her as well.

NINE

The sail snapped into place Saturday afternoon as the wind took hold and the boat surged forward, the San Juan Islands in the foreground, sun drenching the scene enough that Dana and Perry both wore sunglasses.

They sailed for a time in silence, the briny smell of the sea and the slap of the water against the hull of Perry's boat enough to fill Dana's mind and imagination. She'd been working too many hours at the radio station, battling to keep her job, battling the pressures of sales goals that never grew easier to meet. And anytime she wasn't there she spent working on the classes she taught at Well Spring to the ever-growing number of trainees. She needed this break.

When she and Perry had gotten together at the end of summer last year to talk things out it had been healing, better than expected, and their getting together every three or four weeks had been unexpected as well. He hadn't pushed her to go deeper during the past eight months, which of course made her go deeper with him at times than she'd intended. She liked him. Enough for a serious relationship? No. She didn't think about a future together. Today and maybe tomorrow was plenty.

They anchored off Friday Harbor and Perry motioned toward the front of the boat. "If you want to get comfortable up there, I'll go down here" — he pointed below deck — "and bring up some food and some adult refreshments."

Dana eased toward the bow as the wind whipped through her light brown hair and lifted it off her shoulders. She knew what she wanted. But what did Perry want? Did he think they were dating again? He hadn't tried to kiss her which was a bit shocking and a relief. She didn't want to be forced onto the path a kiss would certainly lead them down.

Stop it. Hadn't she just told herself to think about today only? She was having another relaxing afternoon with a friend. Nothing more. What was wrong with that? Even if she and Perry grew back into something more, what fault could that contain?

She reached the bow and stretched out, one leg over the other, leaned back on her elbows, and watched the green waves and the seagulls cantering on the wind, the sun lighting up their wings like snow. If heaven was better than this, she didn't think she'd be able to stand it.

Perry emerged from below a few minutes later with a plate of strawberries surrounding a small glass bowl of melted chocolate and a bottle of champagne, his dark curly hair begging for a trim. "Voilà!" He grinned and climbed out to the bow to join her. "This should keep us occupied for a few minutes at least."

As she stared at him and the strawberries and champagne, Dana didn't know whether to laugh or grab a life jacket and jump overboard. Strawberries and champagne? It was all too clichéd and over the top for just friends. Did she want more? Yes. No. The fickle nature of the undecided human heart, like a garden of flitting butterflies that can't decide where to touch down.

"You're not getting all romantic on me, are you?"

Perry reared back his head. "I'm shocked you would think that."

She laughed. "What am I doing here with you?"

"Soaking in the sun, the wind, the waves . . . soaking in each other. Same thing we've been doing for the past ten months."

"Nine months."

"Nine and a half."

"Fine." She took a sip of the champagne. "Soaking in the first three on your list can work, but the last one isn't on the menu. Sorry."

Perry grew silent and took off his sunglasses.

"What?"

"Can you take off your sunglasses?"

She did.

"I want to soak in each other."

"Don't go there, Per—"

"Don't blame it on me. You've changed. You're more open — way more open about what's going on inside you. You've cut up the sixty-foot pole that kept people away. There's a . . . peace around you that was never there before. It's like you flipped a switch. It's hard not to think of the future."

"Try harder and don't think about it. It's been nice the way it is. Let's keep it that way." She grabbed a strawberry and tossed it overboard.

"Hey!"

"It's symbolic of what I'm going to do if we don't take our relationship one day at a time."

Perry scratched his cheek and fiddled with

the sunglasses he held. "I suppose if you jumped in, I could rescue you from drowning."

"Stop it."

They said nothing for five minutes or so, taking the time to dip the strawberries in the chocolate and savor their taste. When Perry spoke he thankfully changed the subject.

"Tell me more about this group of yours. The one you went to Colorado with and seem to meet with on a regular basis. Do they know we're seeing each other?"

So much for changing the subject. Dana sat up and dipped another strawberry in the chocolate. "We're not seeing each other."

"We're not?" Perry frowned.

"Do you want to hear about the Warriors Riding?"

He nodded.

"You haven't shown much interest all this time, and now you want to know about them?"

"I figure the question is long overdue."

"We're doing amazing things together. Things I never would have believed. My eyes have opened to the spiritual realm in ways I never even imagined could be true."

"This I need to hear about."

How much should she tell him? Probably

more than a little, but much less than all. She didn't want to overload him, but without some concrete examples of what the Spirit had done her statements would be vague platitudes. So she told him about how God had spoken new names to each of them, talked about deep intercessory prayer and how each of their little band had been healed of some of their deepest wounds. But she didn't go so far as to tell him they'd sent their spirits inside each other's souls.

She told him about teleporting their bodies to various places around the country by the power of God's Spirit. About their experience fighting the vine that tried to burrow its way into Brandon's chest at his concert, and how they'd been running frequent four-day training sessions at Well Spring in Colorado for hundreds of those who wanted to go deeper into the things of the Spirit.

When she finished she took a long sip of her champagne and gazed at Perry. "Do you think I'm nuts?"

"Wow." Perry blinked and rapidly shook his head. "No, I don't think you're nuts, but wow. I'll have to take a little time to get my head around this."

"You think we're crazy."

"Maybe a little." Perry dipped a strawberry in the chocolate and bit off half of it and looked in her eyes. "One more question."

"Sure."

"You said one of the four of you is named Brandon Scott."

She nodded.

"But this isn't your ex-fiancé, Brandon Scott, is it? The names are just a coincidence, right?"

Dana shook her head and put her sunglasses back on.

"Are you kidding? You spent four days in Colorado with him? And now you do training with him? And get together as a group on a frequent basis?"

She nodded again.

"Wow." Perry popped his strawberry into his mouth and took a long time to chew and swallow. "Isn't it kind of weird being around him?"

"It was at first." She folded her arms. "It still is a tiny bit, but not much. We worked it out."

"Worked it out? Really? How do you work out something like that?"

The memory of Brandon being in her soul and the war that they waged flooded her mind. The closeness she'd experienced. The fractions of seconds where it felt like it did when they were engaged. "It's part of the healing Jesus did. I'll tell you about it sometime."

"You're okay being around him a lot?"

"It's okay. It's even good." She hesitated. It was good at times. But then there were those moments when she didn't know what to feel. When she wished for . . . no. She wouldn't entertain insane thoughts about Brandon. "Most of the time it's good."

Perry folded his arms and stepped back. "Do you still have feelings for him?"

"They're gone." She turned and focused on a seagull flying low over the water to her right.

"You're sure?"

A tinge of warmth spread across her face and she hoped Perry couldn't see her blush. "Why is that so important?"

"Because if we're . . ." Perry took a sip of his champagne.

"If we're what? We're friends, right? Taking it one day at a time? I thought we just had this conversation."

Perry squinted out over the sound toward Lopez Island. "True. My apologies. Your feelings or lack thereof toward Brandon should be none of my business. For now." He glanced at her, then back to the island. "But if certain scenarios play out, it might become my business."

Once again her emotions whipped back and forth like a loose sail in a prevailing wind. She should feel good about Perry's thinly veiled insinuations about their future. For the first time in . . . forever, she didn't want a guy in her life. More important, she didn't *need* a guy in her life. Which made her want to have someone in her life. It made no sense and all the sense in the world.

"When's the next time you're going to see him?"

"Tomorrow night at our Warriors Riding meeting."

"I see." Perry sucked in a deep breath and let it out slowly.

What do you want? The Spirit spoke to her so softly she almost missed it.

I want to love again. She turned and gazed over the water.

Yes. I want that for you too. Is Perry the one?

It was a question she should be asking the Spirit, not the other way around. Right? No, she knew the truth. Knew the answer because it was as clear as the cobalt sky above her.

She turned and looked at Perry. "There's nothing going on between us." Nothing between her and anyone. Except for the gnawing feeling deep down inside that she wouldn't even tell herself about. She took off her sunglasses once more. "And there never will be. I don't think we should see each other again."

They didn't speak on the way back to shore and their good-bye was short and tense. Where did she go from here? Not Perry. Certainly not Brandon. No way, never. If God truly wanted her to find love again he would have to create the painting of romance. Because as far as she could see, the canvas was utterly blank.

Dana shifted her mind to the meeting tomorrow night and the strange line Doug's cryptic e-mail portended for their meeting. *". . . when we meet you will go deeper than you've ever gone before."*

It sounded like the gathering would be one to remember.

TEN

Reece felt the hands of his watch on Sunday, wishing his meeting with Tamera was already over. Twenty minutes till she arrived. He had a feel for what she wanted to talk about, and the answer he would give her certainly wouldn't be the one she wanted.

He sat on his back deck, the late afternoon sun on his face, the image of what the maple trees looked like at this time of year filling his mind, leaves full of light from the sky turning them a more brilliant green, tiny veins weaving through their form. How he missed seeing them.

Nineteen minutes later a knock came from the front of the cabin. Reece heard Doug invite Tamera in. A creaking came from the living room floor and Reece imagined the woman bouncing across the floor as if trying to burn off some of the perpetual energy she stored inside. Then closer, into the kitchen and out through the screen door that led onto the back deck. The shuffle of two pairs of shoes went silent.

"Tamera is here to see you."

Reece turned to the sound of his voice. "Thanks, Doug."

"My pleasure."

Reece imagined his friend giving a slight bow, a smile, and a flick of his upturned hand toward Tamera that would have fit into eighteenth-century England like an ivory-colored glove. Tamera and everyone else who saw it wouldn't understand it was Doug's dry sense of humor on display for anyone who had eyes to see.

The sound of Tamera sitting in the chair across from him pushed the image of Doug from his mind. "Hey, stranger."

"Good afternoon, Tamera." He pictured her as he'd last seen her. Short blond hair, fair skin, in excellent shape of course.

"Thanks for taking time for me."

"Not a problem."

Her chair creaked. "But it has been a problem, hasn't it?"

"Excuse me?"

"It's been a workout trying to get a one-on-one audience with you. This is our first just-the-two-of-us meeting since . . . I don't remember when."

"Life has been busy. You know that. The

training school at Well Spring. The mundane things of living taking longer due to this." He pointed to where his eyes used to be.

"I understand that, but the last time we really talked and I asked to be part of Warriors Riding, you said you'd most likely invite me into the inner circle once I went through the training at Well Spring."

"No, I did not say I'd 'most likely invite you in.' I said I'd consider it, pray about it. See where the Spirit led."

"So now I've been through the training at Well Spring. Well over three months ago."

"Yes?"

"Marcus, Brandon, and Dana said I had a number of substantial breakthroughs."

"They conveyed that to me."

"And since then I've been growing in the Spirit and seeing him do amazing things through me."

"I agree."

"I'm learning to love like I've never done before."

"Again, from what I've been told, I would agree."

"I'd like to join you."

"I don't understand. You have joined us. You're one of a select group of warriors Jesus is raising up."

"No, I want to join the inner circle. The

one that was formed at Well Spring when you and the others went there a year ago. I blew it. I've told you that many times. I should have been there. It's something I regret every day. But stop making me pay for my mistake. Let me into the inner circle and be one of you like I was meant to be."

"That choice isn't up to me. It's up to the Spirit."

What sounded like Tamera slapping the side of her chair filled the air. "Cut it, Reece! That's such an easy cop-out. You don't want something to happen so you blame it on God and it's his fault."

"The truth is never a cop-out."

"You invited me to Well Spring. You chose me." Tamera's voice rose in volume and pitch. "I was one of the four and now I'm just another grunt in the tribe following the great man."

Reece let the silence grow till Tamera spoke again.

"You have no answer for me? Figures."

"You know about the prophecy, yes? During your training at Well Spring it was shared with you. And you heard of the truth that surprised all of us, most of all me. Do you remember what was told?"

"That you're supposedly the Temple and not me."

Reece uncrossed his legs. "You can still be an integral part of this mission but there are four to the prophecy, not five."

"If it had played out as you intended and I'd gone to Well Spring with you last year, it would right now be Dana, Marcus, Brandon, you, and myself. That's five. So why can't it be five now?"

"You chose not to come. I'm sorry for your regret and the weight of that, but the tapestry is what it is at this point. Neither you nor I can go back and unravel what has been done."

"That's not fair, Reece. Where is the grace you supposedly speak of so frequently when you train people at Well Spring?"

"This isn't about grace or absence of grace. It isn't about what the Spirit did back then, but what the Spirit is doing now. And in this now, there are four Warriors Riding. Not five." Reece tapped his armrest in a slow cadence. "Is there anything else?"

"You're making a mistake, Reece."

"Oh?"

"I could do such powerful things for this ministry. I have my own exercise TV show. I have the ear of producers who would be able to put you in front of millions. I have a newsletter of more than seventy-five thousand people. I have a Facebook page with over thirty thousand likes. I have a book contract."

"I don't want to be in front of millions. I don't want be in front of thousands. I want to be in front of the remnant of warriors who want to go deeper and are willing to pay the price that will entail. There will never be many."

"I get that. But to get to the few, you need to get to the many. You need me, Reece. Think about it. If you're trying to find a needle in a haystack you have to figure out a way to spin through a lot of hay."

"Tamera, you've learned much and grown in love as we both said a moment ago but you've failed to realize your place in the tapestry."

"What's my place? I've found my place. I'm making huge changes in people's lives."

"Yes, I believe you are."

"And you need me to do the same for you."

"No, I don't need you, Tamera. You're not needed at all."

"What?" The scrape of Tamera's chair filled Reece's ears and her voice came from above him. "You're wrong. I have so much to offer you. I'm worth something."

"Sit down."

"How do you know I'm standing?"

"Sit down, friend, and listen. I don't need you just as he doesn't need me. His purposes will be accomplished with or without me. All God's offering is an invitation into his story, the greater story, the things he's doing on a grand and microscopic level."

"I want to be needed. I need to be needed. I want to feel like what I'm doing matters. That God is using me to make a difference, to create some kind of legacy. I want to know I'm worth something. Is that so wrong?"

"And what if the legacy you create is simply one of loving the Father, Son, and Holy Spirit with all your heart, mind, soul, and strength?"

"I couldn't live with that. I need to be able to point to something."

"Open your heart to my words, Tamera. Don't you understand what that means? It means he values you for who you are, not for what you've done or what you might do for him or others. There is no earning his favor, his grace, or his mercy. There is no action you can take to make him love you. He already does. More than you will ever imagine. But you're not wrong to want to know if you're worth something. You are worth something. More than something. You are worth his being crushed and broken, torn and scourged. Executed against a scorching sun and the utter scorn of those around him. You are worth so much."

The air went still and all Reece heard was a gentle wind in the trees. A few seconds later the cry of children playing floated over the air from at far away. "Do you hear that? It's what we must become. No pride, no self-focused ambition, no —"

"I get the message." The volume of Tamera's voice dropped — Reece couldn't tell if it was from sadness or anger seething just below the surface. He wished he could see her eyes, to know if she was about to explode or let the truth in.

"Why is this so important to you? It sounds like you have a tremendous career in fitness going."

"Because I want the power you four have. I want to be around it. Learn more. Do the things you talked about that are on the fringe. I want to experience it all."

"I don't know which way the wind will blow tomorrow, Tamera, but the answer in this moment is to wait."

"I'm done waiting."

"I'm sorry. This is not about you or your worth before God. It's about what he is doing. It's possible I'm not hearing correctly from the Spirit, but I believe I am, and this is not the time and I don't know when it will be."

"You'll regret this, Reece. So will the others."

ELEVEN

Marcus arrived at Reece's house on Sunday evening at 7:05 and scanned the driveway. Brandon's and Dana's cars were already here. He didn't get out. Should he tell them about the bizarre incidents that happened on Friday? Or just let it go like Brandon suggested?

Nothing similar had happened for the past two days. Perchance it was a result of stress or a dream that seemed so genuine he hadn't been able to distinguish it from the real world. A somewhat common occurrence in human dream states.

Marcus stepped out of his car, shut the door, and rubbed his hands as if ridding himself of his visions of Abbie and Kat from Friday afternoon. If Doug and Reece were finally going to tell them about the Wolf and they were about to set their strategy, the focus shouldn't be on his hallucinations. It should be on the coming melee.

■ ■ ■ ■

A firm rap on the front door of Reece's home startled Dana. She'd been wrapped up in studying a site map she'd developed for the Well Spring website. At some point they'd need to expand it beyond the splash page and she was hoping the Warriors would use some of the photos she took at the ranch.

She stood as Brandon opened the front door and ushered Marcus inside. A few minutes after she greeted him, Doug descended Reece's lightly stained wooden stairs and settled onto the couch in the living room. He rubbed his hands together as if getting ready to sculpt an object out of the air in front of him.

"Remember me saying last spring after the victory you had in Reece's soul that you've just begun your journey into the vastness of God? That you've only started down the path of joy and freedom?"

Dana nodded along with Marcus and Brandon and she studied Doug's eyes. They were bright and playful like a little boy's, as if he were about to show them one of his favorite toys. She hadn't ever seen him this animated.

"Today I'm going to show you more of the path. You have seen marvelous things so far but going into souls is only part of what God has made available to us if we only believe and are willing to let the Spirit take us deeper. There are far more tantalizing wonders to be explored for those who want to fly on wings like eagles."

"Here we go again." Brandon smiled.

"Oh yes." Doug returned the Song's smile and laid his hands on his knees. "Most assuredly, yes."

"Are you telling us we're going flying?" Dana flapped her hands like a bird.

"Something far better, yet at the same time I think there might be a bit of flying involved. We will have to see where the Spirit takes us." He winked, opened his Bible, and for a few moments the only sound was the rustle of pages as he searched.

He stopped toward the front of the book and then glanced at each of them, his eyes even brighter. "Are you ready to hear this?" Doug started reading without waiting for a response. He read in a soft voice that built to a crescendo by the end of the passage.

" 'How awesome is this place! This is none other than the house of God; this is the gate of heaven.' Genesis 28:17."

"Are you saying — ?" Brandon pointed the forefingers of both hands at Doug and then at the sky.

Doug held up his hand and patted the air as if to silence Brandon and used his other to paw toward the back of his Bible. " 'I know a man in Christ who fourteen years ago was caught up to the third heaven. Whether it was in the body or out of the body, I do not know . . . I know that this man . . . was caught up to paradise.' "

Marcus looked up from his ever-present notepad and tapped the air in front of him with his pen. "In an effort to accurately summarize your insinuation, you're articulating the view that we can voyage into supplementary spiritual and heavenly realms with as little exertion as we've expended to journey into the souls of others."

Doug stared at him with a bemused look on his face.

Brandon laughed. "Come on, Professor, give it more effort next time. I'm sure you could have stuck five or six more words in there to make that sentence one only your fellow geek-brains could understand. As it was, I understood over a quarter of it."

"Sorry." Marcus shrugged. "You're saying we can send our spirits into spiritual dimensions other than souls?"

"Yes." Doug winked at Brandon. "I am, and we can."

Brandon stood and pretended to hand something to Doug. "I have to take the gold medal from the current record holder and hand it to you, Doug. I've always thought Reece was the outright winner of the On-the-Fringe Olympics, but you're clearly sprinting past him with this one."

Doug smiled. "This is probably true. But I accept the medal with a humble heart and assure you I was taught by another just as I'm about to teach you." He spread his arms wide. "This evening, my friends, we shall go through the gate and see wonders beyond wonders. Are you ready?"

Dana glanced at the others, then settled her gaze on Doug. "Where is Reece?"

"He's upstairs and he'll be praying for us during the time we leave our bodies and then join us toward the end of the evening when we talk about where we need to go from here."

"He's not coming with us." Dana said it more as a statement than a question.

"No."

"Why not?" Brandon said. "We've sent our spirits into seventy-four souls over the past ten months and he hasn't been along for the ride even once."

Doug hesitated before answering. "He says he feels for the moment he's to stay out of souls and the heavens. That the time hasn't come for him yet to reengage in that way. He feels the three of you are doing powerful work — setting others free, bringing them healing — but it's not for him to join in on that front yet."

Dana folded her arms. "In other words, he's letting the enemy convince him he'd be of no use inside a soul or anywhere else in the heavenly realms without his sight."

"Reece is strong and will join you again when he is ready. In the meantime, we shall extend our friend grace." Doug set down his Bible and held out his hands. "Now, let us have an adventure together that will be most enjoyable."

Dana reached for Marcus's hand on her right, then extended her other hand to Brandon on her left. The moment her fingers touched his, her body went weightless and Reece's living room vanished.

She blinked twice, then opened her eyes fully to find herself floating on a current of air. The sensation was like river rafting down a surging rapid, only faster, but there was no undulation in the atmosphere beneath her. A few feet ahead was Doug. Brandon and Marcus were on either side of her.

She looked down and saw they floated miles above an ocean smooth as glass that extended as far as her eyes could see in every direction. Lush green islands dotted the sea, some massive, some not more than an acre across. Far below, birds, seagulls maybe, rode the same currents that must be gliding them toward the horizon and a massive descending sun.

At first she didn't move, concerned the wind wouldn't hold her up if she did. But after a few minutes she twisted and realized no matter how she turned, it wouldn't affect the river of air around her. She turned to her side, then her back, then onto her stomach, and as she did, laughter pushed out of her in waves. Dana spun and twisted and was a little girl again, rolling down the tiny green hill in the park near her school and then sailing to the heavens on her old, rusty, light blue swing set in her childhood backyard.

Dana looked for Brandon and spied him to her left and slightly behind doing somersaults through the air. "Whooo-hoooooooo! Try this, Dana!"

She did and her body raced with adrenaline. After seven rotations she stopped. Laughter burst out of her and she grinned at him. His eyes lit up like they did back in the days when they were engaged. Whoops. She needed to dial it back. Be careful. No mixed signals, even in here.

To her right, Marcus flew spread-eagled, the wind whipping around his clothes and through his thinning brown hair like a hurricane, his face a cascade of joy, laughter pouring out of his mouth in a torrent. Even Doug had joined the celebration, doing cartwheels through the air and yelling like a crazed U-Dub football fan.

The whole thing was so natural and so absurd, both at the same time. All fear of the future, all worry about what would happen with Perry and where Brandon fit in her life, the always-present strain of her job slipped away. And whatever scenario the Warriors would face with the Wolf melted away and joy unspeakable buried her.

As they cavorted through the sky, the river of air grew stronger and they picked up speed. After what seemed like hours, Dana squinted toward the horizon again. The sun had sunk lower in the sky and now she saw a thin smear of colors. As they streaked toward it the smear turned into a wall and grew larger till it towered above them, a mile at least, probably more.

The four of them were traveling so fast she doubted they would survive the same velocity on earth. The greens and blues below her blurred. She should be frightened but she couldn't touch even a hint of that emotion. Only an overwhelming sense of love and joy she was sure would explode out of her in seconds. And still they moved faster.

Then the wall of colors was before them, looming too far above to see the top and too far to the sides to take in its vastness. Only seconds now and they would slam into the crimson, emerald, turquoise, gold, and aqua wall and certainly be destroyed, but Dana didn't care. She stretched forward with her fingers and pulled at the air as if swimming, as if she could draw herself into the wall with more speed. And she was laughing and crying and shouting and coming closer to exploding every second.

Then in a flash she reached the wall and smashed into it and she slammed her eyes shut and waited for death to come but it didn't. As she burst through the wall, the sense of love she'd felt earlier was a drop in the Pacific Ocean compared to what she felt now. The colors wrapped themselves around her and pushed into her and through her and each color was a hand of God that held her in infinite tenderness and strength.

Their speed slowed and they flew lower

and soon a landscape took form in front of them. She glanced at the others, their faces basking in the splendor of the moment, then back to the world appearing in front of her. Mountains and valleys and deserts and forests and seas grew and vanished as they flew over the splendor.

None of them tried to make conversation. What would they say? Words would crash to the ground in epic failure trying to describe what they'd experienced, what they were feeling, what they'd seen, what they were still seeing.

Finally the birthing of worlds around them slowed, and they stood on a plain that reminded Dana of the Australian outback but this one was more vibrant and the air tingled with . . . she didn't know how to describe it. Life was the only word that made sense.

"Where are we?" Marcus's voice sounded strange.

Doug opened his arms and turned 360 degrees before answering. " 'The creation waits in eager expectation for the sons of God to be revealed. For the creation was subjected to frustration, not by its own choice, but by the will of the one who subjected it, in hope that the creation itself will be liberated from its bondage to decay and brought into the glorious freedom of the children of God.' 'Then I saw a new heaven and a new earth, for the first heaven and the first earth had passed away . . .' "

"What?" Dana made her own turn. "Are you saying this is the new heaven and the new earth?"

Doug laughed. "No, no. That is yet to come. Our eyes will not see that till the age we live in ends and all the sons and daughters become the audience as the Great Artist once again creates what was to have been in the beginning and what will be again for ages to come." He made a sweeping gesture. "This is only a foretaste of what that world will be, and not nearly as glorious as what we will see then."

"This is a foretaste?" Brandon widened his eyes. "It'll be better than this?"

"Oh yes." Doug's eyes were white fire. "My educated guess and hope is what you just experienced is the smallest appetizer of what we shall experience at the wedding feast between Christ and his bride.

"C. S. Lewis had it right when he said, 'If we consider the unblushing promises of reward and the staggering nature of the rewards promised in the Gospels, it would seem that Our Lord finds our desire not too strong, but too weak. We are half-hearted creatures, fooling about with drink and sex and ambition when infinite joy is offered us, we are like ignorant children who want to continue making mud pies in a slum because we cannot imagine what is meant by the offer of a vacation at the sea. We are far too easily pleased.' "

The four of them went silent again, soaking in the world Doug had led them to. Then one by one they stood and walked in four opposite directions.

Dana didn't see the colors around her, she tasted them, didn't look on the water of the streams she passed, she was part of it. The air and light were like food and made the most succulent chocolate torte she'd ever tasted seem like dust by comparison.

Too soon Doug's voice called out from behind her. "It is with great regret I must tell you our time here is finished."

She turned and strolled back toward Doug, wanting each step to last forever, watching Marcus's and Brandon's same slow gait and realizing they felt the same.

When she reached him she stopped and frowned. "Why did you bring us here? I'm not sure the ache of going from this place will ever leave me."

"This is true, but knowing this ahead of time, would you have chosen not to come?"

Doug reached for their hands. "After we've returned we will chat about why I brought you here and the lessons to be learned from voyaging through this realm. Let us go."

The moment her fingers touched Doug's hands her surroundings vanished and her spirit slid back into her body in Reece's cabin. She slipped her hands to her sides and rested them on Reece's couch as she stared at the others' faces. They seemed to reflect light and were so alluring she almost gasped.

Doug chuckled. "You see it in the others, don't you, Dana?"

She shook her head and smiled. " 'But we all, with unveiled faces, beholding as in a mirror the glory of the Lord, are being transformed into the same image from glory to glory, just as from the Lord, the Spirit.' From Paul's second letter to the Corinthians, chapter 18."

"Yes, Dana. Yes." Doug patted her hand. "That is right."

Marcus tilted his flushed and bright face toward Doug. "You indicated there was a greater intent behind taking us there than simply to experience utter joy."

"Yes." Doug paused and a cloud came over his eyes. "I wish the only reason was for you to taste that freedom, that joy to come. But it isn't. You needed to see that, to experience the heavenly realms so you know what you are fighting for. Because I fear you'll soon be traveling into other dimensions not so pleasant as the one we just came from. Realms as dark as the one you just experienced are light. Realms where you must take the battle, and where your experience there can inspire and give you strength."

"The Wolf. Doing battle with him," Dana said.

Doug nodded.

Brandon leaned forward in his chair. "Do you know when we'll have to start doing that?"

Doug stood. "Sooner than you or Reece and I would like, I'm afraid."

"Define sooner."

A voice came from the top of the stairs. "We think the attack on each of us will increase in intensity if it hasn't already." Reece clumped down the staircase and eased over to his leather chair. "That's not a surprise, at least it shouldn't be. I will admit I've been on the ropes for the past two or three weeks. And this afternoon I had a conversation indicative of what kinds of things we can expect from the people around us. Do you remember Tamera?" Reece paused. "She's not happy with us."

"Good to see you, Reece." Dana immediately regretted her phrasing but if Reece took offense it didn't show in his face or gestures.

"Why's she putting on the frowny face?" Brandon puckered his lips.

"She wants to be a deeper part of our fellowship than the Spirit wants her to be. I'm not worried about it, but it is an indication of the enemy trying to whack the hornet's nest. Which means we need to be on alert more than ever." He clapped his hands on the armrests of his chair. "Enough of that. It's good for all of us to be together again. I trust you enjoyed what Doug had to show you?"

Dana laughed and the others joined her. "You could say that."

"I'm glad." Reece smiled. "Next time I intend to go with you."

Doug meandered over to where Reece sat and laid a hand on his shoulder. "We welcome that with open hearts and great anticipation." He released Reece's shoulder and sat in the chair next to the big man. "Now, let's talk about next steps."

Marcus opened his notebook and clicked his mechanical pencil twice. "You're finally going to tell us about the Wolf?"

Reece turned his head toward Doug as if he could see him, then turned back to the others. "We are very close to that day, yes. Very close. But first we have to take your training up a notch."

"Do you care to give a clarifying descriptor of 'up a notch'?" Marcus said.

"We'll meet again on Friday night, and during that time the three of you will face a rather arduous test. I don't think it prudent to share anything more than that, but I will encourage you to be in prayer and stay in close communion with the Spirit."

"Anything else?" Dana asked.

"Only this: if the test goes well, Doug and I will tell you what we know about the Wolf, and we will all begin to form our strategy for engaging him in battle."

As Dana drove home, Reece's words filled her thoughts. *Lord, how will the enemy come after me?* Just before she turned into her driveway, a picture of her radio station flashed into her mind and she had the distinct feeling she would soon have a great deal of free time on her hands.

TWELVE

"Robert is waiting for you."

Dana's executive assistant spoke the words softly on Monday afternoon but Rebecca might as well have shouted them. Dana had found out first thing that morning that her general manager wanted to meet with her and even though she'd had a premonition of this the night before, it still surprised her.

"Deep breath, face the music," Dana said under her breath as she walked toward Robert's office. "God is in this." The hallway smelled like carpet cleaners had been there the night before. A fitting symbol for the cleaning her GM was about to do. She reached his door and came to a halt. Another deep breath and a quick prayer for composure. She would find another job. Or Reece could subsidize her to become the official Well Spring photographer. She closed her eyes and imagined the scene about to unfold.

She would step inside, sit on her GM's plush leather couch, and after polite greetings he would say something like, "Although you've done a wonderful job for this company over the years, we think it's time for us to mutually agree it's best for all concerned parties if we go our separate ways."

Then they would negotiate a severance package both Corporate and she could live with, she would pack her things, head home, turn off her alarm, and sleep till noon.

The meeting shouldn't have shocked her. Dana couldn't blame them. All the time she'd been spending on Warriors Riding, all the trips she'd taken to Well Spring to take part in the training sessions had cut into her focus at the station. Her heart was torn between the Warriors and the station and her intensity at the station had waned as her heart and strength went more and more to the mission Reece and Doug were taking them on.

Sure, all the days she'd taken off were from accrued vacation time she'd earned but it didn't mean it was okay. And while her budgets had only been off 3 percent over the past three quarters, she was still 3 percent off. And when her goals were for 7 percent growth, it meant she and her team were consistently underperforming by 10 percent. Not acceptable. Stockholders didn't care if she had the time off coming. And neither did her GM.

She glanced at Robert's executive assistant and he nodded at the door. Dana knocked once and walked in. Oh boy. This wasn't a one-on-one meeting. Next to Robert stood the head of the Seattle division — Spencer Benning — the suit from Corporate who visited a few times a year at most. Great. Two against one.

Spencer smiled, strode over to her, and offered his hand. "Great to see you, Dana. It's been at least a year."

"I think you're right." She shook his hand and offered a thin smile. "It's good to see you as well."

Robert and Spencer sat and he motioned to the couch across from them. She sat in the middle, her hands clasped on her lap. "I'd like to make a request in regard to this meeting."

"All right." Spencer glanced at Robert, then back to her.

"Can we forgo the pleasantries and the details of why you're letting me go and get right to work on a severance package we both agree is fair?"

Spencer glanced at Robert again, then leaned forward, picked up two white folders, and handed one to Dana and one to her GM. "Before we do, I'd like to go over a few figures."

Dana bit her lower lip and stayed silent. This was exactly what she had hoped to avoid but it was obvious her final wish would not be granted. *Go with it. Play the stupid game. It won't kill you.*

"Let's start by taking a look at your team's sales performance over the past four quarters — 2 percent down, 3 percent down, 2 1/2 percent down, 1 percent down, and based on current budgets for this quarter you'll finish at 1 1/2 percent down over the previous year."

This was a complete waste of time. She didn't need to look at these figures. They'd been a splinter in her brain every day for the past year. It had irritated her and made her come up with sales and promotional packages that brought in more revenue than if she hadn't. But it wasn't as important as what was going on with the Warriors Riding and at Well Spring. A year ago she would have found a way to meet her sales goal. Whatever it took, it didn't matter. Now it mattered.

Dana nodded. "Yes, down a little less than 3 percent on average."

"That's correct." Spencer turned a page.

"Look at the next page."

Dana turned the page and looked at a chart tracking her station's rating performance.

"You're probably intimately aware that we've had some programming challenges on your station. Changing program directors twice in one year has not helped. Regardless, budgets still need to be set and met. Not reaching them isn't an option."

Another recap of the obvious. Why were they putting her through this?

"This next page is the Miller Kaplan report for the past year — again a report you've probably glanced at more than once."

This time they were wrong. She hadn't looked at the Miller Kaplan for at least eighteen months. She wasn't sure why. Probably because Robert never paid it much attention and never used it to evaluate her performance. Did it matter what other stations were doing compared to hers? The goal was the goal was the goal as had just been stated.

"As you can see, you've outperformed every station with similar ratings to yours and your revenue is even ahead of five stations who have up to 15 percent higher ratings."

He tossed the packet on the coffee table

in front of him, sat back, and crossed his legs. "That includes three stations here in our own group."

"You're not going to fire me?" Dana blurted out the thought without giving consideration to how stupid it would sound. She glanced at her GM who offered an affirming smile.

"This is true. We had hoped to go in a bit different direction."

Robert slid a sheet of paper across the glass coffee table and tapped it twice. "Before you look at that sheet let me apologize. Based on your request at the start of this meeting we obviously have done a poor job of conveying our view of your performance and what we think of you. With that in mind, take a moment to peruse this sheet that will give you a better feel of what our thoughts are with regard to your future with this company."

Dana picked up the paper. It took only ten seconds to read but she stared at the words and figures for over a minute.

- Dana Raine new position: station general manager
- Salary: $285,000
- Vacation days: six weeks paid
- Bonus structure: Immediate $15,000,

and $15,000 per percentage point over goal each quarter from the previous year

• Start date: May 20

Was this real? She looked up. "You're promoting me." Another obvious comment, but they didn't seem to take offense.

"Yes." Spencer smiled. "You've done an excellent job. And not only with the numbers. As surprising as this might seem we do care about more than the bottom line. We care how our leaders treat the people they lead. Why? Because people do better in an atmosphere where they feel encouraged, believed in, and fought for. We know you've stood in the gap for your salespeople. We know you fight for them in promotion meetings. We know you've gone far above and way beyond to make sure they're appreciated. When people have a leader like that, most of them will overachieve. Which you can see from the Miller Kaplan, they have done and continue to do.

"I guess in that sense that brings us back to the numbers so maybe that is all we care about." He laughed. "We talked to your salespeople and eight of the nine said your leadership over the past ten months has been stellar. Better than it's ever been."

"I . . . I thought . . . I don't know what to say."

"Say yes to a significant advance in your career."

"I didn't apply for this. I didn't even know you were looking for a new GM."

Robert leaned forward, elbows on his knees. "They tell me I've had a good run here, Dana. Good enough that I'm being bumped up." He smiled and waved his thumb at Spencer. "I'm taking his role, so someone needs to fill mine. They're going to let me work out of Seattle, so we'll still get to work together." He pointed to the sheet in her hands. "So what do you say? Would you do me the honor of succeeding me?"

She glanced at the paper in her hands, then up to her GM. "Yes."

The rest of the meeting was a blur. She thanked both of them, shook their hands, and stood, her body numb. They told her to be expecting a contract on her desk in the morning and to take her time looking it over and have her attorney look it over as well.

Dana was still in a daze as she pushed open her office door and slumped against her desk. Really? Had she really just been offered the chance to run the station? She'd been noticed. She'd been seen.

And suddenly life was good.

Sure, it was balanced out on the negative side with wanting a special person in her life and having no prospects on the horizon, not to mention her weird quasi relationship with Brandon. But still, on the whole her life felt solid and the future was full of hope. Warriors Riding continued to propel her deeper with Jesus than she'd ever imagined was possible and they were doing amazing things for the kingdom. The school at Well Spring was going extremely well and now this promotion? If this was the enemy's attack she wanted more.

THIRTEEN

Marcus pushed through his front door at six thirty on Monday evening, the smell of spaghetti filling the small entryway of his home. His gaze fell on the picture of an eight-year-old Layne sitting on the credenza next to the coat closet, reminding Marcus for the millionth time of what he'd done.

No, take every thought captive. It was over and he couldn't go back.

You've been forgiven.

The words of the Spirit were hollow in his mind, the pain in his soul like thunder. But he'd gut through it just like he always did this time of year.

Kat peered around the corner of the kitchen as he took off his shoes and pushed them toward the basket next to the front door. "Hey." She winked at him and disappeared back inside the kitchen.

He walked up to the kitchen door and stood in the entry. "I thought I was supposed to cook tonight."

"You were, but I got home early and figured I'd get things started."

"Sorry I'm late."

"You're not that late." Kat glanced at the clock on the wall above the breakfast nook. "How was your day stimulating young minds?"

"Not as strange as Friday." He set his satchel down on the kitchen counter and gave Kat a quick kiss. "I swear I stepped into two different versions of your shop. It wasn't a dream. It wasn't a vision."

"But you decided to let it go. So do it."

"You're right, you're right, I know you're right."

"Then truly release it and enjoy the evening, okay? You haven't been sleeping. You've been stressed over this possible book deal with Tim, and you're always a little out of sorts on the first day of a new quarter. Isn't it possible your mind was playing tricks on you?"

"Yes."

"Could you say that with a little less enthusiasm?"

Marcus laughed and lifted his hands in surrender. "Let me change and I'll set the table."

"No need. We're eating in the dining room

tonight."

"What?"

"We're having a dinner guest tonight and you're going to be nice." Kat glared at him, a paring knife in her right hand pointed directly at him.

A dinner guest? This couldn't be good. If he hadn't been consulted on the occasion it meant the guest was one of Abbie's or Jayla's friends. And it wouldn't be Jayla's. Her friends didn't come for dinner. Neither did Abbie's unless they happened to be over and Kat extended an impromptu invitation. Which gave high credence to the hypothesis that this guest was not female.

"There's a boy coming to dinner tonight? Here?"

"Come on." Kat put her hands on her hips. "How did you know that?"

"It didn't take a great deal of analytical prowess to reach that conclusion."

"Yes, it's a boy." Kat turned and stirred the spaghetti sauce.

"From where? How old is he?"

"A friend of Abbie's from high school. He's seventeen."

"I seem to have acquired a considerable amount of wax in my ears in the past two seconds. I thought you just said he was seventeen."

Kat spun and glared at Marcus again. "Your ears are fine."

"This *boy* is three years older than Abbie?"

"Yes, he's a senior this year."

"She's not going to date anyone, let alone a young *man* who is three years older than she is."

"She's not dating. This isn't a date. They're just getting to know each other. As friends."

"Coming to the parents' house is more than just getting to know each other. And no seventeen-year-old is simply a friend of a fourteen-year-old girl."

"Would you rather she hid it from us?"

"How long have you known about this?"

Kat set down the knife, sashayed over to Marcus, and slid her fingers under the collar of his shirt. "How old were you when you went on your first date?"

"If memory serves me accurately, twenty-three."

"We were married at twenty-three."

"Then my first date must have been at twenty-two."

"Do I need to remind you of what your father used to say about your dating habits during your teen years? That you had more girlfriends than fleas on a dirty dog's back?"

"That wasn't until I was at least . . . seventeen."

"Try fourteen. The same age as your daughter. I remember stuff like that, remember?"

"The dating equations that pertain to boys are severely different when applied to girls."

"Care to explain that?"

"I was that age once. I understand fully what is going through a teenage boy's mind."

"And what is that?"

"Have you met this kid who has hormones racing all through his body like a particle accelerator?"

Kat nodded.

"And?"

She took a loaf of sourdough bread off the counter and put it in the oven. "You'll like him the second you meet him, I promise."

"I'm sure I will." Marcus gritted his teeth. "And when will said senior in high school be arriving?"

"He's in the family room with Abbie. Dinner will be ready in ten minutes. Remember, be nice, if not for his sake, for the sake of your relationship with Abbie."

Marcus frowned. "It's not right."

"What's not right? Calen is charming, handsome, an athlete, gets decent grades from what Abbie says . . . goes to youth group — he's the total package."

"That's the kind of description that worries me."

"Why?"

"I don't like perfect people. They're usually not."

"Don't be worried. I'm sure he has flaws like the rest of us. And maybe this is God's way of bringing a little light into what has been an unusual past year, to say the least."

Marcus headed upstairs and tried to wrap his mind around the idea of Abbie dating a seventeen-year-old. It wouldn't be easy.

"Good to meet you, Mr. Amber." The kid shook his hand with a firm grip and looked right in Marcus's eyes when he spoke. His smile was relaxed and he didn't hang back but wasn't overly eager.

"You too, Calen. Welcome to our home."

"Thanks." Calen hooked his thumbs on the front of his belt, then immediately released one of his hands and pointed at the bookshelves to his left. "I'm trying to read your book."

"Trying?"

Calen's face flushed a pinch. "I'm dyslexic and reading has always been a challenge. So it takes longer for me to read books than most people."

"Calen has a 3.75 GPA," Abbie said and smiled at Marcus.

Dyslexic? And still got good grades? Great. Could this situation get any more clichéd? Sir Calen was not only a star but circumvented his weaknesses to light the way for others with learning disabilities. When dinner was over, Marcus would be shocked if the kid didn't propose to clear the table and do all the dishes.

He needed to relax. Why couldn't he accept Kat's idea that God was bringing something good into Abbie's life? Because he wasn't ready for another male to waltz into Abbie's world and become her main influence at the same time he was starting to find his way back into her heart.

True, he'd alienated her by spending far too much time on his career at the university when she was younger, but he'd been more than on board for the past two years. And lately their relationship had grown significantly better.

After they were seated, Marcus said a quick prayer and watched Kat gracefully steer the conversation. "Abbie tells me you're new in town."

"Yeah, we've been here for only a month but it's been great so far." Calen glanced at

Abbie. "But like it says in John's gospel, the wind blows where it will, and I have to think the Spirit brought us to Seattle for a reason." He glanced at Abbie again and she flushed and gave him a shy smile.

That night as they lay in bed Marcus tried to accept the fact Abbie wasn't ten anymore. Or even twelve.

"Don't blow it." Kat patted his leg.

"Something is off about this kid."

"No, for you there is. No one else. Something is going to be off for you with every guy Abbie brings home. It's okay to feel that way but your feelings don't make it true."

"A large part of me cannot comprehend that we're having this discussion."

"Be wise." Kat poked him in the shoulder. "I mean it. This is a good kid. Yes, he's a senior but he's good for her. Haven't you seen it? She's lighter than she's been in a year and it's good for your relationship with her. Tell me you saw that tonight. And that you're not going to crush her."

"What are you insinuating?"

"That he asked her to the prom tonight, and when she tells you, you're going to smile and congratulate her."

"What? Wait a minute. When did this turn from 'a friend' to going to the prom? Let me guess, you wanted to ease me into it? Meet the kid, agree he's great, then roll over and say yes?"

"You and Abbie have done pretty well over the past several months. If you're going to tell her she can't go with Calen I suggest you do it with a great deal of tenderness and tact."

"She's just a little girl."

"I wish that were true."

"It is true."

"It's not."

"I don't care if she's twenty."

Kat didn't answer and turned over. Within minutes she was asleep. Slumber didn't come for Marcus till nearly an hour later. And fifty minutes of prayer didn't get him any closer to knowing what he was going to do.

The next evening at nine thirty Abbie slumped onto the couch in their family room next to Kat and skewered him with her eyes. "This is where you tell me I can't go to the prom with Calen, right?"

"I'm only saying I want to discuss it."

"Let's cut to the final scene, Dad. Do you approve or not approve? Can I go or not?"

"He seems like a nice kid but —"

"He's not a *kid*! He's a senior and he's

almost eighteen years old. He's nearly an adult."

Marcus took a deep breath. "Exactly."

"What does that mean?"

"He seems like a nice *adult* but —"

"But I'm too young to date, he's too much older than me, blah, blah, blah, and I can't go to the prom with him."

"I'm just trying to —"

Abbie grabbed the back of her long red hair and pulled down, her eyes closed. "To what, Dad? Protect me? Keep me from getting my heart broken? I just want to go to a dance together and if that goes well maybe a movie. Take a hike in the mountains. Go to a Sounders game together. Hang out with him at youth group. I'm not going to bed the guy."

"Abbie!"

"What?" She kicked the coffee table and yanked her arms across her chest.

"Statistically young girls . . . women . . . who start dating early have a much greater chance of winding up in relationships that will hurt them and taint their marriages for years to come. I know emotionally this doesn't register with you, but please consider the logic of this." He glanced at Kat for support but she shook her head. "You're only fourteen years old and you'll have years of time to date when you're older."

"Technically I've lived on earth for fourteen years so I'm really in my fifteenth year of living."

"Abbie."

She scowled. "Marcus."

"Don't call me that."

"Then be my dad, not a professor lecturing me on the ills of holding hands with a boy at my age. Can't you trust me just a little bit? I've prayed about this by myself and with Mom and I'm not blind."

He stared at her pleading eyes and an image of the dinner they'd had almost a year ago at the Space Needle flashed into his mind. And the times since then where they'd watched TV together, went for mountain bike rides, and how her face lit up for a few seconds when he framed a picture he'd taken of her playing soccer and gave it to her for no reason at all. He didn't want to lose the ground they'd gained.

And logic? Yes, it was logical to let her go. It was one date. She wasn't getting engaged. And he could keep a very close eye on where things went from here with Calen.

"Okay, you can go." The words sputtered out of his mouth, and the moment they did he wished he could take them back.

Abbie leaped from the couch and threw

her arms around his shoulders. "Thanks, Dad. I'm so glad I don't have to cut you out of my will now."

Marcus tried to smile. "Me too." He stood and glanced at Kat who mouthed, *Well done.* Then he walked out of the room and upstairs, trying to ignore the sensation in his stomach telling him he'd made an extremely poor decision.

Marcus sat at his desk in his den. *You made the appropriate choice.* But had he? Where was the line between being a strong father and protecting his daughter and letting her go? How much of their strained relationship played into it — should play into it? Had he let her go just to keep their relationship going in the right direction? Did it mean he'd always be a slave to Abbie's desires? The desires of a fourteen-year-old?

A shuffle of feet in his doorway made him look up. Kat, with a smile on her face.

"Thoughts?" he said.

"You hit a few bumps, swerved a few times, but got the car back on the road by the end of the conversation." Kat eased over to his walnut desk and leaned against it.

"I hope we're even supposed to be on this stretch of the highway."

"I'm thinking what's left of today still has

136

enough to worry about, so why don't we put tomorrow's worries off till tomorrow?"

"Well said."

"Are you coming to bed?" She turned to go.

"In a few minutes. I need some time to wind down."

"Don't think too hard. It's all going to work out." As Kat left, his den light flashed off her wedding ring and Marcus glanced around his den. Everything looked exactly the same.

He leaned back in his chair, closed his eyes, and stayed that way for a long time. He needed to relax. Trust that God had Abbie in his hands. He repeated the idea to himself along with verses that seemed like clichés. Finally he opened his eyes and came forward. Time for bed. Kat was probably already asleep.

He pulled a couple of pens out of his pocket and tossed them onto his desk. They came to rest against a small stack of photos tucked underneath a book he'd been studying. He reached for them and slowly drew them closer. He didn't remember the photos being there the day before yesterday. Were they? Marcus lifted the stack and his pulse spiked. Whether the photos had been there or not was irrelevant because the one on the top of the stack shouldn't exist.

FOURTEEN

Marcus slumped back in the leather chair in his den and stared at the photo clutched in his hand as if it were proof UFOs were real. Where had the shot been taken? He racked his brain for the answer but his mind offered no solutions.

The picture was of Dave Damrell and him standing on the top of a rocky, nondescript cliff, their arms wrapped around each other's shoulders, wide grins under their mirrored sunglasses. A sweeping view of snowcapped peaks forty or fifty miles behind them appeared to be an ideal backdrop to capture a memory of male bonding.

The only problem was, Marcus had no recollection of the picture being taken or where he and Dave were standing. He turned the photo over. Eight words on the back, scrawled in his handwriting, made his body go numb: *On top of Little Annapurna — Enchantments trip '93.*

Was this some kind of joke? The first four photos were of jade-green alpine lakes and sweeping mountain views and goats with molting fur. But the last one was of Dave and him on a trip in the summer of '93 he didn't go on.

The trip he'd regretted missing ever since. Dave, Ricky Totten, and Mark Effinger had all gone and raved about it for years afterward — needled him was a more accurate description — and he'd never forgiven himself for canceling at the last minute so he could . . . Marcus couldn't even remember why he'd thrown the trip away. Probably studying for a test for his PhD.

He turned the other photos over. There was a lack of notation on them. He set the photo of Dave and him in the center of his desk and shoved the other pictures to his right. A thick sensation of dread grew in the center of his stomach. There was no logical explanation for how this photo could exist. But it did.

"Would you like to explain to me what has just occurred, Lord? Along with the scenes in the bakery? Are they tied together?"

He clutched the photos in his hands and tiptoed out of the den toward his bedroom. The door creaked as he opened it — he had to WD-40 those hinges. The lights were off and Kat's rhythmic breathing told him she was asleep. He turned and eased back to the den. He needed to talk to someone now. Reece? No. That would be a ghastly choice. Their leader didn't need anything reminding him that taking or looking at photos would likely not be in his immediate — let alone long-term — future.

Brandon. He was most likely still up and Marcus didn't have to explain what had happened on the Ave last Friday. He pulled out his phone and dialed the Song.

"Professor. You have a physics question for me?"

"Sorry to call late."

"I'll be up for another hour at least. Talk to me."

"I found a photo of myself standing on a mountain I couldn't have been standing on."

"Cool."

"No, not cool." Marcus explained what happened. "I need to know where that photo came from."

"Do you feel like something weird spiritually is going on?"

Nothing in his spirit felt off in the slightest. Once again the situation felt neutral. "It feels the same."

"What's he do for a living?"

"What does who do for a living?"

"Your pal Dave. How does he produce cash-o-la? Put bread on the table, you know?"

"He teaches computers and video production at a junior high school." Marcus leaned back, his leather chair bumping up against his bookshelves.

"Ah yes, that makes perfect sense. Which I believe gives us the answer to your one-question quiz."

"I'm not following you."

"Hello?" Brandon laughed. "I thought you were supposed to have the exceptional mind, Prof."

"Apparently stumbling upon photos I know weren't part of my life has stunted the flow of blood to my prefrontal cortex." Marcus bit his lower lip and continued to stare at the picture.

"Would it be in the nature of this buddy of yours to do some Photoshopping as a practical joke?"

"You're brilliant." Marcus smiled as relief flooded his body.

"Thank you very much . . ." Brandon did a bad Elvis impersonation. "Ol' Dave is a practical joker, huh?"

"He rightfully holds the title of emperor.

The twentieth anniversary of the hike is coming up later this summer and this is precisely the kind of thing Dave would do to remind me of my . . ." Marcus trailed off.

"Regret?"

"Yeah."

"And even though Dave snuck the photos into your house and stuck them on your desk in fun, it's the perfect circumstance for the enemy to use to make you wallow in what didn't happen, right?"

"Well said." Marcus spun his chair back around and gazed out the window at the dark night.

"Take it captive. No regrets. Fight back. Speak truth and all that."

"Thank you, Brandon. I will." Marcus hung up and set his phone down. Finally, a mystery solved. As he hunched farther over his desk to examine the job Dave had done, the light from his emerald-green banker's lamp flashed off his silver letter opener. Marcus blinked against the glare, pulled his glasses off, and rubbed his eyes. When he opened them again perspiration broke out on the back of his neck and forehead. The photos were gone.

Marcus grabbed his phone and redialed

Brandon. "They vanished."

"Professor?"

"Yes, of course, who else?"

"What vanished?"

"The photos. They're gone. I closed my eyes, opened them, and they disappeared."

"Okay . . . I'm sure at some point you're going to tell me what you're talking about, but how 'bout you do it now?"

"I just talked to you!" Marcus wiped the sweat from his forehead. "The photos of the backpacking trip I didn't go on. Determining where they might have come from."

"You all right, Prof?"

The pounding of Marcus's heart filled his ears. "No."

"I'm guessing you had another one of whatever happened to you on the Ave the other day."

"Yes."

"Was it a vision this time? Maybe?" Brandon said. "Something the Spirit was taking you through to have you face a regret and work through it?"

"Not possible."

Brandon gave a fake cough. "So your vast experience of having one vision makes you an expert?"

"No, but this wasn't a vision. It happened. It was real."

"Just because you know it makes it true?"

"I had a conversation with you."

"That makes it not a vision? Why couldn't you have a conversation with someone in your vision? John talked to Jesus quite extensively during the vision that became the book of Revelation." Brandon paused. "So in your wildest imagination, what do you think is going on?"

"A possibility I haven't wanted to admit to myself or anyone else since it happened the first time." Marcus sighed.

"That your book is more than theory? That you've been taking little jaunts into alternate realities?"

"Exactly."

"Anything else?"

"Yes. That this is only the beginning."

FIFTEEN

Brandon glanced at the parking lot on Wednesday evening, hoping Dana would show up first. He sat on the grass in the middle of Houghton Beach Park in Kirkland on the shores of Lake Washington, wanting to talk to her but not having a clue what he would say. He glanced at his watch. Six thirty-five. Dana and Marcus were both twenty minutes late.

Except for two couples and a family with a toddler, the vast green lawn in front of the water was empty. He stared at a boat making its way across the lake in front of the park and pictured Dana and him on it together with a couple of kids. Ridiculous. Would never happen.

"Hey."

Brandon turned at the sound. Dana. "Nice of you to show up."

"Thank you."

"You could have told me you'd be late."

146

Dana scowled, sat beside him, and point at his cell phone sitting between them. did."

Brandon tapped the text icon on his cell phone. There were two messages, one from Dana, one from Marcus. "Oh. Sorry to accuse you falsely." He slipped his phone into his pocket. "Marcus says he'll be here in five."

Brandon shifted forward and tried to ignore the fact this was the first time he'd been with Dana alone since last year on the way to the hospital to see Reece after he lost his eyes. Sitting here alone with her felt right and awkward at the same time. Did she feel it? He certainly wasn't going to ask her.

"Did you get held up at the station again?"

"No, early dinner with a friend. I lost track of time."

"Anyone I know?"

Dana flushed and gazed at Lake Washington. Interesting. A tinge of jealousy flared inside Brandon. Stupid. There was no reason to be feeling anything. Why couldn't he get it through his thick head there would never be anything between them ever again? He pushed the emotion down, but it was like rubber and bounced right back to the surface.

What's his name?"

"Why do you think it was a guy?"

"Because I know you."

"You don't. Not anymore."

Brandon grinned and wrapped his arms around his legs. "Yeah I do."

"I thought we were here to talk about Reece, Doug, and pray for strength for them as we get ready to go after the Wolf."

"I'm sure we will once Marcus gets here. Does your friend have a name?"

"Perry, but I'm not sure why that should concern you."

"No concern, just curious."

She was right. It was none of his business and there was no reason to press her about it. He should stop and change subjects, let it go. He pulled off his sunglasses. "Do you like him?"

She sighed and turned the back of her head to him. "At one point, yes. But now we're just friends and I needed to make sure he's going to keep it that way."

He stared at her till she turned her head back around, then raised one ear like he always used to do when he didn't believe her. It irked her in the old days and he could tell it irked her now.

"Can we please drop this?"

"Have you ever been more than friends

with this guy? Have his lips been on you
in the past six months?"

Dana spun cross-legged on the grass till
she faced him and pointed her forefinger at
his chest. "If we weren't in the Warriors
together I wouldn't even bother to answer
you. But since we are, listen very closely. If
I had put my lips on another man's during
the time we were dating or the time we were
engaged, it would have been your business.
I would have asked Jesus for forgiveness and
then asked for yours. But that's not the situation." She plucked a finger full of grass
and tossed it into the breeze coming off the
lake.

"So if you can explain to me why you
should concern yourself with my social life,
I'll give you all the details. But if you can't,
please leave me alone on the subject of my
love life."

Brandon widened his eyes and fell backward. "Okay!"

"Don't mock me."

"Sorry, I just thought we were doing better than this. That it might be okay if I asked
what was going on with you outside of the
Warriors. You know, the healing may be
changing the way you relate to people and
everything."

Dana scooted around so she faced the lake

ain. "That healing was one of the greatest moments of my life, and yes, we've worked well together but that doesn't mean you can try to peel back my dating life and probe me for answers like I'm on a witness stand."

"You're part of me because you're part of the team, one-fourth of the prophecy. I need to know how to pray for you and —"

"That's why you are asking? So you can pray for me better?"

"I'm only thinking about —"

"Yourself. You're wondering if our relationship could leap back onto the highway it used to be on because we've found some healing from the past. Right?"

Heat rose to Brandon's face and he didn't answer.

"You know me? Well I know you too, so let me help you out. Yes, we will be friends. Yes, we'll probably be connected for a long time because of the prophecy and what God is doing with Warriors Riding. But you and I more than what we are now? No chance. Let it go. That time is irrevocably gone. I thought you would have figured that out over the past ten months."

"Dana, I —"

"Put it out of your mind. Whatever was wrong with me when you broke our engagement is probably still there."

"Come on. You know I didn't break t
because of you, but because I was scare
you'd leave after I gave you all of my heart."
Brandon tugged his fingers through the turf.
"Like my mom did."

"Give up the idea of us. Forever." Dana
stared at the lake. "For both of our sakes."

Brandon blinked and didn't try to hide
his pain. She would take one look at him
and know it anyway. She'd always been able
to read his eyes. She'd told him his eyes
turned a shade darker when his sorrow ran
deep, so they were probably two shades
darker now. He thought he was over her,
over them. Wrong. He turned to her, not
sure what he would say, but as he started to
speak he spied Marcus over her shoulder
ambling toward them.

"There's the professor."

"Thank goodness," Dana muttered.

Marcus settled down next to them. "Everything okay?"

"Great," Brandon said.

"Fine." Dana gave the professor a thin
smile.

"Liars."

Both Dana and Brandon laughed and it
broke the tension.

"I apologize for being detained, and not
to hurry things but can we get right to the

ject at hand?"

"Yes." Dana placed her palms on the grass and stared at the ground. She opened her mouth to speak but stopped as she glanced over Brandon's shoulder.

Brandon turned. Two men strolled their direction. One had brown hair and was probably in his late twenties or early thirties. He was a little shorter than average with a lean build and a baseball hat turned backward on his head. The man next to him looked like he'd probably enjoyed deluxe double-bacon cheeseburgers a few times too many and was trying to cover it up with a Hawaiian shirt straight out of the sixties. Reece would love it.

They stopped three yards away. "Are you Brandon Scott, the fiction writer?"

"The what?" Brandon laughed. "The writer?" He'd heard "the musician" thousands of times, but "the writer"? Never. Where in the world would they get that idea? He'd started a blog three weeks ago but his name wasn't on it and he hadn't told anyone about it. Not Kevin, not Doug. Not even Marcus, Dana, or Reece.

"Yeah, the writer or blogger or whatever it is. The one who writes at www.godeeper.me. Isn't that you?"

"Why do you think it's me?" Brandon

frowned and apprehension shot thro
him.

The guy with the baseball hat flipped I.
thumb back and forth between himself anc
Hawaiian Shirt Man. "We're techies. And
big fans of your music. So when we were
doing a little searching online we found
traces you left that identify you as the owner
of the site."

"I didn't think I left a trail."

"Yeah, most non-techies think that."

"Right." Brandon grimaced and glanced
at Marcus and Dana, then back to the man.

"Are you kidding me?" Dana tapped him
on the elbow. "You have a blog?"

The guy with the baseball cap continued,
"You're prolific. Three posts a week with
almost six hundred words each time —
that's a lot of verbiage. And the story you're
writing is certainly intriguing. The ideas in
it are, uh, not commonplace within Christendom."

Dana leaned in. "What kind of story are
you writing?"

"I'm a little in shock anyone is reading it."

Hawaiian Shirt Man smiled and motioned
to his friend. "Both of us are reading it."

Brandon turned to Dana and Marcus. "I
started writing a story on a blog."

"We deduced that rather easily," Marcus

"But not as private as you intended. y didn't you simply write it on your mputer?"

"What inspired the name of the story?" Cap Man sat and the other man did as well. "Do you mind if we sit down?"

"Uh . . ." Brandon glanced at Dana and Marcus who stayed silent. "No, fine."

Dana poked Brandon's shoulder. "Let me guess. You're basically making a story out of everything that's happened to us over the past year in a thinly veiled exposé for the world to read and see?"

"No one is supposed to see it." Brandon shrugged. "At least not yet."

"Wonderful." Dana slumped back on her arms. "What's the tagline?"

Hawaiian Shirt Man grinned. " 'Skating on the edge of the universe.' " He motioned to Cap Man. "We like it. It sounds like us." The man rubbed his hands together. "How close to the edge do you get?"

"Who are you guys?"

The man with the baseball cap said, "I'm Jotham, and this is Orson. We're both 'Softies' and we love the Mariners. Now you know our entire lives."

"Orson?" Brandon said.

"It's a nickname."

"Okay." Brandon pointed at Orson. "And

you're 'Softies'?"

"Microsoft," Dana said. "They both ⟨...⟩ for Microsoft."

"Got it."

Jotham leaned forward. "So, how close t⟨o⟩ the edge?"

Something about these guys seemed . . . different. Not evil, just different.

"Close."

Jotham turned and grinned at Orson, then shifted his gaze back to Brandon. "Do you really believe all that stuff you're writing in the story? I mean, have you really truly been going into other people's souls, or are you simply having fun?"

"It's a story, not nonfiction."

"Really? That surprises me. The way you're writing it gave me the impression it's more than a story to you."

"Why do you say that?"

"Let's just say I'm reading between the lines."

These guys were playing a game and were a lot smarter than they were letting on. "Let's just say you're going to tell me how you acquired your between-the-lines reading skills."

"It's pretty obvious for anyone with eyes to see."

Brandon glanced at Marcus and Dana,

back to Jotham and Orson. He still
t get the sense these two were evil, but
e was more to them under the surface
d Brandon had a feeling the lake was
eep. They liked the Mariners? Good. He
decided to throw them a fastball.

"You're right, it's not fiction." He motioned toward Dana and Marcus. "My
friends and I send our spirits inside other
people's souls to help set them free."

Jotham nodded and the expression on his
face didn't change. Either he didn't understand what Brandon had said or he was trying to play it cool. "Ah yes. That makes
sense now given the story you've been telling."

"You're not surprised?"

"No."

"This is something you're familiar with?"

"I am." Jotham motioned again to his
companion. "We are."

"Who are you guys again?" Dana said.

Before they could answer, the attention of
all of them was stolen by a tall man who
strode toward them over the grass, a big
smile on his face. Brandon smirked. Why
didn't it surprise him? Tristan Barrow, his
own personal blond-haired stalker, had appeared once again.

He pulled up between all of them and

glanced back and forth. "I see you've
my friends, Brandon." He sat and smile
Marcus and Dana. "Can I meet yours?"

The guy was too comfortable, too confi
dent, too assuming.

"Make yourself at home." Brandon glared
at him.

"Thanks, I appreciate that." Tristan ignored Brandon's look and addressed Dana
and Marcus. "Did Brandon tell you he and
I met a few nights back after one of his
concerts?"

Dana and the professor shook their heads
and eyed Tristan with wariness, and Dana
scooted a few inches backward. "And now
you've bumped into him again. Something
tells me this isn't a chance encounter."

"That's true, Dana. It's not."

Tristan didn't continue so Brandon asked
the obvious follow-up question. "Then at
what point are you going to explain why
you're stalking me?"

"Not just you, Brandon, all three of you.
And Reece as well. And to a lesser extent,
Doug." Tristan smiled as he said it but no
one else joined him.

Marcus pressed his glasses closer to his
face and frowned. "Since you've been
forthcoming with your behavior perhaps

would be so kind as to describe your ...t."

"Simple." Tristan glanced at his friends. "To help you."

"And if we don't want your help?" Dana said.

Tristan winked, the look in his eyes playful, as if he were answering a child. "We've taken enough of your time. It's good to meet all of you." Tristan and the other two men stood in unison. "Maybe we'll run into you again someday."

"Yeah, maybe. Maybe not," Brandon said.

The three strolled out of the park as if they were on a tour of the Seattle Art Museum. As soon as they were out of earshot Dana said, "Demons? Angels? Christians? Overeager fans? New Agers? Something else?"

Brandon scoffed. "Not thinking those three are angels, and I didn't get anything remotely demonic. Maybe they're just spiritually attuned wackos."

"I didn't get anything either." Dana continued to watch the three walk away. "But they were pretty obvious even if they didn't feel demonic."

"Meaning?" Marcus asked.

"These guys should have *Monkey Wrench* stamped on their foreheads because that's what I'm thinking they're going to us."

"Agreed," Marcus said.

Brandon got to his feet and took a toward the parking lot. "Then are you thinking what I'm thinking?"

Dana stood and brushed off her shorts. "Follow them."

"Exactly. I want to know what we're dealing with." He glanced at the professor. "Well?"

The three of them jogged to the sidewalk just beyond the parking lot and glanced left and right. "There!" Marcus pointed north. Tristan's head bobbed along the sidewalk seventy yards in front of them, Jotham and Orson on either side.

Marcus lunged forward and picked up speed with each stride, but Dana caught up to him and shoved an arm across his chest. "Let's not be spotted, okay? A discreet distance, don't you think?"

As they slowed down and followed the three, Dana asked the exact question spinning in Brandon's mind. "So if they're human, then what are they all about?"

Marcus pulled out his cell phone and stabbed his thumbs at the screen like a miniature jackhammer. "There's three possibilities. First, they are evil and our discern-

his is being hindered somehow. we're out of touch with the Spirit e signals are there, but our reading y has waned. Third, the Spirit is block-us."

"What about what I just said? Just ordinary wackos who we will need to avoid?" Brandon said.

"That certainly seems incongruous with their behavior and even a cursory examination of the evidence. First, there is no neutral zone for us these days. I doubt you would postulate this being a chance encounter. I believe it is either for evil or for good. Second, do you really think people asking those kinds of questions are ordinary people? And third —"

"Do you always have to lay out our options like a professor?" Brandon snapped his fingers.

Marcus's face turned red. "But I am a —"

"It's a joke, Prof. Relax."

"I am relaxed." Marcus slid his phone back into his pocket and pushed his glasses back up on his nose.

"Uh-huh. You're melted white chocolate, you're so silky smooth."

Up ahead, the man who called himself Orson crossed the street, leaving Jotham and Tristan on the other side. Another block up,

Jotham crossed the street as well.

"Do we want to split up?" Dana asked.

"No, let's stay on Tristan."

Thirty seconds later Tristan stopped next to a gold Pontiac Grand Am and reached into his pocket.

"You think he can see us?" Brandon said.

"Unlikely at this distance and angle," Marcus replied.

Tristan opened the door of his car, then turned and waved at them before getting in.

"I think he spotted us," Dana said.

"How'd he know we were following?"

"First, we are not as skilled in subterfuge as we would like to believe we are. Second, we were —" Marcus stopped, pointed at Brandon, and laughed. "I'm going to stop doing that sometime in the next ten years, I assure you."

"I hope not." Brandon grinned and watched Tristan pull away.

"Of course." Marcus smiled, then looked skyward, a puzzled expression on his face.

"Why the strange look, Marcus?"

"Two items for contemplation."

"Spill it."

"First, the three of us didn't talk about Reece." The professor rubbed his temple. "But it appears the Spirit had another agenda in mind."

"True, and the second?"

"Your stalker reminds me of someone who might be stalking me. And I have the sensation he's getting ready for a second visit very soon."

Sixteen

Marcus wrapped things up in his office at four fifteen on Thursday afternoon, which meant the chance to get in a workout at his gym before heading home but he never got there.

He decided to walk through Red Square to break up his normal routine when heading for his car. It would take a few more minutes but that was fine. It would give him a little more thinking time — to continue to wrestle with the idea that he truly had switched into another reality on the Ave, at Kat's bakery, and in his den two nights ago.

It couldn't have truly transpired. But that's what he would have said about all the things Doug and Reece had shown them over the past year.

The campus smelled of summer trying to make itself known in the midst of the perpetual dampness of a Seattle spring. A few students wore shorts as if they could hasten its arrival. Others wore jackets, un-convinced of the power of the descending sun poking through thick white clouds.

Marcus strolled by a man he'd long ago dubbed Jeremiah and watched him speak to ten or eleven students in his soft, husky voice about how to experience heaven on earth. As he passed by, Marcus winked at him and Jeremiah returned the gesture. They'd chatted once or twice a month about life and even about a few of his experiences with the Warriors. Jeremiah always ended their conversations by saying, "Go with it, I'll pray for you," and Marcus believed the man did.

In the far corner some spray-paint artists created images for the freshmen who stared at their works in fascination. The painters would be kicked off campus soon enough, but not before three or ten students "do-nated" thirty bucks to their art fund in exchange for a custom painting.

Directly in his path, in the far left corner of the square, a crowd of thirty, maybe thirty-five people stood in a semicircle around a man dressed in black. Marcus took three more strides toward him, then stopped as if he'd slammed into an iron door.

It was him. The man on the street corner who had tried to get cozy six days back. His prediction had come true. They were seeing each other again. At least Marcus was seeing him. He eased up to the back of the crowd and avoided the man's line of sight.

He was dressed the same as the other day: black jeans and a dark red shirt. The man darted back and forth from one side of the crowd to the other, shoulders slightly stooped, not from old age but because they followed his head and neck that were thrust forward as if he were a large bird looking for seeds among his audience.

Finally he stopped on the side of the group opposite Marcus and swept his gaze over the crowd. "Students of this university and students of life, you are about to see a miracle."

He made a quarter bow as if the miracle had already taken place, then stood straight with a broad grin washing across his face. The man turned to a short brunette and offered his empty right hand as if it held something. "You, take it, please." He turned over his hand in the air above hers. "Don't drop it, thank you. Now, take the deck and lift it up for everyone to see."

"I'm not holding —"

"It's invisible." He said it in a mock whisper, then leaned forward and winked at her. "You must believe."

She offered a droopy grin, raised her hand palm up, and the magician pointed at the invisible deck on top of it.

"If you would do me the favor of choosing a color: red or black."

"Red."

"Splendid. Please give the deck to the person to your right."

She pretended to hand the deck to a student who looked like Alfred Hitchcock must have looked like when he was young. "The color red offers us two choices: diamonds or hearts." The man glanced in Marcus's direction, then back to the student. "Please choose either, my young director."

Marcus squinted at the magician and took a few steps closer to the front. How did the man know Marcus was thinking the student looked like Hitchcock? It was either a disconcerting coincidence or an impressive bit of mind reading and he didn't believe in the latter.

"Do you have it? You've chosen a suit, yes?" He rubbed his teeth across his lower lip.

"Diamonds," the student answered.

"Do you want to change your mind?" The magician shuffled one step to his left.

"No."

He shuffled back. "So you're saying you're happy with the mind you have?"

Mild laughter fluttered through the crowd.

"Yes. I'm quite satisfied with the mind I have." Young Hitchcock smiled.

"I'm sure you are. Now hand the deck to the person next to you."

After the student mimed the transfer, the magician spoke to the young bohemian-looking woman who now held the deck. "Please choose lower cards, middle cards, or upper cards."

"Upper."

"Wonderful. Splendid. Superb."

To the next holder of the invisible pack of cards he asked, "Will you give us the name of a card in the upper diamonds?"

"Jack."

"The jack of diamonds?"

"Yes."

He spun in a 360, arms out to the crowd. "Amazing. Truly astounding." The magician closed his eyes and gave little shakes of his head — a thin smile on his face. He took a deep breath, opened his eyes, and beamed at the crowd.

"The card we arrived at was completely random. It was completely unknown to any of us until this moment. The choice of card was utterly and undeniably free. Yes?"

He glanced at the crowd who murmured their agreement.

"And yet last night I had a dream of strange portents." He closed his eyes and bowed his head. When he looked up and opened them, he looked ready to explode. "I dreamt of a card, in a dream so vivid that when I woke I immediately grabbed a deck of cards, found that card I'd dreamed of, and reversed it in the pack. I didn't know what it meant. I didn't know why I was compelled to reverse the card. I simply knew it had to be done."

The magician reached into his back pocket and pulled out a red deck of cards by the tips of his thumb and forefinger. He set it on the palm of his hand and stared at it.

"Unbelievable," he muttered.

He pulled the deck from the case and spread it between his hands. "Look. All these cards are faceup. Aces and eights and kings and fours and every other card." He spread them farther. "All of them."

Marcus squinted to see and pushed to the front of the crowd.

"All except one." Toward the end of the spread a reversed card slid into view, its red back in stark contrast to the other cards. "Fifty-one faceup cards. One card face-down."

The magician grinned, slid it out of the pack, and held it up for the crowd to gawk at. Marcus knew what had to be coming next but it still surprised him. The magician turned the card around and held the jack of diamonds high in the air as he slowly waved it back and forth.

"You were amazing." He pointed at each of the people who had helped choose the card. "Well done. If you'd chosen any other color, any other suit, the lower or middle cards or any other high card, well" — he motioned toward a brown leather bag with green bills overflowing from it — "I fear the others among you wouldn't be as kind with their donations as I'm hoping they will now be." He picked up the bag — the money still sticking over the edges — and passed it through the crowd.

As the bag circulated, the magician squatted and stared at the ground as if trying to figure out what to do next. When he sprang back to his feet, he grinned at the sky, then turned to Marcus. His slate-gray eyes seemed to bore into Marcus's brain and shout, "I told you we'd meet again today, of course I couldn't have it any other way." He spun in a slow circle on his heel, eyes closed, thumbs hooked over the front of his jeans.

When he opened them, he addressed the

crowd but his gaze locked onto Marcus. "We're about to do an experiment. Not a magic trick, not some manipulation of your senses to force you to choose in the way I want you to, but a true experiment that might or might not work. Simply put, I'm going to read your mind." He nodded at the crowd as if he'd just offered all of them a winning lottery ticket they couldn't refuse.

"But before we begin I should warn you this experiment will change at least one of your lives in a significant way." He bowed his head and opened his palms. "So if you suspect it might be you and are wondering what to do . . . if you'd like to remain in the cocoon you call your life, I suggest you leave now and give no chance to stir up strife."

The sensation that the magician was talking specifically about him surged through Marcus's brain like a rogue ocean wave, but he shrugged it off. Apparently not everyone could do so as about a quarter of the crowd shuffled away.

After the sound of their echoing steps off the red bricks of the square faded, the man lifted his head and sighed with seeming contentment. "Ah yes. The faithful remain." He rubbed his hands together. "Good, I think we're ready."

The street magician glanced at each of

the remaining people as if evaluating pieces of machinery. When he'd finished he looked up and to his left, then blinked three times at half speed. Then he turned and smiled at Marcus. "Would you like to help?"

"With what?"

"The experiment of course." He sauntered toward Marcus and stopped with three feet between them. "Are you ready to get on this pony and take a little jaunt together?"

"You're going to read my mind?"

"Yes. But without anything being written down as so many of my brethren must do and without asking you a single question. As I already said, this experiment is real. No smoke, no mirrors, no cheap trick thrill."

He glanced at the rest of the crowd, an expectant look on their faces.

"No thanks."

"No worries." He turned to Marcus's left. "Then let's do something else. Would anyone like to help me prove the existence of alternate realities and explain why a woman would wear the same outfit to her job at a bakery two days in a row?"

Marcus blinked. "What did you say?"

The magician spun back to him. "I don't believe your hearing failed you." He beckoned with his fingers. "Now, can I try to read your mind? I promise to be ever so kind."

"How do you know about that?"

"Do you want to help?"

"How did you know?"

He leaned toward Marcus and spoke in a stage whisper. "Are you sure we should have that conversation right now in front of students who will likely report on the details of what we talk about to others at this university, or should we arrange for a more appropriate time to chat?"

Marcus didn't answer. He wanted to grab the magician around the neck and shove him up against a wall until he told Marcus what he knew about Kat. All this guy needed was a gold coin to flip to convince him it was Zennon.

After a few minutes of pretending he was finding something in the battered leather briefcase at his feet, the magician asked once more, "Will you help?" His eyes said the only acceptable answer was yes. Marcus nodded.

"Splendid." He turned to the crowd and opened his arms wide. "Let us begin." He paced three steps to the right and then three back to the left, stroking his chin as if he were playing a vaudeville stage back in the 1920s.

"Please think of a photograph you own. Any will do. Concentrate on it. Form a picture of it in your head. Now attach an emotion to the picture. Anger, fear, happiness, regret — anything you like." He stopped pacing and stared at Marcus. "Ready?"

"Sure."

"You're thinking of a photograph of the Enchantments. Your arm is around a good friend and the emotion you're feeling is . . . regret."

Marcus stepped out from the crowd and turned to face them. "Show's over. My new friend and I are going to have a chat. Right now."

"Was he right?" a young man asked.

"Yes, he was right." Marcus stared at the magician and motioned him toward Drumheller Fountain at the south end of campus.

Marcus stood next to the fountain, arms crossed, his gaze drilling the magician. "What's your name?"

"Simon."

"Last name?"

Simon waved his hand. "Simon is enough."

"Fine. I suppose I don't have to tell you mine then."

"No, you don't. I picked that up while reading your mind." The man grinned.

"I don't believe that."

"You're right, it was much easier to find it online in the U-Dub faculty directory."

Marcus glanced to his left and right. No one near. Good. "Are you Zennon? Or some other demon?"

"No. Who is Zennon?"

"I think you know full well who Zennon is."

"Maybe, maybe not, but I swear on the stars beyond the stars beyond the many layered realms of alternate realities that I am not him." Simon took a coin out of his pocket and rolled it over his fingers. "He uses a gold coin. As you can plainly see, mine is silver."

"Are you an angel?"

"No." Simon sat on the edge of the fountain and patted the beveled concrete. Marcus stayed standing.

"Then what are you?"

Simon leaned back and laughed. "Are you always this direct?" He didn't wait for an answer. "I meant it when I said we would become friends. Or I should say, I hope we become friends. So let's ease into things before we talk about diamond rings. Get to know each other a bit first. Chat about the

174

mundane things of the world, then let the deeper things naturally unfurl." He leaned forward and looked at Marcus from under his eyebrows. "For example, wouldn't you like to ask me about the invisible deck trick?"

"I'd prefer to be enlightened on how you knew about the Enchantments photo."

Simon wiggled his fingers. "The deck first."

"Fine." If he had to play Simon's game for a spell, he would. "Were the people in the crowd plants? Did you tell them what card to finish with?"

"In other words, did I cheat in order to accomplish my stunning feat?"

"Yes."

"I did not."

"Then how could you anticipate they would pick the jack of diamonds?"

"I didn't."

"I don't understand."

"It doesn't matter what card they choose. It will always be the one reversed in the deck."

"So how did you accomplish the trick?"

"As my son said when he was young, 'maaa-gitch.' " Simon frowned and spoke more to himself than Marcus. "I think I had a son. I did, didn't I? I mean a real one."

"Simon, are you quite well?"

The magician whipped his head up and scratched his salt-and-pepper goatee. "Sorry, can't keep it all straight most of the time. I definitely had a real son." He smiled as if he'd figured out the meaning of quantum mechanics but then his face turned dark. "But he died when he was very young. Years later my wife died too and that's when —" Simon stopped and waved his hand as if to bat the thought away. "No, no, I won't be able to explain the trick." He looked apologetic and bowed his head. "I'm unable to break the magician's code. But it's only a trick — not real magic."

"It's one of the best I've seen." Granted, Marcus hadn't seen a lot of street magic, but if it was true, that the crowd could have picked any card, the trick seemed impossible.

Simon shook his head and chuckled.

"Is there something intrinsically humorous about my comment?"

"Many versed magicians look down on that trick because it's so common and so simple to do." He smiled and rubbed his thumbs together. "Overused they'd call it. Beneath them. It relies on a gimmick — trick cards. Not pure sleight of hand, they say."

"Regardless, the crowd was enamored. If they hadn't observed the trick previously —"

"Exactly." Simon snapped his fingers. "What is common for some is a miracle for others. It's all a matter of perspective."

"As was my perspective with the bakery incident or the photo of the Enchantments."

"Precisely. You're as bright as advertised." Simon rolled his silver coin around his fingers again and it vanished on the second pass. "This switching. Common for you, common for me."

"Not so common for me."

"Or for most of mankind. But it should be for you. You wrote the book. And trust me, they will become more common for you. Of that I'm sure." He frowned. "Almost sure. Close to sure, you know? Can't ever tell for certain. When you've lived in over four hundred different realities, you can't be certain about anything."

"Four hundred realities?"

Simon gave a quick nod. "Maybe a few more than that. Lost count."

Marcus stared at Simon and asked the Spirit what he was. Human didn't come into his mind. But nothing else did either. A few seconds later the magician clapped his hands and handed Marcus a business card.

All it contained was *Simon* and a cell phone number.

"Well now, that was an excellent first session together, don't you think? In our second session let's be sure to talk about the Wolf, okay?"

Heat rose to Marcus's face. "How do you know about the Wolf?"

"In time, Mr. Amber, in time." Simon picked up his leather bag and strolled off.

Whoever Simon was, he would obviously have a role in this play. Marcus glanced at his watch. In a little over twenty-four hours he'd be with the other Warriors. The time couldn't come soon enough.

As he walked toward the garage that held his car, he pulled up his calendar. Tomorrow night: Warriors. Saturday night: Calen over for dinner. What would that be like? Marcus let out a soft moan. He felt like Jesus was telling him it would be far from an ordinary family gathering.

SEVENTEEN

Reece sat at his fire pit on Friday evening at seven waiting for the others to arrive, knowing he would need to be exactly what Doug said he would need to be in the coming days: stronger than he imagined, able to hear the Spirit with ears that listened well, and fully engaged in their coming battle with the Wolf. He couldn't see. So what.

The Spirit had told him the confrontation with the Wolf would be far from what he expected. And that he needed to be ready for that. Wonderful. He had no idea what the battle would be like but he was supposed to anticipate what it would be like?

The sound of footsteps broke Reece out of his mulling. Had to be Doug. Amazing how he'd learned to identify people by the way their feet fell on grass or floors or ground.

"How is my fire, Doug? Did I build a good one?"

"Yes, can't you feel the heat?"

"Just checking." Reece held out his hands and let the flames warm them. "If we send them in tonight, it will be brutal."

"It will be brutal any night. They need to go through this," Doug said, his voice soft.

"I don't want to do it."

"Neither do I."

When Dana arrived the others were already seated around the fire pit in Reece's backyard. She hated being late, but for some reason the emergencies at the station didn't care that she had other commitments on her calendar.

As soon as she sat next to the professor, Reece invited them all to describe what had been happening during the past week. First Marcus told what had happened at the bakery where Kat worked, about the Enchantments photo, and about the strange magician, Simon, he'd met in Red Square at the U-Dub.

Brandon was next, telling them about his first encounter with Tristan Barrow and then the second one in the park with Dana and Marcus. When he'd finished, Reece turned to Dana.

It felt odd for her not to have something to describe other than give her impression

180

of the meeting in Kirkland with Tristan and his two companions. She felt as if she'd done something wrong since there was no specific weirdness she could point to. She told them about her promotion simply to have something to say and received congratulations from Brandon and Marcus, but Reece stayed silent. Doug didn't.

He cleared his throat. "Just because it isn't obvious, it doesn't mean you're not on the enemy's radar, Dana. And please consider the truth that a subtle attack can often be far more effective than a direct assault since an attack of subterfuge and nuance is often not noticed till the victim has crawled into the middle of the spider's web."

"Are you talking about my promotion?"

"Just be aware."

"Thanks. I think."

Reece slid forward on the bench and turned his head in a slow semicircle as if he could see each of them. "My own story is mundane. The enemy has tried to discourage me and belittle me due to my sight being gone. He's tried to tell me I'm no longer fit to be your guide. Not subtle. Not unexpected. But nonetheless effective at times. Whether the attack is more overt as in the case with Brandon and the professor or more subdued as with Dana and me, the solution is the same. Stay close to Jesus. Listen to the truth of the Spirit and make no agreement with the lies of the enemy." Reece sat back. "Doug?"

"Well said." He sighed. "My own battle has been with dreams that bring terror to my heart and a lack of sleep that results. However, he is with me, you are with me, and I am with all of you. We must stay strong, dear friends."

Reece rubbed his knees. "As you know, if the attacks are intensifying, then we are making the enemy nervous. We need to take heart from that thought. And now let's get to the next phase of your training. Any additional thoughts, Doug, before the three go in?"

"We're going 'in' tonight? In where?" Brandon said.

Doug clasped his hands together. "Yes, you are. More on that in a moment." He turned and looked at Reece. "To answer your question, Reece, I do have a few thoughts. While we must be aware of the enemy's schemes, do not let your full concentration be on him. He is not the goal. He is not our focus. Do not give him more power than he has. Jesus is setting captives free, and those captives are stepping out of their chains. That is what we will celebrate and keep at the forefront of our minds. We will press deeper into the Lord daily. That is what will give us the strength and ability to advance with power as we step further into this war."

"So be it," Dana said.

Brandon pulled a bag of sunflower seeds out of his pocket. "Now about this exercise. This is part of us getting in shape to face the Wolf-man?"

"Yes." Reece sighed.

"I don't like the sigh, big guy." Brandon popped a handful of seeds into his mouth. "Are you coming with us? Is this the 'next time' you talked about?"

Reece shook his head and stayed silent.

Doug gazed for a few seconds at each of them. "This will be far from easy. But it won't last long. Seven minutes perhaps. Ten at the most."

"Any advance intel?" Brandon said.

"No." Doug shook his head. "I'm sorry."

"When will this excursion take place?"

Doug took a deep breath and looked at Reece. "Right now."

Instantly Reece's backyard vanished and the only thought in Dana's mind was it was the first time they'd gone into any spiritual realm without holding hands. Apparently it wasn't necessary. Might have been nice to know.

A moment later Brandon, Marcus, and she stood in a small meadow bordered on one side by cliffs of granite. The ground was charred as if a fire had recently swept over the ground and burned the grasses.

"I can see why Reece didn't want to come," Dana said.

Brandon poked at the burned ground with the toe of his shoe. "No kidding."

A cry pierced the air behind her. Dana spun and gasped. It wouldn't be fun dealing with what rushed toward them.

EIGHTEEN

Three hawks or falcons, Dana couldn't tell, streaked down from the sky at them, screams pouring from their beaks. They were a hundred yards away, talons out. Even from this distance they looked razor sharp.

"Move!" Brandon grabbed her arm and dragged her toward a thick row of alder trees fifteen yards to their right. Marcus followed and they reached the trees, turned sideways, and pushed through the narrow opening between the trunks. The falcons would get through easily. Dana spun to face them with . . . what? They had no weapons.

But the birds raced by and banked hard to avoid the cliffs and flew off.

Dana stared at Brandon. "What, that was just to scare us?"

Brandon didn't answer. She turned to see what he was focused on. The air shimmered in front of them as if heat were moving toward them in waves. Then came wind.

Hot. Searing.

The heat slammed into Dana and sent her to her knees. "Unhh!" She shut her eyes against the scorching current of air and tried to breathe steady. It was cooler near the ground, but the swirling air pushed particles of loose dirt into her mouth and nose. What kind of soul had Reece sent them into? And why?

Dana coughed and opened her eyes. Brandon and Marcus knelt in front of her, both pulling in choking gasps of air as she was doing. "Are you all — ?"

"Look out!" Brandon leaped toward her, grabbed her, and rolled over three times with her in his arms. The ground shuddered and Dana turned her head. A massive slab of granite sat two inches from her nose.

"Professor!" Brandon pushed off Dana and glanced behind him.

"I'm good." Marcus's head swiveled back and forth as he studied the cliff above them. "And I'd like to stay that way. Any theories on how that state of being can be assured are heartily welcomed."

Brandon stood and lifted Dana to her feet. "We have to get out of here now!"

Dana's throat tightened as she drew in the burning air. "Agreed, but it's going to be hard to stand and hold hands and get in a state of mind to get out of here when it's raining bus-sized rocks and breathing is like being on Venus."

"Reece's estimate was we'd be here seven minutes." Marcus shouted to be heard over the increasing intensity of the wind. "We've only been in here two."

"And if we stay for three we're going to die."

The sound of boulders cracking high above them split the air. She glanced up. The top of the granite wall shook. Dana clutched Brandon's shoulder and jabbed her finger at a clump of trees at the base of the cliff. "We have to go there. Now!"

As she staggered toward the rock wall, Marcus shouted, "It's inadvisable to head toward the source of the stone that seconds ago nearly —"

Dana kept running and shouted over her shoulder, "I don't have time to debate this right now, Professor. Come on!"

A dull splintering sound came from above, and two seconds later the ground trembled like a giant had jumped from the sky. She turned back to the spot they'd stood in five seconds earlier. A jagged boulder the size of a Volkswagen Beetle filled the space.

Wham! Another boulder slammed into the ground to their right, then another landed and shook the ground to their left. They pushed through the trees to the base of the granite wall. Dana whipped her head back and forth, scanning the rock. "There!" She pointed to a thin, dark opening fifteen yards to their left. "Let's go."

"We're going in there?" Brandon said.

"No choice."

"You might get through that opening but what about Marcus and me?"

"You'll make it," Dana sputtered. "You have to."

The instant they sprinted for the opening, the ground shuddered with another rock that landed in the spot where they'd just been. Dana reached the dark slit in the rock first and flung herself to her belly.

"You first, Professor."

"No, you, Dana." He gave a weak smile. "No time to debate."

Brandon grabbed her shoulder. "Wait. How do we know this whole thing isn't going to come down on us if we crawl in here?"

"We don't." Dana turned her head sideways and put it flat on the ground. Maybe two inches to spare. She dragged herself forward with her elbows, inches at a time, the jagged rocks on the floor of the cave digging into her arms and torso and legs. Faster. She had to move faster, but it made her breathe deeper and breathing was almost impossible.

The air outside was a winter's day compared to the heat inside the cramped cave. Each breath felt like the air inside a sauna ten times hotter than she'd ever been in. But no boulders rained down inside the cave and a sense of peace told her what she'd felt the Spirit saying while they were outside: This cave was safe. That this was their eye of the tornado and their place to escape to. She needed it to be. They all needed it to be.

Dana reached for the ceiling. The height of the tiny cave was three feet at most. It didn't matter. She was alive. But where were Marcus and Brandon? She crouched and blinked against the light coming through the cave. *Keep them safe.*

She spun and laid her face at the entrance, but the wind and dust made her clamp her eyes closed. "Come on, guys. Get in here!"

No sound came back. No, this couldn't happen. *Your protection, Lord.*

"Brandon! Marcus!"

Again there was no response. *No, stay strong. He is our protector and shield.* Dana's chest tightened. Yes, she was safe. But it didn't matter if Brandon and the professor weren't. She couldn't stay if they were in

189

trouble. Dana had just started to crawl back out when a head filled the light streaming into the shallow cave.

"You have to move aside, Dana!" Marcus moaned as he crawled in beside her.

"What took you so long!"

Marcus pulled himself farther in. "We had a slight disagreement as to who should enter the cave next."

"I would let out a disgusted, 'Men!' but it would be a waste of words and I don't have the energy."

Moments later Brandon crawled through, accompanied by assorted angry grunts. "Okay, we've all made it to the party room. What do we do now? There's obviously not enough room to dance."

It was an excellent question. There were no demons to overcome on this one. Their enemy inside this soul wasn't an entity they could focus on. It was nature attacking them and how could they fight that? But it was still the enemy causing the boulders to fall and the heat to assault them and they could fight against that, right? But how? Then again, maybe they didn't have to fight. Stay in here seven minutes? Forget it. It was time to go now.

"It's getting downright toasty in here," Brandon puffed out.

Dana sucked in a breath that felt like fire. "Which is making it harder to breathe in case you hadn't noticed."

"If these conditions accelerate" — Marcus coughed like he was dying — "we'll have no choice but to crawl back outside so we don't suffocate."

"We're not crawling anywhere. We're going back." Dana fumbled to find Brandon's and Marcus's hands. "Grab hold, let's get literally the hell out of here." She clamped down on the others' palms and closed her eyes, then emptied her mind of everything around her and focused on the Spirit. "Take us." But nothing happened.

"This is not good," Brandon said.

"Why are we still here?" Dana ground her teeth. "We've been doing this without a hitch for ten months."

"This is not a soul," Marcus said.

In the next instant the ground right outside the cave shook like a bomb had been dropped, and the feeble amount of light that had come through the opening vanished. A moment later the sound of cracking started over their heads.

"I think there's a high probability this cave is about to collapse," Marcus said.

What was Reece thinking sending them in here? "We can get out of this. We have to,"

Dana puffed out. "Talk to me, Teacher. Now would be a good time for a quick lesson. Are you getting anything?"

Marcus started to mumble as if to himself, then paused and spoke clearly. "Going in and out of souls has been accomplished without incident — like strolling in a garden. We haven't had to think about it, concentrate on it, give it much thought or worry. It has ceased to require an element most would consider critical to a vibrant relationship with the Father, Son, and Holy Spirit. One Doug, Reece, and the three of us would acknowledge as —"

"Professor!" Dana grabbed Marcus's arm. "Can we get to the end of the lesson and get out of class? The bell is about to ring."

"Right, right, yes of course." Marcus coughed. "Faith is confidence in what we hope for and assurance about what we do not see. This is what the ancients were commended for. By faith we understand the universe was formed at God's command, so that what is seen was not made out of what was visible.

" 'By faith Abel brought God a better offering than Cain did . . . By faith Enoch was taken from this life, so that he did not experience death . . . By faith Noah, when warned about things not yet seen, in holy

192

fear built an ark to save his family. By faith Abraham, when called to go to a place he would later receive as his inheritance, obeyed and went, even though he did not know where he was going.

" 'By faith Abraham, when God tested him, offered Isaac as a sacrifice . . . By faith Joseph, when his end was near, spoke about the exodus of the Israelites from Egypt . . . By faith Moses' parents hid him for three months after he was born . . . By faith the people passed through the Red Sea as on dry land. By faith the walls of Jericho fell, after the army had marched around them for seven days.

" 'By faith the prostitute Rahab, because she welcomed the spies, was not killed with those who were disobedient . . .' And without faith it is impossible to please God."

Marcus breathed deep. "A few verses from Hebrews chapter 11."

"Are you kidding me?" Brandon said. "How do you get all that Scripture to stick in your head? I've tried memorizing Romans 8 for years and haven't gotten more than ten verses in."

"I have most of the New Testament memorized. In multiple translations."

"Really?"

"The curse of a brain that retains almost

everything I ever read."

"Guys! Talk more later." Dana grabbed their hands. "Let's. Get. Out. Of. Here. Now!" She ignored the stinging sweat trickling into her eyes and called out to the Spirit of God, "We acknowledge you are the one who takes us into and out of the spiritual realm. By faith in who you are. On our own we can do nothing, with you all things can be done. And nothing can be done if we don't believe." She paused and gripped Marcus's and Brandon's hands even tighter. "In faith, we ask, please take us home."

Instantly the familiar rush of going through a gate filled Dana's mind and heart and body. Her next breath was one of the cool air of Reece's Pacific Northwest backyard. Her breathing slowed and she glanced at Marcus and Brandon. The professor sat with wide eyes, but Brandon had already turned toward Reece, who now stood on the grass a few yards to the right of the fire pit. "What was that?"

Reece raised his eyebrows but didn't speak. Brandon glanced at Doug, then back to Reece. "What were you two thinking? Why did you send us in there? Do you know how close we came to being killed? There wasn't even time to figure out how we were supposed to fight. We're not even close to ready for something like that."

"Exactly," Reece said.

"You're insane, Reece." Brandon slumped back and folded his arms.

Marcus rocked back and forth on the bench. "My assessment is that's precisely why Reece sent us through that particular gate into that particular realm. I'm assuming he had no knowledge of the specific kind of attack that would come against us, but he knew it would be one we couldn't handle."

"Okay, Professor Genius, tell me why."

Dana leaned forward, elbows on her knees, and answered before Marcus could speak. "Exactly what we realized when we were inside. If we're going to take on the Wolf, we need our belief to grow. We need to rely on the Spirit more than ever before. We need to take to heart we can do nothing without Jesus."

"Yes, that's the most significant part of it, Dana." Reece eased back over and sat next to Brandon. "But there is another part as well."

"Which is?"

"As you know, I believe we're about to enter a phase of battle far more intense than we've experienced up till this point. You needed to see the severity of what the enemy can bring. You needed to see how the enemy can sometimes attack without a specific enemy to fight against. How do you fight against nature inside the spiritual realms? What are the weapons you can wield? If you think you can do it on your own, you will die.

"If you surrender to Jesus and put your faith in his providing what you need, those weapons and ideas will come precisely at the moment you have to have them. I could have told you these things, but would you have grasped the lesson and the need as thoroughly as you now have done? I think not. And you all need to grasp it firmly."

Reece stood. "I suggest we take a short break to allow the emotions of your journey to settle a bit more, get something to drink or eat from my kitchen, and then we'll gather here once again. Let's say in ten minutes."

"And the point of discussion?" Dana asked.

Reece cracked his knuckles. "It's time to tell you about the Wolf."

NINETEEN

Finally they'd get answers about the Wolf. Brandon snatched a grape Powerade out of the refrigerator and stepped onto Reece's back deck. Who it was or what it was. How they would go after it. What kind of attack plan they'd put together, and the steps on putting it in motion to destroy the beast. Brandon gazed toward the fire pit.

Part of him relished the idea of taking down the Wolf. And part — if he was brutally honest — was scared. He'd seen what the demons had done to Reece's eyes. What if the Wolf came after his voice? Or Marcus's brain? Could they be as strong as Reece seemed to be after losing one of his greatest pleasures — taking photos, seeing the beauty of the world all around him — if something happened to one of them?

A strange feeling swept through Brandon. That he would soon have to face that question. Was it a premonition? Or a thought from the enemy? Singing had been his life since he was fourteen. He was the Song. He had to sing, right?

The back door opened and Marcus shuffled up next to him. "Are you ready?"

"Yeah, let's go."

They made their way over the hundred yards to Reece's fire pit. The others were already there.

As he and Marcus settled into chairs, Doug rubbed his knees and glanced at all of them. "The past ten months have been stunning. We've made significant progress and our numbers are growing. Of the ninety-six men and women who have gone through the training school at Well Spring, ninety-two say they want to go through the advanced training once we start those courses. And these men and women have taken the Warriors Riding message of freedom back to their friends, their families, their communities.

"They are leading their own retreats, in their churches, at retreat centers, in private homes, and in cabins across the nation. And over the past three weeks I've received e-mails from groups starting Warriors Riding retreats in Australia, South Africa, Wales, France, and Brazil. This message, dear friends, truly is starting to spread to the nations. The prophecy is coming true.

"But . . ." Doug clasped his hands. "The Wolf has risen and is growing stronger daily. The time has come for you to act on the reason you were brought together in the first place."

Doug glanced at Reece who somehow picked up that it was his turn to speak. The big man adjusted his sunglasses and pushed back his beat-up dark tan Stetson. "As you might have suspected, who and what the Wolf is isn't obvious. A direct assault, while often brutal, isn't the most efficient or most thorough way to destroy an enemy."

Marcus looked up from scribbling notes in his journal. "It's to accomplish it from the inside out. The most strategic course of action is to present seemingly important distractions or inconsequential battles to take the focus off the major assault."

"Exactly," Doug said. "While you're fighting the enemy attacking your home out front, there's another contingent setting charges in your crawl space and you don't realize it till it's too late."

Dana pulled her hair back. "In other words, you're saying the Wolf isn't something like the government trying to restrict religious freedoms, or Hollywood and some of the garbage they're putting out, or atheistic groups trying to shut down Christmas."

"Well said."

"I'm loving this intro and discussion, I really am, but can we get on with the show?" Brandon wheeled his forefingers around each other in a circle. "You know? Go ahead and give us the name of the Wolf? Him, her, them, whatever?"

"The Wolf is not a human." Reece massaged his fist.

"I'm lost," Brandon said.

"But while we can't know with 100 percent certainty who the Wolf is, we believe the Spirit has shown us a specific person to go after."

"Now I'm not only lost, every map in the universe has vanished." Brandon ran his fingers through his hair. "The Wolf isn't a person, but he is a person. Do I have it straight?"

"Yes." Reece smiled.

"What? Am I the only one who feels like he's not making any sense?" Brandon glanced at the others, then broke into song. *"Just a sphere of perplexity, that's what the universe is these days . . ."*

" 'Ball of Confusion,' the Temptations, 1970, Motown," Reece said.

"How do you do that? I didn't say the words even close to right, plus sang the wrong melody. I'm never going to stump you. You're a music encyclopedia."

"Only from 1962 through '78. After that all the good music died."

"Why '78?"

Doug cleared his throat. "Gentlemen."

Reece nodded and leaned forward, elbows on his knees. "Think back to last year when we went to church together and the professor's eyes were opened and he saw demons masquerading as mundane ushers. Remember how the pastor challenged his audience not to drink even a sip of alcohol or go to even one R-rated movie for a year? And how Marcus saw the demons putting stones inside the backpacks of the people in the congregation? There is nothing wrong with making a personal choice not to drink alcohol or go to R-rated movies. But for one Christian to weigh another down with rules and regulations that are not their own . . . that is the greatest enemy of Christianity. Religion. It's what Jesus hated the most. What he fought against with the Pharisees. And his onslaught against religion is what got him killed.

"The spirit of religion is an enemy who is crushing churches, dividing fellowships and friends, turning God from a person into a manifesto of dos and don'ts that crush the spirit and turn Christianity into a program devoid of true godly power and devoid of love."

Brandon leaned back in his chair. "I like the speech, but I'm still tempted to sing another verse of the Temptations song."

Dana folded her arms. "I'm still confused as well. I get it about the spirit of religion, but there has to be a more clearly defined expression of the Wolf than that."

Reece turned to Marcus. "Professor?"

"I would surmise that in the spiritual realm the Wolf is the spirit of religion, but in the physical realm that spirit manifests itself in a variety of different ways, including that of human nature. So while the Wolf is a spirit we must be aware of, and probably at some point engage, it is highly likely the Wolf can also be manifested in human individuals who are being used by the Wolf to carry out its design." Marcus pushed his glasses up on his nose. "Is there any accuracy to my assessment of the situation?"

"Ever the teacher, eh, Professor?" Brandon grinned.

"And ever the student as well. It is difficult to teach if you are not open to learning those things you do not yet know."

"Yes, you are accurate, Professor," Reece said. "Completely."

"So even though there's no way the Wolf is using only one person, there is a person you've targeted. That we need to confront."

"Yes." Reece turned toward Doug and opened his palm.

Doug placed a piece of wood on the fire. "For over a year we've sensed the Spirit telling us the Wolf is using a man named Carson Tanner."

"The radio show host?" Dana sat up ramrod straight. "On the cover of *Christianity World*? Named one of the new century's most influential evangelicals? I met him at the National Association of Broadcasters four years ago. He was just starting to get big, but now he's pulling in serious numbers. Plus he's got columns in two major magazines and is a frequent guest on TV shows and podcasts. People follow what he says. You're not serious when you say you think he's —"

"What about you, Brandon? Heard of him?"

"Yeah, don't know many people who haven't. The best-selling books, the filled arenas when he does his speaking tours . . . people love him. They call him hard-core. Radical. That he's getting people back to the Bible and to living a pure Christian life."

Dana laughed. "You're going to have to

sell me hard on the idea of Carson being the Wolf, Doug. He's charming, smart, knows his Bible cold." Dana smiled. "He's handsome."

"What do his looks have to do with anything?" Brandon frowned. "I think we all know what he looks like. We don't need to dwell on —"

"I'm not dwelling on his thick blond hair, his tan skin, or his trim athletic build, Brandon. I'm thinking that Marcus might not know what he looks like, and I'm trying to give the professor a visual to work with."

"I'm aware of him," Marcus said.

Brandon snorted out a breath. "Yeah, Dana, I'm sure that's exactly what you were —"

"Enough." Reece raised his palm, the reflection of the flames of the fire pit turning it a dark red. "Have you ever listened to his program?"

"Yes," Dana said.

"How long ago?"

She shrugged. "I don't know, a year and a half ago. Maybe two and a half years."

"When he first started he did a lot of good for a lot of people. But as his audience grew, he changed. We don't think he's one of the most influential evangelicals today. He is *the* most influential. He is allowing the enemy — through his ministry — to put rocks in his listeners' spiritual backpacks the size of Volkswagen Beetles. But let's be clear. Our enemy is Carson and it isn't Carson."

"Great. More confusion." Brandon rolled his eyes back in his head.

"Carson is only the Wolf because he's allowed the spirit of religion to embed its claws into his life and soul."

Dana pulled her sweatshirt tighter against the rapidly cooling evening. "All right, for argument's sake let's say Carson is the Wolf — what is our action plan?"

"We're going after him," Reece said. "The enemy has been hunting us, trying to take us out. Now the hunters will become the hunted."

Marcus twirled his pen. "Will we look for an opportunity to engage Carson directly, or try to gain permission to enter into his soul, or proceed into some other spiritual sphere to engage the spirit or spirits influencing Carson?"

"My suspicion is all three. But Doug and I haven't sought the Lord on the answer to that yet. Or our next steps."

"Why not?" Brandon said.

"Because we are the Warriors Riding plural, not the Warrior Riding singular. We will seek the answer together."

"Shouldn't we do something in the meantime?" Brandon stood and paced. "Like send out an e-mail blast to our trainees telling them to boycott the guy and tell their friends and family to do the same?"

"Crawl, walk, run," Reece said. "First we will pray about it. Together and individually. Then we'll gather to hear what the Spirit has said to each of us about what actions to take from here." Reece turned to Dana. "Are you with us here, Dana?"

"Yes, sorry." She slid her cell phone into her pocket and looked up. "Crazy days at the station."

Doug stared at her for a long moment. "Too much to handle?"

"No, it's going really well."

Reece stood. "My friends, as usual, it has been an intense evening so let's bring it to a close. A reminder that we're headed to Well Spring next week for our next round of training. We'll see you all here at my house on Thursday at noon."

Brandon walked with Marcus to their cars. "You okay, Professor? Weirded out about the Wolf? Or still dealing with the whole thinking you might be switching back and forth between realities thing?"

"I've put that behind me. I don't have the

bandwidth to analyze it at this point."

"Okay, way to go. So it's this going after the Wolf thing that's bugging you?"

"In a sense, yes, but I have another concern that is a more imminent threat that is occupying the vast majority of my prefrontal cortex."

"I'm guessing that's part of the brain."

"In rudimentary terms it's the area of the brain where we make decisions."

Brandon scrunched up his face and pressed his finger into his cheek. "What does *rudimentary* mean?"

"It means —"

"I'm kidding, Professor." Brandon laughed and punched Marcus playfully in the arm. "I did go to school for a few years, you know." As they walked on, Brandon said, "So what's the big decision?"

"Tomorrow night a young man who is dating Abbie is coming over for dinner for the second time."

"And you're trying to decide whether to be nice to him or not."

"Yes." Marcus stopped and turned toward Brandon. "How did you assess that?"

Brandon smiled. "Unlike you, I was a teenager once and had a lot of those dinners where the dad didn't like me. Or thought he didn't like me just because I was male."

"I assure you, I was a teenager once."

Brandon laughed again and shook his head. "No, I mean the meeting-a-girl's-dad thing. You told me you didn't have to face that gauntlet very often in high school."

"Then I misled you. I faced it far too frequently." Marcus turned and continued toward his car as he recalled a few times where he thought his date's father was going to take out a shotgun. "You're right. I should lighten up. He's a nice kid from what I've seen and Abbie seems quite enamored with him."

"Then be nice."

"Agreed." Marcus frowned. "But still, I would ask that you pray for the dinner and for my attitude toward Romeo once you wake up."

"Done. And don't worry, Prof. It'll be fine."

Brandon watched Marcus pull away as he sat in his car and pictured himself with a daughter Abbie's age. If he did have a girl he'd feel exactly like Marcus. Because if this kid coming over to the professor's house was anything like Brandon was in high school, Marcus should be worried.

TWENTY

Marcus stood at the window of his den on Saturday night looking down on the street, waiting for Calen to pull up in his beat-up Ford truck. Marcus glanced at his watch. Three minutes to six. Calen would be on time. He was a good kid. Which should make Marcus happy. But he wasn't. Fourteen was too young for Abbie to be dating.

At 5:59 Calen's truck chugged to a stop in front of the house and he stepped out, ran his hand over his hair, and stared at Marcus's house. The kid reached into his pocket, smiled, and pulled something out but kept his fist closed around the object.

Irritated. That was the emotion Marcus felt toward the kid. But he shouldn't. On the surface there was no good reason. Which irritated him more. Calen made Abbie happy and that made Abbie happier with Marcus.

Calen put his hand back in his pocket and

released whatever object it was he'd held. For an unknown reason the movement reminded Marcus of someone, but he couldn't determine who.

Marcus went to his desk and prayed hard for five minutes, then strode out of his den to the top of the stairs and took two long breaths. He made a slow descent, the feeling of unease intensifying with each step. He felt like he'd slid into a gladiatorial arena where he had no sword and no shield.

Abbie stood in the entryway, her arms wrapped around Calen, his wrapped around her. She turned and spotted Marcus. "Hey, Daddy, Calen is here."

"That I can see." Marcus reached the bottom of the stairs just as Kat stepped into the entryway.

Kat held out both hands and gripped Calen's. "Great to have you here again, Calen."

"Thanks, fun to be here." He smiled at all of them.

Marcus stepped forward. "Before dinner I want to have a brief chat with Calen."

Calen pointed at himself, eyes mock wide. "You want to chat with me?"

"Yes."

"Sure, sounds good." Calen grinned at Abbie and winked.

"Play fair, Dad." She poked him in the side and smiled.

Marcus stared at Abbie but didn't answer. "It didn't rain for once so why don't we go out back?"

He walked down the hall, through the kitchen, and through the back door onto the patio. Calen followed. Seconds after they settled into two of the patio chairs out back, Kat stepped outside with a glass of strawberry lemonade in each hand. "How can men talk without something to drink while they do so?"

Calen stood and gave a light bow as he accepted the drink from Kat.

"You don't have to stand —"

"My pleasure, Mrs. Amber. Thanks for the drink."

"You are entirely welcome." Kat turned and gave Marcus an isn't-he-a-catch smile.

Marcus whispered a prayer to himself as Calen sat back in his chair. *Show me what I cannot see and bring your truth.*

A flash of darkness shimmered across Calen and in the next instant Marcus knew what the object was that resided in the young man's back pocket. But was it him?

"So did you have something in particular you wanted to talk to me about, or is this just a chance to get to know each other a little better since Abbie and I have been getting to know each other a lot better?"

"My hat is off to you." Marcus set his drink on the armrest of his chair and leaned forward, his gaze drilling Calen. "You're a master, Calen. I'm impressed. It took me a long time to figure you out. In fact the equation didn't fall into place till just now."

"And what is that?"

Marcus glanced at the kitchen windows. "I know what you are."

"A teenager in love?"

"No. You took an object out of your pocket as you approached my house. I know what it is."

Calen reached into the same pocket he had five minutes ago and pulled it out, but kept his fist closed. "You think you know, huh?"

"Show it to me."

"You're sure? You really think it will help the situation?"

"Show me."

Even though Marcus knew what was coming it still sent a chill down his back when Calen held out his fist and uncurled his fingers one at a time to reveal a gold coin. He flipped it in the air and caught it on the back of his hand and then spun it around his fingers just as he had done in Reece's backyard almost a year ago.

A sensation of ice spread down Marcus's arms, down his legs. Zennon. Sitting three feet from him. The demon who had tracked and assaulted each of the Warriors Riding a year ago. The one who had murdered Reece's wife and daughter. Who had appeared in Marcus's class at the U-Dub, showed up in Dana's office, and almost killed his daughter Jayla. Who had destroyed Reece's eyes ten months ago.

Calm. He had to stay focused. Act in the power of the Spirit. No fear. "Hello, Zennon. We knew you'd show up sooner or later."

"Congratulations." Calen set the coin on his armrest and slowly clapped three times like the gong of a grandfather clock striking three. "Now it's my turn to be impressed. You figured it out much quicker than I imagined you would. When did you first suspect?"

"In retrospect, the first night I met you. But as I said, I wasn't certain till a moment ago."

"I've been looking forward to the instant when you realized it was me."

"Sure you have."

Zennon didn't answer.

Marcus leaned forward and pressed into

the fear trying to tear at his mind. "And it explains who Simon is as well."

"Does it?" Zennon rolled his finger around the edge of the gold coin but didn't take his gaze off Marcus. "He's not exactly like us."

"What is he then? Who is he? What part does he have in this?"

"Let him tell you."

"I'd like you to."

"Well, to paraphrase Mick Jagger from many years ago, we can't always get the things we desire, but if we try with diligence, we can often acquire what we need." Calen grinned and played an air guitar. "What, you're not a Rolling Stones fan? Reece is. You should borrow a few of his CDs some-time."

Adrenaline pumped through Marcus. "I need you to listen to me very closely."

"Hmm?" Calen picked up the coin and massaged it between his thumb and fingers.

"You're going to walk into my house and tell Abbie your relationship is over. You're not going to contact her from this point forward. You're going to leave this host body you're in and never bother Abbie or Kat or Jayla in any way, shape, or form ever again."

"That is certainly one option."

"That's the *only* option."

"Do you really think so?" Calen flipped

the coin from one hand to the other. "I would respectfully disagree. I say there's another option, which is that I continue to worm my way into your daughter's and your wife's and your other daughter's lives till I have them precisely where I want them."

"You take option two, I'll tell her exactly what you are."

"That's your plan?" Calen leaned forward and downed half his lemonade. "I think that strategy is fraught with problems. Why? Because Abbie won't believe you, will she? Her first love, the boy who treats her like a princess, is a demon?

"The senior who treats her with more attention and tenderness than her father ever has just so happens to be a spiritual being out to destroy her and her family? She'll buy that trinket? Nay, I think not. She'd look at you like you're crazy and trying to steal from her the happiest season of her life."

A smoldering anger rose in Marcus. "She'll believe me."

"Really?" Calen pointed toward the house. "I think you're delusional. I think you'd have a hard time convincing Kat about what I am, let alone Abbie."

"You're going to leave and you're never going to see Abbie again if I have to be with her twenty-four hours a day."

"Okay, that's one option — and I won't even comment on how stupid that sounds since you have a job and your precious Warriors to attend to. Do it. Ban her from seeing me. Forbid her from texting me or talking on the phone. Make her swear to avoid me at school. Go to the principal and tell her you need a restraining order against me because I've . . . well, I've been . . . wow, nothing is coming to mind at the moment. Model student. Youth group leader . . . athlete, good grades, hmmm, any ideas?" Calen laughed.

"Sure, you can forbid her from seeing me, but I'm thinking that won't do wonders for your relationship." Calen shook his head. "So sad. Just when the ice was starting to crack between you two."

Marcus's mind raced with ways to respond. But each of them seemed preposterous. Zennon, or Calen, was right. Abbie wouldn't believe him. Neither would Kat.

"Just curious." Calen's eyes grew dark. "Does it bother you more to realize I've had my tongue down your daughter's throat, or that there's nothing you can do to stop me from doing it again?"

Marcus gripped the arms of his chair hard and came forward, his heart pounding.

"Would it bother you if I told you about the times I've touched her in areas I don't think would be pleasing for you to hear about?"

"You're lying."

"She's weakening. And she's going to give in very soon. I have extensive experience in these matters. I'm sure you can trust me on that."

Marcus flung his glass of lemonade to the patio and it shattered. A moment later the back door was flung open and Abbie lurched onto the deck. "Dad! What happened?" She glanced back and forth between him and Calen.

"Go back inside, Abbie. Now!"

"What is going on?"

"Nothing. We're fine. Calen and I have to conclude our conversation and then we'll be back inside."

Calen mouthed, *I love you.* Abbie smiled and returned the sentiment.

Calen glanced at the broken glass strewn across the patio. "In the second book of Timothy it says God gives Christians a spirit of self-control. Pity they skipped you on handout day."

He stood, sauntered over to one of the smaller pieces of glass, bent over, and picked it up. "This would hurt if someone swallowed it. I wouldn't want that to happen to Abbie." He tossed it in the air and watched it spin in the fading sunlight, sending off tiny reflections of light. "No, I've grown fond of Abbie." He glared at Marcus. "But Jayla? I barely know her. If she swallowed it, I don't think it would bother me at all."

"I'm going to kill you."

Calen's thin smile grew into a grin and he strolled back over to Marcus and patted his hand before he could yank it away. "No, you're not, because you know you can't kill me. You could wrap your hands around my neck right now or send a bullet through my brain, but it wouldn't do a thing to me. No, what you're going to do is stand up, straighten your preppy little professor shirt, go back through those doors, and pretend everything is okay. And you're going to back off on the little spiritual adventures you and your pals have been having. You're going to tell Reece you're taking a little break from the group, but you'll probably be back in late fall. You're going to let the others go after the Wolf on their own. Because if you don't . . ." Calen pointed toward the house and circled his tongue over his lips. "Do we understand each other completely?"

Calen didn't wait for an answer. He tossed

the glass into one of Kat's flowerpots on the edge of the patio and glided toward the back door. Abbie slid it open and smiled at him. "Good talk with my dad?"

"Yes. He's an amazing guy. We had a great chat." Calen turned and drilled Marcus with his gaze before spinning back to Abbie. "I think we're going to get along really, really well."

"Dad?" Abbie called to Marcus over Calen's shoulder. "Are you coming in? Dinner's just about ready."

Marcus nodded and stood. He'd never felt so alone and so inadequate. He had no idea what to do next. No clue how to fight Zennon in the form of Calen. But it didn't matter. He fought tonight for Abbie, so he would fight well. He would call on the Spirit and the Spirit would answer.

He strode for the back door with a confidence he didn't feel, because he chose to believe by the time he sat down at the table he would have a solution.

TWENTY-ONE

Marcus sat in his den, clenching his hands together tighter and tighter till the strain on his fingers grew into a sharp pain. He released his fingers and leaned forward, arms on his desk, and tried to stop sucking in breaths like he'd just completed a four-minute mile.

He'd come in from outside with confidence the Spirit would give him an answer, but his mind was clouded as if the Spirit was speaking but his ears were too clogged to hear. All he could consider was how impossible it would be to sit through a meal with Calen three feet away, using his allure to draw Abbie, Kat, and even Jayla into his dark pit of hell. That was not going to happen.

But what could he do? Calen — no, not Calen — Zennon, was right. If he kicked the thing out of his house, then Zennon would use the scene to play Abbie against him. If Marcus tried to tell his family right there at the table what Calen was they would shoot him down like a clay pigeon.

But he had to show up. He had to get down there now. He couldn't stay up here and let his wife and daughters dine without him. He stood and walked toward the door of his den. He stopped and his gaze fell on two framed movie posters side by side.

One was of *The Matrix,* the other of *The Terminator.* What would it be like if Neo and the Terminator met in battle? If it was in the real world, Neo would be slaughtered just like Marcus had been out on the back patio. But if it was inside the matrix, the outcome would be vastly different.

Of course. That was it. He'd been fighting in Zennon's arena. An intellectual one where he could never beat the demon. Arguing with him was like a billy club going up against a lightsaber. He needed a nuclear bomb. What was that verse Reece continually quoted? *"For the weapons of our warfare are not of the flesh but have divine power to destroy strongholds."*

Marcus almost laughed. Hadn't he learned anything over the past year? He clomped down the stairs knowing exactly what to do. As he stepped into the dining room, he recalled Isaiah 42:13, *"The LORD will go forth like a warrior, He will arouse His zeal like a man of war. He will utter a shout, yes, He will raise a war cry. He will prevail against His enemies."* Be with me, Warrior God.

Chicken Dijon was stacked on a plate in the middle of the table. Thin wisps of steam rose from a bowl of mashed potatoes sitting next to a Caesar salad and next to it a bowl of corn on the cob. Norman Rockwell would be proud. Such a picturesque meal. One he was about to destroy.

"Nice of you to join us, honey." Kat glared at him.

Marcus smiled as wide as he could, moved to the head of the table, and sat. Kat was to his left and Jayla was next to her. To his right sat Abbie and to her right was Calen.

Here we go.

"Forgive my slight delay. May it not hamper in any way the enjoyment of this fine dinner and the pleasure of having with us once again our stimulating guest, Calen." Marcus took a deep breath through his nose and spread his napkin on his lap. "Calen and I had an extremely illuminating chat out on the back deck, and I feel like we truly had the chance to get to know each other intimately." He stared at the demon and the irises of Calen's brown eyes grew till they filled his pupils and turned to the color of a moonless night at 3:00 a.m.

"Now, before we begin, we have a tradition around the dinner table in our family that I'm starting tonight, and I know all of us would love to have you participate in it, Calen."

Abbie frowned at him. "What are you doing, Dad?"

Marcus held up his hand. "As you know, Calen, we are a family that follows Jesus and have surrendered our lives to him. Abbie told me that you have done the same, which is wonderful. And apparently you're an integral part of the youth group at your church, so what we're about to do will likely feel very comfortable to you.

"With that in mind, from this evening forward, we will go around the table and declare our commitment to the Father, Son, and Holy Spirit by saying the following: 'I confess now before you, Lord, as well as before the friends and family now near me, that Jesus Christ is God come in the flesh, the King of kings, and all authority, all rulers, all principalities are under his feet.' "

Marcus turned and drilled Calen with his gaze. "As our guest, I'd be honored if you would do us the favor of going first." The air seemed to freeze and no one spoke.

"Why are you doing this, Dad?"

Marcus looked at Abbie and narrowed his eyes. "I need you to be silent for a bit, Abbs. And I need you to trust me."

"Marcus?" Kat laid her hand on his arm and squeezed hard. "Do you really want to create a scene at this moment?"

"It's a good question, Mr. Amber," Calen said. "Why are you doing this? I think your saying a short word of grace should suffice for the meal, but anything more will likely make your entire family as well as me quite uncomfortable."

"I appreciate your opinion, Calen. But tonight that will not suffice." Marcus turned to Kat. "Trust me that this is true." He turned back to Calen. "We need to hear our guest tell us Jesus Christ has come in the flesh and that he is God. It's not a difficult request for one who has surrendered to the Nazarene."

Calen's eyes went dark and his breathing grew shallow. He gripped the table and his fingers turned white. "I choose to respectfully decline."

Marcus raised himself up to his full height, sitting in the chair ramrod straight. "I insist."

He glanced at Abbie, whose eyes pleaded for him to stop, and then at Kat, who looked like she'd just swallowed a mouthful of gravel. He gave a slight nod to each of them, and the look in his eyes must have been like steel because they both dropped their gazes to the table and stayed silent.

Calen pulled his hands off the table and laughed. "I'm so sorry, Mr. Amber. I realize it's not my place to say this, but I think you're embarrassing your family and you're making me feel a little awkward as well." He motioned toward Kat. "Your beautiful wife has cooked a wonderful meal and it's getting cold. And if I'm being totally candid, I've never been good at saying grace, and on top of that, I've forgotten the words you wanted me to say. Can you just say a word of thanks so we all can eat?"

"Please, Dad? Please?"

"Calen, humor me and take part in our new tradition. I'm not asking you to say grace. And there are no words for you to memorize. Simply in your own words tell us Jesus is the Son of God, and that he is God come in the flesh."

Marcus waited a moment, then leaped to his feet, and as his chair smashed into the china hutch behind him, he shouted, "I command you by the blood of Jesus Christ to confess that Jesus is Lord."

A shudder went across Calen's shoulders and saliva bubbled onto his lips. His eyes narrowed and he leaned toward Marcus. "You don't want to do this."

Marcus stepped around the corner of the table. "By the blood of Jesus Christ, the power of his resurrection, and the power of his ascension, I command you to tell us who you are and what your true name is. I bind you with the blood of the Lamb. I command you to do this by the authority of Jesus Christ our Lord."

Calen snarled and grabbed the table with both hands. "You have no idea what you're dealing with. You're in so far over your head, you're looking up from the bottom of the seabed."

"Tell us, Calen. I command you by the blood of the Lamb. Tell us who you are."

The demon's face distorted into that of an elderly woman, then to a middle-aged man, then back to the face of Calen. "You have no power over me." His breathing came in gasps now and his hands slid across the table into the mashed potatoes, which slid between Kat and Jayla over the edge and smashed onto the floor.

"Tell us!" Marcus thundered.

"I am . . . I am . . . Zennon." Calen stood, stumbled back, knocked over his chair, and pointed at Marcus. "You cannot stop us. I'm one of millions and we are not going to destroy you at some point in the future — we already have. And you don't even know it."

Marcus stood. "Get out! In the name of Jesus! Go!"

The demon spun and flung his hands at the mirror on the wall. The glass shattered and rained down on them like hail.

"Daddy!"

Calen staggered out of the dining room and came to a halt at the front door. He turned and stared at Marcus. "You're going to lose this battle, Professor. You've already lost it. Just wait till you see what we've cooked up just for you. I worked on it personally. It'll have you wishing you'd never gotten near the hornet's nest. We're coming for you. And for the others. And it won't end till you're dead." He waved his finger at Abbie and Jayla. "And then they will join you."

"One more thing." Zennon opened the door and pointed at Kat. "If you don't tell her soon, we will. And she'll know what you did to him. She'll know the catastrophic secret you've kept hidden from her forever."

Marcus screamed and sprinted toward the front door, but before he could reach Zennon, the door slammed shut and Marcus thumped against it hard. Adrenaline pumped through him and the back of his shirt was damp with perspiration.

After three deep breaths with his eyes closed he opened them and turned to his family. Abbie sat on the floor curled up in a ball in a corner of the dining room, her body shaking. Jayla was still at the table, eyes wide, face the color of copy paper. Kat's arms were spread wide, one in the direction of each girl, and her head darted back and forth as if she couldn't decide which of their daughters to go to first.

Marcus strode back into the dining room, slid down beside Abbie, and motioned Kat and Jayla to join them.

"It's okay. We won. He's gone. He's gone." Marcus prayed, stopped after a few minutes, then prayed again. Three or four minutes went by and he prayed a third time.

"I think I'm going to be sick." Abbie squeezed Marcus's hand. "I . . . I kissed him, Daddy."

"I'm so sorry, Abbs." He pulled her tighter into his chest. "I should have seen it. I should have warned you."

"You did. And I wouldn't listen."

"It's okay."

The four of them sat in silence for what seemed like a half hour. He finally looked at Kat, who stroked Jayla's hair in between kissing the top of her head. She looked up at him, tears in her eyes but also peace.

"You're right, Marcus. It's not going to be easy. But it's going to be okay."

Marcus lay in bed that night pretending he didn't know the secret Zennon had spoken of. Of Layne's death. Of how Marcus could have prevented their son from dying.

Marcus turned over, his back to Kat, and tried to push the memory from his mind. If she knew the truth it could destroy everything. It was a door he thought he'd successfully locked and bolted shut. But if Zennon had his way it would be flung wide open and Kat would be standing there when it was.

Twenty-Two

As Brandon clipped toward the stage in Oregon on Sunday evening he popped three cherry-flavored throat lozenges into his mouth and prayed they would get him through the concert. In the back of his mind he knew he had more than a sore throat going on.

His voice strength had been waning for the past three weeks and he'd never had a sore throat hang on this long. But with everything going on at Well Spring and with Warriors Riding, plus a concert schedule that never seemed to slow down, there was little time to think about it, let alone get to a doctor. And if he told anyone about it they'd force him to go see someone, which would be a waste of time.

His voice was just tired. It needed a little rest. So did he. Another month and he'd get some. His last concert before a two-week break would be in his backyard, at

Marymoor Park in Redmond, Washington. It was a prime spot to end the tour, in front of friends and family.

Brandon stepped onto the stage and the lights fired up and bathed the band and him in their brilliant yellows, reds, and blues. "Hello, Portland! Do you want to live with freedom?"

The crowd roared their answer and Brandon grinned, then turned to the band. "Slight change in the song order. I want to kick things off with 'Final Race,' okay?"

The band ran through their first set as tight as they'd ever been. God was there and the Spirit moved through the music to bring people into deep worship.

As Brandon started into their second set and reached to hit his falsetto on the chorus, a sliver of pain shot down his throat. Then another and his voice faded. He glanced at Anthony, his bass player, who gave a questioning look. Brandon tapped his throat and shook his head, then mouthed the words, *Voice is gone.* He pointed at Anthony, then his microphone. Anthony picked up the hint and finished the song.

"Sorry, folks," Brandon rasped out. "I've been fighting a sore throat lately and it looks like it just won. My voice is shot as you can hear, so Anthony is going to carry this concert the rest of the way home."

Anthony's solid voice boomed through the speakers out over the crowd and the concert ended strong. Afterward Brandon went out into the crowd and tried to greet the people, but he couldn't speak in more than a whisper.

When he reached his dressing room, his manager, Kevin Kaison, was standing outside of it, arms pulled tight across his lean frame. "You've been keeping this from me, haven't you?"

Brandon shrugged and sighed.

"How long?"

"Three weeks," Brandon rasped out.

"Not good, pal."

"I know."

He did know. Depending on what he'd done, he could be out anywhere from a few days to forever. He didn't mean to get dramatic, but if it was nodules on his throat and he'd pushed it too far, he might never sing again like he once did.

First Reece with his eyes and now Brandon's voice. It seemed his premonition might be right. What was next? The professor would sprain his mind? Dana would lose her ability to lead? He needed to talk to Reece about it. Get the Warriors to pray for him. Get healed fast.

Brandon scowled at the floor, then glanced at Kevin. "It's no surprise. The enemy is trying to take me out. Reece said this would happen."

"Uh, maybe it's not the enemy." Kevin cocked his head. "Maybe it's just you being stupid."

"Wow, thanks for the sympathy."

Kevin tapped his foot in double time as he rubbed his brown hair. "Sorry to be harsh, but it's easy to blame the enemy on something you should have taken care of. You had to know it was more than a sore throat, but you kept it to yourself and kept pushing your voice till it snapped. Couldn't it be as simple as that?"

Brandon shrugged.

"I'd find out quick. I'm getting an appointment for you in the next day or two."

Brandon nodded.

He sat in his hotel room that night trying not to swallow and trying to figure out if Kevin was right. He hadn't taken care of his throat. So was it the enemy who did this to him, or just Brandon's neglect? But regardless of the cause, he had a feeling there was a deeper plan in the works that would make the sore throat a blip on the screen in comparison.

■ ■ ■ ■

On Tuesday afternoon, the doctor slid the images of Brandon's throat onto his table and grimaced.

"I don't like the look in your eyes, Doc."

"Yeah, I wouldn't either." He poked at the shots with a mechanical pencil. "But it's really not that bad."

"Define 'not that bad.' " Brandon rubbed the edge of his chair and braced himself. To him, not that bad would mean go home, drink some tea with honey, and not sing for a few days. Anything else would be a disaster.

"The good news is, I think you'll be fine. This happens to singers more often than people hear about." The doctor nodded at the statement. "The bad is, you won't be belting out the hits for at least five weeks. And that's after the surgery."

"Surgery?" Brandon shook his head. "Not an option."

"You've been mightily unkind to your vocal cords. You could take care of this with six months of no singing — that's what Celine Dion did, but it sounds like you don't want to take that long. Plus, in your case I'd recommend the surgery anyway."

234

"I need to be singing faster than that."

"Nope. Sorry." The doctor leaned back and put his hands behind his head.

"I have a concert out in Redmond at Marymoor Park in three weeks."

"You'll be recovering from surgery three weeks from now, so unless you want to lip-synch —"

"Can I put off the surgery till the first part of September?"

"Sure." The doctor leaned forward and gathered the photos into a stack. "You can put off the surgery forever. But if you want to sing again, I'd recommend having the procedure done sooner than later."

"How soon is sooner?"

"Since I like your music, you could persuade me to do the surgery tomorrow."

"Tomorrow?"

"Yes."

"Don't you have to get prepped for something like this?"

"When Kevin called and set up the appointment, he persuaded me to act fast. I did. Plus I'd like to see you up and singing, maybe not as fast as you do, but pretty close. So are you in?"

TWENTY-THREE

"Outstanding work your first ten days in the new role, Dana." Robert popped his head into Dana's office on Wednesday mid-morning and grinned. "You made me look like a hero when you were a general sales manager and you're already making me look that way as GM."

"Already?"

"Yes. I've noticed the restructuring you've been doing."

"Thanks for pushing for my promotion."

He waved his hands. "Nope, I won't take any credit. The only thing I did was say yes when they asked if I thought you'd do a good job as general manager of the station."

"I appreciate it anyway."

"Listen, are you and Perry still on for joining my wife and me a week from tomorrow for dinner?"

"I'm not really seeing him anymore."

"Oh, is that right?"

She nodded, then waited for the invitation to be withdrawn. As a couple she was desirable. Single? Not so much. Dana knew how the game was played.

"So you're coming solo? That will still work if you're okay with it. We'll have a great time."

"I thought —" She stopped, not knowing how to put her thoughts into words.

"You thought we were just doing the polite couples thing?" Robert spread his arms wide, placed his palms on Dana's desk, and leaned forward. "We like you for you, Dana. Period. You don't have to have a date to be around us." He straightened up. "But if you want me to try to fix you up with someone . . ."

"No. I'm okay."

"Great."

Dana smiled as Robert whapped the door frame of her office and strode away. She'd always liked him, but before the promotion she wouldn't have described their relationship as a friendship. A good working acquaintance? Yes. But hanging out together and possibly becoming friends with Robert's wife? She hadn't ever considered it.

But even though it had only been ten days since her promotion, she already felt as if she'd been given membership in an exclusive club where there was no official card to get in, but there was a card nonetheless.

Her cell phone chimed and she glanced at the reminder. Oops. Ten minutes before the staff meeting and half an hour of work to do before she got there. She'd never worked harder during the past week and never loved it more. Everyone in the station had responded positively to her promotion and a significant amount of revenue had been booked in the past week. Huge blessing.

A knock came on her door frame. Rebecca. "Your buddy Reece on line one."

"Thanks." She picked up the phone while reading an e-mail regarding a TV spot they were developing to promote their summer jam concert.

"Reece, hi."

"How are you?"

"Good, but busy. No time to talk."

"I'll be brief. Just confirming you're still coming to Well Spring next week to help train our next batch of recruits. We leave next Thursday at noon, back Sunday night late as usual."

Dana rubbed her eyes and moaned inside. "Didn't you get my e-mail?"

The line went silent for a few seconds. "E-mail isn't the most effective way to communicate with me these days."

"I thought you were going to set up computer reading software for your e-mails."

"I don't see much need when I'm sensing the Spirit is going to heal me soon. What did your e-mail say?"

"I can't go, Reece. I'm sorry."

"What?"

"I have another commitment." Dinner with her boss and his wife was a commitment? Yes, it was. She'd earned it. She needed it. She wanted it.

"The mission of training these people is critical, Dana."

"I'd love to hear of one mission over the past year that hasn't been critical."

"None, but that doesn't change the importance of the time and the fact the entire team needs to be there."

"Point taken, but that doesn't change the fact that I can't make it."

"Why can't you?"

Heat rose to her face. "I don't have time to get into it right now."

"I think you should make the time."

She glanced at her watch. Eight minutes till the meeting. "I'd love to be able to make time, create it out of nothing, and add it to the twenty-four hours I get every day, but I can't. Twenty-four is all there is and all there

239

ever will be."

After she hung up, Dana glared at her phone and shoved it across her desk where it teetered on the edge, then dropped off and thumped onto the carpet. She was mad at Reece, mad at herself, mad at the emotional energy the Warriors and always fighting the enemy took, and mad that her excuse for not going to Well Spring would melt under any kind of honest scrutiny.

Was it so wrong that she finally felt like she belonged at the station and wasn't alone in her job? That a group of people she liked didn't center around activities that exhausted every fiber of her? That she might get a social life going where she could enjoy simple pleasures like going to dinner or a play and maybe even at some point going on a blind date with one of Robert's friends?

She glanced at her watch. Six minutes till the meeting. She'd have to fake it. And try to ignore the tiny neon beacon in her heart telling her she was going the wrong way down a one-way street.

TWENTY-FOUR

Kevin sauntered into Brandon's hospital room on Wednesday evening, leaned against the wall, and pointed back into the hallway with his thumb. "They told me the surgery went well this morning. That it couldn't have gone better."

Brandon flashed a thumbs-up.

"That's the good news. The bad is, it sounds like we have to scrap the Marymoor concert."

Brandon shook his head as he motioned his manager-agent to come farther into the room. No, they wouldn't have to cancel. The solution was simple. As long as Kevin would go along with it, and Brandon didn't think it would take that much persuading to get his manager behind the idea.

"No?"

Brandon shook his head and beckoned Kevin closer. When he reached the hospital bed, Brandon rapped out a message on his laptop.

The show must go on.

"There's no way the doctor I just talked to will let you sing at Marymoor. It's too soon. I suppose you could stand up there and talk for two and a half hours, but I'm not thinking that's what the audience will be coming to hear."

We can still do the show.

"Let's get serious. You want to explain how that's going to happen without your being able to sing? The concert is in just under three weeks and the doc just told me he won't even let you speak till next Thursday, and singing again won't come for another four weeks at the earliest."
Brandon smiled and typed out another message.

I have an idea.

"Let me guess. You want me to play videos of you in concert on a big screen? Or are you going to lip-synch?"
Brandon shook his head, moved his mouth as if singing, played an air guitar, and then

pointed at Kevin.

"Me?" Kevin shook his head.

Brandon nodded.

"Nah, nah, nah, no way."

Brandon grinned and typed out another line.

This could be a big step, a nice break for you.

"Yeah, right. Nice break like break my career into a million pieces before it starts? I'm not ready to headline an entire concert. Plus I'm not going to make my debut trying to step into the monstrous shoes of Brandon Scott. I'm telling you, they'd figure out really quickly I wasn't you."

Brandon whipped his fingers over the keyboard.

You have a hit song, bro. Big hit. They're singing it in churches. A lot of people are starting to know your name. You're working on an album so you have those songs as well. You'll sing yours and some of mine. You know all of them by heart. It'll be a combo pack. They'll love it. I've already worked out all the details with the band. They're ready to rehearse. I've talked to the promoter, and she's good with it. And every ticket holder has been sent an e-mail explaining the situation, and they've been offered a full refund if they want.

Plus Spirit 105.3 is promoting it on air and on their website. And I convinced them to say, "Come hear Kevin Kaison, the inspiration behind Brandon Scott, the one who believed in him and cared for him and supported him and made him into the man he is today."

"What? That makes it sound like I'm your wife. They aren't really saying that."

The hospital bed shook and creaked from Brandon's silent laughter. He bent over his notebook computer again.

No. Not the last part, but they are pushing the concert.

"I don't know, man. That would be too weird to have me up there."

Pray about it. Think about it. I believe it's the right moment for a live crowd to discover Kevin Kaison and his stunning song-writing and singing ability. And "I'm scared" is not a valid excuse. Not after all the speeches you've given me over the years about pushing through fear.

Kevin's eyes grew brighter and Brandon knew his friend would accept.

"I need a day to mull this over."

Really?

"No, not really." Kevin stuck out his fist and bumped Brandon's. "I'm in."

You're going to kill. I guarantee it.

■ ■ ■ ■

"Tell me you got Brandon Scott to come on the show."

Sooz slouched against Carson Tanner's door frame, a few strands of her hair hanging in her face. She flashed a thumbs-up and smiled. "I got Brandon to come on the show."

"Are you serious?" Carson lurched forward in his chair, his knees bumping his thick glass desk.

"No. Of course I'm not serious. You know this is mission extremely improbable. You made multiple attempts yourself. Remember when you liked Brandon and his music and tried for months and months to get him to come on? He doesn't do interviews. He hasn't for a long, long time. No exceptions."

"I never stopped liking him, which is why

I want him on the show. I'm trying to bring him back to the truth. Keep him from getting too wrapped up with this modern mystic Reece Roth wacko." Carson rocked back in his chair, cradled the back of his head with his hands, and stared at the ceiling. "I don't get Brandon. In this day and age where you're supposed to connect with your fans — have give-and-take — interact with them, and the guy won't —"

"He does connect with his fans. You should hear what he does after every concert. Apparently he stays for hours talking to people, praying with them. He just doesn't connect with interviewers. Like you."

"Any other discouraging news?"

"Yes. He just went in for some kind of vocal-cord surgery so he'll be out for who knows how long recovering from that. Probably step out of the public light for at least a couple of months."

"Those kinds of surgeries don't take that long to recover from." Carson tossed his pen across the room and it smacked into the wall.

"I'm just saying."

"I'm not giving up on this, Sooz. I'm going to keep believing God is in this because

I know he is. And that he will make it happen."

"I still say you could get some of these people who are doing mini Warriors Riding retreats on the show —"

"There's no point in cutting off the heads of dandelions. We could do that all day and they'd just grow back. We have to take off the head of the snake. Dam up the river at the source."

"That's three metaphors. I think one will do."

"Just get him. Soon. Okay?"

"I'm not giving up either. And like you, I believe. This battle is God's and he will not fail us."

TWENTY-FIVE

As Reece clomped down his stairs at noon eight days later, he heard his front door open and a voice he didn't expect.

"Good morning, Reece."

He smiled at the sound of Dana's voice as she said hello to Brandon. A pleasant surprise. He'd put the odds of her showing up today to head for Well Spring with them at a hundred to one.

"You're going?" Reece asked.

"I am indeed going. Don't sound so shocked."

"You were able to get out of your seemingly unbreakable commitment?"

She hesitated. "Yes, I was."

The sound of the door opening again and footsteps on the wood floor of his entryway and a bag being set down filled his ears. It had to be the professor. "Looks like all members of the entourage are present."

"Where's Doug?" Dana asked.

"He's meeting us at the ranch."

"Hey, Marcus," Brandon said.

"Your voice is quiet, but overall sounds quite adequate," Marcus said. "All is well?"

"Yeah, the doc says I'm going to be fine. Won't be singing for a bit, but things look good and it shouldn't be long before I'm back onstage."

Reece took a step in the direction Dana's voice had come from. "Do you care to expand on how you escaped your obligation?"

"Not at all. Doug's words the other night were simple but profound when he said, 'A subtle attack can often be far more effective than a direct assault since an attack of subterfuge and nuance is often not noticed till the victim has crawled into the middle of the spider's web.'

"You all probably saw it the whole time. I don't know why I didn't. My promotion — obvious to everyone but me that the enemy was using it to distract me, distance me from the game."

"True." Relief fell on Reece. He'd expected a much longer struggle to get Dana back firing on all cylinders.

"Why didn't you try to tell me?"

"I did."

"I mean, tell me specifically that it was

the enemy."

"Would you have listened?"

Reece heard Dana shift in her chair. "No."

"So what does this mean for your job?"

"I'm not sure, but I am sure I'm all in with the Warriors."

He took another step toward her and reached out for her shoulders. He wrapped an arm around them tight. "You're a treasure, Dana. Never forget that." He released her and motioned with his hands. "Gather 'round, let's get ourselves to Well Spring."

"I don't care how many times we've done this teleportation thing. It still feels very, very strange," Dana said to Brandon.

"I know." Reece heard the smile in Brandon's voice. "That's why it's such a cool rush. I'm ready. Beam me up, Reecy."

After they settled in at Well Spring, they all gathered in the main cabin. Over lunch Marcus told of his encounter with Zennon. Dana tried to imagine what it would be like to have a daughter go through what Abbie had just endured. Sometimes not having children was a very good thing.

"Excellent," Reece said when the professor finished.

"Excellent?" Brandon said. "Are you kidding? I wouldn't describe what the prof and his family went through as excellent."

Doug set down his fork and patted Brandon's arm. "What Reece means is —"

"I know, I know . . . things are on the right track, we've got the enemy upset, my throat, Dana's promotion, Reece's eyes not being healed yet, Zennon's attack on the professor — how that's all a good thing because he's trying to take us out before we confront the Wolf, blah, blah, blah." Brandon glanced around the table. "But don't you ever get tired of the battle? Wouldn't you like some peace and quiet sometimes?"

"Yes." Reece smiled. "Absolutely. We all need a break. That's why we're going in this afternoon before the new recruits get here. To a place of peace. Refreshment." He laughed. "I wish I could see the stunned looks on your faces, which I'm positive are there. Yes, I'm finally going to go back in. Scout's honor." He held up his fingers in the traditional Boy Scout's salute.

"You feel prepared?" Brandon said.

"Funny," Reece said as his countenance grew serious. "Yes, I am prepared, for whatever the Spirit has for me."

Dana looked at her watch. One thirty. The new trainees wouldn't be here till six, so they had plenty of time to go into wherever Reece wanted to go, get back out, and make any necessary last-minute prep to the ranch. The guys of course thought the place looked great. Reece had an excuse now, but the others should be able to see a bit of touch-up was sorely needed. These were the moments she wished another woman was part of the Warriors.

"Are we ready?" Doug glanced around the room, a look of glee on his face.

Dana opened her Bible. "Can I read something first?"

"Please." Doug nodded.

She glanced at the others before focusing her gaze on Reece. "I don't want to create any false expectations or stir hope without reason, Reece, but as I was unpacking before lunch I think I heard the Spirit saying when you went in again, you'd like what you found there." She flipped her Bible to Isaiah. "And then I saw this verse: 'I will lead the blind by a way they do not know, in paths they do not know I will guide them. I will make darkness into light before them and rugged places into plains. These are the things I will do, and I will not leave them undone.' "

Reece didn't comment but he nodded and put his hand on hers.

"Amen and so be it," Doug said. "Anyone else?" No one spoke. "Then let's do a quick cleanup and be off."

Ten minutes later they took hold of each other's hands. Dana closed her eyes and waited. Less than a moment later she opened her eyes and found herself standing on a beach that reminded her of Costa Rica, no, maybe it was more like Jamaica or Fiji. Tiny waves lapped at a white sand beach, the breeze off the crystal-blue water was perfect, and the warm sand felt like cotton against her bare feet.

As it had been in the realm of the Wall of Colors, the hues were far more brilliant here than on earth and they filled her soul with wonder. She turned to look at the tropical foliage behind her but was interrupted by the screams and roars of delight that poured out of Reece.

"I can see!" Reece bounded down the beach and sprinted through the water, his arms waving like he was trying to fly. He probably was flying, in his mind and heart and spirit at least.

Dana laughed and shouted, "Yes!" in chorus with the whoops and cheers of Doug, Brandon, and Marcus. She hadn't known this would happen, but she had known.

After a few minutes he splashed back toward them through the water and stopped five feet away. He grinned, reached for his glasses, and pulled them off like he was unveiling his greatest photograph. For the first time in almost a year she looked into his brilliant blue eyes. Amazing. Full of love, and joy, and freedom. And even more penetrating than when she'd last seen them, if that was possible.

Dana continued to grin as Reece danced in an awkward circle, kicking up sand and letting out another whoop. She turned to Doug and frowned. He was smiling, but there was a deep sadness in his eyes she didn't understand.

For the next ten minutes she and Marcus wandered up and down the beach. Brandon stepped into the sea and swam out to a tiny island of rocks sixty yards off the shore, and Doug pushed into the thick jungle behind them. It was exactly what Reece had said it would be. Refreshing, restorative, invigorating. Too soon Doug's voice rang out over the beach. "It's time to go back."

They gathered at the spot they'd started from, all of their faces radiant and full of life.

"Do you know what this means?" Reece pointed to his eyes and grinned.

Brandon pointed at the big man. "What happens in here —"

"Becomes reality in the physical world." Reece held his arms wide. "I'm healed. The prophecy has been fulfilled."

Doug didn't comment and motioned them together with his hands, his eyes down. "Are you ready?"

"You're kidding, right?" Reece grinned. "Not even close. Five more minutes, friend. This is a moment to celebrate. It's been a long time coming. I need to soak in a little more of this beauty."

"I wish it could be longer." The same look Dana had seen a few minutes ago passed over Doug's face. "A few more at most."

Reece walked to the water's edge and turned his head slowly from one side to the other. Three or four minutes later he turned and trudged back up the beach. "Okay, Doug, I know we need to go. Seeing here is nothing like seeing back on earth. But trust me, I'm not complaining. I have a lot of photography to make up for. So yes, let's go."

Doug didn't respond as he clasped Dana's hand on one side and Marcus's on the other. Reece grabbed the hands of Marcus and Brandon and an instant later they were back in the living room at Well Spring.

Dana whirled to find Reece. He was on his knees in the center of the room, his head resting on the area rug. "Are you okay, Reece?"

He didn't answer and she looked at Doug. His face was ashen, and as he returned her gaze she realized why. He'd known this was going to happen, but there was nothing he could have done. Nothing any of them could have done to prepare Reece for the emotions of the moment.

The big man lifted his head and turned to them. He whipped off his sunglasses and stared at her and the others with the black, seared tissue that a moment ago had been his brilliant blue eyes. Reece opened his mouth. No noise came from his lips, but Dana could imagine what it would sound like if it did. Utter anguish.

She looked at Brandon and Marcus. At first their faces registered shock, then understanding, then horror. Doug glanced at her, then waited till Brandon and Marcus looked at him as well. Then he stood and motioned her and the others outside. No one spoke as they shuffled through the front door. None of them spoke as they stepped away from each other, all in different directions. There was no need. All of them would ask the Spirit why Reece wasn't healed, and all of them would ask him to fall on Reece with a peace their guide couldn't ignore.

■ ■ ■ ■

That night after their first session — without Reece — and after the new students had settled into their cabins, Dana sat at the fire pit and stared at the coals as the last of them winked out. She lifted her gaze at the sound of shoes on the stone path to her right. Doug.

"May I join you?"

"Of course."

He sat next to Dana, hands clasped, concern etched on his face.

"You knew this would happen to Reece, didn't you?"

"I didn't know." He sighed. "But yes, I suspected."

"Why weren't his eyes healed here if they were healed there?"

"I don't know, Dana. But I do know this is not the final chapter of any of our stories."

The Friday, Saturday, and Sunday sessions went well. There were breakthroughs for almost all of the students and Reece took part in every class. If he had been taken down by what happened — what didn't happen to him — nothing in what he said or did showed it. But still, he didn't seem himself.

Ninety percent of the trainees committed to being prayer allies and starting their own groups when they got home. On Saturday night Reece spoke powerfully about going deeper in the Spirit and where the students needed to go from here. But while his words resonated, the fire behind them had gone dim.

As the last of the cars with the trainees in them pulled out of the ranch on Sunday late morning, Dana turned and walked north along the river. She needed to get away. Find a slice of silence to sit in and let the intensity of the past three days slide off of her, along with the fear Reece's eyes would never be restored.

By the time she'd gone one hundred yards she felt better. By the time she'd gone two hundred a sense of hope welled up inside. It wasn't over yet, and until it was, she would keep praying for the healing of Reece's eyes and believing it would happen. She took five steps off the path toward the river to watch the currents as she prayed.

"Hey!"

Dana spun at the sound of the voice. Brandon sat twenty yards to her left behind three pine trees, smiling at her — the same smile that melted her heart when they'd first met. Ugh. She was not going to go there even for a second. She'd been down that path so often in the past year her footprints were stamped on the trail like concrete.

She was done with Brandon forever. She'd told him that. She meant it.

"Want to talk for bit?"

No, she didn't. Yes, she did. Why did she have to be so schizophrenic when it came to him? Probably the curse of once being in love with the idiot.

"Sure, why not."

TWENTY-SIX

"Do you think we'll survive when we go after the Wolf?" Brandon said as Dana shuffled toward him.

"Survive the Wolf?" Dana sat next to him and let out a puff of laughter. "I'm focused on recovering from the past four days."

He knew how she felt. The last of the new trainees had left the ranch an hour ago. It had gone extremely well. Each of the four retreats they'd done over the past year had brought great freedom and healing to the men and women who had come, and this one was no different. But the training left him feeling like an air mattress after all the air had been expelled.

He turned from his view of the river below and lifted his hand to block the late afternoon sun flowing around Dana and into his eyes. She sat with her arms wrapped around her knees, light brown hair pulled back and tied up with a red scrunchie. No makeup.

No need for it. She was beautiful.

"I agree." Brandon stared at her eyes, hoping she would turn and look into his. "It's exhilarating and exhausting at the same time."

The sound of the river soothed him as if God were washing away the dirt that seemed to cling to his soul after every training session was over and the new recruits had gone home. Reece said the enemy tried to spread fear and sin to them like a virus from the people they were training and setting free, so there needed to be a time of restoration and refreshment. Brandon didn't understand the theology behind the statement, but he did know he felt like he needed time to detox every time after they were done and it seemed Dana felt the same.

He turned and looked at Dana again till she returned his gaze. "Do you ever wish you could go back to the way your life was before Well Spring?"

She shifted and drew her finger along the pine needles they sat on. "Yes and no. Do I wish we weren't the ones leading the charge into a battle that probably won't end till we die? Yes. Do I wish I could slip back into the chains I wore before coming here a year ago? Not a chance. What about you?"

"Same. But there are some things I'd like

to go back and do differently."

"Such as?"

Maybe someday he'd tell her. Not now. It would still be a long time before he stepped into that rowboat. But it didn't mean he couldn't explore the condition of the oars.

"How's Perry?"

Dana picked at a spot of pitch on her hand. "Are we going to get into this again?"

"Not at all." Brandon raised his palms in surrender. "I'm genuinely asking."

She frowned. "Why don't I believe you?"

"Hey, don't believe me. It's fine." Brandon watched a leaf move from as far up the river as he could see till it disappeared downstream before he spoke again. "Are you worried about Reece? Do you think he'll be okay, that he'll make it through this?"

"He's probably good."

"You think so? It helps to hear you say that, because to get his sight back, then come out and discover he didn't get healed. Wow."

"Perry is probably good. Once I told him there was no chance of anything more between us than friends, he stopped calling."

"What?" Brandon turned and grinned. "Sorry, I thought you were answering my question about —"

"I know." She offered him a rare smile and her green eyes danced like they used to in the age when they'd been together. "I figured that out."

"Sorry, I just —"

"I'm teasing." She nudged him with her elbow. "Yes, I'm worried about him."

"Why are you worried about Perry?"

"No, I'm not, I'm worried about —"

Brandon grinned. "Now I get to say I knew that."

They both laughed and leaned into each other, and as they did a shot of adrenaline surged through Brandon. Instantly it felt like it was four years earlier and his engagement ring was still on Dana's finger, and his resolve not to ask the question till ages had passed melted away. He stared at her till Dana met his gaze.

"I know I'm asking again. The question I'm not supposed to, but do you ever think about us? What might have been if I hadn't . . . ?"

She dropped her gaze to the ground, then raised it to once again look at the river. "Let's walk, okay?"

"Where?" They stood and dusted off their jeans.

Dana pointed west and they started out on the trail that led toward the cabins.

"That's what you'd do differently, isn't it?" She kicked at sticks and pinecones as they shuffled along the trail leading past the cabins toward the zip lines and ropes course. A team of workers had installed it last fall so students could learn to conquer physical fears in order to face spiritual fears. Reece hadn't talked about putting in a strip of burning coals. Yet.

The silence between them stretched and Brandon let the subject drop. "Tell me what you're thinking about Reece."

Dana stopped, put her hands on her hips, and laughed. "I'm impressed. We're having a fairly digressive conversation and yet you never lost any of the threads."

"As you might suspect, I've bumped into a few women over the course of my life, so I've had practice."

She frowned at him playfully. "You're saying women often can't talk in a straight line?"

"That's exactly what I'm saying."

Dana laughed and walked on. "Yes, of course I'm worried. As mature as Reece is in the faith, you can't lose your sight and your greatest passion, think you've been healed and find out you haven't, and not have it tear at your mind and push you into decisions you wouldn't have made before."

"Have you talked to Doug?"

"A little bit the other night."

"Did he have any insight?" Brandon blinked. "Sorry, wrong word."

"Not really, just to pray."

"You know, we could go crazy and pray for him right now."

She smiled. "Let's go crazy."

They settled down in a small grove of alder trees just past the ropes course and slipped into silence. They'd prayed so often together over the past eleven months neither needed either to start or even pray out loud. After five or so minutes, Brandon opened his eyes and gazed at Dana till she opened hers.

"What did you get? Anything?"

Dana nodded, her eyes wider than normal.

"I'm not liking the look on your face."

"I kept getting this feeling of imminent danger and a picture of a hockey team."

"A what?"

"I know, I've never even been to a hockey game and couldn't tell you one team name, but I had a clear picture of one, their uniforms, the colors. I could almost hear the scrape of their blades on the ice, their streaking toward the other team's goal. It was vivid."

"The hockey team was in danger?"

"No, not them, but they had something to do with the danger or were the cause of the danger."

"Wow. Left of left field."

"Yeah, I know. What about you? Anything?"

"Nothing." Brandon shrugged. "Except an image of something white."

"What was the something?"

"I don't know. It was white. That was it."

"Like ice? Were you seeing the hockey rink?"

"Sure. Maybe. I have no clue." Brandon glanced at his watch. "We should go. We're supposed to be meeting with Reece and Marcus and Doug in a few minutes. Final debrief before we get ready to head home."

They both rose and ambled back toward the main cabin, listening to a lark bunting warble out an afternoon song. Dana glanced at him, then turned her gaze to a blue sky speckled with wispy clouds.

"I'm not trying to avoid the question. I just don't know how to answer it."

"You mean the 'do you think about us' question?"

"Once again, I'm impressed."

"You don't have an answer, or you don't want to give it to me?"

"I have an answer, but not one I'm ready

to speak out loud."

"How often?"

"What?"

"How often do you think about us?"

"That's a different question, Brandon."

"Yes."

"With work and Warriors Riding and the healing still going on inside me . . . I try not to think about how often I think about us, or what we used to be."

They walked the rest of the way back to the main cabin in silence. She hadn't given him an answer, yet at the same time she had. She did think about the two of them. How often? It didn't matter. The two of them came into her mind — and for the moment it was enough to say.

When Dana reached for the doorknob, Brandon put his hand on top of hers and stopped her from opening it. "Dana, I —"

"Don't ask me about it anymore, okay?" She smiled but her eyes were full of sorrow. "I think about us, yes, but that life is over and I don't see it ever returning. That part of my heart is gone. I'm sorry if that's hard to hear, but you and I happened in another age." Dana sighed and lifted his hand off of hers. "We should get inside. Reece and Marcus are probably wondering where we are."

She turned the knob and stepped into the

cabin. He waited for her to look back, to give him another sad smile or a glance that said she didn't truly mean what she'd said, but all he saw was the back of her head as she strolled into the cabin and turned the corner into the living room.

"Hey."

The sound of Dana's voice filled the main room of the cabin along with the clop of her shoes on the heated hardwood floor. Then Reece heard another pair of shoes. Had to be Brandon since the professor and Doug already sat around the fireplace.

"Glad you two are back. I want to talk about our plan for going after the Wolf. Find out what we've all heard from the Spirit. See how and where Jesus wants to take us next."

Reece heard Brandon and Dana take seats across from each other and a slow sigh from Brandon.

"How is the Song today?"

"He's doing awesome."

But Brandon wasn't good. His voice betrayed him. Interesting that although Reece could no longer see body language, his sense of hearing had been so heightened he could gauge people's emotional state by the slightest nuance in their tone of voice.

268

"You're sure?"

"Yup. I'm sure."

It had to be something going on with Dana. Or the lack of something going on. Even though Brandon rarely discussed Dana with him, it was clear to anyone with a modicum of perception that the musician still loved her. It was also clear she either didn't feel the same or was refusing to let her feelings surface.

Reece shook his head. No time to think about that now. They needed to move on to the Wolf. "Who wants to start?"

The tap of a pen on a notebook came from Reece's left. Marcus getting ready to speak.

"The impression I received was we were to take our first step by going right to the source."

Reece smiled. He'd gotten the same feeling. "You mean engage Carson directly?"

"Precisely." Marcus's tapping increased. "But I don't mean confront him. I mean watch him in action, get a sense for what surrounds him spiritually. Do a reconnaissance mission."

"I agree, but how do you suggest we do that? I doubt Carson has any idea who we are, and he's not going to invite someone he doesn't know to drop by for coffee and

269

donuts."

Reece heard someone shift position on the couch. "Easy," Dana said.

"How so?" Reece cocked his head in her direction.

"Have Brandon go on his show."

Reece laughed. "Of course." Given Brandon's level of fame, Carson had to know who the musician was. "Does he interview musicians?"

"Often," Dana said.

"I don't do interviews." From the sound of Brandon's voice and the scrape of his clothes against his chair, it was apparent the Song had stood and turned his back to the group.

"Why is that?" Reece said.

"I haven't done one in over four years."

Dana scoffed, "Is that part of your branding? You want to stay mysterious to your fans?"

Reece heard Brandon's feet shuffling back and forth over the cabin floor. Finally his feet stopped and it sounded like he turned. "But if the rest of you think this is what the Spirit is saying, I'm in."

TWENTY-SEVEN

Sooz stood in Carson Tanner's doorway late Monday afternoon, grinning like the Cheshire cat and bouncing on her toes double time.

"That's a good news smile." He rose and sauntered over to her. "No, that's a great news smile."

"You're not going to believe this." She pointed toward the heavens.

"I believe, help my unbelief."

"Guess who just called me?"

"The only person I can't believe would ever call you is Brandon Scott."

"He asked if he could come on your show."

"Unreal. God comes through."

"I've booked him for June fourteenth. And get this. We're not talking a phone interview. We're talking he's going to be in town to see his label so he wants to come to the studio."

Carson shook his head and sniffed out a laugh. "Just making sure I heard you correctly here. He called you. Not his manager. Him. Asking to be on my show. Plus he wants to come into the studio? Here? In person?" He bent down and pounded the floor with his fist.

"Yes."

"Why?" Carson rose up. "Please tell me what changed."

"No idea."

"I have an idea." He grinned at Sooz. "God is most definitely on the move."

She nodded and laughed.

Carson lurched back around his desk and sat, his hands moving like a windmill. "We're going to promote the garbanzo beans out of this. I want a new audio stinger, thirty-second promos running four times an hour every day till the interview, notices on all our social media sites, the blog, and at least three e-mail blasts to our subscribers. We're going to have the biggest audience we've had in eons. And Brandon and what the enemy is doing through him and his buddies will be hit like a fleet of Mack trucks."

TWENTY-EIGHT

Late afternoon on Saturday Kevin Kaison stood backstage at Marymoor Park, trying to keep his legs from bouncing. Why did he tell Brandon yes? This was too much. Sure, he wanted to do the concert. But unless his nerves quieted, he'd be so amped up and nervous his voice would make a soprano sound like a bass.

He rubbed his hands together. Both were damp with perspiration. His hands would slide all over his guitar — and he didn't play slide guitar. His mouth ached. He didn't realize he was clenching his teeth till the pain worked its way up into his jaw. He was a basket case.

Kevin slumped onto a stool, closed his eyes, and laid two fingers across his wrist. Wow. Relax. How could his heart race with Indianapolis 500 speed when all he was doing was sitting?

■ ■ ■ ■

By seven the crowd started ambling in over the expansive grass of the venue and picked spots to lay their blankets or set up their red and blue and green folding chairs. And it was a crowd. He'd hoped for three hundred people to show up; he'd expected a hundred. He glanced at his watch. Still an hour till showtime and there had to be at least seven hundred people already through the gates.

They knew Brandon wasn't playing, right? Then again, reducing the ticket price by half might have something to do with people still turning out. But still, who would want to see Brandon Scott's manager? Yeah, Kevin had a hit song, but that was hit song, singular. Did they really want to plunk down hard cash to see some guy they'd barely heard of?

Anthony, who wasn't much thicker than a javelin, sauntered up to him as he sucked on a milk shake Kevin surmised was his usual concoction of ice cream, butterscotch, and a healthy dose of wheat germ.

"Looks like you've got a decent crowd shuffling in."

"Yeah, a few anyway."

"Nice guerilla marketing move, K2." Anthony took a big gulp of his shake.

"What move?"

"Sending everyone who bought a ticket an MP3 of your soon-to-be-released next song." He wiggled his forefinger at the crowd. "Looks like a few of them liked it."

"I didn't . . ."

Brandon. He must have sent the song out to the list. "They heard my next song."

"Uh, yeah."

Kevin grabbed his phone and called Brandon. He picked up on the second ring. "You sent out my second song?"

"Did it work?" A light chuckle floated through the phone.

"Yeah, I think it worked." Kevin snaked through the stack of amps at the back of the stage and settled into a chair next to his guitar.

"How many people in seats so far?"

"Getting close to a thousand."

"One thousand? Sweet. See you at the top, bro."

"I don't know what to say."

"Say thanks."

Kevin got up and went back to the front of the stage. He peered around the curtain hiding him from view of the crowd laying blankets on the thick June grass and lying

275

back and letting the late afternoon sun soak into them. "Why are you doing all this for me?"

"You're kidding, right? After all the years you believed in what we were trying to do — even when it was lean? Talking me off the ledge millions of times? Telling me I had it when no one believed it but you? This is a very small payback for all those years."

"Thanks."

"Now go out there and go crazy. Sing like there's no tomorrow because there isn't. There is only this moment. Take it. It's yours."

"I needed those words and to say I appreciate it sounds so . . . stupid."

"Rock it, bro."

Kevin let the growing rumble of the crowd's conversation seep into his heart. They weren't here for Brandon Scott. They were here for him. Kevin Kaison. Not the manager. Not the agent. The musician. "I should go."

"Something else," Brandon said. "This is important. Ready? You might want to make a note of this. I'm serious."

"I'm ready."

"Try your best when the moment comes, and you walk onto that stage . . . not to puke."

Kevin laughed. "I'll try."

"K2? One more thing. Serious this time."

"Yeah?"

"God is in this and since he is, nothing about tonight is about you. It's about him. And if it's about him and he is in it, whatever happens is gold."

"Love ya, bro."

"Same. Kick it hard. I'll be praying."

As Kevin started the fifth song, something flickered in his peripheral vision. A thin line of something translucent with a light green tinge to it slithered through the grass to his right and left and up toward the stage, but when he stared at the matted grass he saw nothing. A memory flashed through his mind. Of Brandon's concert last year where Reece's and Dana's and Marcus's spirits had shown up onstage to fight . . . he couldn't remember. A vine? Some kind of evil but what? Brandon had never really talked about it, and Kevin shook his head. He couldn't let himself get distracted. This was his shot.

The crowd had been appreciative up till now, but he felt a shift, saw it on their faces. They loved him. And he loved them. And if he could admit it, he loved that they loved him. For once in his life the praise wasn't all about the god of Christian music: Brandon Scott. The roars of the crowd were for Kevin Kaison, stepping into his glory. No. Leaping into his glory — with arms stretched to their limit.

For the rest of the concert he did exactly what Brandon had told him to. He went crazy, forgot about playing every chord right and hitting every note perfect and just played with abandon.

By the time the last chord on the last song filled the dusky night air, he knew he'd hit a grand-slam home run. He raised his guitar to the audience and loped offstage, adrenaline and sweat and exhilaration all pouring over him.

The roar of the crowd ended in shouts of "Encore!" and Kevin strutted back onto the stage and again raised his guitar high in the air. The crowd erupted and his grin felt like it wrapped around his head. He was home for the first time in his life and if he had anything to say about it, would never leave.

An hour later Kevin sat alone in the center of the empty stage. The shouts of a late-evening soccer game under the Marymoor Park lights floated toward him from a half mile away. And the shouts of the crowd at the concert still echoed through his head.

Cheering for him. Loving his music. His dream had come alive.

Holding the case his bass rested in with both hands, Anthony bounced over to Kevin. "Congratulations, K2. I knew you could do it. The band knew you could do it. Most of all Brandon knew you could. Well done."

"Thanks." Kevin gazed over the matted grass again, and an image of the crowd again filled his mind.

"How are you going to juggle being a rising star and being Brandon's manager slash agent at the same time?"

A surge of adrenaline filled him, but he shoved the emotion down. "Easy. This was a one-time thing — my hobby getting a few moments in the sun. Managing Brandon is my true calling."

"Do you practice that insipid line every day?"

Kevin turned to Anthony and stared at the bass player's grin. As he did, an impression formed in Kevin's mind. Anthony was right. He wouldn't be going back. His days were on the verge of change. He'd just hopped on a sixty-foot wave and his surfboard was pointed straight down — he was about to go on the ride of his life.

Kevin turned to look out over the venue

as if in slow motion. "I'll do it for you, Anthony. Because I think you're right."

"Don't do it for me, or anyone else, do it for you. You deserve it. You've earned it." Anthony frowned. "What? You're worried about what Brandon will think?"

Yes, he was. Brandon had given him incredible support, so why was Kevin worried? Because he knew Brandon better than almost anyone. And while Brandon wanted him to succeed, he didn't want it to come at the expense of losing Kevin as his manager.

As he drove home that night, two questions wrestled for his attention. How soon should he tell Brandon, and how would Brandon react?

TWENTY-NINE

Marcus finished up his last class on Monday afternoon and called Simon's cell phone again. This would be the third message without a callback, but Marcus didn't care. He wanted to talk to the magician again. Simon hadn't been on campus for the past three weeks, or if he had, Marcus hadn't seen him. The magician had implied they'd talk again but it hadn't happened.

He wanted to ask Simon why the switching had stopped and why it had happened in the first place. And he wanted to talk about the Wolf. How did Simon know about that? What part was God going to have the magician play in this game?

Marcus didn't trust him, but the conjurer had at least some kind of answers, of that Marcus had no doubt. And more than anyone else could offer. As Marcus walked toward Red Square, the call went to voice mail. *"Simon here. Do you believe in magic?*

The Lovin' Spoonful did. I do too. Leave a message."

Marcus smiled. Reece would love that message.

"Simon, it's Marcus. I'd like to talk again. Call me. You have the number from my previous calls. I apologize for the persistence, but I want to continue our discussion from before."

Marcus trudged across the bricks that made up Red Square toward the parking garage but on a whim turned left and headed toward Drumheller Fountain. It's where he'd last seen Simon. Why not?

When he was still one hundred yards from the fountain, Marcus spotted what looked like Simon. It had to be the magician. Who else would be balancing on one leg, the other in the air along with his arms, reaching for the sky? And doing it up on the concrete ring of the fountain dressed in all black. When Marcus was still twenty-five yards away, Simon turned and hopped onto the ground like a cat.

"Professor of time and all it contains, what do you do when realities rain down all around you like lightning and snow, and when the bough breaks, where do you go?"

Simon hadn't mentioned his ability to look more than a little crazy while spouting his somehow-ingratiating rhymes. The magician's gaze darted from the fountain to Marcus to the sky to the ground back to the fountain.

"It's good to see you, Simon."

"Is it?" Simon blinked and rubbed his eyes. "Good to be seen in this reality. It is real, isn't it? I'm choosing to believe so."

"Did you receive my cell phone messages?"

Simon rubbed his head as if he were scrubbing a one-hundred-year-old grease spot off a silver chalice. "I've been having a tough few days. Not sure if I have a cell phone here. Can't remember."

"Here? As opposed to where?"

"Other places, the other places, the other places. Stop asking about it. I don't want to go there. Got free of that finally. Never going back."

Simon bent over and squeezed and unsqueezed his fists like pistons working overtime. "What do you want to say today, and hear with ears that might not listen, to flashes and glistens, that take your mind, to many lives of another kind?"

If this was the result of Simon's tough days, the days must have been difficult indeed.

"Are you with me here, Simon?"

"Most assuredly, yes. Ask me, ask me anything."

"I want to discuss my supposed forays into other realities. And the Wolf."

"The Wolf, the Wolf, the Wolf of confusion, he always spins a compelling illusion."

"Are you all right, Simon?"

"I'm good. I'm fine, really. It's just that it's a contusion, this ball of confusion." Simon straightened and fixed his gaze on the fountain. "Talk? You would, you would, and I think you should. We should, we could, and we should."

"Simon. Slow down."

The magician's head swiveled like his neck was made of rubber, his eyes moving everywhere except to look at Marcus.

"Tell me about the Wolf."

"Wolf bad. God good. Wolf bad, God is good. The Wolf is very, very bad. God is very, very good."

"What do you know about the Wolf — the spirit of religion?"

"I used to have cream with my coffee all the time." Simon paused and blinked again like he was sending a Morse code message with his eyes. "Or did I?" He stared hard at Marcus. "Do you know?" He dropped his gaze and seemed to study his palm. "Hard to keep track of what is real and what isn't.

284

Too many layers. Hard to keep track. Very difficult to keep track."

Marcus leaned in. "Simon, are you sure you're all — ?"

"Did you know in some realities they don't have crème brûlée creamer? How crazy is that? Very challenging to deal with." He bit his lower lip like a chipmunk trying to crack a nut. "Yes, I'm fine. I know what you're thinking. But I'm not. I'm not insane. Not. Not. Not. Just having a bad day today. Too many memories to keep track of. Makes me jumpy and talk gibberish. I know that. Don't you think I don't know that?" His eyes flashed anger.

"What happened, Simon?"

"Chose the wrong door, you see. No, that's not right. That's wrong. Reverse that. Strike that. Didn't choose the door. Should have gone through it but didn't. Didn't, didn't, didn't. Want to go back and walk through it, because I think it would be good, but I can't now. What's done is done. Over. Finished. I went the other way. Didn't even put my hand on the knob." Simon looked up, his gaze darting back and forth between Marcus and the fountain and his shoes. "Had my chance."

With a mixture of fascination and horror pinging through his mind, Marcus stared at

Simon. This wasn't the same man he'd watched perform in Red Square the other day.

"You'll have to make the choice someday, Marcus Amber, professor of physics. The Teacher will need to learn how important choices are. And the most difficult ones will, of course, without doubt, without question, teach him the most important lessons." Simon stopped fidgeting and his body went stiff. "Don't you agree?"

"The switching has stopped."

Simon laughed and clapped Marcus on the shoulder. "Sure. Sure it has. I believe you. It has, certainly. But of course it hasn't stopped and you know that down there." The magician jabbed his finger at Marcus's stomach. "And it won't stop till you choose."

"Choose what?"

"Can't tell you that. No sir, no can do. Not yet."

Simon rose and pulled a silver coin from his pocket and tossed it in the air. Marcus tried to follow the flight but it had vanished. A second later Simon reached behind Marcus's head and pulled the coin into view for a quarter second, then slapped it on the back of his wrist.

"Heads or tails?"

"Tails."

Simon grinned and slowly lifted his hand. The coin was gone, replaced by a small golden ticket. "You're just like Charlie. Willy Wonka is going to hand you a ticket, but you'll have to choose to go through the factory door."

THIRTY

"You were supposed to get me out of that, bro. Now I'm looking stupid."

Brandon tapped his sandal against his deck at his home near Snoqualmie Ridge on Thursday afternoon. Sandals in mid-June. Nice. The month was typically full of rainy days. But today was sun and low seventies. Perfect.

Brandon stared at the Douglas fir trees in his backyard and gripped his phone tighter. Ever since Brandon gave him the show at Marymoor Park, Kevin had dropped the proverbial ball multiple times. There'd been complaints from the road crew as well. Nothing big in and of itself, but added all together it bothered Brandon. His manager was slipping and the cause was pretty obvious.

"Get you out of what?"

"I get a phone call this morning from a producer down in LA wanting to know what time I want to meet on Friday to go over what my cameo is going to look like on their TV series. I told you I wasn't going to do it."

"But you're going to be in LA anyway to meet with your label."

"That's not the point. I asked you to cancel it. I'm not going on the show."

"Yeah," Kevin muttered.

"Yeah what?"

"I spaced."

"You never space." Brandon strolled onto his lawn. "And you haven't exactly been Speed Racer lately with e-mails or phone calls."

"You mean it takes me more than an hour to respond to an e-mail or voice mail?"

This conversation wasn't going to end well if Brandon didn't get off the track, but the road seemed to have rails on it with no place to exit. "Try seven or eight hours."

"I'm allowed to have a life, right?"

"One hit song and one successful concert and you're suddenly a superstar copping an attitude."

"Knock it off, Brandon. I'm trying to keep a million plates spinning."

"Too many are falling off the poles. I think your brain is in the wrong spot and you need to figure out where you want to be."

Kevin didn't respond and Brandon's gut agreed with what his mind had been telling him for the past five days. "When do you want to leave?"

"What?"

"Become my ex-manager."

Brandon heard Kevin's quick breath through the phone. "You're not ticked —"

"I knew we'd get here someday, didn't you?"

"No . . . I mean I hoped . . . but I didn't know how to tell you."

Brandon wandered back inside and stared at a photo of Kevin and him skiing up at Whistler. "But you have to find me someone as good as or better than you before you ditch me entirely. Which is, of course, an impossible task."

"I don't know what to say."

"Say you're looking forward to us going on tour together."

Kevin laughed. "All the way. That will be the top."

Brandon switched gears. "Reminder. I'm headed out to see the label tomorrow. Anything going on there you want to help me with? Anything you've said to them about me I should be aware of?"

"No, it's all good on all fronts. Just trying to get my album finished."

"Sweet."

Brandon hung up and walked toward l home studio. Yeah, Kevin was dropping few plates only because his dreams we coming true. Brandon needed to relax. Bu he couldn't get the feeling out of his min that one of the larger plates was about t drop on his head.

THIRTY-ONE

Reece's cell phone rang on Tuesday evening with a generic ring, which meant he didn't know the caller. He'd assigned all his inner circle specific ring tones since he lost his sight, which meant he probably should let the call go to voice mail. But something told him to pick up.

"It's Reece."

"Hello, Reece Roth. This is Tristan Barrow."

Interesting. Brandon's stalker. The one who had found the Song, the Leader, and the Teacher down at Houghton Beach Park.

"Good morning, Tristan. I understand you're getting to know some of my friends."

"Trying, yes." The tone of Tristan's voice made it sound like he was smiling. Who was this guy?

"And what is your interest in them?"

"The same as my interest in you."

"Which is?"

292

"From what you've heard about me from the others, do you believe I'm here to help or here to hinder you in your quest?"

"Why don't you end the suspense and tell me."

"If I said I was here to help, would you believe me?"

"I'd like to look into your eyes as you said it."

"I'm sorry for your loss, Roy, but there is purpose in it."

Reece's pulse spiked. Roy? How did Tristan know the name Jesus had given him a year and a half ago? Roy Hobbs from *The Natural* — Roy Hobbs who was washed out but stepped back into the game to fulfill his destiny. Just like Reece. Had one of the other Warriors told Tristan that name? Highly unlikely.

"How do you know about that?"

"Why don't we meet, Reece Roth, and we can talk about that and other things as well. Always better in person than over the phone."

The man's voice was powerful, his tone one of confidence but not cockiness.

Jesus?

The answer from the Spirit was immediate. *Go.*

"Will your two friends Jotham and Orson

be joining us?"

"No, they have other duties they must attend to."

"Fine. Maltby Café on Friday morning at eleven o'clock."

"Excellent."

"And, Reece?"

"Yes."

Tristan went silent.

"Do you have something else to say?"

For a few more seconds the only sound was the hum of the phone. "You will see again."

"Enough. How do you know about the name? What do you know of the proph— ?"

"I'll meet you at the café on Friday. I'd like to ask you a favor when we do." The line went dead.

THIRTY-TWO

When Brandon stepped through the doors of Windfire Records Friday morning at nine o'clock his stomach said something was wrong. A moment later the receptionist in the lobby confirmed the feeling.

"Take a seat. Audrey is wrapping up a meeting but should be done shortly. As soon as she is, someone will be right down to get you."

Take a seat? In the fifteen-plus times he'd been in this building over the past six years he'd never had to "take a seat." Sure, in the early days he'd waited, but that was ages ago. There had always been someone waiting for him and he was escorted immediately to whichever office he was visiting.

Fifteen minutes later Logan Hall stepped out of the elevator and clipped over to him. "Sorry, Brandon. I hate to keep people waiting — especially you." Logan patted Brandon's shoulder. "You look good, really good.

You've been well?"

"Sure, and you?"

"Fine, yes, and tell me, how was your flight? And is your hotel okay? I tried to get you first class but it wasn't available, and they were booked at the Hilton. Next time it'll be back to normal, okay?"

They headed to the elevators and Brandon relaxed. Maybe nothing was wrong. Logan seemed normal, without any hint of unease in his eyes. As they rode up the elevator, Logan kept up a monologue about the label, other labels, who would have the biggest release in the fall — the normal Logan commentary about everything and nothing.

It didn't hit Brandon till they passed the sixth floor that this was the first time in years there wasn't a sign at the front desk with his name on it welcoming him. He pushed the thought away. Big deal, so they forgot to put it up one time. Still . . . he tried to shake off the feeling something was off balance, but it didn't work. He needed to get his mind off himself and onto someone else.

"How is Kevin's single doing?"

"Record breaking." Logan smiled. "Big records."

"Really?"

"It's already gone gold. Platinum looks

very attainable."

"Serious? That is so cool. Kevin didn't tell me."

"We've never had a single sell this big this fast. Everyone around here is so grateful to you for discovering Kevin."

"My pleasure."

The elevator doors opened and they strolled down the open, cubicle-filled ninth floor. Half the desks were filled; a few people were on the phone. Windfire's lead cover designer glanced up, gave Brandon a quick wave, and then picked up her cell phone and dialed. On his right, Katie Bostic, Windfire's publicist extraordinaire, met Brandon's gaze and instantly looked away and became fixed on a file on her desk. Was the staff avoiding him, or had his imagination shifted into overdrive?

A few seconds later they reached the office of Audrey Decket, head of Windfire Records. Logan did a 180-degree spin before giving a slight bow and motioning his hand toward her door. "Here you are, Brandon."

"Thanks, Logan. Always good to see you."

"Likewise."

Brandon turned, peered into Audrey's office, and grinned.

She looked up from her desk. "Long time,

stranger."

"True." Brandon strolled inside and gave Audrey a quick hug. A framed, blown-up cover of his latest CD hung along the wall over her mini conference table along with seven or eight other artists. Same ones as last time, and the time before that. Wait. There was a new one on the end. Kevin Kaison's.

"You've already finished the cover art for K2's album."

"He's on the fast track. As well as his single has done, we need to get the CD out last week."

"Congrats."

Audrey smiled and nodded. "How are you, Brandon?" She settled back into her chair and steepled her fingers. "You look good."

"Is that the line today?"

"Hmmm?"

"Same thing Logan said to me."

"There was a memo from the parent company this morning telling us to greet everyone that way." Audrey got up and closed her door. "Ready to get to business?"

"Sure. Is there anything on the agenda other than starting talks on a new contract?" Brandon crossed his legs.

"Yes."

Brandon bit his lip. He didn't like the way Audrey said yes. "And that is?"

"The music industry is changing. Has changed. Is changing more."

"Yeah." The office seemed to grow warmer.

"Brandon, you've had a tremendous run. Phenomenal. But the past three albums have sold fewer units. Yes, I realize people aren't buying albums as much anymore, but you haven't had a breakout hit in almost two years, and no one is downloading your backlist. They used to. But the river of sales has become a trickle."

"Hold on. My concerts have been packed for the past eight months, and six out of my next eight shows are already sold out."

"Yes, that's true." Audrey walked to the window overlooking LA. "Congratulations." She turned back to Brandon. "But we don't make a lot of money on the concerts, you know? You do. We need to make some cuts."

Brandon's gut went tight. "Define cuts."

"Budgets have to be overhauled from time to time, to get them in line. As you know, we lost money last year. And the year before that. And the year before that."

"You're cutting me."

Audrey ran her fingers over the surface of her desk. "Not really."

"What does 'not really' mean? That my latest album is the last one with Windfire?"

Audrey waved her hands. "No, this is coming out sounding far worse than it is. It's not like we're dropping you. We're even willing to look at a new contract. We definitely want to keep making records together, but the terms might be a little different."

"How different? And what about support for my upcoming album?"

"Only a slight change there. We're going to reduce the amount of marketing behind it."

"How much?"

"A portion."

"We've been together too long for games, Audrey." Brandon stood and folded his arms. "What percentage?"

She narrowed her eyes and her tone was flat. "Eighty percent."

"Eighty? You're cutting my marketing budget by eighty percent?" Brandon pointed at the album covers on Audrey's wall. "I've sold over eighteen million albums for this label."

"Sold. Past tense. If this next album does better than your last one, we can look at bringing your marketing funds back up to where they were."

"Unbelievable." Brandon stared out the

window at the Los Angeles smog. "I need to talk to K2. He's going to take you to the mat on this one. We have a contract that clearly spells out what kind of marketing support you'll give me."

"No, that's not in the contract. It's in a memo."

"Same thing."

"You know it's not and besides, it's already done. We've funneled the money into a newer artist. I'm sorry. It wasn't my decision."

"What a crock! Maybe it wasn't your decision, but you approved it. You could have stopped it, blocked it, you're the head of the label." Brandon jabbed his finger onto her desk, his voice rising with each sentence. "At least talked to me before you lit the fuse!"

"It's been decided. As far as everyone around here is concerned, the question of whether we make the move or not is dead."

"When Kevin gets on the phone, it will be resurrected, trust me. There's no way he'll let this happen." Kevin was a superb manager and even better when he played the role of an agent. Kind? One of the kindest men he'd ever known when people were fair with him. But when they weren't, K2 was the Tasmanian Devil. Brandon was looking

301

forward to setting the devil loose.

"I don't think bringing Kevin into this is a good idea."

"Yeah, I wouldn't either if I were you." He paced between the windows and the door.

"Would you like to sit down?"

"No." Brandon stopped and stared at Audrey's phone. "Let's get Kevin on the phone right now and get this thing worked out."

"Brandon?" Audrey leaned forward and lowered her voice. "Let's not."

"Let's do." Brandon pulled out his cell phone, set it on her desk, and put his face inches from hers. "Now."

"We're giving the money to another artist. End of story. Listen, Brandon, we've been friends a long time. I think we should end this meeting before one of us says something that will damage that relationship."

"Who is the other artist?" Brandon pulled back.

"That's not the point."

"Who is it?"

Audrey sighed and closed her eyes.

"What? Is it some big secret?"

She sat in her chair and pressed her lips together for a long time before opening her eyes. "It's Kevin. And he's okay with it."

The words felt like he'd been hit with a medicine ball in the gut. "Wha . . . what?"

"I'm sorry." Audrey tapped the tips of her fingers together. "After Kevin's concert at Marymoor Park, iTunes went nuts with downloads. We have to ride this horse hard. We're a for-profit business."

Brandon sat stunned. It felt like every ounce of his energy had spilled onto the carpet and melted through it to the floor below. "You're sorry? I don't believe this."

He left Audrey's office in a daze. All he needed was Reece or Marcus or Doug to stab him in the back and life would be complete. By the time he reached his car and slid behind the wheel, Brandon's numbness had morphed into a smoldering rage. As he turned out of the parking garage onto the street he pulled his cell phone out and dialed Kevin.

THIRTY-THREE

"Kevin Kaison."

"Why do you answer like that? You know it's me." Brandon spit out the words.

"You all right?"

"Yeah, I'm great. Life is excellent. Couldn't be better. How 'bout you?"

"I'm picking up the slightest tinge of sarcasm. Want to tell me why?"

"I just called to offer my congratulations."

"For what?"

Brandon gunned the engine of his rental car and passed two cars in front of him. One of them laid on the horn and the other screamed words that would probably scorch his paint if he got too close.

"Getting my marketing funds. Nicely done."

"What?"

"I just finished with an interesting meeting with Audrey and she tells me you're getting my marketing funds for your debut

304

album. When were you going to let me in on this?"

"What? Look —"

"Playing stupid doesn't look good on you, pal. I stood up and boldly told her, 'Kevin won't stand for this. He'll fight it.' And you've known about it all along. Just before leaving town I asked you if there was anything going on at the label concerning me, and you said no. Unbelievable."

"Slow down, Brandon. Yes, I knew they were taking funds from somewhere else, but I had no clue where it was from and no clue whatsoever it was coming from another artist and no idea it was coming from your budgets. All they said was they found some additional marketing funds to promote my first album. Why would I ask where the money came from?"

"They said you were okay with it. With getting the money, which meant you knew it was coming from me."

"Of course I told them I was okay with it. That doesn't mean I knew it came from you!"

"You're my manager and my agent. Don't add traitor to your job description. You're going to talk to Audrey and get it fixed."

"What does that mean?"

"You're going to get my money back.

You're going to tell them you can't take it."

"Hang on, Brandon. We need to talk about this."

"You want a career in this industry? You need me, so you're going to stop talking and start acting."

"Really? You still think I need you? Are you blind? I'm in the middle of negotiating a multi-album deal that will make me very comfortable, and I'm getting invitations from venues and promoters all over the country. Need you? You want to know the truth? It's the fall of your career and winter is coming on fast."

"A year ago you were scared to play one song for me. We would not be having this conversation if not for me."

"Wow, praise Brandon. All glory to Brandon. God had nothing to do with it, huh?"

"Shut up, Kaison."

"I appreciate what you did, I really do, but don't make me the arsonist for a fire I didn't set."

Brandon pulled onto the freeway and revved his car up to seventy-five. "Get this thing fixed, Kevin, or you're gone."

Kevin's voice slowed and seemed to drop an octave. "Gone? What do you mean, 'gone'? I was leaving anyway."

Brandon wiped the perspiration from his

forehead. "I just moved up the timetable. You're done as of now. You're finished, Kaison. So is our friendship."

He ended the call and tossed his cell phone to the floor of the passenger seat. After a few minutes he cooled and glanced at the phone. He'd call Kevin back right now. He'd lost it. Did he think Kevin was lying? No. Which meant he didn't know about the marketing funds.

Brandon glanced at his phone again. Now? No. Wait a few days. Give them both time to cool down. Weird. One of his best friends and he'd shredded the guy without hesitation. He gripped his steering wheel harder. But Kevin had shredded right back and his words seeped into the gash Windfire had made in his soul. Maybe a few days would turn into never.

What did Reece always say? "They drop the bombs where the enemy is the strongest." But Brandon didn't feel strong. It felt like his career was coming apart. And that a nuclear warhead had just detonated inside his soul.

THIRTY-FOUR

Tristan Barrow was charming when Reece joined him for their late breakfast on Friday. It didn't surprise Reece. His demeanor on the phone had been strangely engaging and Reece didn't expect his in-person persona to be any different.

The smell of one of the Maltby Café's giant cinnamon rolls filled Reece's nostrils as a waitress carried it by their table. Even someone without an acute sense of smell would know that aroma.

They'd talked for half an hour but Reece felt only inches closer to knowing the identity and nature of the man and what he was after. The words from Tristan about the work of the kingdom were right, his insights into what Reece and the Warriors were doing were penetrating and even challenging, but something didn't ring true about the man.

"Might I ask about the favor I spoke of on

the phone?" Tristan said.

"Sure," Reece answered as he continued to work on his California eggs Benedict.

"Jotham, Orson, and I want to come to one of your training sessions at Well Spring."

Not the favor Reece had expected Tristan to ask for. Of course this didn't seem the type of man who was easily figured out. "And why is it that you'd like to come to Well Spring?"

"God told us to go." He said it as if it were the most obvious thing in the universe.

"I see." The scrape of forks and knives on plates and conversations from all over the restaurant filled Reece's ears. Not knowing who was listening made it more difficult to speak freely, but he hadn't wanted to meet Barrow without others around. "We would want to know more about you before accepting any of you as students."

"My fault." Tristan's fork clanked against his plate, and from the pronunciation of his words, Reece could tell the man was chewing. "I didn't communicate well our desire. We don't want to come as students. We want to come as support. To pray for protection for you. To counsel the trainees if needed. To fight for the success of the week in prayer as you do it through your teaching."

"I just met you and you think I would let

you three come and be part of my team?"

"Yes."

"Your thinking was incorrect."

A chill seemed to sweep across Reece's hands as if a miniature air conditioner had been set on the table and turned on high. "Even if I did agree, why would you offer your services?"

"As I already said, God told us to."

"You did mention that."

"You're skeptical."

Was the man serious? Of course he was skeptical. The word Dana, Brandon, and Marcus had agreed on when describing Tristan, Jotham, and Orson was *enigmatic.* And so far, Reece agreed. Based on their conversation so far it was clear Tristan was well versed in all things spiritual. And something about the man was magnetic. But that didn't mean he was safe and it didn't mean he was of God.

"God has told many people many things throughout the ages and much of the fruit that came out of those ventures proved conclusively God wasn't the one who had spoken."

Tristan laughed. "I understand and most assuredly agree with you. I pledge to you, that is not the case this time. The Spirit is behind this request."

"How do I know you're not the Wolf?"

Reece heard Tristan take another bite, then a long drink before his glass or cup thunked to the table.

"You don't. That is a question you must take to the Spirit, because no matter what I answer, you will likely doubt my words."

The confidence in Tristan's voice made Reece want to invite him to Well Spring right then. But that's what worried him. The enemy was coming at them in all forms, and as an angel of light was always high on his tactical-maneuvers list. Everything the man had said about faith and freedom and warring for the souls of others was perfect, but that was far from enough. If only he could see the man's face, study his countenance, see what light or darkness danced behind his eyes.

They ended their breakfast and agreed to speak again, but Reece wasn't convinced he hadn't just told Tristan a lie. If they spoke again it would be Tristan initiating the conversation and even then Reece wasn't sure he would agree to be on the other end of the line.

As they parted, Tristan's voice rang out with a clarity Reece hadn't heard before. "I know you're going after the Wolf, which is a good thing. But remember, it's highly likely the Wolf is coming after you in return."

THIRTY-FIVE

On Friday afternoon at twelve forty-five, Brandon walked into the den of the Wolf. He pushed open the doors of Carson Tanner's offices and studio hoping his spiritual eyes and ears were wide open. His row with Kevin certainly wasn't the best warm-up, but he wasn't going to let that distract him. He'd worked through the emotions of his meeting with Windfire and his talk with Kevin. At least he told himself he had. He needed to be ready for this interview.

Could he live without doing albums anymore and huge concerts? Yes. He didn't need the money. And he could go back to indie recording and still do concerts. Not being able to sing would end him, but all he needed was his voice and his guitar. And those things would always be there.

"Excuse me." A woman who looked to be in her mid- to late thirties walked toward him. "I believe you're Brandon Scott." She

313

extended her hand. "I'm Sooz Latora, the executive producer of Carson's show. Great to meet you. Thanks so much for coming."

"Good to meet you, and it's my pleasure."

"Right this way."

Sooz motioned him to follow her and they walked down a long hallway. Reece and Doug had said to play it cool, and that's exactly what Brandon planned on doing. No controversy, no uncomfortable conversations. Just the chance to get a feel for the spirit of the place, get to know Carson Tanner, start getting an idea of the kind of game he played, and see if Brandon could find out who the players behind the players were. See where the spirit of religion lurked.

A door at the end of the hallway flew open and Carson popped out of it. He smiled and half walked, half jogged down the hallway till he reached Brandon.

"Sorry to keep you waiting." The host's booming voice filled the hallway and made Brandon think of a movie trailer he'd seen last week. Dana was right. The guy was fit and good looking.

"You didn't keep me waiting at all." Brandon offered his hand.

"Shoot, it would have made me look important." Carson shook his head, then Brandon's hand and laughed at his own joke. "Stupid, sorry. I'm just a little nervous. Big fan of yours and all that. I know I have almost fifteen million listeners these days and the books and the speaking tours, and I'm supposed to be some sort of big deal, but it doesn't feel like that. It still feels like I'm in my basement trying to create a radio show a few people might listen to someday."

"Congratulations on all the success you've had. I wish I could say I've listened to your show but —"

"No worries, there's only so much time, right?"

Carson led him to the studio where another of the host's producers set him up with headphones and positioned him to the left of one of two microphones directly across from Carson's board. The host settled into his chair and bounced up and down a few times before grinning at Brandon. "We're on the air in about forty-five seconds, so since we have all this time on our hands, do you mind signing this?"

Carson handed Brandon a black Sharpie and his latest CD. Brandon scrawled his signature across the case and handed it back. This guy was a fan. Which meant the interview should be cake, leaving him enough bandwidth to focus on the spiritual atmosphere of the place. Maybe the guy was the Wolf but so far he had poodle written all over him. If the wrong kind of spirits were camping out in the place, they were lying so low they were asleep.

After the show's prerecorded intro, Carson pointed at him and grinned. "Very special show today, folks! You've been waiting for it, so have we. He's here, five feet from me ready to talk about the truth — it's the man, the legend, the machine — multiplatinum recording artist Brandon Scott." Carson leaned back and clapped. "We're going to be talking about his music, his ministry, and of course anything you want to talk about.

"No question is off limits, so get on the phone and we'll get to you soon. But first I get to toss out some of my own questions to this ultrapopular, ultratalented musician. Great to have you here, Brandon." Carson winked and pointed at Brandon's mic.

"Great to be here."

"All right, we never waste time on my show so let's dive in. Talk to us about your most recent CD. The one that came out, what, six months back?"

"That's right."

"My friends say it's your strongest album to date. That the songs are fresh again, full of life. It feels like the Brandon Scott from the old days. I agree. Do you? And if your answer is yes, what's changed?"

"Yeah, I agree. I never thought I'd like an album more than my first one, but this has become my favorite."

"What happened with this one?"

"I've been singing about freedom for years, but for a while there that idea was more in my head than in my heart. Now it's more in my heart than my head. I've been changed. I feel like I've had a rebirth and I want others to have happen to them what's happened to me."

Carson adjusted his headphones and narrowed his eyes. "And this change came from . . . ?"

Brandon hesitated. How much should he say? How little? What Reece, Dana, Marcus, and he were doing wasn't a hard-and-fast secret, but it wasn't something to shout from the rooftops either. And if this guy was the Wolf . . .

The Spirit had told them to stay under the radar as much as possible. And talking about going into other people's souls was completely off limits. Trying to explain that part of Warriors Riding would be like playing Russian roulette with a chamber full of bullets.

"I've been getting together with a group

317

of friends for the past year. Deep healing has come out of it, and that's spilled over into my music."

"What about hearing from God?" Carson's eyes narrowed further.

"What do you mean?"

"Hearing his voice. Him telling you what to do, where to go, who to talk to, whether there are demons here or there or everywhere?" Carson's gaze had turned cold.

"Yes, I believe the Spirit speaks to us. That talking to God should be like any other conversation. A back-and-forth dialogue. In the gospel of John, Jesus says his sheep will hear —"

"That's a controversial idea among some Christians."

"Among some, sure."

"Have you had any kind of backlash?"

"Backlash? About trying to listen to God?" Brandon frowned. Where was Carson going with this?

"No, over the extrabiblical ideas you've gotten into lately. Your going way beyond the idea that God speaks."

"What are you talking about?" Brandon's body chilled.

"Ah, folks, this is going to be fun. Here's the scoop with a bright red cherry on top: Brandon Scott has been getting into some pretty wild and wacky ideas lately, but I didn't want to get into it without Brandon here to defend himself." Carson laughed as the sound effect of a drumroll blasted through Brandon's headphones. "Okay, heeeerrre we go."

Carson leaned in close to the mic and lowered his voice. "What I've heard, from reliable sources, is you and these new pals you mentioned a minute or two ago have immersed yourselves deeply in occult practices such as astral projection, soul travel, turning invisible, hearing from the dead, and . . . wow!" Carson threw his hands up. "God knows what else."

Brandon's body went from ice to volcano. He stabbed a finger at Carson and spoke into his microphone to protest, but nothing came through his headphones. Carson had muted his mic. Brandon yanked the headphones off his head, tossed them onto the counter in front of him, and stepped toward Carson.

"Folks, I think we've hit a maaaaajor nerve here. You can't see this, but it looks like Brandon Scott is getting ready to rummmmble." The radio host grinned and raised both his fists in a mock boxing posture. "It's true! Brandon Scott is out of his chair and looks like he's ready to plant

319

his fist into my jaw. Or are you just joshing around, Brandon?"

Brandon sat down hard in his chair and glared at Carson. He had to stay calm. Play the game. Get a chance to speak the truth. "Nah, just stretching my back." He squeezed out a laugh.

"That's what I thought." Carson stared at him with a look that was the exact opposite of his words. "Now, I gotta ask, haven't you been at all worried your fans will get wind of you wrapping yourself up in a bunch of New Age garbage?

"Aren't you worried people will discover you now believe you can turn invisible with some sort of real-life Harry Potter invisibility cloak? That you can instantly beam yourself across vast distances in some kind of spiritual *Star Trek* machine?"

Brandon's body went numb and he pulled shallow breaths in through his mouth. *Stay calm. Ride it out.*

"Have you given any thought to the fact that if it gets out that you're not just dabbling, but embracing the occult head-on that you'll lose some fans? Or even worse, shatter the faith of those who have looked up to you for so long?" Carson paused and raised his eyebrows. "And worst of all, you're teaching other believers this is truth, aren't you? You and your buddies have been doing training seminars out in Colorado for hundreds of people, and those people have been doing retreats with your material all over the United States and even other parts of the world. The heresy is spreading like a rampant virus."

"Are you going to let me speak this time, Carson, or are you going to hit the mute button again?"

Carson waved his hand. "Oh, by all means, speak on, dear friend."

"I'd be curious who you've been talking to. Because what you're describing is not what my friends and I are exploring or what we are teaching others."

"So you are exploring something, hmm?"

Brandon gripped the sides of his chair. "Everything we do is based on Scripture —"

"Based on?" Carson leaned in. "Did you say 'based on'? Kinda like some movies are 'based on' a true story when only 10 percent of the story is true?"

"No." Brandon glared at Carson. "What we are doing is setting people free, healing them of wounds, helping them —"

"From the research I've done, I think you're full-out immersed in the kind of things people in the Old Testament were stoned for." Carson widened his eyes and cocked his head. "Right? C'mon now, Brandon. You're exploring dark parts of the forest that should be left for the animals and the Wiccans, not for Bible-believing Christians. What has happened to you?"

"You're badly mistaken." Sweat seeped down Brandon's back and his heart rate had to be over one hundred. From adrenaline. Anger. The poodle had indeed turned into the Wolf.

"Whatever you've heard has been distorted by someone with a vendetta against us. It's pure slander from those on the outside looking in who don't know what they're talking about."

"I don't think so. This ain't hearsay. We've talked to a friend of yours who told us not only are you delving into areas of darkness yourselves, but you're brainwashing others to think the same way. Would you like to hear what they have to say?" Carson didn't wait for a response and pushed a button on his computer screen. A familiar voice Brandon couldn't quite place filled his headphones.

"*I really truly think they're trying to do good things with their training out at Well Spring, but they've become a little misguided. Okay, they're a* lot *misguided. They've pulled a seri-*

ously large muscle in their spiritual physique. I mean, wow, they're telling people they can do stuff so far out there it makes the Wiccans and the New Agers look like they're Quakers."

"Like?" Carson's voice asked.

"Astral projection. Teleporting around the world like Star Trek *gone mad. Going inside other people's minds and doing psychotherapy on them while they're inside, turning invisible in a crowd. Going inside other people's souls. This is where Reece Roth, Brandon Scott, and the others are telling people they need to take their walk with God. They're telling people this is real and right and true. And that scares me because their influence is growing like mad."*

Carson tapped his computer again and stared at Brandon. "As you might have figured out, that was Tamera Miller who most of you out there probably know has a nationally known show on fitness. She's all about keeping the spirit healthy and keeping the body healthy. She has a book coming out this fall. She's well respected.

"In other words, this isn't some derelict off the street with a skewed view of Christianity. And you know her, don't you, Brandon? Of course you do. She went through your training. So how do you explain her comments? Did you teach her and other people the things she's talking about or didn't you?"

Brandon clenched his teeth and ignored the voice inside telling him to stay silent. "Yes, we have gathered select groups of people over the past eleven months and have taught them how to go deeper with God. And yes, Tamera went through our training. But she isn't happy with us because —" Brandon stopped. What could he say that would have any relevance to Carson's audience? That wouldn't come out sounding divisive? Plus it wasn't anyone's business why Tamera wasn't part of their inner circle, and it would be pure gossip to talk about her this way.

"Wooo, love it! So you're saying this is a revenge move on Tamera's part? Wow, the soup gets thicker fast!" Carson grinned. "Doesn't sound like Tamera got set free."

Brandon's body felt like Jell-O. His phone vibrated with a text message and he struggled to lift his phone. It was from Dana. GET OFF THE AIR. THERE'S NO SALVAGING THIS. CARSON HOLDS ALL THE CARDS AND HE'S NOT PLAYING FAIR AND WON'T START ANYTIME SOON. AND SOMETHING DEMONIC IS FEEDING HIM HIS LINES.

Dana was probably right. It was unlikely Brandon could say anything to stop the tsunami that had just crashed on him. But he would try.

"We'll get to more of your thoughts in a few minutes, Brandon, but first let's take a few calls."

Carson snapped a finger toward the window in front of him behind which sat Sooz. He glanced at his computer and winked at Brandon. "Welcome to the show, Lisa. You have a question for Brandon Scott?"

"More of a statement than a question but —"

"Fire hard."

"Brandon, I've listened to your music since the beginning and have all of your albums, and I don't understand how you could have slipped away from Jesus into the occult. What happened to you? What went wrong? Do you realize how many people you might take to hell with you?"

The woman's voice echoed in Brandon's head as he grasped for words that would stop this nightmare.

"What we're doing at Well Spring isn't occultic. It's being led by the Spirit of —"

"Wait, wait, wait, Brandon." Carson waved his hands. "I'm sorry, you know I love you, but I can't let that statement slide by. You're talking about sending your spirit into other people's souls? You're talking about walking

325

through walls? You're talking about beaming around the universe like Scotty? Are you trying to tell me that's from the Spirit of God?"

"I get it. I understand why you're skeptical. I was too until —"

"Until your brain got washed on the full load cycle?"

"If you look in your Bible, you'll find verses that support what we're —"

"Sure. Of course. Just like I can show you verses that teach you to kill babies, but I'm not thinking that's going to be happenin' in the church anytime soon. Or hey! Wait! Do you guys teach that too?"

"I know why you're coming after us, Carson, and you won't win."

"Just looking for the truth, baby, and keeping the sheep from being devoured by men like you."

Brandon started to respond but Carson had cut off his mic again. Brandon's phone vibrated for a second time and he glanced down. Another text message from Dana. Do YOU BELIEVE ME NOW? GET OUT!

He read the message a second time, then blinked as if coming out of a trance. As he pulled his headphones off his head a second time, he stared at Carson and again struggled not to leap across the five feet

326

between them and strangle the man. Brandon stood and turned toward the studio door as Carson's deep bass voice seemed to vibrate through the room.

"Sorry, folks. Brandon Scott has tucked his tail firmly between his legs and appears to be heading for the hills. I'll be back after our sponsors talk about a few offers you'll probably like, and then I'll take a few calls on why you think Brandon and his band of merry men have strayed so far from the truth. And whether this is the beginning of the end of Brandon Scott's singing career. And finally, we'll talk about what you can do to shut down these Warriors Riding retreats that are popping up all over the country. It's about the truth, baby!"

Carson turned off his mic and slid off his headphones. "Thanks for coming on the show. That was a rough one, I know."

"The enemy has his claws deeply embedded in your life."

"Nah, just love a good show."

"You set me up. You have to know Tamera is a loose cannon. Why?"

"I'm only trying to get to the truth."

"What we're doing at Well Spring is the truth."

"The place you spread your lies. But not anymore. We just took a major step toward shutting off the lights."

"You don't know what you're talking about. You don't know the situation."

"I know a topic that needs to be discussed when I see it. You're one of the most famous musicians singing Christian music in the world today. You could lead a lot of people astray."

Brandon thought of five different responses and rejected them all. His wrestle was not against flesh and blood. He pulled open the door of Carson's studio and strode for the station lobby, his head down, muttering ideas of what to do next, his mind still swimming in an ocean of disbelief at what had just happened.

The sound of voices brought him out of his daze. A crowd of at least ten men and women milled about the lobby chatting with subdued voices as if they worried a stray microphone might pick up their scattered conversations.

"There he is!" A lady in a dark blue blouse and black slacks jabbed her finger in his direction. Great. Apparently the interview wasn't over. Brandon spun back the way he'd come and looked for an exit sign, but all he found was Carson standing in the middle of the hallway with a hand placed on the walls to his right and left, a wry grin on his face.

Brandon turned and strode toward the lobby. He had to be careful. If he pushed through the crowd, they'd say he fled the scene. But if he made any comments, they could easily be twisted into a negative and stories would pop up online and in magazines shredding the ministry. And shredding him. Carson was right. What would this do to his career? Audrey wasn't going to be giving him *any* marketing funds after this. And another contract? Uh, no. He had to turn this thing around now.

He stopped and put his hands up to quiet the crowd, but as he did the Spirit spoke.

Let it go.

Did he hear that right?

Let it go, Brandon.

"I'm sorry. I don't have time to stop and chat at the moment, but let me assure you we are not what Carson implied we are. All I can say is seek the truth. Seek Jesus."

"Nice cop-out, Brandon," said a journalist with a smirk on his face. "If you think you can defend Carson's accusations, then tell us here and now."

Let it go.

Brandon gritted his teeth to keep from responding. There was no question the Spirit had spoken. The tough part was obeying. He blinked twice and turned to the journalist.

"Sorry, guys, not this time." He pushed through the throng and stepped through the lobby doors. A few reporters followed, but he took the stairs and quickly distanced himself from the questions they shouted as he descended.

The Wolf, one. Warriors, zero. And Brandon knew this was only a skirmish compared to what was coming.

THIRTY-SIX

The next night Reece gathered the other Warriors at his home and spent the first half hour debriefing on Brandon's encounter with Carson. The Song had not only taken that shot, but the one with his record label as well. But if it gnawed at him, it didn't show in his voice or the things he said.

"No, I don't need to talk about my pal Carson anymore." Brandon's footsteps echoed back and forth over Reece's hardwood floors. "We've been over it. I had a lot of time to think about it on the plane ride home. I was hammered, yes. But is that a shock? This Tristan character said . . . what'd he say at your breakfast, Reece? That we were going after the Wolf, but the Wolf was also coming after us?" The pacing stopped. "I certainly discovered that to be true. Which makes me more than ever want to know more about this Mr. Barrow, stalker, prophet . . . friend, enemy, whatever

331

he is. I think it's about time we find out."

"I agree," Reece said. "Let's review each of your impressions about Tristan and his friends."

Brandon paced again. "I've never gotten anything. Good or evil. They're spiritual Switzerland."

"Marcus, isn't that what you felt with Zennon when he was trying to infiltrate your home using Abbie? That your spiritual eyes were dulled somewhat?"

"Yes and no. Even though my certainty wasn't complete till the end, something about Calen, or Zennon, felt incongruent from the moment I met him. However, I attributed it to not wanting my daughter to date till she's older. With Tristan, Jotham, and Orson, I'm like Brandon. I've felt nothing."

"I agree," Dana said.

"So Tristan and his friends could be more powerful demons, who have a greater ability to shroud our spiritual eyes and ears," Brandon said.

"Yes."

"Just a thought," Dana said. "It seems unlikely Tristan and his friends would be blocking us if they're good, so can we assume they're not our pals the way they claim to be?"

"It's dangerous to assume." Reece opened the face of his watch and felt the hands. It had become a habit and he did it even when he didn't care what time it was. Maybe symbolic of time growing short and their need to act.

"There is one way to find out where they stand that will give us an undisputable answer," Dana said.

Marcus coughed. "And what would that plan entail?"

"We go in."

"Go through the gate and enter their souls?" Marcus asked.

"Yes."

Brandon laughed. "Whoa, Supergirl, I think you've been sucking on a kryptonite milk shake. It's weakened your brain. Aren't you always the one making sure we don't tear the envelope on the rules of engagement?"

Dana's voice rose. "Am I crazy, Reece?"

Reece didn't answer for a few seconds. "No, you're not. I've been mulling over the same question."

"You're thinking about doing it too?" Brandon sighed. "Are you nuts? What about rule number two? Never go into a soul without explicit permission. That's what got you into — tell me you're not serious."

"Yes, I am. But before we make a decision on that I propose we ask them for their permission to go in. It's a way to call their bluff."

"And if they say yes?" Brandon said.

"Then we will have received their permission and we ask the Spirit if we should go in."

"And if they say no?" Dana said.

"Then we'll have learned something and we'll ask Jesus what the next move is."

"When will you ask the question?" Marcus said.

Reece picked up his cell phone. "Right now." He set his phone on speaker and dialed the number.

Tristan answered on the second ring. "Hello, Reece. Are we coming to Well Spring with you?"

"Before we discuss that, want to talk about something else. You've offered to help us. I'd like to offer something to you in return."

"What is that?"

"We'd like to war for you. Help set you free in the deepest way possible."

"What exactly does that look like?" Tristan said.

"I think you already know what that looks like."

"I believe you're right, but for the sake of

clarity can you state it for me now?" Tristan's voice was light, but somehow serious at the same time.

"We want to send our spirits into your soul."

The phone went quiet and all Reece heard was the ticking of his grandfather clock and Tristan's breathing. "And what would you do while you're inside?"

"See if there are any chains to be broken, any wounds to be healed, any freedom to be fought for."

"When done with the Spirit, that can be powerful."

"Indeed. So? May we?"

"Regretfully that cannot happen. While I appreciate the boldness of the request, that is a boundary I'm unable to let you cross."

"Unable or unwilling?" Brandon said.

"I'd like you to trust me."

"You didn't increase the likelihood of that with the choice you just made."

"Our choices are often not our own. Can you think of another way for us to earn your trust?"

"Not at the moment."

"I understand." Tristan cleared his throat. "Then I believe there's nothing further we can accomplish at the moment."

"Are you for us or against us? What do

you want from the Warriors?"

"We are for you. And what do we want other than your trust? Nothing."

"Who are you?"

"As I've said to all of you, ones who would help."

Reece hung up and turned to the group. "Thoughts? Any impressions as I talked to him? Who do you think he is?"

Dana sighed. "Someone trying to distract us. I say we stay away till we're done with the Wolf, then we can worry about who Tristan is."

Reece turned toward Marcus. "Professor? Do you agree?"

"My conclusion is the same as Dana's. We put Tristan on hold for the time being."

"What about you, Song?" Reece asked.

Reece listened to the sound of Brandon shifting in the brown leather chair to the right. "This guy knows way too much to ignore him. I say we have to find out who he and Jotham and Orson are, now. The big war is coming and I want to know if there's someone who might be outflanking us or might be joining their forces with ours. But going into his soul without permission isn't the way to find out."

Reece didn't respond. He'd asked the Spirit who Tristan was three times and all he'd gotten was silence. But it wouldn't hurt to ask again. An answer came seconds later with stark clarity.

Go in and find out.

His soul, Lord? Without permission?

This time it is permitted. You will understand why.

If Reece could see his own face, he would guess it was pale.

"I believe the Spirit is telling us to go in."

"What?" The sound of Brandon smacking the sides of the chair he sat in echoed in the room. "Maybe you are. Not me."

"I will enter with you." The professor's voice sounded scared.

"As will I." Dana's voice was stronger. "I'm sensing we are to go in as well."

"Did I miss something?" Brandon said.

"Apparently so." Reece heard laughter in Dana's voice.

"Fine," Brandon said. "Let's go on this crazy plane ride once again. It's the only way to die."

THIRTY-SEVEN

Reece spun his walking stick around his hand like it was a sword as the four of them walked to the fire pit in his backyard. Dana caught the hint of a smile on his face. Of course there would be. She watched him as the others built a fire. Inside spiritual realms, Reece felt alive. Valuable. It was a place where he could see in all applications of the word.

After flames blazed from the pit, Reece pointed his stick at the fire. "Are you all ready to find out who we're dealing with? Find out what side of the battle their loyalties lie on?"

"I'm in," Brandon answered.

After Marcus and she said the same, Reece extended his arms. "Grab hands."

Dana slipped her damp hand into Reece's on her right and Brandon's on her left. She didn't exactly feel nervous — they'd done enough soul travel over the past year to make her almost comfortable with it — but still, this felt different. All the souls they'd gone into were known entities — good or evil. Tristan and his friends? They didn't know. And the fact the Spirit had stayed silent on which camp the strangers fell into made this excursion full of apprehension.

"You all right, Dana?" Brandon squeezed her hand.

"Fine."

"Then why is your hand sweating?"

"Because we have no idea what we're getting into."

"Do we ever?"

"We usually know what kind of a soul we're going into."

"But not always."

She dropped the conversation and tried to relax.

"You don't have to go, Dana," Reece said.

"I'm ready."

"You're sure?"

"Yes."

Reece bowed his head. "Get a picture of Tristan in your mind. Let your spirit fly, let the Spirit take you. Here we go."

Dana closed her eyes and let the sensation of falling in upon herself sweep through her. Her mind grew smaller and her spirit welled up from inside and filled her consciousness.

The touch of Brandon's and Reece's hands grew lighter and stronger at the same time and the physical world faded and they were soaring. They would land any moment.

But the landing didn't come.

Going through any soul gate had never taken this long. Seconds turned into minutes and then Dana did something she'd never done when going through a gate, maybe because there had never been the time. Maybe because she'd never thought of it before. She opened her eyes.

Where were they? Stars rushed by her as they streaked through the heavens. Planets appeared, then vanished behind them. Galaxies rushed by her. It seemed they traveled far faster than the speed of light.

She squeezed Brandon's hand, then turned to look at him. No one was beside her. Dana spun to locate Reece, but although she still felt his hand, she saw nothing but the stars rushing by her. She looked down expecting to see her body, but nothing was there either. A particle of thought said this should bother her, but it didn't. She blinked again but didn't know if she'd done so in her mind or in reality. She laughed. How could she blink when she had no eyes to blink with?

They slowed and she found herself looking back on a massive collection of brilliant star clusters. Impossible. But she knew what it was. She'd seen something just like it in eastern Washington last summer on a moonless night. The cluster was made up of hundreds of galaxies, all of which contained billions of stars.

"Do you see this?" In her mind she pointed to the vast collection of light in front of them.

Both Brandon and Reece squeezed her hands. Had they heard her? She laughed. Of course they had — Marcus too. She stared at the galaxies, beyond awe, knowing God held the star systems in the palm of his hand. A moment later the stars vanished and solid ground formed under her feet.

"Wow, what a rush!" Brandon laughed and patted his body. "Nice to be back in my body."

Marcus shook his head. "You aren't in your body. You think you are, but you are not, as it is not possible. You're projecting a mental impression that your spirit has graciously translated into a physical image. Quite effectively if you've forgotten the accuracy of my statement."

"I know, I'm just saying it was weird coming through whatever kind of gate that was and not having any sense of form while we did it."

Dana looked into Reece's blue eyes. "Have you — ?"

"No, I've never experienced anything even close to that."

"What was it?"

"A gift." Reece looked at each of them. "I believe we've just seen a glimpse of the heavens, and in our glorified bodies we'll take journeys like that with high frequency."

They stood on top of a tall hill covered by a thick blanket of heather. A soft wind brought a hint of lilacs and there was a touch of moisture in the wind that soothed her face. In the distance to their right were green cliffs thousands of feet high, reminiscent of Hawaii, with waterfalls dividing the mountains in sporadic sections. To their left was an arid plain spotted with massive red-rock bridges and formations that made Sedona look like a one-sixteenth scale model by comparison.

And in front of them, stretched out across a green field dotted with small patches of the most exquisite trees Dana had ever seen, were rows of doors, thousands of rows, millions maybe. Door frames of gold and silver, ones that looked like they were carved from marble, others carved from concrete, others from stone. Thick wood frames and frames made of thin branches no thicker than a cattail. All different. All captivating in their beauty.

As she stared at them, Dana realized they were more than door frames and doors. They were gates. Could these be . . . ? Some gates appeared to be made of glass and some of ice and even some of swirling clouds.

Directly in front of them, a long, winding set of stairs led to a flat area about halfway down the hill that supported a wide platform made of dark wood. A group of figures — too far away to make out if they were men or women — moved across the large dais, stopping in front of each other for a few seconds, then moving on to descend the stairs on either side of the platform to the field of gates below.

The sensation of peace that surrounded them was so strong, Dana felt like she could taste it. A tang of honey and raspberry and smoky cheddar cheese all blended together.

She caught Brandon licking his lips. "You taste it too?"

"It's unreal." He grinned at her, then turned to Reece. "Quite a soul this Tristan Barrow has."

Dana sniffed out a laugh. "I'm thinking

343

we made a wrong turn and probably didn't end up in Tristan's soul."

"Lucky guess," Brandon said.

"I think we need little confirmation we are not in Tristan's soul," Marcus said. "But that does solicit the question of where we have ended our journey."

"I have a very good idea." Reece smiled.

"So do I," Dana said.

"Come then, let's find out if we're right."

THIRTY-EIGHT

Dana watched Reece stride down the smooth steps of the stairway, his shoulders back, a song on his lips. As they grew closer to the platform of people, a few of them raised their heads and smiled. When they reached it, a man who looked to be in his seventies strolled over to them. His hair was thin and almost silver, but his eyes were young. "Enter in, with freedom, with joy."

Reece bowed his head. "It is our honor to be here."

"No, the honor is mine." He motioned toward the other men and women passing them on the dais. "The honor is ours."

"Can you tell us where we are?"

The man's eyes sparkled. "You've always gone right through the gates, haven't you? Never stopped to examine what it was you were passing through."

"I didn't know it was possible," Reece said.

"Now you do." The man smiled and turned to Dana. "You see what they are, yes? That they are not simply door frames and doors?"

"They're the gates into people's souls."

"Yes."

She gazed over the field. "And do you know who all of the gates belong to?"

"Yes, every one. All six billion of them."

"What?" Brandon stepped closer to the man. "Six billion?"

"How can the number be any other than the one just stated?" Marcus pushed up his glasses. "A gate for every soul on earth."

Reece put his hands on his hips and stared at the field. "Can you show us a specific gate? Take us to it?"

"Of course. You are welcome here and anywhere within the fields. And while you are here, you will have safe passage. I can take you to any gate you like."

Brandon tapped the tips of his fingers together. "Not to be skeptical, but with the spacing you have with the gates we can see, means with six billion gates this field has to be — help me, Prof, with a rough guess — five thousand square miles?"

Marcus blinked and looked up and to his right. "My estimation would be closer to eight thousand one hundred and thirty-five square miles."

The man smiled at Marcus, then turned toward Reece, a questioning look in his eyes.

"We were attempting to enter the soul of a man named Tristan Barrow."

"Ah yes, Tristan." The man nodded. "I see."

"You know of him?"

"Of course. And I'm guessing if you met him, you've met his friends Jotham and Orson as well."

"Some of us have, yes." Reece shifted his weight. "Can you take us to Tristan's gate?"

"No, I cannot. There is none here for him. Nor for Jotham nor Orson in case you care to know."

Brandon jammed his finger into his ear and wiggled it. "Uh, the hearing must be going. Thought you said you'd take us to anyone's gate we wanted to get to."

"Tristan and his friends have no gate here in the field."

"They don't have a soul?"

A thin smile formed on the man's face as he glanced at Reece, then back to Brandon. "Not in the same sense you do."

Brandon spun to Reece. "Do you know what he's succeeding at not explaining very well?"

"Yes." Reece smiled. "I think it's obvious

and the answer I've expected for a while now."

"Are you going to share the secret with the rest of us?" Brandon said.

"Why didn't we see it?" Marcus laughed. "The dilemma has been solved."

"I was hoping for an answer that was a bit more expansive," Brandon said. "Come on, Prof, want to enlighten your fellow Warrior?"

Marcus stepped up next to Brandon and rested his hands on the wooden railing of the platform overlooking the field. "Tristan is an angel, as are Jotham and Orson. The Spirit has sent them to fight for us and with us, which I suspect they've already been doing for a lengthy amount of time."

"Oh, wow." Brandon twisted to face Dana. "Did you know this?"

"I figured it out, yes. But not until we reached the platform."

Brandon spun on his heel and nodded with his arms raised to shoulder height. "So I'm the only stupid one here?"

Laughter broke out and even their host joined them.

"Marcus Amber is right. Tristan, Jotham, and Orson have been warring for you and will continue to do so."

For the next few minutes the men discussed the implications of that, but the conversation faded from Dana as she stared at the field. If she kept her eyes fixed on a certain area, her eyes acted like a telescope and gates that at first were far too distant to see grew close as if she stood right in front of them.

"Will you tell me what has captured your attention so completely?" The elderly man stepped next to her.

"I see a gate of magnificent splendor." She pointed.

"The one on the bank of a small stream next to the poppies. Right where the brook curves to the north."

"Yes, how did you know?" Dana smiled.

"This is a different realm than the one you live in."

Of course. Maybe here there were no secrets. Nothing hidden that wouldn't be known.

"Do you like that gate?"

"It's captivating." What looked like diamonds formed a border just inside the frame of the door, and inside that was another border made of rubies and sapphires. As she focused she could see the frame itself was made of a dark wood with splashes of lighter wood that spoke of strength and power.

"Yes, it is."

Its exquisiteness filled Dana, but along with the splendor came pain. A sense of loss rose up in her and soon overwhelmed the beauty.

"I don't understand." She looked into the man's eyes for the answer.

They were full of sorrow and a heaviness so great she was tempted to turn and run away. The sadness seemed to seep into her spirit and the weight of it threatened to crush her.

"Watch the gate, daughter." The man's tone grew somber. He braced himself on the railing as tears fell from his eyes and dropped onto his hands. "Watch the gate, Dana."

She turned and stared at the gate. It seemed to grow in stature — the jewels reflecting the sun like a kaleidoscope of light — but then shrank a moment later to half its former size. At the base of the gate a thick purple vine grew and entwined the gate as it snaked up the sides and over the top. The creeper's thorns grew deep into the wood and in seconds the gate vanished beneath the thickening vine.

Then the vine and gate exploded together and turned the jewels into a million shards of light that fell onto the grass like November rain. The remains of the jewels along with the twisting vines and what remained of the wood grew darker, then black, then seeped into the soil and vanished, leaving a charred gouge of soil where the gate had stood.

The grass grew over the scar in the ground and filled it with its emerald carpet, and if Dana hadn't seen it, she could not have been convinced a gate had ever stood there.

"What happened to the gate? Why did it happen?"

"Every soul that is born must die. We cannot thrust immortality on them and force them to live forever. It is their choice alone."

Reece's voice sounded behind her. "Is this the only reason you brought us here?"

"No." The man pointed at the field. "Look to the very edge. Tell me what you see."

As before, as Dana stared over the field, the distance seemed to shrink, and her eyes could see far beyond what her normal vision could show her. Slowly a low ring of smoke or a cloud came into focus. It was twenty or thirty feet high and pulsed as if pushing to get to the gates. As she watched, a razor-thin column of the smoke shot out from the ring and circled one of the gates for a moment, then retreated. All along the ring, millions of tendrils shot out, crossing thousands of miles across the field in an instant, then merged back into the dark cloud.

"Do you know what that is, Reece Roth?"

The answer struck Dana just before Reece spoke it.

His voice was deep and sounded marinated in anger. "The spiritual manifestation of the Wolf. The spirit of religion."

"Yes." The man turned from the field and waited till all their eyes were on him. "I am praying for the time when you must confront it."

THIRTY-NINE

Marcus arrived home from the university at six on Monday evening and reached for the doorknob as a ray from the sun flashed off of it. He stopped with his hand inches from the door. Had he just switched again? He couldn't tell. Nothing felt different. But it hadn't the other times either, so why would it now?

He grabbed the knob, opened the door, and stepped inside. Marcus knew immediately he'd switched. "Where's Layne's picture?" It popped out of his mouth before he could stop it. Marcus stared at the antique credenza in the entryway.

"Is anyone home?"

"Upstairs!" Kat's voice called out and then another higher voice spoke from the top of the stairs. "Hi, Daddy!"

Impossible. Marcus shuddered as the boy whipped down the stairs — a blur of green shorts and a white top.

He braced himself against the railing and croaked out, "Layne!"

The blur on the stairs slowed and came to a stop halfway down and pointed at his chest. "That's me!"

Words tried to bubble out of Marcus's mouth, but nothing came. His son. Too full of life, too vibrant to deny he was real. His green eyes smiled at Marcus as if Layne hadn't seen him in forever. How true that was. His brown hair fell forward as he peered up at Marcus.

"Your face looks funny, Daddy."

"I imagine it does," Marcus sputtered out.

His knees weakened but he refused to go down. He'd clearly slipped into the alternate reality again. Layne held out his arms and Marcus didn't hesitate. He scooped up the young child and held him tight, his head buried in Marcus's chest, his lips raining kisses on his son's head.

He squirmed. "You're going to make my stuffing come out, Daddy."

He loosened his grip, tears pouring down his cheeks. "Sorry, I just haven't seen you in so long."

"I know. Between morning and now is a long time." Layne gave a goofy smile with his head tilted to the side.

Alive. The word kept ricocheting through

his brain. Layne was alive. Marcus didn't care if this was an alternate reality. Here his son was breathing, laughing, living, and Marcus wanted to stay forever. How old was his son here? Four? Five? Would he die in this reality three years from now as he had in the real world?

He tried to swallow his emotions. "Today made it seem like a long time since I've seen you."

"Your eyes are leaking."

Marcus laughed through his tears. How could he have forgotten? In preschool a boy had made fun of Layne when he cried, so he and Marcus had come up with this terminology to describe it.

"Yes, they are." He squeezed Layne again. "And you're the one causing the leaks."

Marcus sat in his den at eleven o'clock that night trying to figure out what to do. The previous switches hadn't lasted anywhere near this long. This one was going on five hours. He leafed through a stack of books on quantum mechanics trying to find a reason why these switches were happening, but he knew he wouldn't find an answer. He'd written a book giving those answers and they were all wrong.

The only light came from the lamp on his

desk. Its forty-watt bulb cast a warm gold glow on his scrambled mass of notes and on a glass of Coke the melted ice had diluted into thin, brown sugar water. But it wasn't his desk, wasn't his Coke. Marcus rubbed his hair and closed his eyes.

A rap on the door frame startled him, and he knocked a stack of books to the floor as he sat up straight. They sounded like thunder as they smacked into the hardwood floor of the den. Hardwood? The floor in his den was carpeted. Just another reminder he wasn't in Kansas at the moment.

He looked up to find Kat standing in the doorway.

"Are you okay?"

"Yes."

She eased into the room, her arms folded and her eyes narrowed. "Really?"

"I'm fine."

She strolled by his desk and slid onto the couch under the windows. "What happened today when you came home? Layne told me you acted funny. And then you almost wouldn't let me put him to bed tonight. And squeezed him like it was the last time you would ever see him."

"Nothing happened."

She glanced at her watch. "It's late and I don't want to drag the truth out of you. So if you'd just like me to leave, I can do that. But if you want to talk, I'm here, okay?" She scooted forward on the couch as if to stand.

"If I described what I'm thinking about, you'd call the gentlemen with the white coats." Marcus clasped his hands behind his head and stared at the notes on his desk.

"Try me."

"Right now I'm enamored to a much greater degree with this reality than the true one."

"This reality?" She looked around the room and laughed, the laugh that captured him decades ago. "It's the only one I know of. Do you know of others?"

"Yes."

"Is this something you're delving into in class, or is it an extracurricular activity?"

"A smattering of both."

"How long are you planning to continue this somewhat boring line of conversation?"

"In other words, why don't I just come right out and tell you what is going on."

Kat nodded.

"You aren't real."

"I'm not?"

"No."

Kat squeezed her upper arm, her tan fingers a stark contrast to her white blouse.

"It feels so lifelike."

"You're part of an alternate reality."

"What, like that movie *Family Man,* something like that?" She leaned back and put her arm along the top of the couch. "How wonderful."

"I'm dead serious."

"I see. Do we live in the same house in the other reality? Do I work at a bakery? Are you a physics professor?"

"Yes to all of the above."

"And how long have I been a projection of your imagination?"

"Not my imagination. To me it's as real as the other side."

"So Layne is a figment of your imagination as well?"

"It's why I reacted the way I did this afternoon." He gazed into her eyes. "In my true reality, Layne isn't alive."

For the first time since she'd come in, Kat grew serious. "That's not funny."

"I'm not laughing."

"What do you mean he isn't alive? That would devastate you."

"Yes." He turned and slumped back in his chair.

"I don't know why you're talking like this."

"You're right. I apologize." Marcus lurched forward. "Let's drop it."

"You've gone this far."

He swallowed and closed his eyes. "Could you forgive me?"

"For what?"

"If I was the cause of Layne's death. Could you stay with me if I'd done that?"

"But you didn't do that. Layne is alive, sleeping in his bed right now."

"But if I had."

"But you didn't —"

"Please, Kat. How would you respond?"

"Tell me what you think you did in this dream world of yours."

"It isn't a —"

"What happened?"

The memory rushed in on Marcus like a flash flood.

"Dad, look at this!"

Layne pumped his pedals and his bike shot toward a jump in a field at Matthews Beach Park. He and three older boys had set up a ramp and had been jumping off it for an hour. Layne's bike smacked into the ramp and launched his son three feet into the air. At eight years old it must have seemed like thirty feet. Marcus glanced down at the paper he was presenting at the university that coming week, then back at Layne as joy broke out on his face. He circled around and sped back toward Marcus.

"Did you see that? Did you see it!" Layne slammed on his pedals and his bike skidded to a stop right in front of Marcus. "I was sooooo high!"

"It was excellent. I'm flummoxed that you didn't scrape your head on the clouds." Marcus grinned and turned back to his paper. "Nicely done."

"Do you want to watch me do it again?"

"I would love to, Layne, but I'm right in the middle of finishing up a project here, okay?"

Layne's gaze fell to the ground. "Sure, I guess."

"But next weekend we can come back, and then I'll even bring my camera and get some photos of you flying through the air. I promise. No, wait. I pinkie promise. How does that sound?"

"It sounds good." Layne looked up, a grin on his face. "But do you have your camera now? Could you take just one shot?"

"Layne." Marcus tapped his papers with his mechanical pencil. "I wish I could. I do. Unfortunately I have to concentrate right now, but next weekend I'll get a bazillion pictures and we'll make one of them into a poster and put it on your bedroom wall, okay?"

"Yeah, okay."

Layne pedaled off but was back two minutes later. Marcus set his pencil down, rubbed his eyes, and sighed.

"Dad?"

"Yes?"

Layne pointed to the three other boys he was jumping with. "Is it okay if I go with them to the store?"

"What store? Where is it?"

"Just up the road . . . it's not very far."

"That would be great."

"Really?"

"Yes. Just promise me you'll be careful."

"Of course I will be! Really, very extra careful."

"All right." Marcus glanced at his watch. "It's 2:33 now. I want you back here by three at the latest. Okay, buddy?"

Layne jumped off his bike and grabbed Marcus around the waist. "I love you, Daddy. You're the bestest in the westest."

Marcus smiled. Layne hadn't said *Daddy* for over a year. That wasn't a bad thing. It was good, an indication his son was growing up. But hearing Layne say *Daddy* reminded him there was a little boy still inside who would be a little boy for many years to come.

Three o'clock came and went without a whisper. At three fifteen, Marcus couldn't wait any longer. He pulled his keys from his pocket and strode for his car, trying to ignore the sick feeling growing like thistles in his stomach. As he inserted his key into his car door, sirens sliced through the air of the summer day and the temperature seemed to drop thirty degrees.

Marcus looked up at Kat through eyes blurred with tears. "I never got a photo of him doing the jump."

"I don't understand what you think you did, Marcus." Kat took his hands in hers. "What could you have done? You let him ride his bike with his friends. How could you have known what would happen?"

"I did know. I did." Marcus wiped his eyes. "Something inside me said, 'Don't let him go.' It was as clear as anything I've ever heard. But I let him go anyway." Marcus rubbed the corners of his eyes with his thumb and forefinger for a long time. "I was so wrapped up in that idiotic paper, I paid no attention to the voice inside."

The pace of Marcus's breathing increased and he repeated the last words Layne ever said to him. " 'You're the bestest in the westest.' "Their secret saying for each other.

Marcus went silent, and after a few minutes Kat slid closer and put her arms around his shoulders. "He got hit by a car."

Marcus nodded, his vision blurred by tears. Long minutes later he asked Kat again, "So could you? Forgive me?"

"I don't know." She turned and picked at her fingernails. "When a child is lost, marriages have a hard time surviving it. If I knew you could have prevented it . . . I would try, but I don't think —" Kat sat up straight and stared at him, fire in her eyes. "But it doesn't matter. You didn't do it, Marcus!

"If Layne was on a bike or a boat or a swing or a ski slope or . . . or anything, if you heard that voice inside, you wouldn't let him go. Neither of us would. You'd keep him from going and I'd never ever have to face what you say happened and you wouldn't either."

With that Kat pushed herself off the sofa and shuffled out of his den. In this Kat's world, he would never do what he'd done to Layne. It's the only perspective she could see — the only possible outcome. But in his true reality the angle of vision was much different.

Marcus sat in the silence for ten minutes,

maybe fifteen, before slowly rising and easing into Layne's room. He lay next to his sleeping son, kissed his head, and pulled Layne to his chest. The last thought before sleep took Marcus was how his boy's hair smelled exactly how a five-year-old's should and that he would do almost anything not to lose it.

FORTY

"I need answers." Marcus paced in front of Simon at Magnuson Park, his untucked shirt ruffled by the breeze coming off Lake Washington. "Why is this happening to me?"

"In case I haven't been clear enough, let me do so now." The magician's gray-streaked hair was pulled back in a ponytail and his usual black coat was replaced by a gray sweatshirt. "There are alternate realities within alternate realities. Layers upon layers upon layers. The deeper you go, the less you know."

"Know what?"

"What is real."

"But where I've been can't be real."

"They can't?" Simon reached in his pocket and brought out his silver coin. He twirled it around his fingers as he stared at Marcus. "Not true. Those alternate realities cause chemical reactions in the brain where we store memories. And once that memory is planted, how can we know if it's real or not? Too many memories of too many realities means sifting through too many scenarios, and it's almost impossible to keep them all straight."

"They're dreams, visions."

"You know they aren't."

Simon was right. Marcus did know. Holding Layne the other day wasn't a dream or his imagination. And it had stirred up a pain so deep it would bury him if he couldn't contain it again. "It's a malevolent act to shove me into other worlds without my permission."

Simon lurched backward as if he'd been struck. "Faugh! I'm not the one doing the shoving."

"Who is?"

"You'll figure that out. You need to."

"Is it God or Satan or something else? And what is your role in it? Are you my enemy?"

Simon spread his arms to his sides and smiled. "I am your friend."

"As if I can trust your answer to be the truth."

"I told you the switching would continue till you made the choice."

"What choice?"

"I bet he's going to give you lots of options to choose from." Simon pulled a deck of cards out of his pocket. "He did me. And I chose them all. I answered the call, of the siren's song that drew me along, into years of living, devoid of giving, my heart to the One who shines like the sun."

"Who?"

"Who what?" Simon blinked like he'd just woken.

"Who is going to give me myriad options from which to choose?"

Simon squinted and tilted his head back and to the side as if he were a gunman in the Old West about to suggest a duel at fifty paces. "Do you like card tricks?" Simon whipped his hand up. "Wait! Stop! Don't answer that. I'm going to show you a trick whether you like 'em or not, so your answer doesn't matter."

He slid eight or nine cards out of the deck case and spread them out for Marcus on the picnic table Simon sat at. Marcus stopped pacing and stepped up to the table. All of the cards were different.

"Here's what we're going to do, Professor. I want you to pick a card." He brought the pack together and one at a time pulled a card from the top and put it on the bottom. "Not with your hand, just tell me when the card you want comes to the top of the stack." Simon tapped his head. "But before you choose, let me warn you: I'm going to try to influence your choice. Yes, ladies and professors, there is one card in particular I want you to choose and I'm going to use everything in my power to make you choose that card. Ready?"

Marcus nodded. What exactly were Simon's powers? He still didn't know if the magician was human or demonic or angelic. He was fairly confident he could strike the latter categorization from his list, but the other two were fifty-fifty in his mind.

Simon slowly took each card from the top and placed it on the bottom. When the three of clubs came to the top the second time, Marcus said, "Stop."

"This one? The three?" Simon flicked the edge of the card with his thumb twice, then pulled out the card that had appeared just before the three: the eight of diamonds. "You're sure you don't want the eight? The eight is a wonderful card."

"Yes."

"Positive? Not a doubt in your mind?"

It was just a magic trick. So why was there a part of him that wanted to choose the eight? Was Simon pushing him to choose the eight because he wanted him to or because he'd wanted him to choose the three and by pressing the eight it would cause him to stick with the three? Was it that simple for Simon to manipulate his thinking?

"Sure, you're right. The eight is a great card. Let's go with that one."

Simon brought the eight from the bottom of the stack and placed it on top of the three, then brought out the new bottom card — the ace of hearts — and put it on top of the pack. "Are you positive you don't want the ace?"

"Yes."

"The eight, not the ace?"

"The eight."

"At the risk of insult, I'll ask once more. You want the eight, not the ace."

Marcus frowned and nodded.

Simon placed the eight faceup on the table, then showed him the backs of all the remaining cards in his hands. Each of them was red.

"It's fascinating to me that you chose the eight. But then again, it happens every time." Simon reached for the card and flipped it over. It had a blue back. "The only card among all of these with a blue back. Exactly the card I wanted you to choose."

Marcus had felt nothing in his mind. No manipulation from Simon. The choice was free. Yet there, staring him in the face, was the only card among the stack that didn't have a red back. His face grew hot.

Simon leaned in and whispered, "You play his game, the only choices are his. No choice is free. No choice with him comes without a significant price tag. I know. I paid. I'm still paying."

"What if I'd chosen the ace?"

"I'm glad you asked, Marcus, because I really do like you and I really am trying to help."

Simon placed the ace faceup on the table, then showed the backs of the other cards. All of them were now blue.

"How did you accomplish that?" Marcus stared at the cards. "That's impossible."

"It's a card trick, Marcus. A simple one. One you can find in twenty magic books in hundreds of libraries across America. What's important is the lesson it teaches: He doesn't play fair and every choice is his choice no matter how much it seems like it's yours. Every choice leads to death, okay?" He clapped his hands. "Can I see your phone for a moment?"

Marcus handed his cell phone to Simon who opened a calendar.

"Really! It's already Tuesday. Time certainly dies, doesn't it? I have to go."

"You mean time flies."

"No, it dies. And the chance for choice in that moment dies right along with the passing of the seconds. As I've said before, Marcus, your time for choice is coming. I pray you choose well and you do not allow the moment to die."

FORTY-ONE

Reece's watch beeped, telling him he'd been on the climbing machine for an hour. One more to go. He shifted the day pack full of weights and fumbled for the keypad that would increase the speed of the stairs under his feet. *More intensity. Make the lungs burn.* As if taxing his body to its maximum could distract him from the fact that this coming summer — for the first time in twenty-seven years — he wouldn't be climbing one of the Rockies' fifty-two tallest peaks. He'd tried hiking with a seeing partner, but within twenty minutes he knew it wouldn't work. The man had tried.

"Sorry, Reece! I didn't see that branch."

"You've done this before, right?"

"Not for this kind of hike."

Reece rose from the ground and rubbed his right knee where he'd taken the brunt of his fall and his fingers came away wet. Blood. "How bad is the cut?"

"Oh, wow, that doesn't look good. Let me see."

For the next five minutes the man had cleaned and bandaged the cut on Reece's knee. Then for the next half hour the man called out obstacles as they trudged along.

"Large rock middle of the path, three feet ahead."

"Tree branch at six feet high about four yards in front of you."

It would likely take years of bloody knees and hands to understand what "four yards ahead" really meant. And when they reached a level, smooth part of the climb, Reece felt like a Ferrari following a Yugo. This guy was supposed to be in great shape? That wasn't fair. Reece didn't know many who could keep up with him — which made the dream of finding someone to hike with even more impossible.

Reece turned up the volume on his cell phone and tried to lose himself in the classic rock pulsing through his earbuds, but it was useless. He'd never listened to music in the mountains, why do it here? Because here there was nothing to see and too much to think about. It should be the perfect time to seek the Spirit and hear his counsel.

But it didn't work that way. Other people said exercise was their thinking time, being with and hearing from God time, the time answers to life's conundrums would show up in their minds and hearts. It had never been that way for Reece.

Part of the joy of hiking was pushing his body further than it thought it could go. But a tremendous amount of scaling mountain peaks was what he saw. That should have been obvious. Taking thousands of photos every minute with his eyes and reveling in the artistry of the Spirit. But Reece didn't realize the extent of that part till the enemy had destroyed his eyes and shredded the ability to immerse himself in his greatest passion.

It didn't matter. This wasn't about him. Wasn't about him. Wasn't about *him.*

A rap on the door of his recently constructed workout room spiked Reece's pulse and his Polar heart monitor beeped. Over the top range of where his heart rate should be. No matter how many times Doug or anyone else knocked on a door, Reece didn't think he'd get used to it.

"Come in." Reece pulled his earbuds out.

The door gave a slight creak as it opened and a moment later the sound of Doug's shoes padded across the workout room and stopped three feet to his right.

"How are your workouts progressing?"

"Progressing?"

"Yes." Doug sighed. "I've never known you to exercise without a goal in mind — most often which mountain you were going to climb next. I'm curious what object of motivation you have in mind currently."

Reece continued to pump away, his legs like pistons. The climber was now on the maximum resistance and still his breathing and heart rate weren't as high as he'd like them to be.

"My workouts are fine."

"That's not what I asked."

Reece's watch went off a second time. Good. He was done.

"I know." He stepped off, fumbled for the towel hung on the back of the machine, and turned toward the sound of Doug's voice. "My goal is for God to give me my eyes back. Being able to see inside the spiritual realm was a start. The first part. I expected too much, that the second part of the healing would come at the same time. The second part will be in this world. It's coming."

"And what if he doesn't heal you?"

"He will. I believe the prophecy. Don't you?"

Doug didn't answer.

"Fine, next subject. Have you been reading any of the e-mails that have been coming in from the website?"

"You mean the ones where people are threatening to find Well Spring and burn down the ranch if we don't stop the training sessions? Yes. A pristine example of the religious spirit at work. Carson is doing his job."

"He's replayed the interview with Brandon at least twelve times." Reece rubbed the sweat off his forehead.

"I think it will be played many more times before this is over."

"So do we shut him down?"

"How would you propose doing that?"

"I have no idea."

"Nor do I, but I have a sense Jesus is saying a way is coming that will surprise even you."

"I can't wait." Reece threw his towel over his shoulder and felt his way to the door. "I gotta take a shower."

"Did you say you were going to a place tomorrow night where you can see?"

"Yes. It'll be good for them. And good for me."

"Be careful, Reece."

"I'm always careful."

He climbed the stairs and latched onto the belief he would be healed. It would hap-

pen. He would see again. And in the meantime he would go to where his eyes still
worked. The Warriors could use another jolt
of refreshment before they went after the
Wolf, and Reece sensed the time was approaching quickly when Jesus would tell
them to go in and do battle. So tomorrow
night he would take the Warriors into one
of his favorite realms.

FORTY-TWO

"Tell me this isn't one of the most spectacular views you've ever beheld?"

Dana smiled as she looked from Reece to the mountain ranges buried in snow for as far as she could see. If she was guessing she'd say every one of the peaks would dwarf Everest by miles. And breathing up here was like drinking water. Every breath filled her with life and peace. She studied Marcus off to her left and Brandon to her right. From their posture it was apparent the air was doing the same for them.

After what felt like another ten minutes, she turned to Reece. "How long have we been inside this realm?"

"Not nearly long enough," Reece said, a grin on his face.

"I'm serious. Aren't we getting close to the edge of needing to get back out?" Dana jammed her hands into the pockets of her coat. "You know it's time, Reece."

He gazed down on the vast ranges below them, then slowly turned his head ninety degrees, the blue light in his eyes blazing. "You're right. Absolutely right." But Reece didn't move except for his head, which continued to turn back and forth, a brilliant sunset lighting up his face like gold.

"Just a few more minutes. Take this in, Dana. It is a feast for the eyes from the true Artist. You and I can't take a photo of this, but we can remain long enough to burn the image into our memories. I need this. We all do."

Reece motioned toward Marcus who stood forty yards to their left staring at the deepening red and orange clouds. "Look at the professor. I imagine he's doing the same as we are. Whatever is going on with him and these alternate realities, it's drained him. Let's not deprive him of rejuvenation and of obtaining a memory he'll hold forever, much as we are doing. A few more minutes is all I'm asking."

It wasn't right. It seemed right, it should be right, but staying here even a second longer was wrong. The strong, calm voice of the Spirit was shouting at her to leave. And for some reason she couldn't get the image of the hockey team she'd seen while at Well Spring out of her mind.

"No. Not a few more minutes. We have to get out now." She turned to her right. "Brandon! Let's go."

The Song turned and trudged through the pure snow toward her. When he reached them he said, "Yeah, I'm thinking and feeling you're right."

"Professor!" she called out over the snow. "We have to go now."

Marcus nodded and twisted toward them. He broke into a slow jog, but before he'd gone seven paces, a small crack appeared in the snow halfway between them and the snow under her feet shuddered.

"Hurry!"

"I see it." The professor broke into a run, but before he'd taken three more strides it was already too late. The crack grew as wide as a footpath, then to half the size of a country road. Within ten seconds it was the size of a four-lane freeway.

Dana stuttered up as close to the edge as she dared and peered down. The crevasse was too deep to see the bottom. She whipped her head up and stared at Marcus's horrified expression.

"It isn't possible for me to leap across an expanse that wide."

Reece shuffled up next to her on the right, Brandon did the same on her left.

"It's okay," Reece said. "We'll find a bridge or a way over it where the crevasse isn't as wide or where it ends."

Even as Reece spoke the words, Dana knew the attempt would be futile. She glanced at the massive gash in the snow as far as she could see in both directions. The crevasse didn't narrow, and she knew they would walk for miles and never find a way across.

"Ropes." Reece clenched his fists together as if he held a rope in both hands. "We have to create ropes or a bridge to lie across the gap. Or heal the rift and bring the edges back together. This will be a good exercise for us."

"Dana?" Brandon's face had gone almost as white as the snow they stood on, and he looked ill. "I think we might have a bigger problem than the crevasse."

"What's wrong?"

"Think back to Well Spring. When we prayed together in the grove of aspen trees for Reece. That's pinging so hot and heavy in my brain I can't picture anything else."

"Yes, I got it, get to the point."

"You saw a hockey team, right? And had an overwhelming feeling of danger. And I saw white."

"What does that have to do — ?"

"What were the colors? What did the uniforms look like? Can you remember any symbols or markings on the jerseys?"

"Sure." She frowned. "They were red with blue sleeves and they had the initial *A* on the front."

"Oh boy." The remaining color drained from Brandon's face. "We should have figured it out. We should have stuck with it right then, pressed into it till we got the answer."

"Figured what out?"

"The hockey team you saw was the Colorado Avalanche."

"So?"

Brandon didn't answer except to turn and look up the slope to her left.

"No," Dana whispered. "You don't really think —"

"Yeah, I do."

She turned to Reece. "We need to get that bridge now and get Marcus over here so we can leave!"

Marcus stepped to the edge of the crevasse, his toes sticking over the edge. "Forget the bridge. Let's just go. Try to get out."

"Impossible," Dana said. "You know the answer, Professor. We must go together. All four of us have to be physically connected."

"But that one time . . ."

"Are you willing to take that chance this time? I'm not."

Reece cupped his hands over his mouth. "There would be no way for you to control where you end up when you go back through the gate. And no way for us to know where you've gone."

"Haven't you ever run into this type of situation before?" Marcus said. "Where someone is separated from the group but you have to get out?" The crevasse rumbled and widened by another two feet. "You have to have encountered this scenario previously."

"Yes. I have."

"And what happened?"

Reece pressed his lips together till they turned white, started to answer, then stopped. "We have to get you across to us or us across to you. And you and Dana are right, we need that bridge now."

As Reece finished speaking, a dull roar at the top of the mountain filled Dana's ears. She slowly turned her head toward the sound knowing exactly what she would see and wanting to pretend it wasn't happening.

Avalanche. A half mile above them. At least three hundred yards wide and picking up speed. A churning giant wall of snow and ice and granite shot out tendrils of smaller chunks that it consumed seconds later as it fed upon itself and grew larger. How long did they have? Forty-five seconds? A minute at most? Maybe. Maybe less. Unless they could build an instant way across, they would either die together or be separated and Marcus would end up in a place probably not even Reece could predict. What had they been thinking?

Stick together. Pretend you're a scuba diver. Make sure you're within one breath of your partner at all times. Reece had taught them that as rule number three or four — it didn't matter because they'd broken whichever rule it was and right now, unless the miraculous leaped up in front of them, they were going to lose the professor.

Reece had his head down, hands clenched in front of him. A moment later he threw his arms wide and a bundle of wood and rope appeared in his arms. "Yes!" he shouted and stepped up to the edge of the crevasse, half his boot over the side, teetering over the expanse.

"Here!" Reece called to Marcus across the chasm as he shook the rope and wood slats in his hands. The big man somehow had conjured a rope bridge, and he spun twice like a discus thrower, then flung it toward the professor. It streaked out from Reece's hands like a rifle shot and lay against the bright blue sky. It seemed to float in slow motion toward the professor while the river of snow thundering down on them to their left moved faster.

"Come on!" Brandon shouted.

But the bridge wasn't enough. Not even close to close. The edge of the ropes only reached halfway across the chasm where they fluttered down and bounced against the side of the crevasse they stood on.

"Longer, we have to make it longer." Reece staggered up to the edge of the crevasse, his boots sending tiny bunches of snow over the edge, and dragged the bridge up from the depths. "Concentrate with me. Believe! We have to believe."

What was Reece thinking? Even if a bridge appeared long enough to reach the other side it would take anyone but a world-class tightrope walker at least thirty seconds to cross a chasm that wide.

"If *any* of us are going to survive, we have to go now, Reece!" She grabbed Brandon's hand and stretched out her other for Reece. "Now!"

Reece's head heaved up and down like a buoy in an ocean storm and his breaths came in gasps. "We can't leave him! If we go, he goes too, but we'll have no way of knowing where."

"We have no choice!" She grabbed Brandon's hand and reached out for Reece's. "Grab my hand, Reece!"

"What about Marcus?"

The pain in Reece's eyes said he didn't know and never would. He turned to Marcus and shouted, but how could the professor hear over the thunder of the avalanche from that far away? "Stay in prayer, trust no one, we will find you!"

The professor shouted a response that sounded like a question, but Dana couldn't make it out. Reece whipped his head toward her with a questioning look in his eyes. He hadn't heard it either. She shook her head violently and pointed at the wall of snow and ice and granite pounding toward them like a giant white wave. They had seconds.

"Marcus will go at the same time we do?"

"I don't know."

"What! I thought —"

An instant before the moving wall of jagged snow slammed into them, the rush of soul travel buried Dana, and the avalanche and the roar in her ears vanished. Brilliant light and myriad colors and the rush of warm wind and a sensation of spinning filled her senses. They'd made it out.

In seconds they'd be back at the fire pit in Reece's backyard.

But the seconds stretched out like a blade and Dana felt a tearing in her soul and in her spirit. Why was it taking longer to get out? Because Marcus wasn't with them? Because the Spirit was joining the professor to them even though he hadn't been physically connected when they left? *Please, Lord, let it be so.*

Her spirit slid back into her body with a jerk, as if all of her bones had been given a sharp yank in opposite directions. "Ow!" Her eyes fluttered open and she glanced at Reece and Brandon. "Where'd that electric jolt come from?"

Reece sighed but didn't answer. Brandon pointed at Marcus's prone body lying on the couch. "I'm guessing since one of us didn't get out, it made our reentry a little bumpier than normal. Reece?"

Again the big man didn't answer but gave a slight nod of his head.

Dana gave a tiny shake of hers. "So Marcus's body is here, but his spirit is somewhere else? And we don't know where that somewhere else is?"

"That's right." Another deep breath from the Temple and again, silence.

Brandon stood and paced, his gaze flitting

back and forth between her and Reece. He shrugged and his eyes opened wider as if asking why Reece had gone comatose and what they should do about it.

"Are you sure he didn't get out?" She turned to Marcus, rubbed his shoulder, and bent down to his ear. "Professor, we're back." She turned to Reece. "Is there a chance he's here?"

Reece shook his head and his voice was soft. "Only his body."

"How can you be so calm? I told you we needed to get out. Why didn't you listen to me!"

Reece stared at her with his dark, unmoving scarred eyes.

"Didn't you learn anything twenty-five years ago?" The moment the words escaped she regretted them. His delay wasn't about arrogance. It was about being able to see again. Being able to soak in the desire that had been the driving passion for most of his life. The desire that had been ripped from him by the demons and the gift God had not stopped from being stolen. And she had not walked in those shoes.

"I'm so wrong for saying that, Reece. I'm so sorry."

"We'll find Marcus. I promise you we will."

Brandon folded his arms. "You said this happened before. And the outcome wasn't good. I could see it in your eyes when we were inside just now. Tell us."

"A long time ago I went into a soul with a number of others. We were separated and we didn't know about staying physically connected. We came out, but two of our party did not. We weren't able to find their spirits and bring them back out."

Reece slipped his fingers around the sunglasses hanging around his neck and slid them over his eyes. "But this time we won't fail. I promise, we will find the professor. We have to."

"More than just because he's one of the Warriors?"

"Yes." Reece took a long breath. "The Spirit told me Marcus is critical to our success in the coming battle with the Wolf. Without him, we are lost."

FORTY-THREE

Just before the avalanche slammed into the others, they vanished, or had Marcus vanished from them? The air swirled and the sound of crashing waves surrounded him as often transpired when they went in or out of spiritual worlds. For a moment he thought the similarity meant he would return to his body with the others. But when silence came and his eyes fluttered open, he wasn't back at Reece's home.

He stood on the ledge of a cliff, maybe twenty-five feet long and five feet wide. A breeze pushed through his hair and brought the smell of giant sequoia trees. The screech of a red-tailed hawk ripped through the air to his right.

Far below him — a rough estimate said five hundred feet down — three tree-soaked valleys wound away from him for miles till they ended at the base of a mountain range at least five thousand feet high. Strange. Not a hint of snow covered their tops. The feeling of an early fall afternoon was on the wind.

He should be at least apprehensive, but with each breath he seemed to be inhaling peace. He studied the cliff wall above him, then turned and stared over the edge. Getting off would be a challenge. Marcus looked at the sun. He had two, maybe three hours before the sun disappeared behind the peaks to the west and then? It could get cold. A night up on this ledge would not be pleasant.

A voice from above floated down on him. "Ho there!"

Marcus whipped his head up to find a man dressed in red-and-black climbing gear hanging from a rope at least two hundred feet above him. The man waved and smiled. For the next few minutes Marcus watched the man rappel down the mountain till he stood on the ledge and stepped out of his climbing gear.

"I hope I didn't startle you from above."

The man was short, not much over five four, and his brown eyes were intense but kind. Brown hair was parted on the side and a three-day-old beard was thick on his face. Not handsome, but not unattractive either.

"Not at all." Marcus glanced around the

ledge. "Although I can't say I was expecting you."

"You probably had no idea what to expect." The man stepped to the edge of the cliff, sat, and took long, slow breaths.

"True." Marcus joined him.

"And" — he smiled at Marcus — "I imagine you're wondering where you are."

"I would say earth, based on the geology and plant life, but there's too much peace here."

"Aye, rightly you've called that one." The man grinned and wrapped his arms around his legs and gazed out over the valleys. "There's few places I'd rather be than right here."

"Am I inside someone's soul?"

"No, you know that feeling by now, and I think you realize you're in a place entirely different. Where were you before you came here?"

"I was inside a spiritual realm with three friends of mine. We were on the slope of a mountain together, but a crevasse opened up between us and prevented me from leaving with them."

"Why didn't you find a way across?"

"An avalanche was bearing down on all of us. We couldn't wait any longer."

"I see."

Marcus studied the man's face. He'd been answering every question without hesitation and with complete openness. It's not that he trusted the man — he didn't know him — but something about his eyes drew answers out of Marcus like water.

"You must not worry, Professor. I am well versed in soul travel as well as the journeys to other parts of the spiritual realm. And I'm here to help you. Whether you accept that help or not is, of course, up to you."

Marcus nodded but didn't speak. It might be wise to talk less and listen more.

"What are your friends' names?" The man drew the name Marcus in the dirt between them.

"Reece, Dana, and Brandon."

He added the names underneath Marcus's.

"And what were you doing together on the side of the mountain?"

"We were finding refreshment from the battle we've been in for a long time now. We've all grown weary, and the enemy has been relentless lately with his attacks as we try to figure out what the Wolf is and how to destroy it."

So much for his resolve to say less. Maybe he was free with his answers because the man seemed so familiar. "Do we know each other?"

"Yes, of course we do." The man's smile went wide. "We just met."

"No, I mean before now, did we know each other?"

"I don't think so, unless you've been here before or to one of the other realms I frequently travel in. But I would have remembered you if you had, I'm sure of that. And I think you would have remembered me."

"It's just that —" Marcus stopped. Just that what? That part of him wanted to tell this man every secret? That whatever this being was, Marcus was ready to open his soul to the man and take whatever help he could offer without reservation?

"Just what?"

"Even though I just met you, I feel you're one I can trust."

"Ah, thank you, Marcus. I hope so. I would indeed like to help you."

Marcus leaned back on his hands and surveyed the valleys below. A low ridge separated each one. The middle was the widest; the other two were the same width. A town sat in the middle of each valley and the layout looked identical. Something about each of them drew Marcus as if he were destined to visit each of them and had no way to prevent that from happening.

"If this isn't earth and we're not inside someone's soul, we must be in one of the other spiritual realms you spoke of. So where are we?"

The man stood, closed his eyes, and drew in a breath as if he were drinking the air. "This is the place where dreams are seen — all dreams, the good and the bad — and where dreams can come true." He turned to Marcus and his smile seemed to make his face glow. "And where some things best forgotten can be. Forever."

"Are you a man?"

"No, but you already suspected that, didn't you?"

"What are you?"

"One who can help you shed your darkest regrets and restore your greatest dreams."

"And you know what those are?"

"Most certainly. I've watched you for a long time, Marcus."

"I thought you said we'd never met."

"Yes, I did, and we haven't. But that doesn't mean I haven't been your friend for ages."

"Then you know about my son?"

"Yes, of course." His eyes grew somber. "That's what I meant when I said, 'Some things best forgotten can be.' The thing buried so deep and so far the others saw no hint of it when they went inside your soul. The one you'd almost convinced yourself didn't happen. The one God has brought to the surface so it can be dealt with once and for all."

The full memory of that day snaked out of the depths, and this time Marcus couldn't stop it.

Marcus slumped forward and dug his fingers into his forehead, his eyes, his cheeks. "You brought that up out of me just now. Made me face it. So I can get rid of the guilt, the remorse, the condemnation, the regret."

"I assisted, yes. But you wanted to face it. So give yourself a bit of credit."

Marcus spotted three hikers climbing a steep trail half a mile below them, one with an oversized backpack that seemed to slow his progress to a crawl. Just like what he'd seen in that church a year ago. Just like he had in his own backpack: a stone he'd placed there that day long ago. And now it was time to get rid of it.

He stared at the man. "I have to tell Kat, don't I? It's time to come clean and beg for forgiveness."

The man smiled and spoke in a voice so

soft, Marcus strained to hear it. "No, that's what I was trying to tell you. You don't. That's the beauty of this place." The man gazed at the sky and the valleys below them.

"But even so, I must warn you, it won't be easy. After we talk and your eyes are opened, you'll have to make a choice of great difficulty. I will help you with the choice and freely give you all the wisdom I have, but I cannot make the choice for you."

"When do we start?"

"We can start now if you like."

"Then let's go."

FORTY-FOUR

The valley in the middle seemed to grow in size, or Marcus's eyes changed so he saw and heard things moving in it. As his focus zeroed in, Kat and he came into view. It was the early days of their marriage when they lived in a one-bedroom apartment with an ugly, swirling, pea green and dark green carpet, and a man downstairs who loved to play Frank Sinatra records at three in the morning with all the strength his speakers could provide.

Kat had no lines in her face and no sadness in her eyes. It was the time before Abbie and Jayla — days when even Layne was only a someday dream and the horror of losing him hadn't woven its fibers into every place in their hearts.

Marcus lounged on their ugly tan couch and tossed a pillow at Kat. "Have you considered the various options for us this weekend?"

"What are you talking about? The weekend is already fully booked. We're going to a movie tonight with Marty and Cindy, Sunday we're going over to my parents, and tomorrow we're watching Kelly and Cecil get engaged at the top of Mount Si."

Marcus leaned his head back and moaned. "I wish we were just watching. Carrying a table and chairs and champagne to the top of Mount Si and then hiding a ring under a rock so Cecil can 'discover' it and ask Kelly to marry him is not watching. It's working. Hard."

"My heart is breaking for you."

The look he'd seen in the mirror for so many years now was gone, replaced by a lightness on his face that brought back the days before he'd made the mistake that had killed Layne. Those innocent, beautiful, ignorant days when life's biggest struggle was deciding what trail to mountain bike down or what new cheap restaurant they should try in the coming week.

Marcus leaned forward on the cliff toward the valley as if he could step into that world and take into his arms the Kat he saw below and start over again from those days. Replay all the years of regret and this time live them right.

"You can, you know."

"Can what?" Marcus glanced at the man, then back to the valley, but the vision of Kat and him was gone.

The man pointed to the valley. "I can offer you that life, Marcus. You can step into it and live it and I promise you will never remember what you did to Layne. It will disappear as if it never happened because in that life down there, it won't happen.

"It's a world where you went on the Enchantments hike with Dave and the others, where you're close to Abbie, and it's a world, Marcus . . . where you didn't lose Layne."

At the last words Marcus's heart tightened. "That's not true."

The man nodded. "Yes, you can have him back. Your son. Returned to you along with all your memories of his childhood. Just give me the word and it will happen immediately."

Marcus spun and stared at the man. "What's the catch? You said the choice would be made with great difficulty."

The man sighed. "Yes, I did. I also said your eyes need to be opened. So before I tell you about the price you would have to pay to live in this world, you must see what will happen if you don't choose the valley you've just witnessed." The man scooted closer to the edge and pointed to the valley on the left. "This valley is what will happen if you tell Kat about your role in Layne's death. Are you ready?"

Marcus nodded and again either they moved toward the valley or the valley moved toward them, and within seconds he watched Kat as she stood in their kitchen, her back to him, her hand clutching the counter as if she'd fall over if she let go.

"Kat?"

She turned. "I want to get it done quick for the sake of the girls." She slid a manila envelope onto the kitchen table.

"Get what done?"

"I'm so sorry, Marcus. I just can't do it anymore. I can't get past it. I've tried for so many years." Tears formed in her eyes. "I've filed."

"You've what? Divorce? I can't believe you filed. I didn't think —"

"But you did think. You heard God tell you not to let him go and you thought about it and let him go anyway."

"Please, I don't want to lose us. I don't believe you want to —"

"I know, and you're right. You are." Kat wiped her tears. "There's part of me that wants to make it work, but I just can't. You allowed my son to die, Marcus, and I so wish I could let that go. But I've tried and tried and tried and it's never going to happen."

A moment later the valley morphed into a courtroom, the air stuffy, the smell of old papers swirling around the space as if pushed by an invisible fan. A judge sat hunched over her bench as if she'd just finished speaking.

"I'm sorry, Marcus." A woman placed her hand on his shoulder. "It's final."

"You're my attorney?"

The woman smiled sadly. "Not anymore, unless you plan on getting divorced again someday."

Marcus turned, his sweat-soaked dress shirt plastered to his back, and stared at Kat who stood and shuffled out of the courtroom.

The scene stopped and grew smaller. In seconds he was back on the ledge.

"And the third valley?" Marcus asked the man.

"Are you sure you want to see it?"

"No."

"You're sure?"

"Yes. I mean no, I want to see it."

"This might be the most painful of the three."

"Can you give me a warning, a precursor

of what will be shown?"

"Yes, it is the valley if you choose to do nothing. What will happen if you stay in your current world, keep your silence, and Kat doesn't find out about what you did to your son."

Marcus nodded and sighed. "Show me."

He stood in the middle of their bedroom, Kat stood at their closet. She pulled down sweaters and jeans and shoes as if they each weighed sixty pounds.

"Are you going on a trip?"

"No."

"Then what are you doing?"

"I'm leaving. Going to my mom and dad's for a while. Sort some things out. Figure out what I'm going to do." She dropped a pair of shoes and they seemed to land on the carpet like bowling balls.

"Do about what?"

"Us."

"What do you mean, 'us'? What's wrong with us?"

Kat turned and dropped the clothes in her hands to the floor. "I'm not sure. But I know when it started. It was the night you discovered Calen was Zennon and fought him right there in our dining room." She paused and looked down and her voice dropped to a whisper. "He talked about a secret, about 'what you did to him.' " Kat looked up. "I can't get it out of my mind that he was talking about Layne."

Heat torched Marcus's face. She knew. At the least she suspected what he'd done.

She picked up the clothes. "Is there anything you want to tell me?"

Marcus tried to imagine saying the words. Confessing what he'd done. But there was no point. He'd already seen what would happen if he did. He stared at her but dropped his gaze as her sad, questioning eyes looked into his and then filled again with tears.

"Don't say it, Marcus. Don't tell me. I don't want to know." A sorrow-tinged smile creased her face. "Just give me this time and who knows, maybe it will be okay."

The scene grew smaller and the sensation of moving backward came over Marcus again till the ground grew hard and he was back on the cliff staring at the three valleys below.

"I'm sorry you had to see that, Marcus." The man's eyes were moist. "So much pain."

Marcus swallowed and tried to swallow again without success, his throat raw and dry. "Why would you, why would God give me the gift of the middle valley? I don't deserve it. What I've done has earned me the valley on the right or the left instead."

"That is true." The man drew three lines in the thin dirt next to them.

"Then why?"

"Because he is good. In James it says every perfect gift comes from the Father . . ." The man hesitated. "And he longs to give good gifts to his children."

"But what will it cost me? You said when I'd seen all three valleys, you would tell me the price. And I believe the price will be high."

The man raised his head and stared at Marcus for over ten seconds before speaking. "Why do you think the price will be high?"

"Because I see it in your eyes."

"It is true." The man turned away and gazed at each of the three valleys. "Your perception serves you well, Professor. And the cost might be too great for you to bear."

"Tell me."

The man stood and walked to the edge of the cliff. "In the middle valley you will retain all of your healing and all of your memories except for the memory of that afternoon with Layne.

"Your life with Kat and the girls will be the one you've longed for since before they were born. Your career, everything will be all you've ever imagined it could be. And Layne will be alive and well and enjoying the full life of a sixteen-year-old."

The man paused and locked his gaze on Marcus. "But one significant element of your life will be missing." The man paused again. "Warriors Riding."

A chill washed through Marcus. "What about them? What do you mean, 'missing'?"

"Although all your memories of Reece and Dana and Brandon will be fully intact, their memories of you will not be. They will not know who you are and will have no recollection of what you've built and experienced together."

"How could they not remember?"

"It's the way it has to be."

"Can I make them remember?"

"No." The man shook his head. "I know it is hard to think of what that would be like. I'm sorry."

"Can I tell them things about themselves no one else would know? Can I convince them those things happened?"

"I don't know." The man's gaze swept across the valleys as if he were searching for the answer. "Over time you might convince them something happened in another reality, but you can never bring back their memories and emotions and convictions about what went on at the ranch or your lives together."

"What about the healings inside Dana and Reece? What about Brandon getting his name and stepping back into the freedom he once sang with?"

"They will not have happened."

"Does that mean they could still happen?"

The man shrugged. "It is possible."

"Where would I start with them?"

"You would have to start over from the very beginning. It would be as if the past year had never happened. Reece would come to you as he did the first time with an invitation."

"So we would all go to Well Spring again?"

"Yes."

"I'd have to relive all of it?"

"Are you up for the challenge of that? Can you live through those weeks again, knowing what is going to happen and not saying anything about it? Can you live with knowing Reece will lose his eyes and knowing you are not allowed to do anything to stop it?"

"I don't know."

"A fair answer."

"Will everything turn out the same?"

"That cannot be known. Man has free

choice. The decisions you make and Reece and Brandon and Dana make might be different next time. As you know, theoretically, the movement of a butterfly's wing in the Amazon can cause a hurricane in Texas." The man hesitated. "But to answer your next question before you ask it, yes, it is highly likely things would turn out very similar to what they are now. Highly likely, but not guaranteed."

The man lapsed into silence and Marcus did the same. There should be more questions to ask — at least he felt there should be. But there weren't. He wanted a fourth option. How could he give up what the Spirit had led the Warriors into? If he went back to Well Spring, how could he fake it and not tell them what he knew? What if things turned out differently, turned into disaster, how could he live with that? Yet the other two valleys were certain death — one fast and one slow. And he couldn't live with either.

"Do I have to choose in this moment?"

The man laughed. "No, it's not like some late-night infomercial where you have to call now, or some business deal where you're offered the world and if you don't grab it, it instantly vanishes forever. This" — the man gestured with both hands toward the valleys

— "is the place where the offer always stands, and you can choose it now, or choose it a millennium from now." He paused and stared at Marcus with eyes that made him want to climb the mountain behind him or leap off the cliff knowing he could fly. "But why would anyone want to put off living the life they've always wanted for even one more moment?"

"I need a few minutes to think and to pray."

"Take all the time necessary." The man stood and walked to the far right side of the edge. "I'll be here interceding for you, that you will choose well."

FORTY-FIVE

Ten minutes later Marcus shuffled over to the man.

"Have you made your choice?" he asked.

"I want to see more of the valley to the right."

"The one where Kat is about to leave."

"Yes."

"Why is that, Marcus?" The man seemed to stare through him — eyes full of kindness that seemed on the brink of tearing up.

"Because she said she needed time. She didn't say it was over. That means if I stay in the reality I live in, there is hope for things to work themselves out, if I stay silent and accept that God has forgiven me and ignore the voice of the enemy screaming at me to tell her."

"Yes, you can see. But only a glimpse. Ten years from now." The man tapped both feet on the ledge in a fast rhythm and stared at the valleys. "I should warn you, it won't be

410

easy. Are you sure you want to go?"

His answer came out in a whisper. "Yes."

There was no movement this time. Marcus instantly stood in front of a tunnel at the base of a smooth stone wall. And this time the man was with him. "In there."

"After you?" Marcus said.

"No. You first." The man smiled and patted Marcus on the shoulder. "But don't worry, I'll be right behind you."

Marcus shuffled down the tunnel, the click of his shoes echoing off the walls. It smelled like antiseptic gone bad. It seemed like there should be stagnant water on the floor of the tunnel but it was dry. Ahead of them, framed in the curve of the opening, sat a man at what looked like an old kitchen table, no tablecloth, the only chair the one he sat in.

Marcus gazed at the man as they moved slowly through the tunnel. "Is that me?"

"You know it is."

Marcus stared at the figure who was him but wasn't him, and a moment later he sat at the small table hunched over a baked potato smothered in sour cream and bacon bits. A glass of vodka sat next to a bottle of Stoli.

Under his left hand was a photo of a young woman who looked to be in her mid-twenties with sad eyes holding a blond baby boy as they both sat on a park bench, the trees in the background bare of leaves. Something about her was familiar.

A ring of a cell phone shattered the silence and he jerked his head to the right and left searching for it. On the small microwave on the counter. He lurched out of the chair and picked up the phone. The face of the woman in the photo filled the screen. There was no button to push to answer. "Hello? Hello?"

"Dad, thank God I got you."

"Jayla?"

"Yeah . . ."

"My daughter Jayla?"

"No, Jayla your son. Who do you think it is?"

"I'm sorry, I just . . . it's just that —"

"You're not drunk again, are you? You just got out of rehab three months ago. At least make it last a little longer this time. The U-Dub has been pretty nice to you, but my guess is their patience is getting tissue-paper thin."

Marcus glanced at the bottle of Stoli again. "No. I'm clean."

"Glad to hear it. Okay, now I know I just asked, so no lectures, okay? I need a little bit of cash. Just a little to get me through to next month. He says he'll get me two months' worth really soon."

"Who is he? And what do you need the cash for? I —"

"I told you not to start, Dad. Please. Kids cost money."

"Yes, I apologize. I mean if you need it, but . . . let me talk to Kat about this. She'll —"

"You're going to talk to Mom? Yeah, sure. And my ex is going to morph into Prince Charming and waltz through my front door this afternoon."

Perspiration broke out on Marcus's forehead. "I talk to her every day."

"Oh, I'm sure you do. I'm sure you and Mom and her new husband sit down over a nightly cup of Earl Grey tea and talk about how she's making millions in the pastry business and you're staggering through your classroom lectures." A sigh came through the phone. "Wow, Dad, I really thought you'd stay sober this time."

Marcus's back grew damp and his hands shook. "Kat is not married to someone —"

Jayla's voice went up three notches. "Listen to me. I know you probably won't remember this once the booze wears off, but once the truth came out about your choice causing Layne to die, she left you.

For good. And she's never, ever coming back. Okay? But I'll tell her you said hello if that makes you feel any better."

Marcus's mind reeled. It wasn't true. He wasn't really here. It was the future. But it felt so real. "Your mom is married to me!"

"You are so living in fantasy land."

"No, I'm not. I'm —"

"Make it a good one this time, Dad. You just woke up, or you were immersed in a novel or a sci-fi film, or you are just about to prove Einstein wrong on his theory of relativity. Any of those will work as to why your brain took a vaction, or do you want to try another?"

"Where's Abbie?"

"Are you on crack? What is wrong with you? Just trying to drop another Stonehenge-size rock of pain into your mind? Dwelling on the might-have-beens?"

A sick feeling swept through Marcus and somehow he knew in whatever reality he was currently in, he'd never speak to his older daughter again. "Tell me where she is, Jayla."

"How should I know? Tibet or Bali or wherever she went when she cut us off entirely, forever and ever amen. If you think you'll ever find her, you're delusional. I mean, it's been eight years for you and three

414

years for Mom and me without a peep from her. Now I don't mean to be rude, but can I have the money or not?"

Marcus spun to find the man who had brought him here, but no one was in the kitchen. His gaze scraped across the worn cabinets and the counter stacked with books and a collection of battered coffee cups. In the middle of the refrigerator a photo riveted his gaze. Kat, the girls, and he stood in front of the Disneyland castle, broad smiles on their faces, bright sun lighting up their Tigger, Winnie the Pooh, Peter Pan, and Snow White T-shirts. Marcus closed his eyes and let out a soft moan. Why would he put up that shot? To torture himself every time he wanted something to eat?

He opened his eyes and called out to the ceiling, then out the small window over the sink that framed a setting sun. "Get me out of here. I've seen enough. I've seen too much."

There was no answer and Marcus slumped back in his chair and over the next hour watched the sky turn to the color of ash, then to black. He stood, walked to the sink, and stared at his reflection in the window. His hair was thinner and streaked with gray, his face gaunt, lines etched into it. And his eyes. Hollow and dead as if their hue had been changed to black and white.

"Are you ready to go?"

Marcus jerked around. The man from the cliff stood in the kitchen doorway, a compassionate smile on his face.

"Where have you been?"

The man took a step into the kitchen and held out his hands. "I'm sorry. In order to fully grasp what is to come, you needed to be alone in the emotion for a good amount of time. If I could have stayed I would have, but I needed to take care of a few other things while the scene played out for you."

"We can go now?"

"Yes, of course."

The man waved his hand and, as if in sped-up reverse motion, Marcus was whisked backward through the tunnel and in seconds sat again on the cliff with the man. Marcus tried to shake the scene from his mind. It wasn't real. But it was. He hadn't just seen it, he'd lived it, he'd been inside the body of the Marcus of the future with all the emotions and horror of that life.

Marcus stared into the valley they'd just come from, its green winding form and the silver snake of a river on its right-hand side belying the desolation that lay within it.

The man picked up a thin stick and broke it into three pieces, then laid them next to each other. One pointing to the left, one straight ahead, and one to the right. "Are you ready to make a choice, Marcus Amber?"

"Yes." Marcus's head slumped forward. "I have to be."

"And what will your choice be?"

The images of Reece, Dana, and Brandon swept across his mind's eye. Then images of all the people they'd set free and the students they'd trained. Then visions of what more they would achieve.

"The choice is difficult in the extreme."

"Yes. It is." The man slid the front of his foot over the edge of the cliff. "And this is the kind of choice where choosing not to choose isn't an option."

As the man's words faded, something inside Marcus snapped. The decision settled on him and lightness filled his mind. Why had it been so hard to choose? The choice was obvious. He turned to the man and began to speak.

FORTY-SIX

Dana reached over, grabbed Reece's knee-cap, and shook it. They'd been back from their razor-close call with the avalanche for ten minutes, and Reece had slipped into a prolonged silence. "Hey, we can't just sit here. We have to take action. Figure out a plan for finding Marcus and how to go after him."

Reece tilted his head toward her. "I am taking action. I'm asking the Spirit for forgiveness for my foolishness and asking for the location of the professor. I suggest you do the same."

She looked up at Brandon, then closed her eyes and prayed. Two words blazed into her mind like neon signs flashing on and off. *Mountain.* And *valley.* Then another word joined the first two: *abandoned.* Great. Her weak spot. Jesus had done such healing in her, but still, the scar was fresh and she knew there was more healing to be done in that part of her heart.

Dana opened her eyes. Brandon's head was bowed, but Reece's head was turned toward her. "Did you get anything?"

"Mountain. Valley. Abandoned."

"I saw the word *mountain* as well. I felt the Spirit saying he would take us to Marcus, and finally, that this won't be easy." Reece clasped his knees. "Brandon?"

The musician glanced at Marcus's body. "I saw a sprinter racing down a track, the field behind him crumbling into darkness inches behind him. He strained to outrun the disintegrating track, but it was gaining on him."

"Interpretation?"

"Pretty straightforward I think." Brandon leaned toward Marcus's body. "If we want to save the professor, we have to hurry."

"I agree." Reece rubbed his forehead, pushing his hat back high on his head. "Our first step is to get through a kind of gate none of us has ever gone through. But the Spirit will take us through and get us to Marcus, although this journey will not be an easy one."

Brandon leaned back on the couch in Reece's home and grinned. "In other words there's a good chance of going down in spectacular flames, dying an excruciatingly painful death at the hands of the enemy, and winding up in heaven."

"Precisely."

"Or in other words, business as usual," Dana added.

Reece smiled and held out his hand to Dana. "Would you like to be my guide out to the fire pit? I think that's where we should go in from."

"An honor, yes."

She took his hand and the three stepped out through Reece's back door. As they walked the familiar path through Reece's backyard to the circle of stones surrounding the pit, Dana realized his request for her to lead him was more about her than him. Over the past eleven months, Reece had certainly taught himself the way to the fire pit without needing help. He didn't need her hand to guide him. But she needed the assurance of his touch. Strength seemed to flow through his giant hand into hers, and although imaginations of the battle they were about to enter into spilled across her mind, a peace settled there as well and it seemed to carry her without effort across the hundred yards to the spot from which they would try to rescue the professor.

After Brandon started a small fire, Reece sat forward and clasped his hands. "Another adventure together." He paused and his head turned down. "This is my doing, my fault, my selfishness, and consequently my battle to wage. I've confessed this to Jesus; now I'm confessing it to you. And because of that, you two do not have to come."

Neither Brandon nor she spoke.

"I take it the answer you both would give if I demanded it from you is you want to come."

"Ahh, I'm not sure I would describe it as *want* to —" Brandon raised his eyebrows.

"I want to come," Dana said. "So does Brandon." She looked at him and winked.

"So be it." Reece lifted his head as he took her hand and Brandon's. "There's a Warrior from among us who is missing. It's time we go find him and bring him home. Strength, truth, hope, and love. Go before us, Lord, and take up guard behind us. Be below us and above. To our left and our right, fill us with life and wisdom and your vast, unending strength."

Reece gave her hand a light squeeze and then she was freefalling, her stomach seizing up as if she'd just leaped from a plane at twelve thousand feet, air rushing past her, the sound of a thousand waterfalls pressing in on her. Then a shaking in her body as if being pummeled by twenty-foot waves and being slammed into the sand only to be picked up by another swell and slammed back to the ground.

She had to hang on. It would be over in seconds. But it wasn't. The feeling intensified till her body felt like it couldn't last another five seconds without breaking apart. Where had Reece taken them? Maybe no one had ever gone through this gate because it was impossible to get through.

She tried to pull in a breath, but there was no air to breathe and she started to panic. But before the sensation could overwhelm her, the wind and the roar around her stopped and she stood on solid ground. Dana bent over, gasped for air, her legs numb and shaking. She let go of Brandon's and Reece's hands and tried to slow her breathing.

"I can't say I enjoyed that a whole lot," Brandon sputtered out.

"Are you all right, Dana?" Reece said.

"It felt like my body was about to explode, but yes, I'm okay. Why was, why did we . . . ?"

"There is little light in this realm. It is owned by the evil one and we are far from welcome here."

She stood up straight and blinked against a harsh sun low in a turquoise sky. Ten small thatched huts surrounded them. The ground at their feet was muddy and wet as if it had rained just before they arrived.

A thick smoke that smelled like burned fish seeped from crude chimneys on top of each hut but didn't rise. It slithered along the top, then fell slowly to the ground where it formed a circle around the outside of the huts and grew darker as more smoke spilled down the sides of the huts onto the ground.

Dana studied the opening of each hut. Most were four to five feet high, a few were taller, one was barely two feet tall. All were dark inside and the feeling she got from all of them made bile rise in her throat.

The sound of a small chime seemed to come from above them, and as the sound rang out, nine men came through the opening of each hut except for the one with the smallest passageway. Their faces were like gray stone, their eyes dark, hair dark or missing; gnarled hands and fingers stuck out of thin, dark brown tunics.

The garb of the men reminded her of the medieval renaissance fair she'd gone to out in Carnation a few summers back. But these people obviously weren't pretending.

Brandon looked behind him, then turned to Reece. "I'm guessing we go through one of those huts to get to Marcus."

Reece did a slow spin. "I'm thinking the same."

Dana glanced at the men's faces. "And I'm presuming our new friends won't be completely enthralled with that idea."

Reece did another slow spin, then addressed a stocky man with a shock of hair that looked like a bird's nest made of black roots and grasses. "We'd like your help."

The man stared at each of them for at least five seconds, his gaze finally settling on Reece. "Speak of this help."

"We have a friend we need to reach. I believe we need to go through one of your huts to get to him."

"You have spoken rightly." The man glanced at the others in front of each hut, then back to Reece. "That is the way for you to reach him."

"May we pass?"

"Yes."

Brandon turned to Dana and whispered, "It may have taken me a few times to get the lesson, but I think that sounds a little too easy."

Dana nodded but kept her eyes on the nine men.

Reece took a step toward the stocky man. "You won't offer resistance?"

"No, you are free to pass through whichever opening you choose." The hint of a smile appeared on the man's face and grew into a full-out grin. The men in front of the rest of the huts joined him, and then all of them burst into laughter. When their mirth finally subsided, the man who had spoken to them shuffled forward a few paces.

"Is there anything else we can assist you with?"

Dana looked at the smoke surrounding the outside of the huts, which had grown into an ink-black wall thirty feet high. Reece and Brandon were looking at it too, and she met both their gazes when they turned back. None of them needed to speak. Unless the Spirit decided to offer up a miracle, going outside the circle of huts wouldn't be their path to wherever Marcus was. Going into one of the huts was their only option.

"Which is the hut that will take us to our friend?"

"Have you not considered the possibility that the gates here are closed to travelers such as yourselves?"

"No, and there's no chance of us considering."

"I understand." The man motioned with his gnarled hand to each of the openings. "In that case please look on the ten passages before you. One of them will take you to Marcus Amber. The others will take you to nothing. And if you pass through one of those gates, you will reside in that nothingness for eternity."

"Is there one you can recommend to us?"

"I am not afforded that honor." The man grinned for the second time and again his comrades joined in his laughter. "Only the one who made the huts has the right to show you which to choose."

Reece motioned Brandon and her toward him. He took their shoulders and drew them in close. "Which one — are either of you hearing anything?"

"Nothing," Brandon said.

"Dana?"

"Same." But a moment later she did and pointed to her right at a hut that sat back from the circle by only a foot, maybe less. "I have a sense that is our path."

"How sure are you?"

"It's only an impression."

Reece stood straight and stared at the opening, then leaned down again. "Since it's the only one any of us have received, we'll go with it."

"I'm thinking we might want to be a bit surer," Brandon said.

"That would certainly be nice." Reece strode toward the hut and stopped at the entrance, waiting for Brandon and her to join him.

The man they'd spoken to started to clap and one at a time the others joined him. Their rhythm was slow and the sound their hands produced was low as if each of their hands were made of tree trunks. Dana came to a halt five feet from the opening, squatted, and stared into the darkness. For an instant a thin ray of light inside the hut shot across her vision, then vanished.

A sign? Again she searched for confirmation from the Spirit and again there was no answer. She stood and walked up to the entrance. The smell of fish was stronger here and turned her stomach.

"Should we try another?" Dana peered at Reece. "It was only an impression and it's gone now."

"No, time is even less on our side here than in the other realms. We must act."

Dana nodded, ducked her head, and forced herself to step through the hut's opening. Again the shaft of light appeared, then vanished and hope stirred in her. But the instant Dana had cleared the opening, something from behind shoved her onto the dirt floor of the hut and she landed hard on her hands and knees. "Uhhhhh!" Then whatever had shoved her forward landed on her back and slammed her to the floor and knocked the wind out of her. She groped for air and struggled, face pushed into the putrid-smelling ground.

"Dana!" Brandon's muffled yell floated through the walls of the hut and she heard him push through the opening. She caught her breath and cried out, "No!" but too late. A second later Brandon lay sprawled out beside her.

"Reece, stay out!" But again she was too late and Reece lay quivering on his stomach next to them.

Desolation swept over her. The blackness inside the hut seemed to grow and her thoughts felt thick, as if the mud they'd stood in outside the huts had filled her mind. She tried to get to her knees, but whatever held her down was like iron. Sharp, tiny rocks sliced into her cheeks and tried to force their way into her eyes.

She reached up to block them, but her hands wouldn't move and the force behind her continued to shove her face harder into the ground. Her vision blurred and blackness started to seep into her mind. Then the ground gave way and she melted through the dirt floor and seemed to be floating down — for how long she didn't know. The darkness swallowed her and silence pressed in on her. She cried out but her voice made no sound. With each second the darkness seemed to grow thicker as if she were sinking into black glue.

Finally her feet came to rest on a damp, undulating surface as if she stood on an old waterbed leaking tar. Dana felt her face with two fingers. Wet. Blood she guessed, but the pain was minimal. The cuts couldn't be deep. Small consolation. A feeling of isolation rose up inside. She was alone in the nothingness. There was no doubt.

"Am I alone?" Brandon's voice, thin and hollow, flittered through the darkness and echoed in her head. Relief thundered through her. "No! I'm here. Reece? Are you there?"

A response came as if from miles away and it echoed. "Yes."

"Where are we?"

Neither Reece nor Brandon answered.

"I made the wrong choice."

"I don't think so," Reece said. "I'm not sure any of the huts would have led us to Marcus. In fact, I'm sure they wouldn't."

"Where are we?" she asked again.

"I don't know," Brandon said, his voice growing fainter.

"Don't leave me!" Dana strained to push through the darkness toward the sound of

Brandon's voice.

"I won't."

But his voice came to her even softer than before.

"Spirit, come." She cradled her head in her hands.

"He's not here, Dana." Only a hint of Brandon's voice came to her now. "You want to know where we are? In nothing. Alone forever."

Her brain felt like it was stuffed with black cotton. "Reece, help me fight this!"

"Fight? Yes, we have to." His voice sounded thick and as if he spoke in slow motion.

"We have to get out of here. There has to be a way." The mud continued to fill her brain and tried to push out thoughts of escape. No, she wouldn't give in. *You say I can do all things with your strength, Lord? Now would be a good time to fill me up.*

"Stay with me, Reece. What would Marcus say if he were here? What would he teach us in this moment?"

"Marcus? The physics professor? He's the one we're trying to rescue, yes? Is that why we're here?"

"What would he say!" Dana screamed the words but the sound sounded like a whisper coming out of her mouth.

"That the observation of quantum events affects the outcome." Reece's words sounded like they came to her from oceans away.

"What else?"

"That in the same way, our faith affects the outcome of events."

"Like this one." The words crossed her lips and fell to the ground, but she had to get them out. And had to keep Reece talking. Speaking truth.

"Yes."

"So one of our greatest weapons is . . . ?"

"Faith," Reece said.

"Another?"

"Hope."

"And the greatest of these?"

Brandon's voice flittered through the darkness. "The greatest is love."

"Yes." It was the first word Dana had spoken since they reached the bottom of the pit that didn't feel like it had fifty-pound weights on it.

Brandon's voice grew fifty decibels in volume. "And the sword of the Spirit, which is the Word of God."

"And with it there has to be a way of escape." Reece sounded like he was right next to her.

A moment later it felt like ice had been

shot into Dana's veins, and a voice that seemed to come from everywhere interrupted them. The tone was that of the stocky man they'd spoken to outside the huts.

"You are wrong. Here you will stay forever. You know this to be true. Separated from the people you love. Separated from your life on earth. And separated forever from the God you have so blindly and futilely served. You made the choice and now you will live with the decision in utter solitude. You know this to be true. After a month you will give up. In two you'll go mad. With thirst, with hunger, but you will not die. In three months you will tear each other apart. You know this to be true."

Dana's head snapped back. "It can't be. That can't be true. It's a lie."

"No, it is true," Brandon muttered.

"Do you think it's true, Reece? What do you believe, Temple?"

"No, I won't believe that . . ." The words sounded like Reece spoke underwater and he gasped for air as he pushed his thoughts out. "I believe this voice lies. I believe all that we see here is deception. I believe we have the power to take these thoughts of evil captive to the obedience of Christ."

The voice of the stocky man spoke again.

"Pretending doesn't make things real. We told you before you went in that if you chose wrong, you would be separated from everything and everyone you've loved, forever. There was no deception on our part. You chose this destiny for yourselves. Now you must live with the consequences of your decision."

Dana sank to her knees. Her fault. They would stay here forever because of her. Despair buried her and tears came. She didn't know how long she stayed like that, but at some point Reece's voice reached her. " 'And who shall separate us from the love of Christ?' "

She raised her head and opened her mouth, but the words wouldn't come. But Dana refused to surrender and she pushed the words out as if lifting a massive stone off her chest. " 'Neither death nor life.' "

" 'And who shall separate us from the love of Christ?' " Reece repeated slightly louder.

" 'Neither angels nor demons,' " Dana said, the words more easily sliding off her tongue.

" 'And who shall separate us from the love of Christ?' "

" 'Neither the present nor the future.' "

" 'And who shall separate us from the love

of Christ?' " Reece's voice went up another notch.

This time Brandon answered. " 'Nor any powers.' "

" 'And who shall separate us from the love of Christ?' " The big man was almost shouting now.

" 'Neither height nor depth, nor anything else in all creation, will be able to separate us from the love of God that is in Christ Jesus our Lord.' "

"The voice lies." Reece's voice sounded out like a clock striking midnight, and the thick, constrictive air around Dana loosened. "Though we stay here forever, the unquenchable love of the Trinity will never leave us." Reece paused and she heard laughter in his voice. " 'Though he slay me, yet will I hope in him.' "

Nothing changed in what Dana could see, and her feet were still mired in whatever she stood upon, but inside a peace grew till she knew if her face could be seen by the others it would be radiant.

She closed her eyes. " 'Who shall separate us from the love of Christ? Shall trouble or hardship or persecution or famine or nakedness or danger or sword? . . . No, in all these things we are more than conquerors through him who loved us.' "

Dana repeated the verses and halfway through Reece joined in. The third time through, all three of them spoke the scriptures with power. As they began the verse for the sixth time, a light the size of a needle point appeared. So small yet so bright in the midst of the darkness it seemed like she stood right in front of a massive lighthouse, its mirrors throwing off a million beams of light. The pinprick of brightness grew to the size of a spotlight, then the light was a torrent, a giant vortex pulling them forward, drawing them into its tunnel.

The instant Dana passed the edge of the tunnel, a feeling of joy and power and love surged through her. Laughter broke from her mouth and she spun and raced through the light at a trillion miles an hour, and still she wanted to go faster.

Their speed slowed and the light parted in the middle of the tunnel, and they were now flying over a series of vast mountain ranges far taller than Mount Everest, then down into valleys that reminded Dana of Hawaii, but these valleys were far wilder, the greens deeper, the churning of the waterfalls much whiter, and the rivers running through them more powerful.

Their speed slowed more and she looked at a mountain maybe a mile away, far below them. As they came closer, Dana spotted two dots on a ledge about halfway up the mountain that morphed into men, and then into Marcus and a man surrounded by a thin, swirling curtain of darkness.

She didn't need the Spirit to tell her they were about to go to war.

FORTY-SEVEN

"I've chosen." As Marcus spoke, a thin smile grew on the man's face. "I will release the Warriors, let them go. I can rebuild with them. I can't give up Kat or the girls . . . and to have Layne back . . ." The words tumbled out of Marcus's mouth as if they were tiny lead anchors, but even after he spoke them, his jaw still seemed to be weighed down.

"Excellent." The man clapped Marcus on the back and pointed behind him. "This is so good. I'm so happy for you. It will only be moments now till you're with them in that valley forever."

The man wrapped his fist in the palm of his other hand. "You've chosen the right pill this time."

"What?" Marcus frowned at the man. Was he quoting from — ?

"Yes, Professor, I'm quoting from *The Matrix.* Some choose the blue pill, some choose the red. You know that scene by heart."

He did. It flashed into his mind fully formed and he saw Neo taking the red pill and turning his world into insanity and pain and great triumph and truth. Red pill. Blue pill. Red cards. Blue cards. Red backs, blue backs. Simon! The magician's words rushed into his mind. *"He doesn't play fair. Every choice is his. Every choice leads to death."*

Neo had chosen the truth. Marcus fell onto his knees, his hands and arms limp at his sides. And he, Marcus Amber, was about to choose a lie. He was about to insert himself into a world that would lobotomize his memory and bury the lie so far down, it could never be dug up, but that was a lie too.

It didn't matter if Kat would never know. It didn't matter if even he himself couldn't remember it. It had happened. It was real. It was true. And nothing could wipe that out of existence. He stared at the man, his breaths came more rapidly, his hands formed into fists.

"Is there a problem?" The man eased toward Marcus.

"You can turn the backs of the cards whatever color you want to, can't you? It's your game and I can't win. The blue pill is the way of the lie."

"No, Marcus, it is the way of salvation for you, for your daughters, for your wife, and for Layne."

"Who are you?"

"I am your friend. And it's time for you to go." He glanced at something over Marcus's shoulder. "And if you don't go, I will help you for I am truly a man who desires the best for you." His eyes grew darker.

Marcus's heart pounded and perspiration seeped down his back. "I've allowed my eyes to be blinded." He stood and stepped back from the oncoming man.

"If you don't follow through on your decision, just like Reece, your eyes truly will be blinded." The man glanced over Marcus's head and reached out his hand as if he were about to grab Marcus around the neck. "Be it your choice or not, you will . . ."

The last of the man's words were drowned out as a flash of light and the sound of boulders smashing together filled the air. The concussion of sound thrust Marcus back and he slammed into the cliff wall. When he regained his balance, he looked up and found himself staring into the dirt- and blood-smeared faces of Reece, Dana, and Brandon.

Brandon strode forward and grabbed him in a firm hug. "It's good to see you, Professor. I hope you haven't been bored since we last saw you. We haven't been."

"I apologize for taking so long, Marcus." Reece riveted his gaze on the man and spoke in a low voice. "Leave. Now, Zennon. In the name of the Christ."

"Hello, Reece, it's wonderful to see you. So sorry to disappoint, but I'm not going anywhere."

The demon stared at Reece, his eyes on fire, the veins in his head and arms pulsing. "You think you can control me? Tell me to leave with a simple sentence? No, Reece Roth. You have no power over me. Not here. Not in this place. Or have you forgotten what happened eleven months ago?" Zennon tapped his skin next to his right eye.

He grinned and stepped toward Reece and the others, his feet stopping with each step as if a great weight were wrapped around his ankles. "This is my domain, not yours. Your simple religious phrases are no help here."

"You have spoken truth. I have no power worth speaking of in this place or any place on heaven or earth or any other realm. But the authority I have in every place because of the Spirit that lives within me is far beyond your ability to fight. Go. By the blood of the Lamb, by the Son of the

Creator of the heavens and the earth, and by the authority that rules the universe."

The demon kept coming but Reece didn't move.

"Really? You truly aspire to that belief? And when I reach out seconds from now and draw my finger across your heart and destroy more than your eyes this time, what will you believe?"

Another heavy step and the cliff seemed to tremble with the weight of the demon's foot. "I feel it." A guttural laugh sputtered out of Zennon's throat. "The fear racing up your legs into your torso and into your mind. Yes, embrace the fear, Reece, embrace the truth of my power over you."

Their leader shuddered and his brilliant blue eyes blinked again and again.

"I will have mercy on you and your friends. I will allow you and the others to live if you leave this place now, but I will not make this offer again." The air around them grew hot.

Reece staggered back two steps and glanced at Marcus, Brandon, and Dana. Fear and strength were both reflected in Reece's eyes, but the strength seemed to flicker like a dying TV.

"The panic growing inside you is the truth." Zennon was now only five feet from

Reece. "Make your choice. Leave or Die. I suggest you choose wisely." The demon turned and smiled at Marcus as the air around them grew hotter.

Marcus turned back to Reece. "He's right. Choose wisely. Choose truth."

Brandon stared at Marcus, the musician's face an odd mix of fear and confusion and wonder and risk as if something inside wanted to burst out, but Brandon wasn't sure if he wanted it to. Brandon's hands balled into fists — he closed his eyes and lifted his head to the heavens. He pulled in a long breath and held it.

A moment later Brandon opened his eyes and stared straight at the demon. He began to hum, a high lilting melody that couldn't have been more than four or five notes but somehow sounded like it was made up of thousands of crystals ringing out amid a soft wind.

The demon rose up, seeming to grow three inches taller, and growled. "Desist, Brandon Scott — before I rip your throat out."

Brandon sang it again, louder, and his voice didn't sound like the voice of a man but that of an instrument made of water and glass and air and forest. Reece grinned at Brandon. "Nice to have you back, Brandon." Then he stepped toward the demon, who stopped, labored breaths pouring out of his mouth. "More. You are the Song."

Brandon grinned and joy spread across his face like a boy getting his first baseball glove. It was the first time he'd sung since his surgery, and the doubt Marcus saw moments earlier was gone.

Brandon glanced at each of them and his eyes shone with the knowledge his voice had been fully restored in the physical realm and that its power was even more potent here. He was the Song, and the music poured out of him like it was the last time he would ever sing.

Brandon raised his hands high and the melody grew louder and more complex and somehow out of his mouth poured melody and harmonies that seemed to sweep around them in tighter and tighter circles. The demon's eyes grew darker — if that were possible — and he lifted a shuddering hand toward Brandon as if to crush his throat.

"No." Reece spoke the word in a whisper, then again louder. "No." The third time it was a shout that reverberated off the mountain like a cannon shot. "No!"

The big man stepped toward the demon, lightning in his eyes. "By the power of his resurrection and ascension, we come against you and your lies and the poison you've tried to spread. By the name of the King of all, Jesus Christ, I command you to leave!"

A low guttural scream came out of the demon. "This is not over. It will never be —!" Zennon vanished. There was no sound, no flash of light, and nothing left behind. A hawk cried far above them and the air cooled in seconds. Marcus slumped to the ground.

"I almost made a profoundly poor choice." A chill raced down Marcus's back as he stared at the valley he'd almost vanished into.

"As did I," Reece said. He stepped to the edge of the cliff and stared down at the valleys. "Forgive me, Marcus."

"For what?"

"For allowing this to happen. For letting my selfishness send you here."

Marcus clasped Reece's hands in both of his. "It's over. Forgiven. There was purpose in it."

"Let's get out of here," Dana said. Brandon, Reece, and she joined hands, but the professor held up a finger and walked to the edge of the cliff and stared down into the valleys below.

"Marcus?"

He turned, his heart heavy. "I have been rescued in this moment, but it doesn't change the future. I'm still faced with a choice I don't want to make. One I feel must be made soon."

"What is the choice?" Brandon asked.

"If I'm going to tell Kat."

"Tell her what?"

Marcus didn't answer, and he had no doubt his eyes told them not to ask again.

FORTY-EIGHT

"Whew. That was a ride on the far side of extreme." Brandon squeezed his legs as if he were feeling them for the first time. "Kinda, sorta, extremely glad that pup is over." His body felt like lead, and if he were home in his bed he had no doubt he could crash for twelve hours without moving. The workout they'd just completed in the spiritual realm had been fully absorbed into his physical body.

"It's not over." Reece lurched to his feet and strode away from the fire pit toward the back of his house as if the experience hadn't affected him at all.

Brandon slowly rose from the bench, Dana stood, and they followed. For a guy who couldn't see, Reece moved fast. Not over? Brandon felt like they'd just finished sudden-death overtime in the Super Bowl and they weren't done?

He broke into a sluggish jog till he caught

up with Reece. "Care to expand on what 'not over' means?"

"Yes, as soon as the four of us are together. I want to make sure the professor is okay."

The three of them reached Reece's back door together and if Brandon didn't know better, he'd swear the big man was seeing again. He reached for the door handle without hesitation and pushed through.

"Marcus?" Reece called the professor's name twice before he got an answer.

"I'm here."

Brandon slogged into the living room and stared at Marcus. His complexion was paler than usual, but other than that the professor looked well. "You're all right, Prof?"

"I'm good."

He stood, then sat back down on the couch his body had been lying on for almost five hours. Marcus breathed like he'd just finished a marathon. Good, Brandon wasn't the only one ready for a break.

"It will take an abundance of time to process the complexity and spiritual implications of what I just experienced, but yes, I truly am well."

"Regretfully, for all of us, there isn't any time for processing." Reece stood like a statue, his long arms folded across his chest.

Marcus gazed up at him. "I don't understand."

"That's two of us, bro." Brandon eased over next to the professor.

A voice rang out from above them. "It's time to go after the Wolf in the heavens, Marcus."

Doug eased down the stairs and came to a stop next to Reece.

"Now?" Brandon said. He glanced at Dana. Her eyes told him she wondered the same thing.

The professor looked down, then raised his head slowly. "It's not."

"It is," Doug said. "I've never heard more clearly from the Spirit. The time is now. I believe Reece agrees."

Marcus shook his head. "Proceeding into that course of action is not a path I'm able to take."

"I realize you've been through a harrowing journey and need time to analyze what has happened." Reece lumbered toward Marcus. "I realize what we all just came out of has exhausted us physically and emotionally as well as spiritually. But there isn't time for recovery right now. You don't think you have it in you to enter immediately into another battle, but you do. You have the strength, Professor, his strength."

Marcus shook his head. "That isn't what I meant to indicate." He rubbed his hair. "Confronting the Wolf is not my path."

"What?"

"I'm not to go in with you and the other Warriors."

"It's the path for all of those of the prophecy." Reece took a step forward, his arms still folded. "We cannot do this without you. The Spirit has told me more than once that you are the key to victory over the Wolf. That without you, we are lost."

"I'm sorry."

Reece turned. "Dana? Brandon? Am I missing something here?"

Brandon hesitated before answering. Missing something? Yeah. Any hint of sanity. Reece and Doug wanted them to go after the Wolf right now? After what each of them had been through? Brandon was at the point of collapse. Dana had to be as well. But it didn't seem that way when she spoke.

"I think Reece and Doug might be right. I feel like Jesus told me the same thing. The time to go after the Wolf is now. Believe me, I don't want to, but I have little doubt of what we are to do." She turned to Brandon and stared at him for several seconds before speaking again. "Brandon, have you asked the Spirit? If yes, what has he said?"

He hadn't even thought of asking the Spirit what their next move was. He was thinking of sleep. But in the next moment the answer came. *Now.* He turned to Marcus. "We gotta go in, bro."

"That might be the state of affairs for the three of you, but it isn't for me. I'm sorry."

Reece stood to his full six-foot-five height and raised his voice a notch above normal. "Marcus Amber, put down your own desires, your self, the thing you feel you should do, and take hold of the thing you know you must do!"

Marcus stared at Reece, his eyes more intense than Brandon had ever seen them, his countenance like granite. As he opened his mouth to speak, a thundering knock came from the front door.

"Well now, it looks like we have a party crasher who wants to join this friendly discussion." Brandon turned to Reece. "Were you expecting guests?"

He didn't wait for an answer and loped toward the front of the house. He glanced back at the others, then opened the door. Tristan Barrow stood on the wood porch, his arms folded and legs spread shoulder-width apart. Behind him and to either side stood Jotham and Orson.

"Hello, Song." Tristan grinned and gazed

at the rest of the Warriors. "We're not inter-rupting anything, are we?"

Brandon stepped back and ushered them in. The three angels clomped down the two steps into Reece's sunken living room and stood in front of the fireplace, Tristan in the middle, Jotham and Orson to his sides.

"Welcome." Reece stood and gestured to the others. "No interruption at all. Your tim-ing is impeccable. We're just about to go in to confront the Wolf."

"Yes, it is time for that." Tristan glanced around the room. "All of you are going in?"

"Yes."

"I see." Tristan looked at the floor for a moment, then raised his head and stared at Reece. "So you don't believe Marcus when he says he knows he's to take a different path?"

"I know what the prophecy says, that the four must face the Wolf."

"Let it go, Reece. Allow Marcus to hear from the Spirit as clearly as you do."

"He's not to go with us?"

Marcus stared at Tristan. Even though he knew he wasn't to go with the other War-riors, he had little doubt no quarter of rest was being offered to him either.

Tristan turned to Marcus, arm outstretched, eyes full of joy. "Will you go with me?"

Marcus didn't respond. The laughter in Tristan's eyes drew him, but whatever journey the angel wanted to take him on would not be all joy. Far from it. Facing what he'd done to Layne and choosing to tell Kat about it were sure to be part of wherever Tristan wanted to take him, and Marcus wasn't ready. He was worn out, exhausted from his ordeal on the ledge with Zennon, and Marcus didn't know if he could face any more potential realities without his brain splitting open.

Because there was no answer this time, no solution he could analyze and formulate that would save him. No principle of quantum mechanics that could be applied to create a happily ever after. Each one of the paths ended in wrenching pain for him, for Kat . . . but where else could he go?

"Will you join me, Marcus Amber?"

He stared into Tristan's eyes, then into Brandon's and Dana's. He held her gaze. Strange. For just an instant it felt like he wasn't seeing Dana's eyes, but Kat's. And in that moment he saw the tiniest flicker of hope.

"Yes, I will join you."

Tristan grinned and his head tilted back

as if he were about to laugh. "I am glad for you. This is the path of truth." He turned back to Reece. "Go. Battle the Wolf. Fulfill the prophecy. He is for you." Tristan reached his hand out. "Marcus?"

Marcus walked over and laid his palm in Tristan's. Tristan nodded at the remaining Warriors and an instant later Reece's living room vanished.

No one spoke. What could any of them say? Dana considered the options. There was only one. Go in without Marcus, but she believed Reece was right. The four of them were to confront the Wolf, not three. And if Reece was right about Marcus being the key to their overcoming the Wolf, should they wait to go in till the professor did whatever he had to do?

Brandon was the first to break the silence. "That kind of puts a kibosh on our plans."

Dana sighed. "Leave it to you to try to be funny at a time like this."

"It wasn't funny? I saw the distinct hint of a smile on Reece's face. Really. You didn't notice?"

"You heard what Tristan said." Reece reached out his hands. "We still go in."

"Are you sure?" Dana moved toward Reece, as did Brandon on his other side.

"Without question."

Brandon asked, "Are we going in from here?"

Reece shook his head. "But we need to get to where we're going in from." He smiled.

"Well Spring?" Dana said. "Really?"

"Yes. Where else?"

"Here we come, Scotty," Brandon said.

Dana moved her fingers toward Reece's hand like she was reaching out to touch a scared fawn. The instant their hands met, their surroundings vanished and the three of them stood on the white-stone porch down the path from the main cabin at Well Spring Ranch.

FORTY-NINE

Marcus gasped. The rush this time was nothing like traveling through a soul's gate. This was faster and more exhilarating than any other time he had voyaged into a spiritual realm. He wasn't in the eye of the hurricane. He was on the fringe, moving a million miles an hour, and he didn't want it to stop.

But within seconds, the earth — or something like the earth — grew solid under his feet and he spun to take in his surroundings. Laughter burst out of his mouth. "Elation beyond anything I've experienced."

"Yes," Tristan said. "Few taste this while still wrapped in the confines of their mortal coil."

To their right and below them a huge golden-hued meadow — of wheat? grass? — spread to a blue horizon. In front of them a massive waterfall thundered hundreds of feet into a pool so clear and so deep, it made

Marcus blink to make sure it was real. To their left ran a forest, and in the middle of the fir trees lay a lake so still the water seemed not to be water but trees planted upside down.

"This place . . . the . . . everything . . . the colors are so . . . vivid."

Marcus laughed at himself. Describing the colors as vivid was as vast an understatement as he'd ever made. It was like saying the universe was somewhat large. The most brilliant blue on earth was dull compared to the azure and cobalt hues that were splashed across the sky and lake. The greens of the trees and gold in the meadow made the richest emerald colors of the Pacific Ocean in midsummer and the deepest golden sun of Hawaii seem pale by comparison. And one breath of the air here rendered all the most-treasured fragrances of earth odorless.

Marcus did a slow spin. "Where are we?"

Tristan laughed. "A place every man and woman longs for even though it does not exist in their wildest imaginings."

"What place?"

"A land where lies cannot live even for a moment. It's a country where the truth is seen by all those who face it."

"Face it?" Marcus said.

Tristan's face grew sober. "Face what would have been if they had chosen differently."

Marcus closed his eyes and pressed hard on one side of his nose. Unbelievable. The answer shouldn't have surprised him — he knew this was coming — but still, the answer did.

"And if I choose to face this truth, what will be the outcome? Will the sorrow of what I would face be too much?"

"I cannot know what will happen to you if you choose to face the memories and then see what might have been. I've never had to face one of my regrets because I've not made a choice that would force that emotion upon me."

Marcus frowned. "How can you insinuate this is a place men and women long for when your description indicates the greatest pain I can imagine lies before me?"

"I invited you to come. It is your choice to face what might have been." Tristan grabbed Marcus's shoulders and peered into his eyes. "But though the truth may slay you, it will also set you free."

The truth would set him free. Did he believe that? Marcus stared at Tristan. "I will go with you."

The angel grinned at Marcus and his eyes

seemed to throw off showers of light making the charge of anticipation and fear that pulsed through Marcus all the stronger.

Tristan held out his palm. "Grab my hand."

Marcus waited for another rush but this time it didn't come. There was no sensation of movement, no swirling around his mind and heart and body. The journey was instant. One moment he stood with the angel on the hill; the next he was in a grassland seemingly as vast as the one that held the field of doors — the souls of all people on earth.

Tristan pointed at a speck on the horizon. "Do you see the object rising out of the ground in the center of the field? Where the sky meets the grass?"

"Yes."

"That is our destination."

Tristan turned and strode off at a pace Marcus had to half walk, half jog to keep up with. After a few minutes a song rang out, and although it seemed to come from all directions at once, Marcus knew Tristan was the one singing. The words were in a language Marcus didn't know, but it didn't matter. His mind filled with images of warriors in great wars and vast fleets of ships battling through thirty-foot waves.

They covered ground quickly. Marcus still couldn't make out precisely what the object was, but it was rectangular in shape. A few minutes later he knew it was a door. When they were ten yards from it, Tristan stopped and folded his arms.

The door rested on a four-tiered concrete foundation. Each tier was smaller than the one underneath it — steps leading up to the door. The sides and frame of the door looked to be concrete as well, and the top was slightly wider than the frame on both sides. A smattering of daisies grew out of the thick jade grass that surrounded the foundation.

Behind the door, ethereal trees moved in an unfelt breeze against a sea-green sky. An arched wooden lattice stood behind the door. The door itself opened in the middle and was made up of four-paneled wood. Enthralling. But what captured Marcus's imagination was the light that seemed to pour from the sides and back of the door in waves. Brilliant light that he was sure would kill him if he touched it.

The air smelled of an early morning day in the beginning of autumn, and he drank it in. The door seemed to beckon him, and yet he couldn't ignore the sense of dread that surrounded the structure.

"What door is this?"

"It's time to choose, Marcus."

"Choose what?" he said even though the answer was obvious.

"Whether you will go through the door . . ." Tristan stared at the structure. "Or turn and walk away. This time will be your only chance."

"What is inside?"

Tristan bent to one knee, his gaze fixed on the door. "You would like to know the answer before you step through?"

Did he want to know? Was it even permissible to ask? "I asked the question with little expectation of you giving me the answer."

"I will answer the question if you want me to."

"Tell me."

Tristan continued to stare at the door as he answered. "It is the door of your memories."

His memories? "I don't understand."

Tristan rose and turned to Marcus. "Inside you will find all of your memories. The ones of joy, the ones of devastation. Ones you have treasured and ones you have forgotten. Played out as real as when the moments happened."

Marcus staggered back a step.

"You will face the memories of what you

have imagined the future to be, of what the past might have been, of what the future might have been had you chosen differently. All are contained inside your door."

The memories of what Zennon showed him in the valleys flooded his mind — Kat trying to figure out if she could stay with him, and her divorcing him, and ten years from now with his life in shambles. He took another step backward on the thick grass.

"Will I see what my life and Kat's life truly would have been like if I hadn't done what I did to Layne and he hadn't died? A memory still to come?"

"Yes." Tristan's face was like stone. "This you shall see."

Marcus's arms and legs grew cold. "I can't face that."

"I see." Tristan shifted his weight and went silent again, his thick arms still folded across his wide chest.

Marcus stepped toward the angel. "Guide me, lend me your counsel."

"The choice to step through the door is yours. None can make it for you, and none can give counsel for this decision but the One."

Marcus asked the Spirit but no answer came. *Jesus, please, tell me.* Again, nothing.

"Are you permitted to tell me what else lies beyond the door?"

"A choice."

"What choice?"

"Open the door and discover it for yourself."

Marcus walked to the door's foundation, closed his eyes, and prayed for strength. A strange mix of peace and dread settled on him. How could he be feeling both at the same time?

Must I, Lord?

This time the Spirit answered. *As my angel has said, it is your choice.*

Will I survive?

No answer.

What will happen to me if I don't go through?

I have already spoken of that to you.

Marcus shook his head. When? How could the Spirit have told him anything about the door, since until a few minutes ago Marcus didn't know it existed? The image of a coin flashed into Marcus's mind. Of course! How could he be so obtuse? He twisted to look at Tristan.

"Simon. That's the answer, isn't it?" Marcus turned back and stared at the door as the magician's words floated back to him once again.

"Chose the wrong door, you see. No, that's

not right. That's wrong. Reverse that. Strike that. Didn't choose the door. Should have gone through it but didn't. Didn't, didn't, didn't. Want to go back and walk through it, because I think it would be good, but I can't now. What's done is done. Over. Finished. I went the other way. Had my chance.

"You're just like Charlie. Willy Wonka is going to hand you a ticket, but you'll have to choose to go through the factory door."

Marcus took a last look at Tristan and smiled. The angel didn't look a bit like Willy Wonka.

Marcus placed his foot on the first step and his legs shuddered. Or was it the concrete step he stood on that moved? A second step. A third, and then he eased his foot onto the last step. The light that emanated from the sides of the door swirled around him and seemed to pull him closer. He took a deep breath, held it, and pushed the door open. The pulsing light on the sides of the door burst out like a flood and immersed him. It felt like liquid, as if he could swim in its currents.

After a minute his eyes somehow adjusted to the brilliance of the light and he stepped forward. He was in a hallway made of stone walls and ceiling — it reminded him of the Alhambra in Granada, Spain. Arched windows were spaced every few feet and gave views of a green, rocky coastline on either side. The crash of waves and the briny smell of sea air filled his nostrils.

A seagull riding the currents to his left seemed to cry in rhythm with his footsteps on the dark stones at his feet as he eased forward. Ten yards ahead was another door. This one had a handle made of gold and it turned without a whisper. Marcus stepped through and stared at the splendor around him.

He was in a lush garden of flowering trees and tiny waterfalls. Was he still inside the structure he'd entered? Or outside? Marcus laughed at himself. Inside what structure? The door of his memories hadn't led to anywhere, but in another sense he knew it led to everywhere.

A path made of leaves wove through the center of the garden and he stepped onto it. The pad of his feet on the leaves was the only sound. The path went on for fifteen yards before it turned hard to the right, then hard to the left for ten yards, then a gentle curve for forty paces before it turned straight.

A canopy of trees was now overhead. As he walked on, the canopy grew closer till he felt like he was walking down a hallway made for a Hobbit. After a few more steps, he had to stoop almost double to keep from brushing his head on the soft branches above him. He craned his neck and saw the end of the tunnel and through it a clearing.

Enter in.

He fell to his knees and crawled through. He was in the middle of a wide swath of Japanese maples. There was no underbrush here, just a carpet of emerald green moss that ran up to the base of the trees. In the center of the clearing, not more than twenty feet across, was a pool. A ring of thick jade grass surrounded it.

Look into the pool. You must see what it contains.

Marcus removed his socks and shoes, giving in to a sudden desire to feel the soft touch of the moss on his feet. There was no movement on the surface of the pool, no breeze in the air, no sound of his feet on the moss carpet.

When he reached the line where the moss and the grass met, he slid his toes onto the grass, the rest of his foot remaining on the moss. A tingling sensation seeped through his toes, into his feet, up his legs, slowly at first, then faster as it surged into his torso, his arms, and then his face and head. He wouldn't have been surprised if whatever it was had rocketed out of his fingertips, but it remained inside and filled him with thundering joy.

Marcus rocked back and forth from his toes to his heels as the feeling intensified as if ocean waves were crashing inside him — each wave made up of his wildest desires answered. The longer he stood soaking in the glory of the Spirit's presence, the more difficult it was to imagine having to gaze into the pool and see what his life could have been, would have been if he hadn't let Layne die. To see what his life with Kat would be in the coming days and years.

But he had to see. It was the only way to deal with the regret once and for all, to slay the beast for all time. With the strength of the Spirit he could more than face it. He could destroy it just as so many of his regrets had been vanquished last year when the three other Warriors had gone into some of the deepest parts of his soul and obliterated them.

But even with the truth of those thoughts ricocheting through his mind, Marcus couldn't make his lead-filled feet move toward the pool. The regret was so deep, so cutting. The consequences so severe. His son had died because of him, and no matter which path he chose, from this moment forward he would lose Kat as well. The memories of what he'd seen in the valleys buried him, and tears rose to the surface. He cried out to Jesus, but the voice that answered him was not the Spirit's, but Simon's once again.

"The Wolf, the Wolf, the Wolf of confusion, he always spins a compelling illusion."

For the second time the magician's words pulled the scales of deception from Marcus's eyes. Simon was right. Illusions. Alternate realities of the enemy's making. How could the enemy know his future? Or what would have happened if he hadn't let Layne go? Why would Zennon show him anything but lies laced with enough truth to draw him into darkness and assault his heart? Marcus closed his eyes and tried to receive the truth.

Are you ready to see?

The voice of the Spirit.

"To see what, Lord?"

You know.

"What my life would have truly been like if I'd kept Layne in the park that day?"

Yes.

No, he wasn't ready, but he never would be. "Though the truth slay me . . ."

Marcus breathed deep three times, once for each member of the Trinity, and lifted

467

his foot, which now felt as light as a butterfly rising off a daisy in the heart of summer.
Then another step, then another, then one
more, and he settled onto the grass at the
edge of the pool and let his feet slip into the
crystal waters.

Instantly the same sensation he'd felt
when his toes first touched the grass rocketed through his body, this time with so
much more intensity his body felt like it was
on fire, burning him with a hint of pain that
seemed to cleanse his body, mind, soul, and
spirit. He must have shut his eyes again
because he no longer saw the trees or the
grass or the moss or the sun cascading into
the glade like liquid, but instead he saw the
universe and other worlds and beings of
power and overwhelming light.

After moments or ages, the fire inside
faded along with the visions and Marcus
opened his eyes. The ripples on the surface
of the pool were fading and seconds later it
was glass again. He gazed at its surface
without hesitation and without fear, the
power of the Spirit surging through him,
giving him the strength and faith to endure
and press through whatever he was about to
see.

Freedom comes.

Slowly a jumble of colors formed on the

surface of the pool and began to form into thin shapes he could almost make out. They faded, replaced by other ethereal scenes of shapes flying and running that again vanished into the water without becoming clear. Over and over the hint of a face appeared, or a gathering of people, a woman, a man, a child, but none of them came into focus.

Each time it was as if a giant hand came and washed away the image before it could settle. And each time the colors and images were washed away, Marcus felt another wave of peace and another surge of freedom enter his heart till there was no fear, no regret, no worry about what was to come. The pool bubbled and churned and when it stopped, the sense of peace and contentment was overwhelming.

He was ready and he knew beyond a doubt that when the pool formed the next image, he would see what would have happened if he had chosen differently that day in the park with Layne.

Nothing came except a feeling of love that grew stronger. He waited, but the water only reflected his own image back to him. Marcus swished his foot through the water and watched the ripples build, then fade back into glass. It didn't make sense. Why wasn't Jesus showing him? There was nothing to see. Nothing to see. Nothing.

I have shown you, son of my heart.

Realization flooded over him as the implications of what he'd seen — or not seen — became clear. Was it possible? Was it true? His would-have-been life couldn't be shown because it didn't happen? The pain of what might have been had no hold over him unless he allowed it to. And the future was not set. Hope filled him as the truth washed over him again and again.

There is one more thing you must do.

"Yes, Lord?"

Offer forgiveness.

"To?" But Marcus didn't need to ask, and in an instant he forgave himself for the choice he'd made with Layne so many years before. Once again he was buried in tears, but this time they were ones of release and unrestrained freedom. Wave after wave of forgiveness engulfed him. After an age the Spirit spoke again.

It is time to go.

Marcus made his way back through the tunnel of trees, back through the garden, and up to the door of his memories that would lead him back to Tristan. As Marcus approached the door, his pace slowed. On the back of the door was carved a verse that shone like gold.

"Do not remember the past events, pay no attention to things of old. Look, I am about to do something new; even now it is coming. Do you not see it? Indeed, I will make a way in the wilderness, rivers in the desert." *Isaiah 43:18–19*

For a moment he was too stunned to move. Then Marcus ripped open the door and leaped from the top step to the grass, then tumbled and rolled like he was four years old again. Finally he rose to his feet, rushed to Tristan, and grabbed the angel as laughter poured from his mouth. When he released Tristan, Marcus stepped back and his breaths came in gasps.

"Marcus Amber, son of the King, the goal of the enemy was to make you live in the might-have-beens, to dwell on them till they destroyed you and those closest to you. But now you have been set free and have been given a choice going forward. To believe the Word of God and live in that freedom, or take up the chains from the past and wrap them around your heart."

Tristan peered deep into Marcus's eyes. "My suggestion is you choose to believe what God has said."

"I choose to believe." Marcus adjusted his glasses and frowned at Tristan. "The alternate realities. Were they real? Was my physical body truly there?"

"Your body truly was there, yes. But were they real? No. As you now know, they were only a life of lies created by the enemy to destroy you." Tristan squeezed Marcus's shoulder. "It is time to go."

"A question before we do."

"Of course."

"Simon."

Tristan smiled. "Yes, a good man."

"He's human?"

"Yes. But years ago he did not make the same choice you made on the cliffs with Zennon, nor did he make the same choice you did at the door of your memories." Tristan squeezed Marcus's shoulder again. "But all is not lost and the day of restoration for Simon is coming. You have not seen the last of him. He has helped you, and I believe in the weeks and months to come you will have the chance to help him in return."

"So be it." Marcus nodded. "I'm ready to leave."

"You're not curious as to where I'm to guide you next?"

"No." He smiled. "I am not."

"Where then?"

"Home," Marcus said. "To Kat."

He took Tristan's hand and the field and the door of his memories vanished.

FIFTY

Reece marched down the path toward the fire pit at Well Spring as if his eyes had been restored and Dana and Brandon followed. The midday sun radiating off the stones was almost blinding. This was it. Excitement, fear, and resolve all competed for Brandon's emotional attention. As the others settled in around the pit, Brandon built a fire. Once it burned bright and hot, Reece cleared his throat.

"I believe this will be the defining moment of each of our lives. It will be the moment we step into a battle we've been destined for since before we were born. If we are successful, the strike against the enemy will be catastrophic for him."

"Do you still believe we can succeed? Without the four of us together?" Dana asked.

"If we obey the Spirit's call to go in and allow him to take us where he wants us to go, we will have succeeded. Anything after that is a bonus." Reece held a hand toward each of them as if to give a blessing. "This is our destiny. He is for us. We will ride together. We will ride with strength." He lowered his hands. "Any comments before we go in?"

"Yeah, if we die in there . . ." Brandon slapped his legs. "No, forget it. I'll tell you when we get out."

"Tell us now," Dana said.

"Okay." Brandon shrugged and smiled. "Warriors Riding is the greatest thing that's ever happened to me." He looked at Dana and hoped his eyes conveyed a piece of what his heart felt and that his voice did the same for Reece.

"Me too," Dana said.

"I agree." Reece nodded. "Anything else?"

"I feel the Spirit saying time to go," Dana said.

"So be it." Reece extended his hands to Dana on one side, Brandon on the other. Brandon took his hand and extended his other to Dana. The instant his hand touched hers, Well Spring vanished and a moment later they stood on the edge of the field of doors where they'd first discovered Tristan's true identity. In front of them, not more than twenty yards away, lay the dark, pulsing ring of darkness that surrounded the entire field. The spirit of religion.

"What are you two getting?" Reece's penetrating blue eyes danced. It was clear the man was ready for battle.

Brandon rubbed his lower lip with his eyeteeth. "Strange as this might sound, I'm getting the impression we're supposed to go through the darkness and find out what's on the other side."

"Why strange?" Reece asked.

"Because if the black cloud is the spirit, wouldn't you think that's what we have to fight?"

"I'm not sure I know how to fight a cloud." Reece turned toward Dana. "Anything?"

"I think Brandon's right. We go through."

"So be it." Before the sound of Reece's words faded, a murky tunnel through the cloud opened up.

"This seems a little too easy," Brandon said.

Dana smiled at him. "It seems you've learned a lesson."

"Maybe."

Reece strode toward the tunnel. "Let's go." He walked toward the misty tunnel and reached it with three of his long strides. Two more and he vanished from sight. Dana went next, and then Brandon stepped into the swirling chaos.

The cloud grew thicker as he stepped farther in, and a sense of evil radiated off of it like heat. Tendrils reached out as if to grab him and pull him into the cloud, but they only flickered near his arms and legs. They never took hold. Seven steps later Brandon was out the other side, breathing heavy, but fine other than that.

Too easy, Brandon thought again. It made no sense. Why would the spirit want them to get through if it's where they were supposed to go? He joined the others who were both staring at the cloud they'd just exited. The tunnel was closed.

"Why did it let us through?" Brandon said.

"I don't know." Reece stared at the cloud for a long time before turning and gazing at their surroundings.

They stood on a dry, hard-packed dirt road beneath a reddish-gray sky. Vast drifts of undulating red sand stretched out for miles on either side of the road. The land held no trees, no plants. No birds flew overhead. The air was still. The heat blistering. There was no sound but the shuffle of their boots and shoes on the dirt.

Wait. A faint buzzing in front of and above them. Brandon looked up. Streaking down on them was a shadowy cloud of . . . he couldn't tell. Birds? No, far too small. Then the sound of thousands of tiny wings reached his ears as the cloud came close enough for him to see what it was.

Wasps, moving faster than he'd ever seen in the physical world.

Dana staggered back. "I'm not a fan of wasps."

"Brandon?" Reece focused his gaze on him and shouted over the roar of the insects. "Do you remember the orbs of fire you conjured up when we were inside Marcus's soul a year ago?"

"Yeah."

"I think now would be a good time to bring them back. And Dana, if you remember how to do them as well, all the better. I'd appreciate it if you'd greet our new friends with a few of them."

Brandon and Dana stretched out their arms and an instant later two white-hot balls of fire rested in each of their hands. Brandon slung his fireballs at the swarm and Dana threw hers an instant later. They exploded as they hit the front of the attack.

They followed the first four with four more and seconds later all that was left of the wasps was a thin black column of smoke that cleared a few seconds later.

"Nicely done."

"I'm guessing there are more assaults where that one came from," Dana said.

"Maybe, maybe not. Expect the unexpected is a wise attitude to cultivate."

"Sometimes you talk almost as weird as the professor," Brandon said.

"Thanks, I've been working on it," Reece said.

Just ahead of them the road sloped downward and grew level in a small valley. Then it rose, with multiple switchbacks as it climbed to the base of a cliff that shot two or three hundred feet almost straight up. On top of a column of dark red rock was a fortress.

Reece turned. "Does this look familiar?"

Brandon stared at the red sand, then to the fortress, then at the road. "Very."

"Do you two realize where we are?" Reece turned to Brandon and Dana and winked.

"Unbelievable," Brandon said. "We're in the professor's vision, aren't we? The one he had a year ago when we first went to Well Spring. Where he saw the four of us riding through that demonic cloud on horses, with Jesus in front, and then the cloud lifted and he was freeing people alongside the road, and then we got to a fortress and Jesus took the enemy down, threw him into an ancient-looking box and then the whole land broke out into grass and trees."

"It appears so."

"So maybe we know how this thing is going to play out?" Dana put her hands on her hips.

"Maybe? I don't like 'maybe,' " Brandon said.

Reece turned and strode down the road. "I think it's going to be more involved this time."

For the next half hour they hiked toward the fortress in silence. Nothing more attacked them, but it gave Brandon no comfort. It only meant something else more ominous was coming their way.

Finally they crested the top of the last switchback and found themselves in a large courtyard of black stone. The air grew cooler as the sound of their shoes against the stones echoed off the castle walls. The pungent odor of rotting vegetation filled the air.

Brandon coughed out a laugh. "This is too cliché. Cue the creepy music and get a vampire to walk out the front door, or Dr. Frankenstein's monster, or a crew of one hundred zombies, or the Hunchback of —"

"We get it, Brandon," Dana said.

Reece looked behind them, then at the

archway of the entrance to the fortress. "Are either of you getting anything from the Spirit?"

Dana and Brandon shook their heads. Reece stood and alternated between staring at them and the long corridor in front of them. "Neither am I. I have no direction on what we're to do."

Dana looked at Reece, then Brandon. "We go on." She walked through the archway and down the long corridor, Brandon and Reece on her heels.

The Leader leading once again. Brandon would probably follow her anywhere. The passageway led them to a door, a mass of dark planks bound together at the top and bottom to rough two-by-sixes, three spikes pounded through each piece of wood. Dana reached up, hands steady, placed her palms on the gnarled wood, then turned back to Reece.

"Barricaded?" Reece asked.

Dana shook her head. "I'm guessing the Wolf has been waiting for us to arrive and wouldn't feel the need to keep us from getting in even if they didn't know we were coming. We are the flies here, not the spider."

"No, Dana." Reece glanced at Brandon, then back to her. "That's exactly what they want us to think. But think back to what happened at the end of Marcus's vision. In the place we now stand, Jesus defeated Satan with no more effort than flicking a crumb of bread off a table."

"But we're not Jesus."

"Yet he lives inside us and we sit with him at the right hand of the Father with all power and authority."

"Good," Brandon said. " 'Cause I have a feeling we're gonna need it."

Dana pushed on the door and it swung open without a sound.

FIFTY-ONE

Did he have to tell her? Of course. But it didn't mean he had the desire to.

Marcus stood in his kitchen and stared through the window at Kat, who sat on their deck in the backyard, head back, eyes closed, listening to music, the late morning sun on her face. The weight of regret over what had happened to Layne had vanished, and forgiveness filled the place of pain, but there was no way to know how Kat would react when he told her what he'd done.

No, Zennon's illusions were not the truth, but that didn't mean the outcome would be positive.

He slid open the screen door in the kitchen, eased onto the deck, and sat in a chair across from her.

She opened her eyes, waved at him, then closed them again. "When Doug called and said you and the other Warriors were going to have a late night, I didn't think he meant this late. It's almost noon."

"He called you?"

"Last night and again this morning. He wanted me to know you were okay." Kat sat up and opened her eyes again. "Are you okay?"

"Fine." Marcus stared at the cherry tree to the right of the house as if it could give him an idea of how to start, what he would say in the middle, and what he would say at the end. Just like a good teacher should do. Work out the lecture in his mind first. Then imagine giving it with confidence and clarity. Then deliver what he'd already practiced with perfection in his head.

But this wasn't class, Kat wasn't one of his students, and the only test was how she would react. "I thought you were working at the bakery today."

"I took the day off. I had a feeling I should. Was I right?"

"Yes, you were." It felt like he was sputtering out chunks of concrete. "I have to tell you something."

"What?" Kat pulled her earbuds out.

"I have to tell you some—"

"I heard you." She pulled her legs up so her feet rested on the edge of the chair and she wrapped her arms around them tight. "I meant what is it?"

"I don't know how to begin this. The words are having difficulty emerging from my mouth." His pulse felt like it was topping out at 180 beats per minute and cold sweat eked out along his forehead.

"Begin anywhere."

"I don't want to hurt us." Marcus sighed. "I don't want to lose everything we are."

Kat's face turned pale and then her eyes narrowed as if she suspected what he was about to say. But how could she know what he'd done?

"This is the secret the demon spoke of that night at dinner."

Marcus nodded and stared at the trees along the back edge of their property as they swayed in the breeze. He stopped and gripped his knees with the tips of his fingers. He was near the edge of the waterfall now. The air seemed too thin and Marcus had trouble breathing. He braced himself for what was about to be unleashed on her, then unleashed on him, then them. It didn't matter. It was the truth. *Jesus, let there be freedom in it.*

"I made a poor choice. The most devastating of my life. And I'm terrified to tell you because I know what will happen if I do. I've seen it — and I can't live with that — but I can't not tell you."

She slipped on her sunglasses even though it was growing dark and pulled her legs in tighter. "If you tell me you had an affair, I won't believe you."

Marcus squeezed his eyes shut. "No, in some ways having an affair would be easier."

Kat went silent and when she spoke it was only two words. "Tell me."

Then he was over the edge of the waterfall hurtling down, the speed increasing as the words of what he'd done poured out of him. Kat's mouth didn't move, nor did her chin or her head or her hands or her body. When he finished, Marcus dragged his hands slowly over his head and slumped back in his chair.

A minute passed. Then another. Kat said nothing.

"Please forgive me. Can you? Is that desire of mine even remotely attainable?"

Still his wife didn't speak, the only sound her slow, steady breathing.

"Please . . ." The word was barely above a whisper. "Talk to me. Say something, anything."

She nodded but remained silent. Kat sighed, let go of her legs, and shifted so she sat crisscrossed. She gazed toward their home, then out over the lawn, then back to Marcus.

"It's stunning," Kat said, then lapsed back into silence.

"What is?"

"How long you've carried this and how effectively the enemy has used it to ravage your soul."

"I don't understand. What do you — ?"

Kat held her finger up to her lips. "As brilliant as you are at most times, your mind and heart have been blinded."

"I don't —"

"Let me speak." Kat took his hands in hers. "Do you not have any understanding of the heart of a mother? I heard that voice in my mind from the moment Layne was born. I heard it when Abbie and Jayla were born, and it has never stopped whispering in my ear.

"I hear it now in almost every moment of every day. I second-guess myself. Don't let Abbie play soccer, she could be badly hurt. Don't let Jayla do gymnastics — she's too young. Don't let them ski or ice skate, or even go to a friend's house for an overnight stay."

Kat squeezed his hands tighter. "Do you remember what I went through the first time Abbie went to summer camp? I was certain a canoe would tip over and there wouldn't be a lifeguard there in time. Do you remember the first time each of the girls got on the school bus?"

Kat swung her legs down onto the patio and pulled Marcus closer. "Every time I say good-bye to the girls, I wonder if it's for the last time. You don't know, you don't know." She laughed. "If I'd listened to that voice every time it said to keep them from going somewhere or doing something with the slightest hint of danger, they'd have never left the house."

"But it doesn't change the fact I let him go for that ride. It doesn't change the fact I was so consumed with my presentation, I . . . wanted him to go." Fresh tears spilled onto Marcus's cheeks. "Do you understand what I'm saying? I wanted him to go."

"Yes, you did. But that doesn't change anything. The enemy has used that lie against you for the last time. Yes, maybe you wouldn't have let him go if you'd been more focused on the moment. Maybe. But would you have saved him that time and lost him the next? Our lives are in God's hands, our hours on this earth are his alone to hold. I'm not going to live my life with regrets because I said yes to my children living life."

"Still I . . ."

"Yes, you let him ride. Yes, I miss him horribly. It's rare for two days to go by without my crying about it during moments alone that you never see. And yes, this time of the year it grows far worse and I wonder how I'll get through the days before and after the anniversary. But that pain has nothing to do with the guilt the enemy has thrown on you.

"For you to have carried this burden all these years makes me so sad. And angry. Such a lie from the pit of hell. Why didn't you talk to me about this years ago?"

Marcus rubbed his face. "It took so much out of you when it happened, and I was afraid if I ever told you, you would . . . leave."

Tears spilled onto Kat's cheeks. "Hear me when I say this, Marcus." She waited till he held her gaze and when she spoke the words came slowly. "I would have done the same thing. Hear me again. I would have let Layne go too."

Marcus sighed and pulled her into his chest and his tears mixed with hers. Neither spoke for a long time.

"You have to let it go." Kat leaned forward and planted her elbows on her knees. "Now listen to me. Hear my words and hear my heart. I mean every word: I forgive you, Marcus. I forgive you utterly and completely even though there is nothing and never has been anything to forgive. It's gone. Don't let it ever sink its claws into you again. Do you hear me?"

Marcus stared at her, tears again coming to his eyes. What was wrong with him? He'd cried more in the past eight hours than he'd cried in the past eight months. Finally he lifted her head and kissed her. "Freedom."

She smiled, the tears glistening on her cheeks making her more beautiful than ever. "Yes. It's what he does."

FIFTY-TWO

Dana, Reece, and Brandon stepped through the curved doorway in the fortress and stopped just inside. Before them lay a long hallway with a low ceiling that ran for sixty yards before ending in front of a heavy blue curtain. They eased down the hallway and stopped in front of the curtain.

"Go on?" Brandon said.

Dana glanced at him. Of course they would go on. They didn't come this far to stop now. She pushed through the plush curtain and the others followed. Ten feet ahead was another curtain — wispy, that looked like it was made of a lace that had faded long ago. They stepped through it into a huge circular room twenty yards across. It towered above them so high, the ceiling faded into dimness. The floor of the room was made of green marble, the walls of a light wood, ash or maple.

In the exact center of the room sat a

young-looking boy — nine, ten at the most — on an ivory chair. Thin blond hair framed a peaceful face. The boy wore dark jeans and a light blue T-shirt with a picture of an eagle on it. His feet were bare. He sat so still Dana couldn't tell if he was alive or a statue.

When they got to within ten feet of the boy, he turned. "Hello." His smile was innocent and full of wonder. "Finally you're here, but where is Marcus?"

Reece took a step in front of Dana and Brandon. "We know what you are."

"No, you don't, but that's okay. It really is. All will be made clear, all will be revealed very soon." He gazed at them with placid green eyes.

"You are the Wolf."

"No." The boy giggled. "It's so much better than you could have imagined. There will be a tiny bit of discomfort, but that is all. The rest will be so very, very good. Are you ready?"

Before the boy finished speaking, he and the stone walls around them faded. The floor under their feet turned from stone to soft grass. They stood on a wide hill that sloped down to a valley filled with cypress trees. Above them was an almost-cloudless blue sky and the air had a feeling of late spring and unbridled joy. Worry slipped off Dana like a lead coat falling to the ground.

"Wow." Brandon spun in a slow circle. "I'm having a hard time not liking it here. Are you guys feeling this?"

"Be careful. Stay alert," Reece said.

"Any idea what we do next?"

The big man answered by pointing to the end of the valley on their right. Dana squinted and saw a tiny cloud of dust rising and then the cause. A rider on a white horse streaked their way faster than would have been possible on earth.

"The Wolf cometh?" Brandon said.

"I'm not getting any sense of evil." Reece turned to Dana. "You?"

"*Triumph* is the word that comes to mind."

"Brandon?"

"Same."

They stood, each of them like stone, and watched the rider flash toward them. In seconds he reached the bottom of the hill. The garb of the man matched the color of his horse. His body was wrapped in a white cloak except for a dark crimson stain along the bottom. In one hand he held the reins of his horse. In the other he held a sword. A thin gold crown encircled his head.

It couldn't be. Brandon was the first one to say it, but Dana was thinking it. Reece had to be as well.

"Straight out of Rev," Brandon said. " 'I looked, and there before me was a white horse! Its rider held a bow, and he was given a crown, and he rode out as a conqueror bent on conquest.' "

"Is it possible?" Dana stared in astonishment.

Reece voiced her next thought. " 'I saw heaven standing open and there before me was a white horse, whose rider is called Faithful and True. With justice he judges and wages war. His eyes are like blazing fire . . . He is dressed in a robe dipped in blood, and his name is the Word of God.' "

An instant later the ground shook as the thundering hooves of the horse dug into the ground ten feet from them, and the rider pulled the stallion back onto two legs as a loud whinny erupted from its throat.

The rider brought his horse back to four hooves and trotted back and forth twice before coming to a stop. The apostle had it right with the blazing-eyes thing.

"Lord." Dana stared at the rider. The word came out as a statement, but in her mind it was a question. It made no sense. How could it be him? This was the lair of the Wolf. The arena in the heavens where they had been led to face him in battle.

The rider grinned as he glanced at all of them and opened his arms wide. "You have all fought so well and so long. Well done, my faithful servants."

"Who are you?" Reece's voice was tight. Controlled. No fear.

"Search your heart, Reece." The rider slid from his horse and stood next to it. "You know it is I."

"Prove it."

"You are right to be cautious, alert, testing the spirits, but the time for rest is upon you." The rider . . . the Lord? Was it truly him? "Come, let me show you something."

He walked to the opposite side of the hill and they followed him but kept a healthy distance between them. The rider pointed toward the horizon. A speck of darkness far away, almost too distant to see, spread across the vast plain. Gold, red, and silver light flashed against the clouds like machine-gun fire.

"There the battle against the kingdom rages, a war with the spirit of religion and all the other members of the demonic host. Its fires will never go out till I come again to earth to bring my beloved bride home, but let us not speak of that for the moment. Yes, you have come to the lair of the Wolf, but it is out there." He pointed again toward the horizon. "Not here." He turned and smiled at them again. "It is so good to see you."

Reece glanced at Brandon and her. "No closer than ten yards till we know if it is really him."

The rider held out his nail-scarred hands. " 'Come to Me, all who are weary and heavy-laden, and I will give you rest.' "

Reece's head moved side to side as if he were studying one of M. C. Escher's drawings and couldn't reconcile how a staircase could keep going up indefinitely. Confusion and joy wrestled on his face. "The Spirit brought us here to engage the Wolf, the spirit of religion."

"Are you sure of that, Reece?" The rider shook his head. "No, I brought you here to explain that you have already battled the Wolf — the spirit of religion — many times and you will continue to wage war against him for years to come."

"If that's true, then explain it."

"With great joy I will, for you all have done well." Laughter swept through Jesus' eyes. "Yes, the Wolf — the spirit of religion — has risen, but don't you see? For the past year you have advanced the kingdom in significant ways. With each soul you go into and set free, you have brought war against the Wolf and weakened his kingdom. With every four-day session of training you do at Well Spring, you damage the enemy more and advance the cause of freedom."

The rider stroked his horse with a strong hand. "The ones you've trained have taken the message of freedom back to their friends, their families, their churches. Think of the e-mails you receive! The phone calls. The cards. The stories of breakthrough and healing and victory over religion and rote traditions. Think of the fruit that is being produced." Jesus raised his arms to his sides. "Don't you see it? What the Father is doing?"

Reece glanced at Brandon and her, but only for an instant, then turned his gaze back to Jesus. "Talk to me, Song. What are you sensing?"

"Relief. I was so geared up for this massive battle with this religious spirit — whatever that was." Brandon snorted out a laugh. "Actually I wasn't geared up. I was exhausted after rescuing Marcus. I have to say this is totally unexpected, but so glorious." He let his head fall backward and he closed his eyes. "Accept the gift of this moment."

Reece's body language softened. "I'm starting to agree. But we have to be sure."

He turned to Dana. "Leader?"

What the rider said made sense. And how could she deny his words? She'd never heard Zennon talk like this. It would be so good to rest. To let go. But a small part of her wasn't convinced. "Why the big buildup? Why take us through the dark cloud? Why set us on the road that was in Marcus's vision and lead us to the fortress that he saw? Why not simply bring us here first?"

"Don't you understand, child? Don't you remember the end of Marcus's vision? In it, I defeated Satan. I locked him in the chest and tossed the chest into a crack in the ground so small human eyes would not be able to see it. But you only *heard* about Marcus's vision. And even he only went so far as to watch my victory from a great distance. I wanted you to experience the victory, step into it yourselves, and celebrate here with me rather than just being told about it. Think about what stirred inside you as I streaked toward you just now down in the valley below. Think of the joy and triumph you felt when you knew it was me! I wanted you to know that feeling because you have earned it."

Dana stared at Reece's face. It was full of peace and adoration. Brandon looked the same. So what was wrong with her? Why did doubts still swirl around her like a swarm of mosquitoes?

"Why haven't you restored Reece's eyesight?"

He smiled with compassion. "Oh, Dana, let your doubts slip away. Have you not understood yet what it says in Isaiah? How my ways are higher than yours and there is purpose in all of them?" He turned to Reece. "How often do I answer you in the way you do not expect?" He turned back to Dana. "Yes, the answer will come for Reece, and I will do what is to be done, but in my way, my timing, and in my wisdom."

"So that's the only reason you brought us here?" She narrowed her eyes. "So we could feel the victory?"

"Ah yes, now we come to it. Good for you, Dana. You've seen there is another reason we must speak of." The Lord's face turned somber. "A father disciplines and instructs every son and daughter he loves. And since you have done so much for the kingdom and sacrificed so much, I desired to bring you here to talk face-to-face about the areas in which you have grown weak."

"What areas?" Reece frowned, his face like a little boy who is told there are no presents for his birthday.

"You have opened the door of freedom to many, Reece. All of you have. But without care of the hinges, care of the foundation, care of the frame that holds the door, the door will tumble — and crush many with its fall."

"I don't understand."

"This might be hard to bear, but he who has ears, let him hear." Jesus glanced at Brandon and her, then back to Reece. "Carson Tanner is not your enemy."

What? Dana's mind felt thick. Slow. How could Carson not be their enemy? It was what the Spirit had shown them. His mission was to destroy the Warriors Riding. He'd shown that when Brandon was on air.

"He is not the Wolf, Dana." Jesus focused his gaze on her. "He is a good man, one of my beloved servants, trying to bring truth to the world. Is he mistaken in areas? Yes. Just as you are. Has he taken things too far? Yes. Did he take them too far with you, Brandon? You know that to be true. Does he have areas to grow in and areas where he needs to be reined in? Yes. But much of what he says is truth."

Reece blinked as if to throw off the bewilderment that must be in his mind as much or more than it was in hers.

"I understand your thoughts and your

500

confusion. Why would Carson tear into the powerful work you've been doing at Well Spring? Exactly because it is so powerful. It is changing lives, Reece. But you've gone too far. Understand and accept that I used Carson to bring you to this place. I placed the idea in your mind that he was the Wolf so you would engage him and bring you here to this very moment so the wheat and the chaff of your lives could be separated. You would not have heard it otherwise. Although this might sound difficult, I want you to forgive what he has done to you and become his friend. Come alongside him and help him grow when he needs growth. And allow him to help you grow where you need growth. Together you can be a powerful force for the kingdom."

Jesus strolled back and forth in front of them. "You speak of freedom, my Warriors Riding, but where do you speak of the disciplines? Of fasting? Of solitude? Of regular gatherings of believers? Of memorizing Scripture? Of study?"

Reece shook his head. "We do speak of all those things. That's part of the training we take people through."

"Yes, but not enough. Your emphasis on freedom can lead people astray, and it has done so in some cases." Jesus opened his arms. "That is the reason I brought you here. To lend correction to your path, to strengthen you, to sharpen you, to make you more powerful for my kingdom than ever before. Will you come?"

Dana stared at the faces of the Temple and the Song. They each held a tinge of sorrow. As if Jesus' words had cut them because they knew the words were true. What was the expression on her own face? Undoubtedly confusion but she wasn't buying what this Jesus was selling. Something was off.

"Are you ready to be restored? Refreshed?" Reece and Brandon gave a slow nod. Jesus turned to her. "Are you ready to enter my rest, Dana?" He beckoned all of them. "Come, take my hands."

"Wait." Dana held her arms out as if to block Reece and Brandon from stepping forward.

"You have warred so hard, Dana. You have led so well. But it is time to rest. There is so much more to be done, and you shall do it, but for now it is time for reprieve and refreshment." Jesus reached out his arms. "Take hold, and I will take you to a place of respite. Come. Enter into my rest."

"No." Dana shook her head and drew her hands into fists. "I don't believe you are who you say you are."

"Why do you think this, Dana? What is your evidence? What can you point to that proves who I say I am is not true?"

There was nothing she could point to. Every fiber in her said this was Jesus. Every fiber but one. A fiber buried so deep in her spirit, she barely felt it. As if she were in darkness and it was the light of a candle a mile away. "I just know it. I feel it."

"Feelings are not truth, Dana. They are emotions only and emotions are not reality." The rider stepped toward her. "Do I speak in the style of our enemy? Do I look like him? Is there anything I've said that is not true? How would you have me prove myself to you?"

"I don't know."

"But I do. You can choose to doubt. It's all right." He smiled. "But come with me now and enter into the place I have created for the three of you, and then you will not be able to deny who I Am and your doubts will vanish in the warm breeze of that land." He reached out his hand. "Come."

"What if I refuse?"

Sadness spilled onto his face. "Then you will stay here and I will take the others, and when they return they will tell you of an ecstasy you will long for the rest of your days but will not experience till you join me for eternity in heaven." The rider had been talking softly, but now his voice grew loud. "Enough. We must go." He stared at her, his eyes kind but intense.

"Are you coming with the others, daughter?"

FIFTY-THREE

Marcus held Kat for a few more seconds, then pulled back to arm's length. "There's someone I'd like you to meet."

"What? Now?" Kat glanced around their backyard. "Someone is here?"

"Yes. They've been —"

"They've been here during our whole conversation? Where?"

"In the front yard but not listening. You'll understand when you meet him."

"I'd better." She cocked her head, a wry smile on her face.

Marcus turned and called out, "Tristan!"

The angel strode around the corner of the house a few seconds later, his grin as wide as Marcus had ever seen it.

"You?" Kat stared at him, mouth open.

Marcus glanced back and forth between Kat and Tristan. "You know him? How is that poss— ?"

"Hello, Kat, it's good to see you."

"Hello, Tristan." She stared at him as her eyes twinkled. "Yes, I know him. We've met once before."

Tristan gave a nod of his head. "This is true."

"Care to enlighten me?" Marcus said.

"On the street, in Seattle's University District. You were the one who saved Jayla almost a year ago from being run over by the car."

"Unbelievable. Utterly unbelievable," Marcus muttered.

"Yes. I'm sorry we didn't have longer to talk that day. It wasn't time."

"I understand." She smiled. "I'm guessing you've taken my husband on some interesting adventures as of late."

"Indeed I have," Tristan said.

"Daddy?"

Marcus turned. Abbie stood in the doorway leading onto the deck. She hesitated, stepped forward, then ran toward him. She threw her arms around him and buried her head in his chest.

"Hi, Abbie girl."

"I'm glad you're okay."

"Why wouldn't I be?"

"I don't know." She lifted her head. "I prayed for you through the night last night."

"You did?"

"I don't know why. I couldn't sleep and I just felt like I was supposed to." She snuggled back into his chest. "Like you did for me with . . . the other day when . . . at dinner, you know? You fought for me. I felt like I needed to fight for you."

"You fought well, Abbs." Marcus blinked back tears as he squeezed Abbie tighter. "Really, really well."

"You all have." Tristan looked at Marcus, then Kat, and then Abbie. "But the fight is not over. I'm sorry to pull your husband from you and your father from you again so soon, but he is desperately needed a little longer." The angel held out his arm. "Take my hand, Professor. You're due on the radio in five minutes. I wouldn't want you to be late."

"What? I'm due where?"

"You're about to appear on *The Carson Tanner Show*. I believe you are more than ready."

The air swirled and an instant later Marcus stood in a hallway that led to a thick gray door. Over the top of it was a red sign, lit up with the words *On the Air.*

Marcus stared at the door seven paces in front of them. "Carson's studio."

"Of course."

"He has no idea I'm here."

"No, that would ruin the surprise." Tristan smiled. "But have no doubt as soon as he sees you he'll be more than willing to scrap his intended show and welcome you on the air as his special guest."

They walked toward the door.

"Hey!" A voice rang out behind them. "You can't go in there."

Marcus turned to find a slender woman twenty paces back striding toward them.

"I'm guessing you're Sooz," Marcus said.

"Yeah, who are you?"

"Marcus Amber, one of the Warriors Riding."

Surprise splashed on Sooz's face, replaced quickly by a gleam in her eyes that shouted, *This is going to be very, very good.*

"A pleasure to meet you, Professor." She pointed over his shoulder toward the studio door. "I'm thinking you'd like to be a special surprise guest on Carson's show."

"If he can squeeze me in."

"I'm almost certain that can be arranged. Do you mind if I let Carson know you're here?" She slid by them on the right and stopped.

"Not at all."

Sooz fixed her gaze on the sign above the door, apparently waiting for it to go off. The three stood not moving, the silence growing awkward. Sooz glanced back at Tristan, then at Marcus. "Who is your friend here?"

"A friend."

"I see."

Sooz opened her mouth, probably to press for a more complete answer, but before she could, the red light above the door went off. "Stay here." She opened the studio door and stepped through.

Tristan put his hand on Marcus's shoulder. "You're about to walk through another door, Marcus Amber. A different kind, but still one that will change you as your door of memories did. Are you ready?" Tristan smiled at him and it filled Marcus with hope and power.

A moment later Carson Tanner strode through his studio door, light laughter filling the hallway. "Wow! Talk about slapping a surprise on my forehead like a God Bless You tattoo. It's good to meet you, Professor, and I hope" — he motioned behind him — "to have you on my show. What do you say?"

"I gratefully accept your invitation."

"No, no, no." Carson waved his hands. "The gratitude is mine. Shall we?"

Forty-five seconds later Marcus sat across from Carson, a pair of headphones on his

509

head, his mind racing, his heart pumping. To his right and behind him, leaning against the wall, stood Tristan. "Are you sure you want to be here, Professor Amber? We're on the air in thirty seconds."

"Why do you ask?"

"Love the sinner, hate the sin. Or put another way, I'm guessing you heard my interview with your buddy Brandon."

"I did."

"In an attitude of truth, since that's what we're all about here, I need to tell you this won't go well for you." Carson grinned. "You still want to go on?"

Marcus didn't answer and adjusted his headphones.

"I'll take that as a yes." Carson kept grinning as he pushed his mic button. "Shake it, bake it, but there's no way we'll take it." Carson shifted his weight back and forth on his chair like he was trying to dance sitting down and the microphone was his partner. "Take what? Lies. No thank you, we don't want 'em! On *The Carson Tanner Show* we're all about truth, and right now I have a very special guest in the studio who might be tempted to tell you mixed truth that isn't truth at all. Just warning you. Keep your minds sharp 'cause we've got with us right now in the studio one of the brightest minds in the country — professor of physics at the University of Washington, Marcus Amber! Welcome, Professor."

"Thank you."

"Folks, just to remind you, we've been talking about this cult-like group called Warriors Riding that Brandon Scott got himself caught up in. That they're spreading their heresy all over the country with their training, and the Lord has told us to do our part in stopping it. Did you catch my interview with Brandon where we exposed the lies? Worth listening to."

Carson grinned and pointed at Marcus. "The professor here is part of the leadership of this group, and I had no idea till three — yeah, three minutes ago we were going to get the chance to talk to him. So let's get to it, Professor. What are you doing here?"

Marcus stared at Carson. It was an excellent question. Why was he here? Tristan obviously knew, but there hadn't been time to ask the angel what the purpose was in bringing him onto the show. He opened his mouth to confess to Carson he didn't know, but the words that spilled out were not an admittance of ignorance.

"I'm here to speak to you about truth and confront the lies of the spirit that have been controlling you. I'm here to talk about true freedom."

"Controlling me? Yeah, baby! That's what I'm talking about." Carson slapped his chair. "See why this stuff these Warriors are spouting about is so deceptive? Didn't the professor sound sincere?" He pointed at Marcus. "Okay, Professor, let's get right to it. What's the truth you think I'm missing?"

Again Marcus didn't have the words, and again he opened his mouth and spoke, his gaze fixed on Carson's eyes. " 'You foolish Galatians! Who has bewitched you? Before your very eyes Jesus Christ was clearly portrayed as crucified. I would like to learn just one thing from you: Did you receive the Spirit by the works of the law, or by believing what you heard?' "

"Professor? You okay?" Carson whipped his head back and forth. "No Galatians in the studio here, and not thinking we have too many, if any among our fifteen million listeners. Want to try again?"

Marcus leaned forward. "Carson, 'Are you so foolish? After beginning with the Spirit, are you now trying to attain your goal by human effort? Have you suffered so much for nothing — if it really was for nothing? Does God give you his Spirit and work miracles among you because you observe

512

the law, or because you believe what you heard?' "

Carson blinked and a look of confusion flitted across his face. "We're not trying to attain anything by our own effort, Prof. We're simply trying to show people what a righteous lifestyle looks like. We're giving Christians a set of standards they can aspire to live up to every day."

" 'Christ has set us free to live a free life. So take your stand! Never again let anyone put a harness of slavery on you. I am emphatic about this. The moment any one of you submits to circumcision or any other rule-keeping system, at that same moment Christ's hard-won gift of freedom is squandered.' "

Again a look of puzzlement appeared on Carson's face and it stayed longer this time. "We're not promoting a rule-keeping system. And we're not talking about whether Christians should have their baby boys circumcised or not. What does circumcision have to do with — ?"

" 'I repeat my warning: The person who accepts the ways of circumcision trades all the advantages of the free life in Christ for the obligations of the slave life of the law.' "

A thick sheen of sweat appeared on Carson's forehead and he struggled to speak.

"Professor, I don't know where you're going with this circumcision thing, but my ministry was founded on the idea of drawing people deeper into Christ. Showing them how to walk the path."

Carson gripped the armrests of his chair. "My Redemptive Reminders are in churches and homes all across America. People memorize them and use them to lead their families and congregations."

" 'Why don't you choose to be led by the Spirit and so escape the erratic compulsions of a law-dominated existence?' "

Marcus stood and took a step toward Carson. " 'I suspect you would never intend this, but this is what happens. When you attempt to live by your own religious plans and projects, you are cut off from Christ, you fall out of grace.' "

"I'm in his grace, don't try to tell me I'm not." Carson wiped the perspiration off his forehead. "Without religion, Christianity gets out of control. Read Corinthians. They went nuts. Religion is to be regarded, respected, and revered."

Marcus took another step toward the radio show host, the cord of his headphones stretching to its full length. " 'In Christ, neither our most conscientious religion nor disregard of religion amounts to anything.

What matters is something far more interior: faith expressed in love.' "

Marcus blinked. A translucent curtain of darkness appeared and seemed to surround Carson as if he were inside a cocoon. It shuddered every few seconds as if being struck by a hammer.

"I have faith. I have love. I started this show with nothing, no one believed it would happen. No one. I've brought people stability. Guidelines. Principles. Challenges. They need it! They want it. Maybe some people don't like it, but it's the truth! And it will make people more moral, more righteous; it will purify their hearts. It will make them holy."

Marcus spoke in a whisper. " 'Legalism is helpless in bringing this about; it only gets in the way.' "

The look now etched into Carson's face said he no longer believed what he just said was the truth, but he was holding on to it like a man drowning. "They need an ideology they can apply to their lives and their kids' lives. Rules are not a bad thing!"

The words poured from Marcus's mouth with power. " 'For everything we know about God's Word is summed up in a single sentence: Love others as you love yourself. That's an act of true freedom. If you bite and ravage each other, watch out — in no time at all you will be annihilating each other, and where will your precious freedom be then?' "

The curtain around Carson shattered as if made of glass and the shards floated to the floor. Carson's eyes went wide and his breaths came quicker. "I'm doing a good work here, Professor. I'm not trying to divide people. We're changing lives. How do I know? Nearly fifteen million listeners tell me I am."

"I believe you, Carson. From what I've heard, 'you were running superbly. Who cut in on you, deflecting you from the true course of obedience? This detour doesn't come from the One who called you into the race in the first place. And please don't toss this off as insignificant. It only takes a minute amount of yeast, you know, to permeate an entire loaf of bread. Deep down, the Master has given me confidence that you will not defect. But the one who is upsetting you, whoever he is, will bear the divine judgment.' "

Carson's face went blank. He opened his mouth to speak three times, and three times he stopped. Five seconds passed. Ten. Twenty. Marcus prayed the power of the Spirit down on the room, but he didn't need to. The hold of the enemy had been shattered.

The dull sound of a fist pounding on glass floated toward them. Marcus turned. Sooz jabbed her finger at Carson's microphone and mouthed the words, *Get him back on the air!*

Marcus turned back toward Carson, the host's eyes desperate, pleading.

"I want to be free."

Marcus grinned and finished the passage from Galatians. " 'It is absolutely clear that God has called you to a free life.' "

He turned and looked at Tristan. "I feel what the Spirit just accomplished has ramifications far beyond this studio."

"You have no idea how accurate you are, Professor." Tristan gripped Marcus's arm. "I have to go, but I'll be back soon. Wait here, yes?" The angel inclined his head toward Carson and smiled. "I think you'll find a friend to occupy your time till I return."

FIFTY-FOUR

The rider smiled, took another step toward Dana, and repeated his question. "Are you coming with the other Warriors, daughter? Or will you stay here while they enter my rest?"

In the next moment three things happened in Dana's brain simultaneously. First, an image of the professor flashed into her mind. *Marcus, where are you?* He was talking into a microphone in some kind of studio with a man sitting near him. Carson Tanner? But somehow she knew the professor wasn't having a conversation. He was quoting Scripture. As the image intensified, a dark curtain surrounding him shattered into a million pieces, and the room the professor sat in filled with light.

Second, the words *confusion* and *deception* were plastered in brilliant white letters against a cloud of darkness. Third, she saw a picture of Jesus standing on a hill just like the one the three of them stood on now. More real, with more glory and power than the false Jesus in front of them could ever display. His words came in a whisper but also as loud as thunder. *Stay strong, Dana. For all of you.*

Peace and power flooded her. Whatever war the professor was waging in the physical realm had just saved them here.

"No!" She pointed her finger at the rider and took a step toward him.

"What is wrong with you?" Brandon grabbed her shoulders. "This is more than we could ever have hoped for."

"No." She bent over and pressed her temples as if to stop the migraine that had flared up seconds earlier. "He's not who he preten—"

"Be quiet, Dana!" She yanked her head up as the rider drilled her with his gaze. His eyes flashed dark for a nanosecond, then returned to light brown, full of life and joy. "Do not quench the Holy Spirit. I am giving you a gift. Do not neglect it. Do not refuse what you desperately need.

"The pain in your head is from the enemy, trying to distract and deceive you." The pretender motioned toward her head and the migraine vanished. "I long to bring you rest and healing, yet I will always give you a choice, even in this. You can turn from this now if you want and I will take Reece and Brandon without you. But I pray you do not. The Spirit desires to do a great work in all of you."

"Let's go, Dana." Brandon took her hand. "It's okay. Didn't he just heal you?"

"Yes." She rubbed her temple again. "But it's not him —"

"What more do you need to see? Let your doubt go. We need this. You need this."

She stepped back and pulled her hand from Brandon's. "I want you to do something for me."

"Sure." He gazed into her eyes and she looked back through the twin windows into his soul. His heart for her had never been this deep. "Anything."

"Be the Song."

"I am the —"

"Sing like you've never sung before. To Jesus. Not to this . . . this . . ." She pointed to the rider. "Close your eyes and sing to the Alpha and Omega with everything you are."

"Now? Right now? Even though my vocal cords aren't all the way back?" He grinned.

"Since we're in the spirit here, not in body, I think you'll sound wonderful." She returned his smile. "And even if you don't,

I think it's about the heart behind the song, not how it sounds."

"I'm sorry." The rider shook his head. "There isn't time for Brandon to sing, Dana. Later, yes, we'll let the song of the Song echo through the heavens. But not now. If you want this gift, we must go."

"There is always time to bring adoration to the King. Always time to praise the one who holds eternity in the palm of his hand."

"So true, my friend." The rider opened his arms and smiled. "I welcome your song, Brandon. Then we will go."

"Sing, Brandon." Dana fixed her gaze on the rider. Maybe Reece and Brandon and this Jesus were right and the enemy was trying to pull her away. But more of her knew it was a lie.

Stay strong, Dana. For all of you. The words echoed in her mind again.

Brandon's song started soft and built, the melody strong and haunting.

Look.

The voice of the Spirit filled her heart and mind, and she intensified her focus on the rider. His arms were raised to the heavens and tears ran down his cheeks. His mouth moved silently along with Brandon's words. Despair flooded her. Was the vision she'd just seen of Marcus a lie? Was the rider who he claimed to be? Wait. Darkness shimmered across his chest so fast, she couldn't be sure if she'd seen it or imagined it.

The song ended and she grabbed Brandon by the collar. "Tell me you saw that!"

"Saw what? I was sing—"

"Reece?" She whirled toward the big man and clenched her fists. "Did you?"

"No." Reece shook his head and looked at Dana. "Brandon is right. Let go of your doubts and fears. It is time to go with him."

"Are you satisfied, Dana?" The rider smiled at her as his eyes danced like joy-filled lightning. There is so much I want to show you! Why did you doubt?"

Dana's legs shook. From fear? From adrenaline? She couldn't tell and didn't care. She knew what she'd seen, and yes, she doubted it. But if she cried out and was wrong, there would be forgiveness from the Lord. If she was right . . . *Jesus, if this isn't you . . .*

Speak truth, dear one. I am with you.

She strode forward two paces — now only five feet from him — and pointed at the heart of the Jesus in front of them. "In the name of the true Christ, King of all realms in heaven and on earth, the crucified, ascended, and glorified Jesus Messiah, I command you to reveal yourself."

For a moment nothing happened. But an instant later the sky darkened and fat rain fell from the heavens and pelted them like liquid BBs. The drops fell on her arms and hands and face and head, but the sensation wasn't like liquid, it was like drops of fire that seared her skin.

"Arrrgh!" Brandon tried to shield his head from the rain, but it only exposed more of his bare arms. Tiny red welts appeared on his skin and on hers as well. But the drops didn't seem to be affecting Reece.

"Reece!"

The big man drew close to Brandon and her and covered them with his arms and body. "You have to fight this just like the three of you did during the testing Doug and I sent you on."

"No caves around here to escape into this time." Dana ground her teeth. "You couldn't just tell us how to fight this, could you?"

"What did you use then?"

"The sword of the Spirit." She closed her eyes against the pain and her body tightened.

"Yes."

Dana's brain spun as the rain fell harder. It pounded into the ground and splashed up onto her ankles and through her pants.

The drops seemed to seep like acid through her skin into her bones. It was like white-hot needles were being stuck into her body in a thousand places.

"Reece!"

"Put on the armor."

A moment later she had it. "Ephesians. Faith . . . 'Take up the shield of faith, with which you can extinguish all the flaming arrows of the evil one.' " Her words rang out and seemed to surround them. She stared at Brandon and shouted through the pain, "Faith. We must believe he is with us. 'The LORD is a warrior, the LORD is his name!' "

His eyes widened and he nodded. She held his gaze and watched determination and belief grow inside and his pain grow into anger. He glanced at Reece, then stepped out from under the big man's covering. The drops of rain pounding down on them didn't lessen, but now they seemed to have no effect on Brandon.

She turned to her own arms in surprise. She'd been so focused on Brandon, Dana hadn't noticed the rain was bouncing off her arms as if a thin invisible force field surrounded her body. She looked up at Reece.

"Well done, both of you."

"Yes, well done."

Dana spun at the sound of the dark voice.

Where the rider had stood was a man with thick dark hair and a gruesome smile on his face. "Your precious faith might have protected your skin, but it won't save you from what is about to be unleashed." He was taller, broader in his shoulders, his eyes somehow darker than the tar black they'd always been, but there was no doubt it was Zennon.

"I'm going to take my time killing you for revealing who I am, Dana."

"Zennon." Reece shook the rain from his face, his countenance one of granite.

"I really thought all of you had fallen for it." The demon cocked his head and pulled his gold coin out of his pocket and flipped it in the air. The raindrops bounced off it like miniature pinballs. "I really did. Why? Because you're stupid. Easily deceived." He slapped the coin onto the back of his hand. "Wow, heads. You all die." He looked up and zeroed his gaze in on Dana. "I'm curious, though. What tipped you off, dear?"

"I'm sorry, Dana." Brandon's words were full of shock.

"The Leader." Reece shifted in the mud at their feet and leveled his gaze on Zennon. "How many times do we have to vanquish you before you will leave us alone forever?"

Zennon scratched at a small scab on his left wrist. He pulled it off and fresh blood formed on his skin. The demon touched his finger to the blood, then brought it to his mouth and licked it off. "I'm guessing yours will taste better, Dana."

She shuddered. "Your strength, Jesus."

As she spoke Jesus' name, Zennon took a step back and pain streaked across his face for an instant. The demon turned to Reece. "What is it like to see again, blind man, knowing you can't see any place but the spiritual realms? What is it like to realize the answer to the prophecy isn't what you thought it would be? Does it claw at your mind in the still night hours? Does it make you wonder what else you're wrong about?" The demon held a finger over the spot where he'd ripped the scab off and pressed down. "Do you miss taking your precious photographs, Reece? I took your eyes last time, but of course I wanted to take much more. Now I will."

"Is there anything else you want to say before we destroy you?" Reece thundered one step forward.

"You and your petty desires. You believe yourself to be this mighty warrior, yet you're consumed with the idea of getting your eyes back. You let it blind you. Your choice to marinate in your selfishness on that mountain almost cost Marcus his sanity, and yet you still pretend you are worthy of being at the head of this band of pretenders."

Zennon turned his gaze on Brandon. "And you, Song. You think yourself worthy of that name? Hardly. Are you proud of your reaction at your record label? Toward Kevin? How would you like me to play a tape of that for all your adoring fans? And what about those fans? So you go out and shake a few hands after your concerts. Say a few insipid prayers. Do you really think that makes a difference in their lives? Come now. The prayers you offer all sound the same. Why not make a recording and have someone else play it over and over again? Face the truth. Your singing career has been about you. Always about you trying to fill the hole left vacant from your childhood."

He turned to her. "My dear Dana. Filling your empty heart with the attention of your boss. Wondering what would happen if his wife were to leave him. I know you've had those thoughts. They've come and you've allowed them to linger in your mind. And you are alone, so alone in this life, and it will always be so."

"Enough!" The cry roared out of Reece's mouth with power. "Accuser of the brethren, you will stop. Be silent, in the name of Jesus."

Again pain flitted across Zennon's face.

"Jesus!"

Reece spoke the name again, and again Zennon stepped back, anger flashing. The demon breathed as if fire would erupt from his lungs but calmed a few moments later. "You have no idea what you're dealing with, Reece. But I think it's time you found out."

Zennon's face quivered. "I might be wrong about this, but I don't think so. I get the feeling you think I'm the spirit of religion." He paused and looked at each of them. "Ah yes, I see I am right." Zennon laughed and clapped his hands softly. "Wrong. I am not the spirit of religion. But since he is the one you came to see, let us delay no further and commence with the introductions, shall we?"

Zennon motioned to his right and left as if he were conducting an orchestra. "Warriors, I'd like you to meet a friend of mine. And I predict he'll want you to meet his army."

An icy gust of wind tore into Dana's clothes and as a second blast slammed into her back, a figure appeared next to Zennon. His height was eight feet plus. Black leather pants covered his legs, and his chest was bare and gleaming with dark sweat. Black hair was matted to his forehead and he held a curved white sword in his hand.

When he spoke, the sound rumbled out of his mouth like two trains smashing into each other head-on. "You will die."

"Nice voice, don't you think? I love it. Scares even people like you three." Zennon laughed. "Now it's time to pick the order. Hmm, let's see." He pointed at her. "Because of the stunt you pulled, Dana — making me show my true nature — you receive the honor of dying first."

Dana sucked air into her lungs in huge gulps and stumbled backward in step with the others. "Jesus!"

Zennon shuddered and his body grew thinner, his skin turned pale, and he grabbed the arm of the demon next to him. But the massive demon at his side only laughed and pointed to something over their heads. She spun. Advancing toward them from the back of the hill were hundreds of demons.

She glanced down the sides of the hill to the valleys on the left and right. Hundreds more climbed toward them with methodical steps. In unison the horde of demons marched up the sides of the hill, their white, dead eyes fixed on the three of them. A low screech filled the air and grew louder every second.

"We underestimated you last time, Reece," Zennon said, his voice laced with rage. "I hope it's obvious that isn't a mistake we've made a second time."

"Believe!" Reece shouted and instantly swords appeared in their hands.

Dana turned back to Zennon and the huge demon next to him who snarled out, "No escape."

The words ripped into her heart and a cloud of overwhelming fear filled her mind. The demon advanced on her, sword raised as iron hands gripped her arms from behind and knocked the sword from her hand. Dana yanked her head to the right. Reece shouted the name of Jesus over and over as he spun and ducked and slashed at the demons attacking him, his boots flinging mud and water into the air. The demons fell before Reece's blade like the rain pounding down on them from the sky, but an instant later more took the place of those who had fallen.

To her right came Brandon's voice, singing like lightning, and the sound of his sword was like a hammer ringing against an anvil, but there were too many of the demons. They came like thundering waves.

She turned to look at Brandon, but one of the demons behind her jerked her head back by her hair before she could spot him — her throat now exposed. The white blade of the demon flashed above her. It was over. She closed her eyes. *I come, Lord Jesus, I come.*

The crash of metal on metal ripped into the air followed by a ragged scream. Her eyes flew open. Brandon stood between her and the demon for a moment before he slumped to his knees. His body shuddered. He dropped his sword and clutched for his throat. The demon stood over Brandon grinning.

"Such a touching sacrifice, boy." The demon's eyes shifted to Dana. "But it won't save her."

Brandon made a half turn and fixed his gaze on her. Blood oozed from a deep gash across his throat. The light in his eyes was fading and he gasped for air.

"No!" She reached for him but was wrenched back and held again by the demons. She looked up and stared at Zennon and the other massive demon. "I bind all of you by the blood and power of Jesus Christ, Son of the most high God. He is our shield and I claim it now against you!"

The demons behind her let go and Zennon staggered backward a step, a guttural snarl coming from his throat. An instant later Reece leaped between her and Zennon, his sword flashing at them, then in back of her at the horde coming from behind. They too had been buffeted back by her words, but how long would that last before they regrouped and attacked again? Any hope of victory seeped out of her and she shivered as fear coursed through her body.

But an instant later the sky flashed with a brilliance that would have blinded her on earth and all the demons surrounding them were flung to the ground. Then a voice rang out, crisp and clear as the dawn, " 'The LORD is a warrior; the LORD is his name.' "

Tristan, Jotham, and Orson stood before them, eyes on fire, blazing swords in their hands.

Tristan glanced at her. "Trust in him, Dana."

"Will Brandon die?"

"Our lives are in God's hands."

Laughter from the massive demon echoed over the hill. "And your life is in my hand, Tristan Barrow. How long has it been? A millennium? Two? It is good to see you. It is a good day for you to die."

"I think not."

The giant demon laughed again. "You think the three of you can defeat my army?" He paced two steps to the right, then back to the left. "The three of you couldn't defeat me alone. You know this to be true. Give up the humans and we will let you remain."

Tristan, Jotham, and Orson together slowly raised their swords and stood back to back, Jotham facing to the right, Orson to the left, and Tristan straight ahead. Tristan's face turned to granite. " 'I saw Satan fall like lightning from heaven.' "

He stepped toward the massive demon — at least a foot and a half taller — and its face contorted, but Dana couldn't tell if it was from fear or rage. Jotham and Orson stayed anchored to the ground, their swords ready. The demons in front of each of them stared at Tristan and their leader.

"Leave!" Tristan thundered.

"I've waited long to destroy you." The demon raised his sword, the end of its blade now only two feet from Tristan's. "But I offer one more chance, for old times, when the ages were different and there was no animosity between you and me. Go from us now."

"So you can destroy my friends?" Tristan grew more like stone if that were possible. "Leave."

The demon answered by swinging his blade toward Tristan so fast it blurred. The angel's body didn't move — just his hands and arms. He easily parried the demon's blow, then stepped to the right. The demon's face registered surprise but only for an instant. The two warriors circled each other, the demon feinting as if to strike. Tristan did not respond and gave no false movement of his own.

Once, twice, then three times the two engaged, their swords exploding against each other, the impact reverberating over the hillside. The two fell back, Tristan's face expressionless but his breaths more rapid. They circled again, both faces like steel. The only sound was their boots sloshing through the mud.

Then so fast Dana almost couldn't follow the movement, the demon flung his sword like a spear toward Tristan's chest. The angel yanked his body to the side but not in time. The demon's sword pierced the angel's side and blood spilled out. Tristan stumbled to his knees, head down.

The demon leaped toward Tristan, yanked his sword out of Tristan's side, and raised it high above his head. The demon's bare torso gleamed with sweat and rain, his face full of triumph. "It is finished."

Dana tried to crawl to the angel but her arms and hands somehow wouldn't move. Time seemed to slow as the demon's blade swung in a wide arc toward Tristan's head. The cold blue steel of the sword threw off a darkness that reached Tristan's neck before the blade. Was what the demon said true? Could Tristan Barrow die? She stared in morbid fascination as the blade streaked toward Tristan's neck. It would be over in an instant. How could this happen?

But just before the blade reached Tristan, the angel moved faster than Dana thought possible, ducked underneath it, spun onto his back, and sliced his sword like lightning through the demon's legs.

The demon screamed — a mixture of pain and rage that reverberated across the sky. The demon crashed to the ground and blood gushed from what was left of his legs. He glanced up at Tristan and raised his sword to strike, but the angel was again too fast.

Tristan leaped forward and plunged his sword into the demon's heart with a scream of his own. Seconds later the giant demon lay facedown in the mud, his lifeless body between them and Zennon.

Tristan fixed his gaze on Zennon. "You will not escape."

"Don't try to steal my line." Zennon motioned to his right and left and instantly the demon horde began to circle them and close in.

"Now! Open the eyes of all remaining on the field of battle, Lord of the heavens," Tristan shouted and the land shuddered.

Dana glanced around the field of battle. A vast ring of angels sat on horses encircling the demon army. All had swords drawn. Their horses pawed the ground and strained against their reins. The radiance coming off the horses and riders was like a thousand suns and many of the demons shielded their eyes against the light.

Tristan lifted his sword high and his shout rang over the hillside. "Engage!"

The next three minutes seemed to move in slow motion as Tristan, Jotham, Orson, and the angel army descended on the demons. Their swords flashed and rang out and the demons fell like water. Dana stood over Brandon as she watched Reece join the angels, his sword decimating as many of the demons as any of the angels'.

Then it was over, and as Tristan, Jotham, Orson, and Reece joined her on top of the hill, the skies cleared and the sun shone down on them.

Dana stared at Tristan. "Second Kings

6:5–17.”

"Yes, the army has been here, waiting to be summoned." He shook his head. "Getting here was far more difficult than I anticipated." He glanced at Dana. "I am sorry we did not arrive sooner. We were detained."

She dropped to her knees and took Brandon's arms. "Talk to me."

A voice she didn't recognize rasped out of his mouth. "It probably looks worse than it is."

"Brandon, no."

He gave her a weak smile and closed his eyes. "I'll live."

Maybe he would. But this was about more than his life. Was his throat not as damaged as it looked? And while Brandon might sing again, she somehow knew his voice would never be the same. She glanced up at Tristan and the angel's eyes confirmed it. Tears spilled onto her cheeks and she held Brandon's hand tight.

"We need to get you out of here."

FIFTY-FIVE

Marcus sat with Carson in his office, neither of them speaking. Tristan had left after instructing Marcus to call on the Spirit to be taken to Well Spring when he was done talking to the radio host but told him there was no hurry. That he should take as much time as was needed with the host.

Carson stared out the window at the LA skyline, his face still wet from the tears that had streamed down his cheeks a few minutes earlier. Marcus held his tongue. He expected a man with Carson's ability to speak would speak when ready, but not before.

"That wasn't the show I was expecting." Carson massaged his knuckles. His voice grew soft. "I've been a fool. I allowed myself to be made into a god. Set up to lead people on the crooked and wide path."

He sniffed out a disgusted laugh. "I started the race well. Back then I talked a balanced mix of justice and grace." He dropped his face to his hands and rubbed his eyes. "I can't point to the moment we started sliding down the icy slope. If I could, I might have stopped it. Where do I go from here?"

"Jesus longs to restore you."

"And how do I forgive myself? Let the past go?"

"That is a choice only you can make." An image of his door of memories flashed into Marcus's mind. "And the choice is this: Will you believe that God wants you not to remember the past events and pay no attention to things of old? Will you choose to believe it when he says, 'Look, I am about to do something new; even now it is coming. Do you not see it?' Will you hold on to his statement that he will make a way in the wilderness, rivers in the desert?"

Carson sighed. "Isaiah 43:18–19. I've quoted those verses many times."

"My assessment of your situation is the moment has come to embrace the verse with a liberal dose of belief. Not here." Marcus pointed to Carson's head, then his heart. "But here."

Carson laughed, tears forming again in the corners of his eyes. "Do you talk to everyone like that, or just people you're barely beginning to like?"

"Only those I'm giving strong consideration to liking."

Carson laughed again. "I know you need to go. Any final thoughts?"

"Might I suggest you give serious deliberation to at some point during the next few months coming to join the Warriors Riding at a small ranch in Colorado called Well Spring."

"After what I tried to do to you?" Carson shook his head. "You can't be serious."

Marcus slipped his card onto the conference room table and pushed it toward Carson. "We would be honored if you choose to come someday."

Late that night Reece, Dana, Brandon, Doug, and Marcus sat in the family room at Well Spring and celebrated their victories. They talked about Marcus's conversation with Kat and how it freed him, about his experience with Carson in the studio and how what he had broken there had broken Zennon's hold on Reece, Brandon, and her in the spiritual realm. They heard what happened when Marcus went through the door of his memories. And talked about Reece's, Brandon's, and her battle with Zennon and the other demons and how Tristan, Jotham, and Orson had warred for them.

But while part of her reveled in what they'd done and the triumph Jesus had brought them, another part couldn't get Brandon out of her mind. Would he make it without being able to sing? Once again, the enemy had dealt a devastating blow to one of the Warriors. Brandon was the Song. How could he be anything else? How would he live without his music?

He didn't say much as they talked. How could he? The gash across his throat would take time to heal, if it healed at all. The doctor who had worked on him in the emergency room at St. Vincent Hospital in Buena Vista earlier in the day said he would keep his voice but gave little hope Brandon would ever sing again like he once did. Ever sing at all. His voice at this point was only a whisper, and it was probably painful to talk.

Dana went to sleep that night trying to accept what he had done for her. In the morning she would talk to him. And say the things that needed to be said.

FIFTY-SIX

The next morning after taking a hot shower and spending a half hour alone down by the river, Dana strolled up to Piñon Bothy — the cabin Brandon stayed in last night — and knocked on the door. He opened the door a few seconds later and stood in the door frame, a look of surprise on his face.

"How is your throat?"

"I'll be okay." His whisper was a bit louder than the night before, and it gave her hope.

"Will you join me down at the listening post?"

He smiled, nodded, grabbed a coat off his bed, then stepped outside. They didn't speak till they'd reached the listening post and settled into chairs on the edge of the patio overlooking the river.

"I suppose you know what I want to talk about."

"Maybe." Brandon smiled.

"I think you know. Because you know me.

Better than anyone." She immediately regretted the admission and then a moment later didn't. It was true. He did know her better than anyone else and it was nice to be known.

"You want to talk about what happened during the battle?"

"Sure."

Would she get used to Brandon's new voice? Before, so smooth, now little more than a rasp, like he'd eaten sandpaper for breakfast, lunch, dinner, and midnight snacks. Yes, she would get used to it because with every syllable it would remind her of what he'd done for her. And that made his voice more beautiful than ever.

"What you did . . ." She couldn't say the words.

"You would have done the same."

Would she have? Dana watched the leaves on the aspen trees starting to bud, their green shoots speaking of new life to come.

"Did you know what would happen to you?"

Brandon stared at her. "In that moment time slowed, and yes, somehow I knew what might happen."

"But you did it anyway."

He leaned forward, elbows on his knees, and nodded.

"Was it worth it? Saving me? Knowing what you know now about your voice?" What was she asking for? For him to tell her he loved her again? *Maybe.* She chided herself for allowing the flame deep inside to flicker to life. Of course she'd known it had never completely gone out.

Over the past year she'd figured out how to frequently douse it with water. But like those birthday candles that stayed lit no matter how hard you blew, whatever emotions she still carried for Brandon simply wouldn't die. Dana reached out, put her hand on top of his, and held it there too long before pulling it away. "I don't know how to thank you without it sounding lame."

"Yes, I would do it again. I knew in that moment that I had to choose. My life or yours."

"Why did you choose mine?"

"You know why."

She did. The only sound for the next five minutes was the rush of the river and the wind through the trees.

"Another part of the prophecy comes true," Brandon finally said.

"What do you mean?"

" 'And for one, death will come before the appointed time.' "

"The death of your career?"

"It's better than the alternative." Brandon picked up a tiny pebble and rolled it between his fingers. "I always thought the part of the prophecy about one of us dying was literal."

"In some ways this is worse." In that moment Dana admitted how much she loved Brandon's music — how much she had missed it after they ended their engagement. "It will be hard not hearing new songs from you."

He let out a scratchy laugh. "Like I just said, I'm not dying. I can still write songs — it's just not going to work to sing them like I used to."

"That's the best part — hearing your voice. No one sings . . ." She hesitated. Should she be that blunt? "No one sang like you."

He didn't respond but he didn't need to. She glanced at him and spoke the words she'd considered since they sat down. "You've asked me to have coffee with you six times over the past year."

He nodded.

She leaned closer to him. "I'm told seven is the perfect number."

"I've heard that too." He smiled at her, his eyes bright.

They lapsed back into silence, but now

they shared it and it felt so right. She didn't worry about what would happen with the two of them in the future. There was only this moment and she would live in it fully and let the days come as they may.

Brandon stood and stepped to the edge of the patio, hands in his back pockets, the sun framing his body and hair. "Does it frighten you to realize how close you came to dying?"

"Not anymore. I've seen too much. Think of the field of doors. Our gates are gone in a breath. We are such glorious flowers that fade from this earth so quickly. Lush grass that withers with one pass of the sun.

"If my door crumbles early, it's nothing in the scope of eternity. And I choose to believe I'm indestructible till my time has come." She stood and stepped next to Brandon. "What about you?"

"We're dead already if we're in Christ. But there is a Life inside me, a new being that is immortal and can never be destroyed." He turned to her and laughed, a choking, raspy laugh, but one filled with joy. "You know what was going through my mind after I dove in front of you and lay with my throat spilling blood into the mud? 'He is no fool who gives what he cannot keep to gain that which he cannot lose.' "

"Jim Elliot."

"You impress me yet again," Brandon said.

"No greater love than to lay your life down for a friend."

"We have seen the unspeakable, Dana. We're four ordinary people who have seen far beyond the extraordinary. And maybe this is what you're feeling too. That those glories of eternity draw me deeper into the here and now and at the same time deeper into the life to come. I'm looking forward to going home."

Brandon turned and pointed toward the main Well Spring cabin. "Ready?"

"Yes."

"Can I ask you something?" Brandon said as they ambled up the path of white stones.

Dana nodded.

"Was what Zennon said true? Have you ever had thoughts about your boss?"

Dana laughed. "Not for an instant. Zennon was grasping for anything. Trying to put thoughts in your head maybe. I don't know." She paused. Should she say it? "There's only one person I've thought of from time to time lately."

Thankfully he didn't ask who it was, but that was only because he didn't have to. She wouldn't have answered if he asked. She'd already said more than enough.

FIFTY-SEVEN

"Where do we go from here?" Dana said.

"Home. Bed," Brandon rasped. "Sleep for nine days. Repeat."

Reece smiled as they all sat around the fire pit for a few more minutes before they headed back to Seattle. It wasn't a bad plan, and certainly one he could support. They'd all earned it. But first they needed to do a final debrief on their battle in the heavens.

"My friends, my fellow Warriors, the spirit of religion is still out there. Our victory over him was major, but it was one battle in a larger war."

"There is more than one spirit of religion?" Brandon said.

"Many."

"So what will be our strategy as we venture on?" Marcus asked.

"It might sound strange, but the answer came from both Zennon and Carson Tanner during the time Brandon was on his show."

"And that is?" Dana asked.

"We continue to train. We continue to raise up other warriors here at Well Spring. We equip others to take the message of freedom to those around them. Here in the US, and around the globe."

Marcus smiled. "I know of a new ally I believe can become a significant warrior on our behalf."

"Who is that, Professor?" Doug said.

"Might I read you something before I reveal who it is?"

"Of course."

"I received an e-mail while we were in Buena Vista at the hospital with Brandon. It is titled 'Reminders for True Life.' " Marcus pulled out his cell phone and began to read. "When you speak, speak words of truth and life and love. All around you are parched souls longing for the living water of the Holy Spirit, and your words can guide them to the place where the water flows.

"Your body is a temple. Worship him through the way you care for it. Offer it as a living sacrifice that you might use it to advance his kingdom in great measure.

"Grow in wholeness — let him into your deepest wounds and fully surrender to his lordship and you will find holiness and will throw off the chains the world and the enemy try to entangle you in.

"Seek the pleasures of this age as shadows, as a foretaste to set your mind on the age to come where we will delight in his gifts in full measure and reign with him in eternity.

"Seek him with all your heart, all your mind, all your soul, all your strength.

"And finally, love your brothers and sisters deep and well, because this is the greatest command and love covers a multitude of sins."

"So be it," Dana said. "Who wrote it?"

"Has to be Carson Tanner." Reece grinned. "I would say he has been set free from the spirit of religion."

"Most assuredly." Marcus smiled as well. "If he stays on the air, I have little doubt his show will take a radical turn from what he has been doing. And I believe in the not-too-distant future he'll sit with us around this very fire pit."

"What!" Brandon's raspy laugh sounded more like a cough.

"During our time in the studio, I invited him to come to one of our Well Spring trainings. I have little doubt he will accept."

"Any other revelations, Marcus?" Dana said.

"Yes, I believe so. During my journey with Tristan, I received the distinct impression we will be visiting the field of doors again soon."

The others asked for details with excited voices and Marcus talked of how he felt the Spirit told him they would all return within the next year. Reece listened to the conversation with a deep sense of peace. The warriors had done well. And he knew all of them would be willing to step into any new quest the Spirit brought them.

He breathed deep, drawing in the smell of burning pinyon pine. The rush of the river was the rhythm guitar to this rock-and-roll symphony of smells and sounds, and a deep joy seeped into every fiber of his body. Brandon would be okay. He would learn to live without his voice being what it once was. He was still the Song and always would be.

"It's time." Reece stood. "Take a few more minutes here, please. Just the three of you. Then grab your things. We'll meet back here in fifteen minutes. Let's go home."

He strode up to the main cabin. When he reached the nine-foot sliding door, Doug's voice spoke out from behind.

"Is there anything you'd like to share with me?"

Reece turned. "What do you mean?"

"I mean, friend, either you've gotten

extremely confident with the repetition of walking these grounds, or something rather miraculous is going on with your eyes."

"The latter description is the most accurate." Reece pulled off his sunglasses. "But you're wondering how that can be when all you can see is two scars where my eyes used to be."

"Yes."

Reece turned his head back toward where the others sat around the fire pit and talked with animated voices. "The prophecy has come true. I can see again, Doug." Reece cocked his head toward his friend. "Not in the same way I used to. Not in the way a normal person does. But I see shapes, outlines — of the mountains, the cabin, the river — in impressions of light and darkness. And not all the time — but often — I can see the angelic warriors and the demonic host all around us."

"How often?"

"In fits and starts. Most of the time it's muddled and fuzzy. But even then I can see enough to orient myself. Don't worry; I'm not going to be driving a car anytime soon."

"What do you see right now?"

Reece turned again toward the fire. Three angels surrounded the fire pit behind the Warriors. "Our new friends are here."

"Tristan, Jotham, and Orson?"

"Yes."

"Fascinating." Doug put his hand on Reece's arm. "Then it's probably time to give you something."

"What?"

"Your journal. I found it out at the fire pit back home behind one of the benches."

"But didn't give it to me because it would be too difficult for me not to be able to read it."

"Yes."

Doug handed him the journal and Reece caressed the leather cover. "I still can't read it."

"Maybe not at this moment, but with your new vision that might change."

"True. Thank you; this was the perfect moment to return it." Reece turned his head toward his old friend. A faint gold outline of light gave a distinct shape to his body. "This kind of sight could be extremely useful and extremely terrifying in the days to come."

Reece took Doug's forearm. "I thought this would be the Warriors' last battle together. I thought finding the Wolf and confronting him was the end. The prophecy fulfilled. But now I'm not so sure. I think more freedom is coming if we desire it. For us, and for others."

Reece focused on where Doug's face should be. "You're smiling. I can see it."

"Yes, friend, I am." Doug chuckled. "Because you're right. There is more coming. Much more. The paths of freedom are breaking out all around us, and he has called you and the Warriors to ride."

READING GROUP GUIDE

1. Which character could you relate to most in *Memory's Door*? Was it Reece, Brandon, Dana, Marcus, or maybe even Simon? Explain.

2. Tristan, Jotham, and Orson turn out to be angels. Do you think angels can be involved in the lives of Christians as they were with the main characters?

3. One of the major themes of *Memory's Door* is finding freedom from regret. Do you have regrets from your past? If so, have you allowed them to keep you from truly living in the present?

4. Why do you think it's so tempting for us to look back on our mistakes?

5. Does the verse from Isaiah 43:18–19 — "Do not remember the past events, pay

no attention to things of old. Look, I am about to do something new; even now it is coming. Do you not see it? Indeed, I will make a way in the wilderness, rivers in the desert" — seem too good to be true? Do you think we really can forget the former things and that God can do and is doing a new thing in our lives? Why or why not?

6. If God has "made a way in the wilderness" or "rivers in the desert" for you, can you describe them? Are there others you see coming?

7. At the end of *Memory's Door,* Reece gets his sight back, but not in the way he was expecting. Have you ever realized God has given you an answer, but it's far different from what you expected? Was it a good different or a hard different? Why?

8. Brandon lost his voice in the final battle against the Wolf. Have you ever lost something like he did and felt like your life was over?

9. Toward the book's end, a Jesus appears that turns out to be a counterfeit. How can we know if we are hearing the true

voice of the Spirit and not a false one?

10. Carson Tanner had a list of "Redemptive Reminders" he promoted on his radio show. Do you know people who seem to carry a list like that even if it's only in their heads? Do they bring freedom to the people around them and themselves or bondage?

11. Have you ever "carried" a list of dos and don'ts in your mind? Has it kept you from freedom or brought you freedom?

12. What do you need to do in your life right now that will bring you more freedom?

ACKNOWLEDGMENTS

Significant thanks goes out to my agent, Lee Hough; my brainstorming friend Ruth Voetmann; my prayer team; all of my team at Thomas Nelson; my editors, Amanda Bostic and Julee Schwarzburg; collaborator Allen Arnold; my sons, Taylor and Micah; my wife, Darci; and last but most certainly far from least, the passionate readers of my novels.

AUTHOR'S NOTE

Dear friends,

The response to *Soul's Gate* has thrilled me. Authors are frequently too close to their novels to know if a story has worked or not, so it's been a rush to hear the book is making a serious impact on people's lives. Some authors write to entertain. I do too, but I also want people to come away from reading one of my books with more freedom than when they started as well as full of the hope that their life can be transformed in significant ways.

With *Memory's Door,* I had the tremendous privilege of continuing to be with characters who have become a large part of my life and I was eager to see where their story would go. I don't use an outline when I write. I just transcribe the movie playing in my head, which allows me to experience the story for the first time just as you do.

Yet at the same time, my stories are never

a complete surprise because they spring from my subconscious. What I see on my mental movie screen is a part of me. I've been asked if there are elements of me in Reece, Dana, Brandon, and Marcus. Yes, without question.

Consequently their struggles are (in part) my struggles. As an author friend of mine says, "My novels are just my personal journals in published form. I'm working the things out in my own life that wind up in my books."

That statement resonated with me at the time he said it and it resonates strongly within the framework of *Memory's Door.* I went through a significant personal and spiritual crisis — and then rebirth — during the time I wrote the novel. It forced me to ask the same question Marcus faces. Can I forget the past, the things of old? Will I open my eyes despite the pain of what has been, in order to see the new thing(s) God is doing and has already done? Can I believe he can and will create rivers in the desert? My answer is yes, I can, because I did believe. And God came through.

My hope for you is you can open your eyes as I did, to see the good he is doing in your life. I don't know where you are on your journey through this reality, but I do know we have a choice every day and in every moment to enter boldly into the unquenchable love, grace, and mercy the One offers to our hearts, our minds, and our souls.

To your joy and freedom,
James L. Rubart
2013

ABOUT THE AUTHOR

James L. Rubart is a professional marketer and speaker. He is the author of the best-selling novel *Rooms* as well as *Book of Days, The Chair,* and *Soul's Gate.* He lives with his wife and sons in the Pacific Northwest.

The employees of Thorndike Press hope you have enjoyed this Large Print book. All our Thorndike, Wheeler, and Kennebec Large Print titles are designed for easy reading, and all our books are made to last. Other Thorndike Press Large Print books are available at your library, through selected bookstores, or directly from us.

For information about titles, please call:
(800) 223-1244

or visit our Web site at:
http://gale.cengage.com/thorndike

To share your comments, please write:
Publisher
Thorndike Press
10 Water St., Suite 310
Waterville, ME 04901